Raves for *Forests of the Night* and *Fearful Symmetries*:

"The private eye tiger hero is a tough, serious minded, but often sentimental character who really makes this story of secret plots, assassins, drug dealers, and political intrigue work. One of the more interesting blends of mystery and SF."
—*Science Fiction Chronicle*

"An entertaining hard-boiled detective novel set in a gritty, relatively near future . . . . If any book was meant to be made into an action-adventure movie, this is it." —*Locus*

"An enjoyable mix of a hard-boiled detective novel with near-future science fiction." —SF Site

"Here is the printed page equivalent of an action movie: a novel as vivid as a cinema blockbuster . . . . Swann has superb technical skills . . . the particular details and variations that he comes up with are inventive and neat. More importantly, he has a style that makes the action leap off the page. Many SF writers who have more famous names could learn a great deal from Swann."
—*The New York Review of Science Fiction*

"A plot packed with action and suspense . . . written with warmth, humor, and intelligence." —*Kliatt*

"As the story unfolded, I couldn't put it down. I look forward to more adventures of Nohar Rajasthan, private investigator." —*VOYA*

THE
MOREAU QUARTET:
VOLUME ONE

S. Andrew Swann

FORESTS OF THE NIGHT

FEARFUL SYMMETRIES

DAW BOOKS, INC.
DONALD A. WOLLHEIM, FOUNDER
375 Hudson Street, New York, NY 10014
ELIZABETH R. WOLLHEIM
SHEILA E. GILBERT
PUBLISHERS
www.dawbooks.com

DAW TRADEMARK REGISTERED
U.S. PAT. AND TM. OFF. AND FOREIGN COUNTRIES
—MARCA REGISTRADA
HECHO EN U.S.A.

PRINTED IN THE U.S.A.

FORESTS
OF THE
NIGHT

Dedication

This is for John, Heather, and their kid(s?)

Acknowledgments

Thanks to a number of people who left their mark on this manuscript. To Dan Eloff, who knows he got me writing again, and to R. M. Meluch, who doesn't. To the members of the Cleveland SF Writer's Workshop, who helped me get the burrs and toolmarks off this novel. To Stacy Newman, who offered to proof this. To Anastacia H. Brightfox, for naming one of the characters. And thanks to Amy, who, if nothing else, helped to give me something to write about.

Tyger! Tyger! burning bright
In the forests of the night,
What immortal hand or eye
Could frame thy fearful symmetry?

In what distant deeps or skies
Burnt the fire of thine eyes?
On what wings dare he aspire?
What the hand, dare seize the fire?

And what shoulder, and what art,
Could twist the sinews of thy heart?
And when thy heart began to beat,
What dread hand? And what dread feet?

What the hammer? What the chain?
In what furnace was thy brain?
What the anvil? what dread grasp
Dare its deadly terrors clasp?

When the stars threw down their spears,
And water'd heaven with their tears,
Did he smile his work to see?
Did he who made the Lamb make thee?

Tyger! Tyger! burning bright
In the forests of the night,
What immortal hand or eye
Could frame thy fearful symmetry?

—WILLIAM BLAKE

Chapter 1

"One day, Nugoya, you're going to screw the wrong person." Nohar Rajasthan raked his claws across the seat of his booth, wishing it was Nugoya's face. Like the rest of *Zero's*, the vinyl on the seat was flashy, shiny, and cheap. The seat shredded.

Nugoya grabbed the collar of the black jacket that was draped over his left shoulder, shaking his head. He looked human, but only at first glance. A close examination of the graying Japanese would reveal joints large beyond normal human proportions and muscles that snaked like steel cable. The light above the booth glinted off the chrome irises of Nugoya's artificial Japanese eyes. "I hire you to find my girl. You find me a corpse. A corpse is worthless. I owe you nothing."

Nohar shouldn't have had the bad sense to let Nugoya hire him. It was becoming hard to contain his anger. "Expenses, and four days of legwork."

Nohar shouldn't have trusted a frank. Japan had been one of the few countries to ever defy the U.N. ban on the manipulation of human genetic material. The INS had tight restrictions on letting human frankensteins into the country and those that made it here found that they had few, if any, rights. That kind of bitterness tended to turn people into assholes—and Nugoya didn't need any help on that score.

Even moreaus like Nohar had a constitutional amendment in their favor.

"I owe you nothing. I should ask back the thousand I paid you. You are an arrogant cat. Were we elsewhere, you would have to show some respect, and pay for your failure." Nugoya held up his mutilated right hand. It was missing two fingers.

Nohar was already scanning the rest of the bar. He picked out Nugoya's people easily. They were all moreaus—a human would not be caught dead working for a frank.

"Twenty-five hundred, Nugoya. Pay me."

It was Tuesday, two in the morning. There were only a half-dozen other people. The civilians—all human since they were downtown—were giving Nugoya's booth a wide berth. No surprise, since two of Nugoya's soldiers were hovering near the table. One was a tiger, like Nohar. The other was a dark brown, nearly black ursine that couldn't quite stand upright even with the relatively high ceiling. Nugoya had a vulpine manning the bar, and a trio of white rabbits sat near the entrance. Nohar knew there was a canine somewhere out of sight, probably in the kitchen. Nohar could catch a hint of the dog's scent.

"You failed. No money."

Nohar told himself that he should just walk out of there. Shut up, leave, and cut his losses. He didn't.

"I found the bitch, peddling her ass on the side for the flush *you* hooked her on. I don't know if it was cut with angel dust or drain cleaner, but her last trip splatted her all over Morey Hill. It's *your* fault she's dead."

Nugoya's jaw clenched, and Nohar could smell his anger. Nugoya stood up. His jacket slid off his shoulder, revealing his artificial left arm and some scarring on his neck. "How dare you, *an animal,* presume—"

That was enough. "And what are you, Nugoya, but a half-pint, half pink sleazeball?"

Nugoya sputtered something incomprehensible. Probably Japanese.

Nohar was glad he was the one facing the rest of the bar. He could feel all hell was about to break loose. Why couldn't he keep his damn mouth shut? One more try at being reasonable. "I just want my money, Nugoya. You aren't going to shake me down like one of your girls."

Nugoya's problem was he couldn't ever be anything but a small-time pimp. He wasn't human and he wasn't a moreau, so neither world would let him have more than a few scraps of the power he thought he deserved.

"I will not take any more insolence. Leave or I will have you removed."

Nugoya motioned with his left arm at the other tiger and the bear. The tiger started moving forward. The bear reached under a table and took a hold of something large and presumably deadly. He kept it out of sight of the patrons.

"It's insolence to think the world owes you respect because some defunct Jap corporation built you like a disposable radio."

That did it. Nugoya had a killer ego, and could only take a little needling before he jumped. In his prime, a Japanese corporate samurai could take Nohar in a fair fight. Nugoya's ego would never let him admit that he was well past his prime. Tokyo was nuked by China a long time ago, and Nugoya had been sitting on his butt for longer than that.

The frank ripped the table from the wall and threw it to the side. The advancing tiger almost tripped over it. Nohar stayed seated and Nugoya went for his neck. Nugoya was fast, faster than any normal human, faster than most moreaus.

Nohar was faster.

As the other tiger manhandled the remains of the table out of his way and the bear pulled out a Russian-make assault rifle, Nohar's right hand shot up and clamped on Nugoya's mechanical wrist. At the same time, Nohar wrapped his left arm around Nugoya's right arm. The frank's three-fingered hand ended up clamped under Nohar's armpit. Nohar had his forearm levered under Nugoya's upper arm, his hand resting on the shoulder.

Nohar pushed down and heard the bone crack.

Nugoya yelled, washing Nohar's face with his sour breath, and tried to escape. But Nohar had lifted the frank off the ground by the mechanical arm. Nugoya didn't have the leverage.

Predictably, one of the civilians screamed.

"That will heal. If I did that to your other arm, who's around to fix it? Call off the muscle."

Nugoya showed some reluctance, so Nohar bore down on the broken arm. Nohar could hear the bones grate together. Nugoya shook his head violently and screamed something back at his people in Japanese. The tiger stopped moving, and the bear set the rifle down on the ground.

The tiger slowly drew his gun from a shoulder holster and dropped it.

"You're dead, Rajasthan."

"Hundred years we'll all be dead. I just want my money."

It was a standoff. Nohar had Nugoya as a shield, but there were six of Nugoya's people between him and the door. The rabbits weren't an immediate problem; the press of exiting civilians was pinning them by the door. The bar-tending fox had pulled out a shotgun, but he had the sense not to point it at his boss. Even so, Nohar couldn't move away from the wall without exposing himself.

He might be 260 centimeters tall and weigh 300 kilos. He might be able to whip anything but that bear and a few franks in a fair fight. But guns were guns.

Nohar stood up, lifting Nugoya by his mechanical arm. The little pimp barely gave his torso cover. Nohar would have preferred kevlar—he would have preferred not being there in the first place.

Nohar could smell the canine, stronger now. The other tiger's nose twitched. The bear started turning toward the bar. The civilians were gone.

So were the rabbits.

What?

Nugoya was still yelling. "Dead!"

The tiger turned toward the entrance. Nohar was smelling it now, too. The copper odor of blood. Rabbit blood. It had drifted in from the open door to the empty bar with the algae smell from the river. Nugoya stopped yelling.

The fox started turning around to face the long mirror behind the bar. The canine's smell was rank in the bar now. Nohar began to realize the dog might not be one of Nugoya's people. The fox must have heard something because he was raising the shotgun toward the mirror.

"Let me down!" There was the hint of panic in Nugoya's voice and more than a hint of it in his smell.

Someone turned on a glass jackhammer and the mirror for the length of the bar exploded outward in a wave, from left to right. It was some sort of silenced submachine gun. The vulpine got in the way of at least three shots, and large chunks of fox flew out over the bar. The shotgun went off, blowing away a case of Guinness that was sitting behind the bar. The fox fell half over the bar and bled.

The smell of cordite, beer, and melted teflon wafted over. Whoever was shooting was using glazer rounds. If the internal injuries didn't get you, the blood poisoning would.

The other tiger was ducking for cover in a booth across from Nohar and Nugoya. There wasn't cover for the bear. All the ursine could do was reach back for the rifle and hope the guy with the machine gun missed.

As the bear was bending over Nohar had an unobstructed view of the assassin jumping out of the broken mirror and on to the bar. Canine. A dog with a shaggy gray coat that tagged him as an Afghani. The dog wore a long black coat over a black jumpsuit that bulged with the kevlar vest he wore under it. The gun was small, the silencer was twice as long as the weapon itself. The clip was the length of the dog's forearm.

The bear was intimidating, but size was the bear's downfall. What was terrifying on the battlefields of Asia was a deadly handicap in the small confines of the rear of *Zero's*. The ursine couldn't turn around fast enough to shoot the canine.

The canine emptied a burst into the bear's back and Nohar got a good look and a good smell of the inside of the bear's chest as the ursine splatted on to the ground.

The tiger had a problem. His gun was on the ground, by the rifle. Nohar could smell the bloodlust rising from the other cat. *No,* Nohar thought, *you don't jump a guy with an automatic weapon.* But the cat was already hyped on adrenaline and Nohar could see the muscles in the tiger's haunches tense, even under the human clothing.

The dog was waiting for the tiger to pounce. Three bullets hit the cat before it got halfway. Blood sprayed the wall and the tiger slammed into a booth, smashing a table and scattering glassware.

Then the dog turned his attention to Nohar and Nugoya.

Nugoya was thrashing like a fish out of water. "Get me out of this, you have your money, you have three times your money—"

The dog licked his nose. The smell of his musk made Nohar want to sneeze. "Drop the pimp."

Nohar didn't argue.

Nugoya hit the ground and collapsed, cradling his arm. He turned toward the dog. "Hassan . . ."

The canine shook his head. "Too late. You were warned last time."

"Can't we deal—"

"No. You knew the rules. Do not tread on our business. Flush is our business. We say who sells, and who to."

Nugoya staggered to his feet. "I needed the money to keep my girls supplied. You're charging too much—"

"Others will be quite glad not to get off as cheaply as you." The canine fired one shot that hit Nugoya in the face. The pimp's head jerked back hard enough that Nohar heard the neck crack. Nugoya fell backward at Nohar's feet, looking upward with only half a face. Only one chrome iris looked up. The other eye had become electronic shrapnel buried deep in what was left of Nugoya's brain.

Nohar looked up from the corpse, and at Hassan. "Me now?"

The dog shook his head and raised his gun. "Not today. This was a lesson. Lessons need witnesses."

Hassan began backing away, keeping his eyes on Nohar.

When Hassan reached the door, he gave the carnage a brief inspection. Then he looked back up at Nohar, who was still standing by the rear wall. "Advice, tiger. Next time be more careful who you work for."

No shit.

It took all of fifteen minutes for the first police to descend on the party side of the flats. In twenty minutes the east side of the Cuyahoga River was illuminated by a wash of dozens of flashing blue and red lights. Even though Nohar was the one who called in the shooting, he had to sit on his tail in the back of a very cramped Chevy Caldera sedan. At least the pink uniforms didn't cuff him—not that they hadn't tried, but this far out of Moreytown they didn't have cuffs that would fit him. They simply deposited him in the back seat and kept their distance.

Nohar squirmed to get his tail in a comfortable position and looked out the windows facing the river. Not much to see, water for a few hundred meters reflecting the police flashers. The water terminated at the ·concrete base of the West Side office complex. The office buildings were so dark at this time of night that they seemed to be trapezoidal holes cut in the night sky, revealing something blacker behind it.

There wasn't much else to watch out the other window. The forensics people were all in *Zero's*. He'd end up talking to Manny later anyway. Not that there was anything to discuss. It wasn't like he was on a case any more.

Twenty-five hundred dollars. Gone. The first of the

month was at the end of the week, and he only had about two hundred in the bank. Served him right for working for a pimp.

Nohar had his pride. He didn't want to have to ask Manny about his old room—

He shook his head. Things would work out. They usually did.

A soft rain began to fall. It broke up the reflections on the river.

Nohar heard the scream of abused brakes. He turned around to face the entrance of the parking lot. A puke-green Dodge Havier that was missing one front fender jumped the curb and skidded to a halt in a handicapped parking spot.

It had to be Harsk.

Indeed, Irwin Harsk's bald head emerged from the driver's side door of the unmarked sedan. Harsk stormed out like an avalanche. Many standards of pink beauty escaped Nohar, but some forms of ugly transcended species. Harsk's black face resembled a cinder block.

It had been only a matter of time before Harsk got involved. He was the detective in charge of Moreytown. He had jurisdiction over anything involving moreaus, and, by extension, any product of genetic engineering. In the case of the shoot-out at *Zero's* that covered the victims, the suspect, and the witness.

This obviously didn't please the detective.

Harsk stood a moment in the rain, looking over the scene—the ambulances, the forensics van, Manny's medical examiner's van, the seven marked and two unmarked police cars. Even over the twenty-meter distance between them, Nohar could hear Harsk grunt.

After giving the scene the once-over, Harsk targeted a lone uniform who was standing by the door to *Zero's*. Harsk looked like he wanted to unload on someone. The cop by the door was the unlucky one. Nohar supposed Harsk chose his victim because of the cup of coffee the guy was drinking. Harsk walked up to the guy, and even though Nohar wasn't great at reading human expressions, the way the poor cop bit his lip and gave forced nods indicated that Harsk wasn't having a nice day and was doing his best to share the experience.

Harsk pointed at the Caldera that Nohar was sitting in and yelled something that Nohar couldn't quite make out. The cop shrugged and tried to say something, and Harsk cut him off. Harsk grabbed the guy's coffee and pointed back into *Zero's*.

Nohar wished he could read lips.

The cop went inside and Harsk started walking toward the Caldera. He took a sip from the uniform's coffee and grimaced. He looked into the cup, shook his head, and dumped it on the asphalt.

Harsk walked up to the door and opened it. "Rajasthan, how did I know you'd be involved in this crap?"

"Deductive reasoning?"

Harsk grunted. "Get the fuck out of that patrol car. The city just bought those and we don't want you shedding on them."

Nohar ducked out the door and stretched. The misting rain started to dampen his fur immediately. He wished he had worn his trench coat to the meeting. "No apology for treating me like a suspect? I didn't *have* to call this in."

"Be glad that some downtown cowboy didn't shoot you. Half these kids are just out of the academy and tend to shit if they see a moreau. This ain't your neighborhood. What the fuck are you doing here?"

"Nugoya was a client."

Harsk looked at Nohar. "So when are you going to start selling yourself to the flush peddlers?"

Nohar had his right hand up, claws fully extended, before he knew what he was doing. Harsk's face cracked into an ugly grin. "Do it, you fucking alley cat. I would love to put you away and get you out of my hair."

Nohar took a few deep breaths and lowered his arm. "What hair?"

A lithe nonhuman form left *Zero's*. The moreau wore a lab coat and carried a notebook-sized computer, the display of which he was reading.

Nohar called out, "Manny."

Manny—his full name was Mandvi Gujerat—looked up from the display, twitched his nose, and started across the parking lot toward Nohar and Harsk. Manny was a small guy with a thin, whiplike body. He had short brown fur, a lean, aerodynamic head, and small black eyes. People who saw Manny usually guessed he was designed from a rat, or a ferret. Both were wrong. Manny was a mongoose.

Manny reached them and Harsk interrupted before Nohar could say anything. "Gujerat, what have you got on the bodies?"

Manny gave Nohar an undulating shrug and looked down at his notebook. "I have a tentative species on six of seven. The three bodies outside were all a Peruvian Lepus strain. From the white fur and the characteristic skull profile, I'd say Pajonal '35 or '36. They all have unit tattoos, and some heavy scarring. Infantry, and they saw combat."

Manny tapped the screen and the page changed. "The bartender was definitely vulpine. Brit fox, Ulster antiterrorist. I think second generation, but I can't be sure. The British ID their forces under the tongue and most of the fox's head is gone.

"The tiger—" Manny looked at Nohar briefly. "Secondgeneration Rajasthan. Indian Special Forces.

"The bear, I would guess Turkmen, Russia, or Kazakhstahn. That's only on my previous experience in ursoid strains. Her species—"

"Her?" asked Harsk.

"Yes. I think she was a parthenogenetic adaption. But as I was saying, her species isn't cataloged. She's either a unique experiment, or one of the few dozen species that fell through the cracks during the war. From the corpse, for all I know, she could be Canadian."

Nohar snorted.

Manny shrugged again. "I supposed you already have a file on the one engineered human. But his strain checks out against what we have on Sony's late human-enhancement projects. The one we have here underwent a massive reconstruction after some major trauma. The hardware in his body was worth a few million when there were people who could make and install the stuff."

Harsk nodded. "Any leads on the suspect?"

"Some hairs from the mirror check out as canine. From that and a description, purebred Afghani, Qandahar '24. Attack strain, one the Kabul government 'discontinued' after the war."

"Enough. Rajasthan, I'll get your statement from the uniforms. Get out of here before you attract more trouble. Gujerat, dump the rest into the precinct mainframe." Harsk started to go toward *Zero's* and paused. "The *Moreytown* precinct."

Manny nodded. "Where else?"

Harsk left.

Manny folded up the computer and twitched his nose. "So, stranger, what the hell are you doing at this bloodbath?"

"Bad sense to let Nugoya hire me—"

"Let me guess. Female Vietnamese canine who shot herself so full of flush that she thought she was avian? The one you asked me to ID for you?"

Nohar nodded.

"I know you don't like my advice—"

"Then don't give me any."

"—*but* something dangerous is going on. I don't think you want to be involved, even tangentially, with anything that has to do with the flush industry."

Nohar leaned against the Caldera. His fur was beginning to itch. "Sounds like you know something you think I don't."

"Something's in the air. The DEA is crawling all over downtown, and the gangs in Moreytown are acting up. Most of the bodies I'm looking at the past few weeks are young, second-generation street kids."

"I can handle myself."

"So I worry. You were once one of those second-generation street kids."

"I can handle myself," Nohar said a little more forcefully.

Manny backed off. "Anyway, we do have to stop meeting like this. When are you going to come back and let me cook you some dinner?"

You've been trying to get me back there for fifteen years, Nohar thought. "I'll make it over one of these days."

"The door's always open."

"I know."

Manny turned and started back to *Zero's,* where a gaggle of pink EMTs were trying to manhandle the ursine's corpse out the door.

Nohar sighed.

"I know," he whispered to himself.

Nohar uselessly turned the collar up on the irritating pink-designed jacked and headed for his car. There wasn't anything left for him to do here.

Chapter 2

Nohar's apartment had holes in the wall, a leaky roof, a sagging floor in the kitchen, and wiring that hadn't been up to code when it was put in forty years ago. However, the place had one redeeming feature. Someone had installed a huge stainless-steel shower that Nohar could fit into. Four in the morning was a god-awful time to take a shower, but Nohar wanted to get the city off of him—as well as pieces of bear and Nugoya.

Nohar stood under a blast of warm water, feeling the grit melt off his fur. Through the open door of the bathroom, he listened to the news coming off his comm and tried to forget the fiasco he had left downtown.

". . . major demonstrations through the Economic Community. However, despite public pressure and threats of violence, the European parliament followed through on its vote to eliminate most internal restrictions on nonhuman movement. The French and German states are braced for a massive influx of unemployed nonhumans from the rest of the economically troubled European nation.

"The French and German interior ministers issued a joint statement condemning the parliament's decision to outlaw screening across internal borders."

Nohar sighed. The pinks in Paris and Berlin were worried about a few thousand moreaus—relatively benign moreaus for the most part. The EEC had a few combat designs in reaction to the war, but it never produced many moreaus. Most of their nonhumans were designed for police and hazardous industrial work.

The European parliament probably would still have considered their moreaus as not better than slaves or machines if the Vatican hadn't screwed everything up with the pope's decision that moreys had souls. The EEC was still dealing with the repercussions of that, even fifteen years after the production lines stopped.

"In a related story, a car bomb exploded in Bern, Switzerland, today outside of the Bensheim Genetic Repository Building. No injuries were reported, and no one has claimed responsibility. Damage to the Bensheim building was estimated at a quarter of a million dollars. The Bensheim Foundation issued a statement to reassure their clients that no damage was done to their inventory of genetic material which is kept in an undisclosed location. The building that was bombed housed only administrative offices. The Foundation says that this will in no way affect its worldwide collection and distribution of semen.

"Dr. Bensheim himself issued a statement from Stockholm deploring the attack, and saying, 'the right to reproduce is fundamental and should not be denied on the basis of species.'

"In local news . . ."

Nohar turned off the water and leaned his back against the cool metal wall of the shower. He couldn't get that two and a half grand out of his mind. How the hell was he going to pay the rent—how the hell was he going to eat? He knew too many moreaus who lived out on the street, and he had already done time there himself.

Nohar slid the shower door aside and Cat looked up quizzically. The yellow tomcat was curled up on top of the john and was looking annoyingly serene. Sometimes Nohar thought there was something to the idea that you shouldn't have pets too close to your own species.

Nohar turned on the dryer and Cat made a satisfying leap out the bathroom door. Served the little fuzzball right for not having the sense to worry about where his next meal was coming from. After a few minutes, Cat peeked around the doorjamb and gave Nohar a peeved expression.

Nohar allowed himself the luxury of standing in front of the dryer until his entire body had aired out. Who gave a shit what this month's utility bill cost. Moot if he couldn't pay it. He needed the time to relax. He was too tense to think rationally.

". . . buried tomorrow. Graveside services to be held at Lakeview Cemetery. The police have no suspects as of yet, and the Binder campaign has yet to issue an official statement other than appointing Congressman Binder's legal counsel, Edwin Harrison, as acting campaign manager.

"Former Cleveland mayor, Russell Gardner, expressed sympathy for his opponent and said that he did not intend to make rumors of alleged financial irregularities in Binder's fund-raising a campaign issue.

"Binder finance chairman, Philip Young, could not be reached for comment."

Nohar turned off the dryer and walked out of the bathroom. He collapsed on the nearly dead couch in the living room. There was the sound of protesting wood and permanently compressed springs. He shifted on his back, and Cat ran up and pounced on his chest. Nohar winced as four *cold* little feet kneaded his fur. Cat curled up to take a nap.

Nohar lifted his hand to push him off, but a loud purring made him stop and simply pet the creature.

". . . more violence on the East Side today. There was an apparent clash between nonhuman gang members on Murray Hill—"

Only newscasters and politicians still called it Murray Hill. It was Morey Hill now, had been for nearly a decade. Nohar sighed. The guy on the news couldn't bring himself to say the word morey—or even moreau. Nohar looked at the guy on the comm. Pink—what else—slick black hair, a nothing Midwestern accent, dead gray eyes, all the animation of a cheap computer graphic. The bodies on the screen behind him were more lively.

"—fifteen dead, all of various species, making this the most bloody incidence of cross-species violence since the 'Dark August' riots of 2042. Local community leaders have expressed concern over the latest escalation of violence in the nonhuman community . . ."

To prove the point, the newscast started to show clips of interviews with said "community leaders." Nohar snorted, with the token morey exception—Father Sean Murphy, a Brit fox who defected to the Irish Catholics, one of two ordained morey priests in the United States—the "community leaders" were all human.

The newscast then went into the obligatory human fear/responsibility versus moreau poverty/empowerment segment.

Same shit, different day. Nohar closed his eyes and listened for something interesting to come on.

Nohar woke to the sound of the comm buzzing for his attention. Grayish daylight streamed through the windows. The comm's display was still on the news channel. More gang violence, even worse this time. It barely registered on Nohar that it had gone down only three blocks from his apartment. Flashing text informed him he had slept through two other calls and nearly eight hours.

The incoming call was from Robert Dittrich. Nohar called out to the comm. "Got it."

The newscast winked out and was replaced by a red-bearded human face. "I wish you'd put on some clothes before you answer the phone."

Nohar growled. "What the hell do you want, Bobby?"

"Tough night?"

Nohar closed his eyes and sighed. "What do you think?"

"Heard about Nugoya. Tough break—"

"Tough all over. What do you want?"

Bobby coughed. "If you're going to be like that. I was going to give you the background I hacked on Nugoya—"

"Great, real useful."

"Did anyone ever tell you that you can be a real asshole at times, Nohar? As I was saying—" Bobby paused. Nohar didn't interrupt. "As I was saying, I was going to give you that data when the Fed landed on my doorstep."

Nohar sat up, fully awake now. Cat tumbled off his chest and ran off into the kitchen. "Shit. You in trouble?"

Bobby laughed and shook his head. "No, apparently I'm still clean. As we all know, everything I do on my computer is perfectly legal."

Nohar shook his head at that.

Bobby went on. "Wasn't me at all. They were asking about you. That's how I heard about Nugoya and last night."

"Me?"

"Yes, thought I'd call you. They wanted to know about your politics, of all things." Bobby put his hand to his forehead and chuckled. "They had this *babe* with them. Was she a hard case—"

"Skip the commentary. What were they looking for?"

"Some hired gun, I think. Named Hassan. I think they wanted to know if they could link the two of you."

"An Afghan canine and an Indian tiger—do they know how silly that sounds?"

"The war's been over for eighteen years. Things change. Just wanted you to know the Fed's interested in you. I got to go. Still want the data on Nugoya?"

"Keep it."

"Don't let the Fed screw you."

"I try to avoid it."

Bobby's face winked out and the news came back on.

Wonderful stuff to wake up to. Not only was he broke and one day closer to eviction, but now the FBI was curious about him.

The comm was talking about dead politicians. Nohar told it to shut up.

There were still two messages on his comm, waiting for his attention. One had been forwarded from his office—

Maybe it was a client.

Yeah, real likely, and maybe a morey would get elected president. Nohar told the comm, "Classify. Phone messages."

"two messages. july twenty-ninth. message one, ten-oh-five a.m. unlisted number—"

The voice of the computer was a flat, neutral monotone. Nohar never understood the urge people had to make computers sound like anything but. He told the comm, "Play."

Nohar didn't like calls that didn't ID themselves. People who called from unlisted locations generally had something to hide.

This caller definitely had something to hide, the screen came up a generic test pattern. This guy either didn't have a video pickup, or had turned his camera off.

"I hope to reach you, Mr. Rajasthan." The voice that came over the comm sounded like it was at the bottom of a well. It sounded bubbly. The words oozed. "I have need of the service of a private investigator. Please meet me at Lakeview Cemetery today at one-thirty p.m. This is not something I can discuss on a phone. I look for you by the grave of Eliza Wilkins."

That was the end of the message.

"Damn. It *was* a client."

"instructions unclear." The comm thought Nohar was talking to it.

Nohar told it, "Comm off," and the comm shut off obligingly.

It was a client, and a damn secretive one at that. Nohar didn't trust the situation one bit. There was little he could do about it. Nohar was so low on cash that he would have to at least meet the guy—

Nohar suddenly realized that it was already fifteen after one.

It took him two minutes to dress and another five to call Lakeview and get a plot number for Wilkins. Nohar did it with the video off, because if they saw he was a moreau it would have taken five times as long.

The first thing to greet him as he walked out into the misting rain was the acrid smell of burning plastic. The smoke made his nose itch. He realized the smell was coming from a burning car up by the traffic barriers.

Across the street from his apartment was an abandoned bus. There was a fresh graffiti logo on it. "ZIPPERHEAD— Off The Pink."

Another gang with it in for humans.

He walked up Mayfield, toward the cemetery, passing a knot of pink cops at the traffic barrier. Apparently this was the latest violence the news was going on about when he woke up. The fire was burning a prewar Japanese compact, an ancient Subaru. The car was wrapped around one of the concrete pylons. The way the thing had gone up—was still going; the cops were letting it burn itself out in the middle of the street—it had to have been wired with explosives. Inductors might explode, but they don't burn very well.

The cops didn't stop him—any other part of town and they probably would have on general principles.

The car wasn't all. It had been a busy morning. A block past the cops, things got ugly. Upwind of the burning plastic, Nohar could smell the scent of someone, multiple someones, who had bought it nasty. He smelled blood, fear, and cordite. The victims smelled canine.

He rounded the old cemetery gate—sealed by a solid four meter concrete wall behind the flaking wrought iron—

and headed down toward Coventry. When he turned the corner, he could see the medics loading body-bags—three vans' worth of body-bags. Canine had been a good guess. Nohar caught sight of one of the victims before the black plastic was zipped over the face. The body was a vulpine female with a small caliber gunshot wound to the right eye. One of the hispanic medics saw him looking over. There was the fresh smell of fear from the pink.

Another day, Nohar would have ignored it. Today, however, he had just had a case blow up in his face, the Fed was taking an unhealthy interest in him, the record July heat and the misting rain were making his fur itch under his trench coat, and—if his luck held—he was going to be late and miss his potential client. Today he was in a particularly bad mood.

Nohar could not resist the urge to smile.

Some moreaus don't have the facial equipment to produce a convincing smile, but Nohar's evolved feline cheeks could pull his mouth into a quite perceptible arc. The same gesture also bared an impressive set of teeth. Predominant among which were two glistening-white canines, the size of a man's thumb.

The poor guy didn't deserve it. Nohar could tell he was nervous enough just *being* in Moreytown. He didn't need to have a huge predatory morey looking at him like he was lunch.

Nohar didn't hang around for the reaction. He was still running late. Two blocks further down, at the intersection of Mayfield and Coventry, was the only open gate on this side of Lakeview Cemetery—seemed appropriate that it was into the Jewish section.

When he reached the right monument, "Eliza Wilkins, 1966–2042, beloved wife of Harold," it was thirty-two after. He was in time for the show. A funeral was progressing below him.

He was out of sight of most of them, and it was probably a good thing. They were planting someone of consequence, and from his vantage, it was pinks only. He thought he saw a morey in the crowd, but—damn his bad day-vision—it turned out to be a black pink with a heavy beard.

Not a morey in the lot, and the *whitest* bunch of pinks he had ever seen. Especially under the canopy. There, he figured on fifty people who got to use the folding chairs, at least another fifty standing back under cover, and a hundred or so milling about beyond some sort of private security line in back of the paying customers. Even with his poor eyesight he could make the types. The pinks who knew the corpse were obvious, they wore their money—he could see the glints of their shoes and jewelry whenever they moved—and they were, with few exceptions, white. The pinks who wanted to know the corpse were just as easily made, and they were closer to the normal mix of human coloring, a few blacks, orientals, hispanics. The black cops were totally out of it, with their cheap suits and their attention on everything but the service. The private security goons—they were white—were better dressed than the cops and were intent on keeping the flow of riffraff behind the tent. Then, the back with the crowd, were the vids. Cameras and mikes at the ready . . .

Some of the riffraff—mostly blacks and orientals—were carrying signs. Looked like a full-fledged protest was going on. The vids were paying as much, if not more, attention to the riffraff than to the service. Nohar wished he could make out more of the signs, but the best he could do was read the occasional word. Lots of isms, "Racism," "Sexism," "Speciesism." The signs that weren't isms seemed to mention capital-R Rights.

The Right to what, Nohar couldn't read.

Nohar wondered who had died—irritating, because he thought he had heard something about this, and the job his anonymous client had in mind probably involved the stiff. Perhaps the guy left all his money to some morey squeeze and they needed to track her down.

Nohar heard a truck, and hoped it wasn't security. The pinks might take offense at a morey walking around the human part of the cemetery. But instead of security, Nohar saw an unmarked cargo van. A Dodge Electroline painted institution-green. It was windowless, boxy, cheap, and either remote-driven or programmed. It wasn't the kind of vehicle Nohar expected to see in a cemetery. It pulled on to the shoulder and backed toward him. When it stopped, the rear doors opened with a pneumatic hiss.

The smell was overpowering. His sensitive nose was suddenly exposed to an open sewer. Nohar was enveloped by the odor of sweat, and bile, and ammonia. Even a pink would've been able to sense it.

He had no idea what this guy was supposed to look like, or who he was—but Nohar did *not* expect another frank. They were supposed to be rare. Despite that, what the opening door revealed *couldn't* be anything *but* a frank.

And a failure at that.

Once Nohar's eyes had adjusted to the nearly black interior of the cargo van, he could see it. The frank was vaguely humanoid and had a pasty white color to its rubbery skin. Its limbs seemed tubular and boneless, and its fingers were fused into a mittenlike hand. It wore a pink's clothes, but its pale bulk was fighting them. Rolls of white flesh cascaded over its belt, its collar, even its shoes. Glassy eyes, a lump of a nose, and a lipless mouth were collected together on a pear-shaped head. Its face seemed incapable of showing any expression. It seemed that, if the clothes were removed, the frank would just slide down and form a puddle on the ground.

The frank also massed more than Nohar did though it was a meter shorter.

Whatever gene-tech had designed this monstrosity had screwed-up big-time. Until now, Nohar could never quite fathom the reason for the pinks' horror at the franks. It seemed bizarre to him that humans, who took all the genetic tinkering with other species in stride, were so aghast when someone tinkered with their own. If this was a sample of what happened, Nohar could begin to understand. *Maybe*, thought Nohar, *pink genes didn't take kindly to fiddling*.

The voice was the same as the one over the comm—deep, bubbly, and, somehow, slimy. "Are you the detective, Nohar Rajasthan?"

Briefly, Nohar wondered if he needed the money this badly—he did. "Yes."

Nohar began to feel warmth coming from the back of the van. Nohar realized that the frank had the heat on in the van, all the way. Back where the frank was sitting it could be fifty degrees. An unpleasant sound emerged from the frank's mass. It could have been a belch. "We have fifteen minutes before van goes to next stop, forgive. I need to smuggle myself out. Have to keep meeting secret."

Nohar shrugged. "Then you better get on with it."

At least the frank took Nohar's appearance in stride. In most of the directories it didn't mention that Nohar was the only moreau in the city with a private investigator's license. For some people, his address wasn't a big enough clue. Of course a *pink* detective would have a problem with this guy, even more so than with Nugoya. At least with Nugoya, a pink could pretend the guy had been human.

"What kind of job? Surveillance or missing persons?"

Nohar heard flesh shifting as the frank moved. "Do you know who is being buried down the hill?"

Chalk one up for obvious conclusions. The stiff was involved. "Rich, human, lots of friends."

Another ugly sound emerged from the mass of white flesh. It might have been a laugh. "The dead man is a politician. His name is Daryl Johnson. He is the campaign manager for twelfth district congressman, Joseph Binder."

Nohar was wondering about the frank's weird accent when he realized that the frank had ducked his first question. "What's the *job*?"

"I must know who killed Daryl Johnson."

Nohar almost laughed, but he knew the frank was serious. "Outside my specialty." So much for the money he needed. "I don't mess with police investigations—"

"There is no police investigation."

Nohar was getting irritated with the frank's bubbling monotone. "I work with moreys. I don't work with human problems. You got the wrong P.I."

"Binder pressures the police, they close the case. I need to know if someone in my company is responsible for Johnson's death . . ."

Nohar looked straight into the frank's eyes. That usually unnerved people, but the frank was as expressionless as ever. "Did you hear what I said?" It took Nohar a while to realize that the reason he didn't like the frank's eyes was because they didn't blink.

"Let me finish, Mr. Rajasthan. You are the only person I can contact for this job. For obvious reasons, I am unable to hire a human investigator—"

"No solidarity shit."

"Practical matter. No qualified human is willing to talk to me. My company is Midwest Lapidary Imports. We're privately owned. We import gemstones from South Africa. The board is formed of South African refugees—"

"All like you?"

The frank showed no offense at the question. "Yes, like me. We retain contacts in the mining industry—" Nohar got a picture of the South African gene-techs trying to create a modified human miner. Hell, maybe the frank's appearance wasn't a mistake. For all Nohar knew, this guy was perfectly adapted for work in a five-mile-deep hole. Nohar stopped musing and waited for the frank to get to the point. "To succeed, the owners of Midwest Lapidary Imports, MLI, need to remain hidden, unnoticed, private. The company will not survive if our existence is widely known.

"With Johnson's death there is the possibility that one of our number is behind the murder . . ."

Nohar sighed. Learn something new every day. A bunch of franks were importing diamonds from South Africa, probably illegally. The pinks would just *love* that idea. The Supreme Court was still debating if the 29th amendment even covered the franks. No one knew yet if the franks were covered by the Bill of Rights, the limited morey amendment, or nothing at all. Before the pinks in this country had even locked down the legal status of engineered humans, here were a few, acting just like eager little capitalists. "You said Binder's blocking the investigation. What are you worried about?"

"One kills once, one kills again. You have no idea what it would mean if one of our number is directly involved in a human's death. The company is a worthy project, but someone may commit atrocities in its name. I cannot, nor can anyone else, abide our secrecy, our existence, if one of us kills to further our ends."

"How is your organization involved?"

"The police call it a robbery-murder because there are over three million dollars in campaign funds missing from his house—"

"Sounds plausible." Nohar realized that he was just leading the frank on. He had some natural curiosity, but there was no sane way he could touch this case.

The frank's bulk groaned and rippled as he leaned toward Nohar. The heat and stench that floated off of the frank's body almost made Nohar wince. "I am the accountant for MLI. The three million that is missing is never there. Campaign records the police use are wrong about this. The money comes from MLI, and *should* be there. But I handle the books and such a sum never leaves our accounts, or, if it does, it returns before the sum is debited.

"I do not go to the police. For now I must retain the secrecy. I can be wrong. I cannot damage the company until my suspicions are proved correct. I can't work within MLI. I have no idea who of my colleagues are involved. And I am closely watched—"

Nohar stood up. "I don't deal with anything involving murder. I have to walk from this one—find an out-of-towner."

"I have a five thousand retainer, and I will pay five times your usual rate, another five thousand when you complete the job successfully."

Nohar froze, his usual rate was five hundred a day. *No,* he told himself, *it's a bad job all over. You don't get involved with killings. You don't get involved with pinks. You don't get involved with things bigger than you are.* Against his will, he found himself saying, "Double the retainer."

It was a ludicrous request. The frank would never go for it. He'd be able to walk away clean.

"Agreed."

Damn it. "Plus expenses."

"Of course."

Nohar had trapped himself.

"Time closes in on us." The frank handed him an envelope. Ten thousand. He'd been anticipated. "Start with Johnson, work back. Do not contact anyone at MLI. I'll contact you every few days. Get any information about MLI through me. We have a few minutes. Any immediate questions?"

Nohar was still looking at the cash. "Why is a bunch of franks backing a reactionary right-winger like Binder?"

"*Quid pro quo,* Mr. Rajasthan. The corporate entity will see its interests served in the Senate. The fact that we're of a background Binder despises is of little consequence. Binder doesn't know who runs MLI. Anything else?"

"What's your name?"

Nohar heard the engine start up again. As the door closed with its pneumatic hiss, Nohar heard the frank say, "You can call me John Smith."

The ugly green van drove away, leaving a pair of divots in the grass. The ghost of the frank's smell remained, emanating from the money Nohar still held in his hand.

Once he took the money, he did the job. No matter what. *No matter what, damn it.*

Nohar put the money in one of the cavernous pockets of his trenchcoat. Now that he was on the job, he pulled out his camera, slipped in a ramcard, and started recording the funeral.

Chapter 3

The ATM was half a block from Nohar's place. To his relief, it appeared to be working. At least the lights were on. He stopped in front of the armored door, and, under the blank stare of the disabled external camera, he pulled his card and slipped it into the slot. The mechanism gave an arthritic wheeze and he feared it was going to eat his card again. Fortunately, the keypad flashed green at him. He punched in his ID number while the servos on the lensless camera followed his every move.

The door slid aside with a grinding noise and he ducked into the too-small room. When the door shut behind him, he finally felt comfortable with all that money on him.

The chair the bank provided was too small to sit on. The best he could do was to lean against it and hunch over, hanging his tail over the back of the seat. Besides, somebody had pissed all over the damn thing.

There was a short burst of static, and a voice came through one of the intact speakers. "Welcome to Society Bank's Green Machine—bzt—Mr. Noharajasthan. Please state clearly what transaction you wish—"

The voice was supposed to be female human, but it was tinny and muffled. Nohar interrupted. "Deposit. Card Account. Ten thousand dollars."

"Please repeat clearly."

"Deposit. Card Account. Ten thousand dollars."

"Please type in request."

Great, the damn thing couldn't hear him. He typed in the transaction on the terminal.

"Is this a cash transaction?"

It didn't believe him. "Yes," he said and typed at the same time.

A drawer opened under the terminal. Unlike most of the ATM, it seemed to be in perfect working order. " —bzt— please place paper currency in the drawer. There will be a slight pause while the bills are screened."

Nohar placed the two packets of bills in the drawer. Nohar knew that the note of surprise he heard in the ATM's voice was in his own head more than anywhere else. "Your currency checks as valid. Thank you for banking with Society, Mr. Noharajasthan. The current balance on your card account is —bzt— ten-thousand-one-hundred-ninety-three-dollars and sixty-five cents. You may pick up your card and receipt at the door. Have a nice day."

Nohar left the ATM and turned up the collar of his coat against a sudden burst of more intense rain. He typed in his ID again at the keypad, blinking twice as water got in his eyes. The ATM released his card and the receipt. As he pocketed the items, he noticed a couple of ratboys hanging around across the street.

An ATM in use attracted vermin.

The two ratboys were crossing the street. Nohar had hoped that his appearance would have put them off. Apparently, they were too zoned or too stupid, perhaps both. As they closed he could smell that they were probably on something. Itching for a fight. both of them.

"Kitty."

"*Pretty* kitty."

Nohar decided to ignore them. All he wanted was to get home and shuck his wet coat. He walked down the road past them.

The damn rodents didn't seem to know any better. They cut around in front of him, blocking his path.

"No, no, *wrong*, kitty." This rat was a dirty brown, shiny black in the rain. His nose seemed to twitch in time to his spastic tail. He wore an abbreviated leather vest and denim cutoffs. He was taking the lead in this idiotic display. "Doncha know who we are?"

This was more than enough for Nohar. "You're two rodent wet-backs too stoned for your own good. You're future road kill if you keep this up."

The big one—well, the relatively big one, maybe 70 kilos, mostly fat—didn't like that. "We the Ziphead, man, and you better up some bucks for that. We rule here . . ."

This was nuts. These guys were Latin American cannon fodder. Honduras, Nicaragua, Cuba, Panama, all the Central American countries went for quantity and quick reproduction. Huge standing armies from zero—most of the rats were never even trained to use their weapons.

Two of those, those jokes, were trying to face down someone whose genes had gone through a multibillion dollar evolution simulation to produce the elite troops of the Indian Special Forces. Nohar had no special training, but it was still ludicrous.

He smiled, teeth and all. He couldn't take this seriously. "Ever occur to you I just made a *deposit*?"

Fearless Leader was put out. "You don't fuck with us—stray—we'll *shave* you."

"We vanish what don't give us respect—"

"*Stigmata de nada.*"

Stupid and stoned. That last line only made sense to them, and they found it uproariously funny. Nohar stepped to the side and left them to their inside joke.

"Fucking stray." Snick. Bigboy had pulled a weapon, sounded like a knife. Nohar slowly turned around. Bigboy had a switchblade out and was showing the world that he couldn't use it. It was long, pointed, and had no edge to speak of. Bigboy was swishing the thing like a baton. Wide slicing arcs that, had they connected with anything solid, might raise a welt and would probably sprain Bigboy's wrist all to hell. "Teach you some respect. I'll have your tail for a belt."

Nohar stowed the comments. He spread his legs apart and bent down, lowering his center of gravity. He thrust his left arm, claws forward, in a defensive posture, while his right arm hung back behind him, hand cupped to slice at any opening Bigboy gave him. He growled, deep in his diaphragm. The sound didn't make it out of his throat.

Bigboy was oblivious in his advance. Fearless Leader had a little more brains and hung back. Bigboy was reeking of excitement and adrenaline. Fearless was almost as jacked, but he was beginning to realize he might have bitten off more than he could chew.

Bigboy swung one of his wide, predictable arcs. Nohar caught Bigboy's wrist with his left hand, remembering Nugoya, and smiled at the rat. Nohar's right hand swung forward in a well aimed sweep that left four light trails of blood on Bigboy's overlarge gut.

"Listen, ratboy, I *could* have pulled you into that sweep. We'd have a nice view of your intestines— Drop the knife."

The knife clattered to the ground. Nohar stepped on it and let Bigboy go. Fearless was still backpedaling. Fearless didn't seem to get the point, he was still on his line of bullshit. "Your pussy bastard ass is mine."

Fearless was reaching behind, into the waistband of his cutoffs. Nohar knew instinctively that the rat was going for a gun. Nohar was about to jump Fearless—he could clear the distance easily before the rat got his hand untangled from his pants—but the action was broken by a burst of high-pitched rapid-fire Spanish from down the street, by the old bus.

They all turned that way to face a snow-white female rodent. She wore the same abbreviated leather vest and denim cutoffs. Her naked tail was writhing, and she sounded pissed. Nohar immediately pegged her as a superior. Bigboy and Fearless seemed to forget about him and began talking back to her in Spanish as well. All babble to him, he just hoped she was cussing the fools out.

Cat-and-mouse is not a smart game to play when you are the mouse.

The three rodents were talking among themselves, and Nohar began to slowly withdraw from the rodent fiasco.

Nohar had nearly gotten to the door to his apartment. Bigboy and Fearless had slunk away, but the white one stayed.

"Rajasthan!"

The white rat was addressing him directly. She wasn't making any threatening moves, so Nohar stopped and waited.

"You are a lucky cat, son of Rajasthan—"

How did she know, how could she— "What do you—"

"I speak! You listen." The force of the rat's voice actually made Nohar stop his question in mid-breath. The tiny rat's body could produce a voice that would intimidate a rabid ursine. "The finger of God has just touched your brow, son of Rajasthan. Those that control want your life for their reasons. They buy you much tolerance."

The rat paused, and for once Nohar had nothing to say. She just stood there, staring at him with eyes that looked like high-carbon steel. Nohar turned toward his door—

"Pray you that God doesn't forget you, Nohar. If the blessing is lifted, Zipperhead will have you."

Nohar punched the combination on his door. He had given the rats enough of his time.

"*I'll* have you, Nohar."

As Nohar ducked inside, the white rat added. "You, or someone you love."

He slammed the door shut. It was a shame. She hadn't been bad-looking. Her triangular face ended in a delicate nose—but she was a die-hard creep just like her idiot subordinates.

She also wore cheap pink perfume. Why would a morey wear that kind of crap?

Nohar had hurried away from the smell as much as the spiel. He took a few deep breaths of relatively clean air before he started up the stairwell.

The humidity was making his door stick again, and it took him a few seconds to unwedge it. The damn thing was heavier than it should have been because it had a steel plate in it, a relic of the previous tenant. Nohar would have questioned the wisdom of sticking an armored door in a wooden door frame.

Cat ran up to the door and immediately began rubbing against his foot. "So you hungry or lonely?" Nohar asked the yellow tomcat as he picked it up. A loud purr from under his hand told him to figure it out for himself. Nohar pushed the door shut with his foot and ducked into the living room. Cat started butting his head into Nohar's chin, and, after glancing into the kitchen to check Cat's dishes, Nohar decided Cat wasn't hungry.

"Sorry I took so long, I got distracted by the local color." Cat closed his eyes as Nohar scratched him behind the ears. "But, lucky us, I got one hell of an advance from a client before the first of the month."

Cat started grooming Nohar's thumb.

"Yeah, right. Look, you little missing link, I have to put you down so I can get this damn pink clothing off. So don't start mewing at me—"

Nohar put him down and Cat started mewing.

He undressed and looked at the comm. Two messages waiting now.

"Comm on," he said to the machine as he started peeling clothing off of his damp fur.

"comm on."

Nohar reclined on the couch. Cat took up a perch on his chest and purred.

"Classify. Phone messages."

"two messages. july twenty-ninth, three-oh-five p.m. from detective irwin harsk, calling from—"

"Play."

Static, then Harsk's bald black head appeared on the screen.

"Sorry I didn't catch you, Nohar." There was a smile on Harsk's face and Nohar couldn't decide if it was ironic or sarcastic. "I thought I'd tell you that another little red light is flashing by your name. The DEA computer has this 'thing' about large cash transactions. Ten thousand dollars? The Fed is curious, and so am I. We're watching you, so—on the off-chance the cash is legit—remember to withhold your income tax."

That was damn quick, even for the Fed. The DEA must have a tap on the ATM down the street. It was irritating, but not that surprising. Harsk knew he was clean, but he'd let the Fed wonder just out of a sense of perversity. The comm was asking if he had a reply.

"Yes. Record," Nohar cleared his throat., "Harsk, don't call back until you have a warrant. End. Mail. Reply."

Nohar closed his eyes and clawed the back of the couch. He told the comm to play the earlier message without really paying attention to it. He wasn't looking directly at the screen when he heard a husky female voice.

"Raj?"

"Pause!" His eyes shot open and he turned to look at Maria Limon. The call had come in close to two in the morning, during his meet with Nugoya. In the pressure of the moment, Nohar had forgotten to call Maria and cancel their date—

This wasn't the first time either. Nohar had a sinking feeling.

She was at a public phone. He could see the streetlights behind her. There was frozen shimmer on the screen where the lights were reflecting off the black fur under her whiskers. Apparently the Brazilians had been more creative with their moreaus. She'd been crying. Nohar doubted his tear ducts could be triggered emotionally.

Maria's golden eyes, her pupils almost round, seemed to level an accusation at him.

Cat tilted his head and gave Nohar a curious look.

"Replay."

Static, then Maria's face reappeared on the screen. Nohar watched as one delicate black hand wiped away the moisture on her cheek. The hand fell and she looked directly at Nohar.

"Raj? I'm sorry about this. I should have the guts to face you, but I can't. You'd say something and we'd end up shouting at each other, or fucking each other—or, God help me, both—I can't do this anymore. I still care for you, but if we keep seeing each other, I won't—" Maria's voice broke, and more tears came. Maria was a strong person. Nohar had never seen her cry before. "Good-bye, Raj, I have to leave while the memories are still worth something to me."

Maria's face vanished as she broke the connection.

Nohar felt like someone had just kneed him in the balls, and he was feeling his stomach drop out just before the pain came.

They had known each other for only two months. It shouldn't have been a surprise. He had been expecting something like this all along. She was right.

Cat must have sensed some of his agitation, because he started butting his head against Nohar's face and licking his cheek. Cat stopped after a few seconds and regarded Nohar with his head cocked to one side. Cat's expression seemed to be asking him what was wrong.

Nohar stayed quiet for a long while before he told the computer to put the message into permanent storage. He tried to call Maria, but her comm was locking out his calls. Maria would want a clean break. He could probably talk her out of it once, maybe twice, more. She didn't want him to.

He spent a few moments in relative silence, stroking Cat and listening to the high-frequency hum of the comm.

Instead of turning the comm off, he called up Maria's message, and paused it. He paused it where the claw on the index finger of her right hand had caught a tear. The small sphere of liquid was nestled between the hook in her claw and the pad on her finger. It refracted the unnatural white of the streetlight behind her, causing arcs of light to emerge from one golden half-lidded eye. It was the kind of image that made Nohar wish he had a scrap of romance in his soul.

Chapter 4

After a while, Nohar decided he had better things to do than stare at Maria.

"Load program. Label, 'Log-on library.' "

"searching . . . found."

"Run program."

Maria's face disappeared as the computer started the access sequence. It showed the blue-and-white AT&T test pattern as it repeatedly buzzed the public library database, waiting for an open data channel. It was close to prime time for library access. It took nearly fifteen minutes for the comm to lock onto the library's mainframe.

Even when the Cleveland Public Library logo came up, there were a few minutes of waiting. The screen scrolled messages about fighting illiteracy, and how he should spend his summer reading a book. Nohar knew that a few thousand users on a clunky timesharing system at the same time tended to slow things down, but it still seemed the delay was directed at him.

He shifted on the couch, trying to become more comfortable. Waiting always made him aware of his tail.

Two minutes passed. Then, with a little electronic fanfare, the menu came up—though you couldn't quite call the animated figure a "menu." The library system called their animated characters "guides." The software was trying too hard to be friendly. It verged on the cute.

The "guide" facing him on the screen wore a sword strapped to his side, and was in the process of contemplating a human skull when he seemed to notice Nohar's intrusion. The effect was spoiled by a glitch in the animation. A rolling blue line scrolled up and down the screen, shifting everything above it a pixel to the left. Nohar sighed. He had no desire to spend his time with a manic-depressive Dane. Especially after that call from Maria.

He spoke before the prince had time to object. "Text menu."

The only library "guide" he liked was the little blonde human girl, Alice.

The text menu came up and the first thing he did, despite Smith's admonition to start with Johnson, was to conduct a global search for information on Midwest Lapidary Imports. He wanted some sort of handle on his client's employer, which was also the home of the alleged suspects.

There was only a fifteen second pause.

The computer came back with the report, "Three items found."

Nohar shook his head. Only three? With a *global* search? That meant there were only three items in the entire library database that even mentioned MLI.

Nohar played the first item and got a newsfax about diamond imports, legal and illegal. The focus on the article was how hard it was to keep track of the gems. It had a graph that dramatized the divergence between the gems known to have come into the country, and those known to be in circulation. In the last fifteen years, a hell of a lot more gems had been in circulation than could be accounted for. It was, in fact, causing a depression in the diamond market. The article blamed the Fed and new smuggling techniques. The least likely smuggling method Nohar read about was casting the diamonds in the heat-tiles on the exterior of a ballistic shuttle. Midwest Lapidary was only mentioned peripherally in a list of domestic diamond-related companies at the end of the article.

The second article was actually *about* MLI, but it was only barely informative. It was from some subscriber service and was just a sparse paragraph of electronic text. MLI, a new company, incorporated in 2038. Wholesale diamond sales. Headquartered in Cleveland. Privately owned. Address.

That was it. Smith was right about these guys keeping a low profile. Nohar pictured most new corporate enterprises announcing themselves with trumpets and splashy media campaigns. It looked like MLI was trying to hide the fact it even existed.

The third item was a vid broadcast from December 2, 2043. The broadcast was dated. The guy with the news was still following journalistic fashion from the riots. Grimy safari jacket, urban camo pants, three-day-old stubble, sunglasses. The outfit had nothing to do with the story. The guy was standing in a snowdrift outside a pair of low office buildings faced in blue tile. Nohar recognized a stretch of Mayfield Road behind the buildings. The guy was only a few miles to the cast of Moreytown.

Hmm, Nohar thought there was a prison there.

The guy was trying very hard to have the voice of authority. "I am standing outside the offices and the laboratory of NuFood Incorporated. Today, came the surprising announcement that NuFood had been bought by a local diamond wholesaler, Midwest Lapidary. There had been speculation that NuFood had been on the verge of bankruptcy when it sold its assets and patents to Midwest Lapidary for an undisclosed amount. Shortly after the sale, NuFood's two hundred employees were laid off in what Midwest Lapidary called in a press release, 'a streamlining measure.'

"NuFood, you may recall from a Special Health Report earlier this year, is the company with patents on the dietary supplement, MirrorProtein. While NuFood has had success creating synthetic food-products resembling natural items, which the human body cannot process, it has had continuing problems with the FDA in getting its products approved. Sources say this created the financial difficulty that led directly to the sale of the company. No one from Midwest Lapidary could be reached for comment."

That was a big help.

So Smith was right. He needed to start with Johnson and work back. Johnson was Binder's campaign manager, so Nohar did a global search using both his name and Binder's.

The pause was closer to a full minute this time. His tail fell asleep. Nohar stood up to massage the base of his tail.

Cat took the opportunity to jump up on the couch and snuggle into the warm dent in the cushions.

The screen flashed the results of the search. Over six thousand items, more like it. No way he could peruse all of it on-line, so he slipped in a ramcard and downloaded the whole mess of data. He leeched nearly fifteen megs in half that many minutes.

He now had his own little database on Binder and his campaign.

By five, his examination of the public information on Binder gave him no reason to alter his first impression of the guy as a right-wing reactionary bastard. It seemed Binder had something bad to say about every group or organization that didn't count him as a member; women, foreigners, liberals, intellectuals, blacks and hispanics, Catholics, the poor, the homeless, pornographers, the news media—the list was endless. Despite the vitriol that coated every word the man uttered, three groups in particular gained his very special attention. In order of the invective he threw upon them, they were: moreaus, franks, and all their genetically-engineered ilk, whose rights he was actively involved in trying to repeal; homosexuals, whose sexual preference Binder seemed to rank primary in his personal list of mortal sins; and the U.S. federal government—the only place Binder and Nohar seemed to touch common ground—whose propensity for spending money was only equaled by Binder's impulse to slash any spending program he could lay his hands on.

Nohar found it hard to believe he was investigating the murder of this guy's campaign manager.

The data on Daryl Johnson was more scattered. Nohar couldn't get a fix on his beliefs. All he got was the fact that Johnson was loyal to Binder and had been with the congressman since the state legislature. He had been recruited out of Bowling Green in the autumn of 2040. The same time as most of Binder's inner circle. Johnson's three classmates were: Edwin Harrison, the campaign's legal counsel; Philip Young, the campaign finance chairman; and Desmond Thomson, the campaign press secretary. Johnson graduated at the age of twenty-three, late. Apparently because of a shift in his major, from chemistry to political science. A bit of a jump. That would make him the ripe old age of thirty-nine when he died.

Not so ripe, Nohar corrected himself. This guy was human, so thirty-nine was barely on the threshold of middle age. Thirty-nine was better than the life expectancy of some moreys.

He was a little more familiar with the situation he was dealing with. That was all. His client wanted to find out if MLI was behind the Johnson killing. So far, he didn't have any connection between the two, other than Smith's assertion that the missing three megabucks came from MLI.

Time to start making some calls. Thomson looked like a good choice. The press secretary would be used to talking to people, if not actually to saying anything.

If he was going to talk to a pink, he'd better put some clothes on. He snorted. Clothes were a needless irritation that wouldn't have been necessary on a morey case. Getting dressed, just to make a phone call, was just plain silly.

He pulled a button-down shirt from a small pile in the corner of his bedroom. The storm had reduced the light in the apartment, so Nohar couldn't quite make out the color of the shirt. It was either a very light blue, or a very off white. Nohar put it on, claws catching on the buttons, and decided to forgo the pants. The comm was only going to show him from the waist up, as long as he didn't stand up.

He ducked into the bathroom and looked in the mirror. Pointless, really. What did a pink know about grooming anyway? Still, Nohar licked the back of his hand and ran it over his head a few times, smoothing things out.

After that, he sat on the couch, shooing Cat away. He set the comm to record and told it to call Desmond Thomson at Binder campaign headquarters. He routed the call through the comm at his office so his credentials would be shown up front.

Oddly enough, though it was only a little after five, no one at Binder headquarters seemed to be answering. After nearly a minute of displaying the Binder Senate campaign logo, the comm at Binder headquarters forwarded his call to Thompson's home. Nohar shrugged. It didn't matter as long as he got through to Thomson.

Thomson surprised the hell out of him by being black. In

fact, Thomson had been the bearded pink that had tricked Nohar's eyes into seeing a morey in the crowd at the funeral. Thomson's hair and beard were shot with gray. He had the bearing of a pro wrestler and the voice of a vid anchorman. "Mister," Thomson's gaze flicked to the text on his monitor, "Rajasthan?" Thomson's voice had begun on a high note, indicating some surprise at Nohar's appearance. However, by the end of Nohar's name, the tone of Thomson's voice had become smooth, friendly, and utterly phony.

"Yes, Mr. Thomson?"

"I am. I see your call has been forwarded from our campaign headquarters. I presume you wish to talk to me in my capacity as Congressman Binder's press secretary?"

The man talked like a press release, and Nohar couldn't get over the fact that Thomson was black. It made about as much sense as having a Jewish spokesman for the Islamic Axis. Nohar nodded.

"I would like to ask about your late campaign manager—"

"Of course. I'll help as much as possible. We've been quite free with what we know about the tragedy. However, things are quite chaotic in the organization with the loss of Mr. Johnson. We've had to give the whole campaign the week off so we can sort out the mess. So my time is limited. I'm sure what you need has already been told to the police or the press."

Nohar could smell a brush-off coming from a mile away. "I only have a few questions. They won't take long."

"Would you mind transmitting your credentials?"

Either Thomson didn't trust the label from Nohar's office comm, or he was politely looking for an excuse to hang up. Fortunately, Nohar's wallet with his PI license was sitting on top of the comm and he didn't have to stand up to get it. He slid his license into the fax slot on his comm and hit the send button. Thomson nodded when he saw the results. "I can give you ten minutes."

At the length this guy spoke, that wouldn't give Nohar much. "When did Johnson die?"

"I am given to understand the time of death was placed sometime in the middle of the week of the twentieth—"

"July twentieth?"

"Of course."

"When was the last official contact with Johnson?"

"As we have informed the police, he attended a political fund-raiser Saturday the nineteenth. He didn't come in to work the following week—"

"Didn't this strike anyone as odd?"

Thomson was undoubtedly irritated by Nohar's interruptions, but he hid it well. "No, it is an election year. It's common for executive officers to be pulled away from the desk for trips, speeches, press, and so on. Johnson was the chief executive under Binder, he often did such things on his own initiative—"

"Do you know what he was doing?"

"No. If it wasn't dealing with the media, it was not my department. Now, if you don't mind, the time—"

It didn't feel like ten minutes to Nohar. "One more thing."

Nohar thought he heard Thomson sigh. "What?"

"About the three million dollars the police believe was stolen from the campaign—"

Thomson interrupted this time. "I am sorry, but I do not have the authority to discuss the financial details of the campaign."

Ah, Nohar had finally run into the brick wall. "I am sorry to hear that. You see, I have conflicting information. I simply want to know if the three million was physically in Johnson's possession, in cash—"

"I said, I can't discuss it."

Try another tack. "Who has access to the campaign's financial records?"

Thomson was shaking his head. He even grinned a bit, showing a gold tooth that had to be decorative.

"Me, the legal counsel, the campaign manager and his executive assistant, and the finance chairman, of course."

"Thank you."

Thomson chuckled. "I'm afraid they can't help you. No one but Binder has the authority to release confidential financial data. Except, of course, disclosures required by law."

"Or a subpoena," Nohar muttered.

"I would call that a disclosure required by law. Now, as I said before, my time is limited. I really must go."

"Thanks for your help," Nohar said, nearly choking on the insincerity.

"You're welcome. It's my job," Thomson replied, just as insincere, but much more professional.

The line was cut and Nohar was left staring at a test pattern.

Nohar ran through the record of the conversation a few times. It irritated him that Thomson was right. Nothing was in the conversation he wouldn't be able to get from the police record or the news. Reviewing the tape didn't tell Nohar anything more, other than the fact Thomson lived in a ritzy penthouse overlooking downtown—Thomson's home comm faced a window.

The comm told him it was fifteen after. It was time to call Manny down at the pathologist's office. Nohar wanted to set up a meeting for tonight. One he hoped would be more fruitful.

Chapter 5

During the night, the rain turned into a deluge. Nohar didn't feel half as uncomfortable under the sudden thunderstorm as he had in the misting drizzle in the cemetery. The dark violence of it suited him.

Coventry suited him.

The three block area was a ragged collection of bars close to the East Cleveland border. It was far enough away from the heart of Moreytown to see the occasional pink in the area. As always, there were two patrol cars, the riot watch, one on either end of the strip. Nohar passed one of them at the intersection of Coventry and Mayfield, and, while it was too far for him to see it, he knew its twin was parked in the old school parking lot, three blocks away.

Like Nohar's neighborhood, Coventry was blocked off from car traffic by three-meter-tall concrete pylons left over from the riots. Graffiti wrapped around the rectangular blocks, as if the strip were trying to escape its arbitrary confines by oozing through the gaps.

The rain hadn't slowed things down. Ten-thirty at night and the street was packed with the backwash of Moreytown.

The downpour couldn't remove the omnipresent smell of damp fur.

Nohar made his way down the center of the old asphalt strip. He passed canines, felines, a knot of rodents in leather vests and denim briefs—he avoided the slight scent of familiar perfume—an unfamiliar ursine, a loud lepus shouting at a rapt vulpine congregation. The people around him only made the briefest impression. A few shouted greetings. Nohar waved without quite noticing who they had been.

His destination, *Watership Down*, was one of the few bars on the Coventry strip that was actually owned and operated by a morey proprietor—Gerard Lopez, a lepus. The reason Nohar chose to frequent this particular bar, out of the two dozen on the strip, was the high ceiling. This was one of the few places he could get fully toasted and not end up bashing his head into a ceiling fan or a light fixture.

Nohar entered the bar, shook some of the rain out of his coat, and took his regular seat, a booth in the back that had the seats moved back for people his size. The table was directly underneath a garish framed picture someone had once told him was an original Warner Brothers' animation cell. It was a hand drawn cartoon of a gray bipedal rabbit in the process of blowing up a bald, round-headed, human. Lopez had mounted a little brass plaque under the picture. It said, "1946—Off the Pink." Even if it was a joke, Nohar was glad that most humans didn't come down to Coventry.

Manny was waiting at the bar. He bore down on Nohar's booth carrying two pitchers of beer. Alert black eyes glanced over Nohar as the quick little mongoose put the pitcher on the table. "Nohar, you look like hell."

Nohar's mind had drifted off the case and on to Maria. He was at once irritated and defensive. Manny was the only real family Nohar had. The mongoose had come to America with Nohar's parents, and had been there when Nohar's mother had died. When he was younger, Nohar had resented him. It was still hard for Nohar to accept Manny's concern with good grace.

It had taken finding his real father to allow Nohar to appreciate Manny.

"Maria dumped me." Nohar poured himself a beer and downed it.

Manny slid into the opposite side of the booth and chittered a little in sympathy. "That's hard to believe. After the last time I saw you two together, it looked like you finally found the right one."

"I thought so myself. Always do."

"Do you want to talk about it?"

"I want to talk to an M.E., not a psychiatrist."

Manny gave his head a shake and poured himself a beer. "Are you sure you want to talk business right now?"

Nohar glared down at Manny. "I didn't ask you to meet me for a counseling session." Nohar reined in the outburst. "Sorry. Been a tough day. Did you bring the database?"

Unlike Nohar, Manny couldn't form a smile, but between them a nose-twitch on Manny's part served the same purpose. Manny took a notebook-sized case and put it on the table and flipped up the cover. There was a pause as it warmed up.

"What happened to your wallet computer?"

Manny gave a brief shrug. His voice held a tone of resignation. "The Jap chip blew. It was a prewar model, so the county couldn't replace it. So, I got this new bug-ridden Tunja 1200. Soon we're going to be back to manual typewriters and paper records . . ."

Manny's head shook, accompanied by a high-pitched sigh. In a few seconds, the screen began to glow faintly and the keypad became visible. "I updated it from the mainframe after you called. Do you have a name for the stiff you're looking for?"

Nohar poured himself another beer. "Yes, but this isn't a normal case—"

"But you want records for a stiff, right?"

"The name's Daryl Johnson."

Manny's whole upper body undulated with a momentary shrug. "Off hand, I don't remember that name. What species?"

"Human."

Manny froze; the sudden absence of motion was eerie on the mongoose. "What?"

"I need the complete forensic record on the murder of a man named Daryl Johnson."

"What the *hell?*"

Nohar could see him tense up. He could almost see the vibration in Manny's small frame. Nohar could smell

Manny's nervousness even over the smell of the beer. "You *can* access those records?"

"Nohar, you said *human,* you said *murder.*"

"I said it wasn't a normal case."

Manny was silent. His black eyes darted from Nohar to his little portable computer and back. Nohar was a little surprised at his reaction. They'd worked together and had shared information ever since Nohar had gotten his license.

But then, until now, it had simply consisted of Nohar making sure the moreys he'd been hired to find hadn't ended up in the morgue.

After nearly a full minute of silence, Manny finally spoke, "Nohar, I've known you all your life. You don't ask for trouble anymore. You've never interfered with a police investigation. You've *never* messed with pink business."

"You slipped, you said the 'p' word." Nohar regretted it the instant he said it. Manny had to work with humans. He was one of perhaps a half-dozen moreaus in the city with medical training, and they would only let him cut up corpses. Only morey corpses at that. Manny was always open to the accusation of selling out, being pink under his fur. Nohar just rubbed Manny's nose in it.

"Forgive me if I don't want to see you mixed up in something that might hurt you."

"Sorry. It's just a case. An important one. I'm trying to find out who killed him."

Manny closed his eyes. His voice picked up speed. "You are trying to find out who murdered a human? You know what'd happen if word got on the street? You know what happens to moreys that get too close to humans—"

"I still need your help."

Manny made an effort to slow down. "I'm not going to change your mind, am I? I'll call up the file, but first—" One of Manny's too-long hands clasped Nohar's wrist. "Remember, my place is as far from Moreytown as you can get."

Nohar nodded.

Manny held Nohar's gaze for a brief moment. Then Manny looked down at his computer and started rapid-fire tapping on the screen. For a terminal with no audio, Manny handled it very efficiently. His hands were engineered for surgery, and their gracefulness permeated every gesture.

He did, however, have to hit the thing a few times to get it to work right.

Manny's nose twitched. "I don't believe it. The file's inactive. It's barely a week old."

"The police are under pressure to drop the investigation."

Manny looked like he was about to say something, but apparently thought better of it. "Fine, well, we have the autopsy report, list of the forensic evidence, abstract of the scene of the crime, a few preliminary statements from the neighbors, as well as the witness who found the body, etcetera. Pretty complete record. Compared to most I've seen."

One of Manny's lithe hands dove into a breast pocket and pulled out a ramcard and slid it into the side of the computer. Nohar briefly saw the rainbow sheen of the card reflected in a small puddle of beer on the table. "I'm running off a copy. Do me a favor and make a backup. Occasionally they *do* monitor access to the database."

Nohar nodded when Manny handed him the card. Nohar slipped it into his wallet, next to the as yet unexamined card from his camera, the pictures from Johnson's funeral. "could you tell me how Johnson died?"

"It's all on the card I gave you. He was shot in the head. Through his picture window. Splattered his brains all over his comm—oh, *that's* interesting . . ."

"What?"

There was the hint of what might have been admiration in Manny's voice. "Are you familiar with Israeli weaponry? Thought not. The forensics team found the remains of two bullets, from a Levitt Mark II, fifty-caliber." A slight whistle of air came from between Manny's front teeth.

"So?"

"Came out of Mossad during the Third Gulf War. It was designed for a single sniper, and, like most designs they came up with, it's made to keep the sniper alive. The bullets are propelled by compressed carbon dioxide. It can't be heard firing by anyone farther away than fifteen meters or so. The ammunition is made from an impact-sensitive plastic explosive impregnated with shrapnel. It's intended as an antipersonnel weapon. I haven't seen an impact wound form one of these since the war. The Afghanis favored them for night raids—Nohar, what the hell have you gotten yourself into?"

"I don't know."

Nohar knew Manny was tempted to try and talk him out of it. However, Manny wouldn't try. Nohar hated when Manny got into surrogate-father mode, and Manny was too aware of that fact.

Such meetings usually ended with them spending a few hours discussing innocent bullshit over too many beers. This time they finished the pitchers in relative silence. Nohar wanted to reassure Manny he wasn't in over his head. But it would have been a lie. Nohar had trouble with lies, especially with Manny.

So, at eleven-fifteen—an early night for them—they walked to the south end of the strip, and the lot where Manny had parked. The rain had intensified, finally chasing the moreys inside. The abandoned trash-strewn asphalt reminded Nohar of pictures of the Pan-Asian war. It was the view of a city waiting for a biological warhead.

They rounded the pylons on Euclid Heights Boulevard and Nohar caught sight of the other cop on the riot-watch. Nohar wondered what it would be like, to come to work each day, to sit and wait for something to explode. The cops would have to be on rotation. Someone on permanent assignment would go nuts.

The cop looked at them as they passed, two unequal-sized moreys huddling through the rain. There was a flash of lightning, and Nohar saw the cop's face. The pink looked scared. In that instant he saw a man, a kid really, no more than twenty-two—young for a human that was, most moreys who made it into their twenties were well into middle age. The pink kid would have no idea what he would do if Nohar and Manny decided to do something illegal. He could imagine he sensed the smell of fear off of the kid, even with the car and the rain between them.

They passed the police car and walked into the parking lot of the old school. Nohar couldn't help but feel sorry for the cop. No one deserved to be placed in that kind of situation unprepared.

They stopped at the van and Manny spoke for the first

time since they'd left the bar. "I can't talk you out of this, but my door's open if you need it."

"I know." Nohar was uncomfortably reminded of last night.

Nohar told himself that there was no reason to accept things on this case to go bad like that. Hell, he'd been paid a hell of a lot up front, things *couldn't* go that badly this time.

At least it didn't look like he was going to be stiffed again.

Manny got into his van, another Electroline. In the dark of the storm, away from the streetlights, the van reminded Nohar of the frank in the graveyard. Both vans were the same industrial-green, the same boxy make, and had the same pneumatic doors on the back. The only difference— Manny's van had a driver's cab and "Cuyahoga County Medical Examiner" painted on all the doors.

As Manny drove back toward downtown, Nohar supposed the van's markings had a deterrent effect on car thieves.

"I said, a *fifteen* by *fifteen* grid with times *three* magnification!"

"instructions unclear."

Nohar almost shouted something back at the comm. Instead, he took a deep breath and stroked Cat a few times. *There are a few things,* he thought, *more fruitless than getting angry at a machine.* Shouting at it was just going to overtax the translation software.

"Display. Photo thirty-five. Grid. Fifteen by fifteen. Magnification. Times three."

This time the comm did what it was told.

Photo number thirty-five was a good, panoramic shot of the seated parties at Johnson's funeral. It was the one picture that had a full facial on everybody. The haze had helped by diffusing the July sun. The indirect lighting eliminated stark shadows, and would help in making the attendees, especially those to the rear, under the tent.

He had enlarged it enough. Most of the faces were clear, which was good. Nohar did not want to wait half an hour while his cheap software enhanced the picture.

Now for the grunt work. "Move. Grid. Left five percent."

One box on the grid now enclosed a face.

He told the program to print it and a portrait of a funeral attendee started sliding out of the comm's fax slot. One down, forty-nine to go.

Nohar spent two hours getting identifiable portraits from the one picture. Most of them, he knew, would offer no useful information. However, the procedure calmed him. It was something he had done hundreds of times before.

The routine was so automatic that his mind kept traveling back to Johnson's murder.

According to the autopsy, the time of death was somewhere between 9:30 p.m. on Tuesday the twenty-second, and 10:30 a.m. on Wednesday the twenty-third. The body was discovered by a jogger who noticed the broken window around noon on the twenty-fifth. There was a violent thunderstorm Thursday night, washing away a good deal of evidence. Presumably, this was why no evidence was found of the party or parties who allegedly stole the three million the campaign finance records said should have been there. Well, that wasn't quite right. The police *thought* the finance records said the three million was there. However, before the cops folded, they only had a brief perusal of the campaign finances over the weekend. Apparently the records never left Binder's headquarters.

The autopsy also said Daryl had been having a good time before someone slammed a mini-grenade into the back of his head. Nohar read at the time of death Daryl had a good point-oh-two blood alcohol, traces of weasel-dust in his nose, as well as a few 'dorphs lying undigested in his stomach. To top it off, he'd shot his wad into somebody in the twelve hours previous.

Seems he died happy.

Nohar pictured him at the comm, riding his buzz, watching some party film or other, air-conditioning going full blast. Daryl might be giggling a bit. Then the sniper takes up his position. The sniper is hiding somewhere. The ballistic evidence gave an approximate trajectory giving a field of fire at the back of Johnson's head. Five houses across the street fit the bill, all occupied, no witnesses. Perhaps the sniper uses a driveway between those houses across the street.

It's night, to give the sniper cover. Night makes sense.

Daryl's been partying. The sniper knows the alarm is off because Daryl is home. He can see Daryl through the sight. The sniper aims at Daryl's head, which might be bobbing to the beat from the comm. The sniper squeezes off a shot. The shot explodes, vaporizing the picture window.

The sniper squeezes off shot number two.

Daryl is sitting in the study, facing his comm, when his head gets blown away by the second exploding projectile belonging to the sniper's Levitt Mark II. It hits six centimeters from the base of the skull—dead center, according to the autopsy.

It hits from behind him, through the picture window in the living room, through the dining room, and through the open door to the study.

The cops found remains of two Levitt bullets. One set in Daryl's head. The other set by the picture window.

There was a problem with this sequence of events.

It was those two words. "dead center."

Daryl Johnson should have turned to see what the noise was.

For Nohar, that was a big problem. Daryl was shot in the back of the head. Nohar couldn't see someone so jazzed-up he'd be oblivious to twenty square meters of glass *exploding* directly behind him—now that he thought about it, the whole damn neighborhood was oblivious. What the autopsy listed shouldn't have zoned Daryl out that bad. Even a reflexive jerk toward the noise, no matter how fast the sniper got the second round off, would have put the shell toward one side of the head or the other.

Also, what was a nine-to-five working stiff doing that jazzed in the middle of the week? Given the time of death, Daryl was doing some heavy partying for a Tuesday.

Finally, even in Shaker Heights, a house standing open like that, two or three days without the alarm or a window, and nothing *else* ripped off? That didn't ring true.

The final portrait ejected from the printer.

Nohar stretched and got to his feet. His throat hurt from all the commands. Someday he was going to have to fix the keyboard. Despite the overstuffed cushions on the couch, his tail had fallen asleep again.

Nohar rubbed his throat and decided he needed a beer. He ducked into the kitchen. As he ripped the last bulb of beer from its envelope, he realized how hungry he was. The only food in the fridge was a plate of bones, and the last kilo of hamburger. Nohar only briefly considered the beef bones, even though a few looked fairly meaty. He grabbed the lump of hamburger and tossed it into the micro as he snapped the top off his bulb.

The cold brew soothed the raw feeling at the back of his throat, leaving a yeasty taste in his mouth. One of the few decent things pinks did with grain was turn it into booze.

Outside the dirty little kitchen window, the storm was worsening. The thunder rattled the glass in its loose molding.

Nohar drank as he watched the lightning through haze glass and rippling sheets of water. If Smith was right, and there never was any three million, why was Johnson killed? What was Johnson doing Tuesday night? Why didn't Johnson, or anyone else, respond to the shattering picture window—

Ding, the burger was warm. Nohar dropped the empty bulb into the disposal and washed his hands in the sink. He pulled the meat out of the micro, and spent a few seconds finding a clean plate. The hamburger leaked all over the plate as soon as he began unwrapping it. The blood-smell of the warm meat wafted to Nohar and *really* reminded him of how hungry he was. He ripped out a red, golfball-sized chunk from the heart of the burger and popped it into his mouth, licking the ferric taste from his claws.

Another thing the pinks did well, picking their domestic prey animals.

Cat was suddenly wide awake, mewing and rubbing against Nohar's leg. Nohar flicked a small gobbet of hamburger toward the other end of the kitchen. Cat went after it.

Nohar ate, standing at the counter by the sink, looking out the window, thinking about Daryl Johnson. Occasionally he flung another chunk of meat away, to keep Cat form distracting him.

Chapter 6

The rain broke Thursday morning and the sun came out.

Nohar barely noticed. He spent a few hours attaching names to the faces he had excised from the funeral picture. The only real interesting aspect of that drudgery was the fact that Philip Young, the finance chairman, had not attended the funeral.

He spent wasted effort trying to get a hold of Young. He tracked down an address and a comm number, but Young wasn't answering his comm. Neither was his computer, which was irritating. He called Harrison, but the legal counsel's comm was actually locking out Nohar's calls.

Nohar had never talked to the lawyer before.

Thomson's comm was also locking out Nohar's calls.

That left Binder. Nohar knew *that* would be hopeless. He tried anyway, going as far as calling Washington long-distance. The guy manning the phones was polite, condescending, and totally useless. Binder was somewhere in Columbus, raising money and campaigning, and the only way to talk to him would be to have a press pass or a large check.

Nohar didn't know if it was because he was a morey, a PI, or because they were hiding something. Nohar would lay odds on all three.

No need to be frustrated yet, Nohar told himself. There were a lot more people employed by Binder than the executive officers. Someone out there knew Johnson, and would hand him a lead.

He scanned through the items he had downloaded from the library yesterday. He was looking for a likely subject to hit. Predictably, the picture that caught his eye was a photo-op at a fund-raiser.

Behind Binder, with the upper crust of his campaign machine, there was an extra player.

Nohar leaned forward on the couch. "Magnification. Times five."

The picture zoomed at him. The resolution was excessively grainy, but he could see the extra person in the gang of four. To Binder's right were Thomson and Harrison, to his left were Young and Johnson—and Johnson's executive assistant. Johnson's assistant happened to be a woman. The picture implied a lot about them.

Nohar ran a search through his Binder database with her name, Stephanie Weir. Every time the software found something with Weir in it, there was Johnson. They seemed inseparable.

Now, here was someone who'd know about Johnson.

But would she talk to him?

He almost called her. However, when he thought it through, he realized this wasn't going to be one of those cases he could run from the comm. He had already seen how easy it was for the pinks to shut him out over the phone. He was at enough of a disadvantage as it was. He'd do this in person.

He should wear his suit for this. He hated it with a passion, but he was going out to the pinks' own territory. They had their own rules. He opened the one closet and took out the huge black jacket and the matching pants. He hesitated for a moment.

Maria wasn't here, but he could smell her tangy musk.

Nohar snatched shirt, tie, and shoes, and slammed the door shut. The memories didn't stay in the closet. He did his best to ignore them as he dressed. The relationship was over. It was only going to be a matter of time before he found one of her tops. She always left them here in hot weather.

He was still thinking about her by the time he got to the tie. The difficult ritual of getting the black strip of cloth properly wrapped around his neck was a welcome distraction. While he did so, he tried to force his mind off of Maria and on to Weir.

Nohar left the apartment comparing Maria's black jaguar fur to the long raven hair Stephanie Weir had in her pictures.

He had to walk three blocks to his car, because of the traffic restrictions. It was parked outside his office—actually a glorified mail drop—on the city end of Mayfield Road. It was a dusty-yellow Ford Jerboa convertible. Nohar wished someone would steal it. It was too old, too cheap, and for Nohar, too small. He could fit in the little thing, but the '28 Jerboa had a power plant that could barely push around its own two tons with Nohar on board.

He unplugged the car from the curb feed and tapped the combination on the passenger-side door, the one that worked. With the door open and the top down, he stepped over the passenger seat. Nohar eased himself behind the wheel, slipped some morey reggae into the cardplayer, and pulled away from the curb.

Shaker Heights was a different world. It was only separated from Moreytown by a sparse strip of middle-class pink suburbia. It could have been on the other side of the city. Driving into Shaker required some effort, since most of the direct routes were blocked off by familiar concrete pylons. In keeping with the neighborhood, these barriers were faced with brick and sat amidst vines, bushes, and tiny well-kept lawns. Nohar actually had to drive into Cleveland proper before he could weave his way into Shaker.

He expected to be stopped by the cops at least once, but he wasn't. Could be the suit. It didn't lessen the tension he felt. The roads were smooth and lined with trees. Not a morey in sight. The cozy one-family dwellings stared at him from behind manicured lawns.

Stephanie Weir lived in one of those intimidating brick houses.

Nohar pulled the Jerboa up to the curb in front of her house. Brick, one family, seven rooms, a century old or so. It was the kind of building that reminded Nohar how young his species was.

Come on, he told himself, *a few questions, nothing major.*

After saying that to himself a few times, he climbed out of the car and stretched. Before he realized what he was doing, he had reached up and started clawing the bark from the tree next to his car. No matter how good it felt, when he noticed himself doing it, he stopped. He hoped the Weir woman hadn't seen. It was embarrassing.

He shook loose bark from his fingers and walked up to the house. He pushed the call button next to the door and waited for an answer.

A speaker near his hand buzzed briefly, then spoke. "Damn, just a minute." There was a very long pause. "Who do we have here?"

Nohar tried to find the camera. "My name's Nohar Rajasthan. I'm a private investigator. I'd like to talk to a Ms. Stephanie Weir."

Another long pause. "Well, you got her. You have any ID?"

Nohar fished into his wallet and held up his PI license.

"Stick that into the slot."

A small panel under the call button slid aside. Nohar tossed it in.

Nohar stood and waited. He was tempted to push the call button again. But, without warning, the door was thrust open. Nohar had to suppress an urge to leap back. Weir offered his license back. "What can I help you with, Mr. Rajasthan?"

Pronounced it right her first try. Nohar was relieved, and a little puzzled, not to smell any fear. He was also grateful Weir didn't wear any strong perfume. She had an odd smile on her face and he wished he was better at reading human expressions. "I'd like to talk about Daryl Johnson."

Weir bit her lip. "Complicated subject. You better come in."

Nohar watched her walk away from the door before ducking in and closing it behind him. He could stand in the living room and not feel cramped. He wondered what she did with all this space. A comm was playing in the background. He recognized the voice from his research, ex-mayor Russell Gardner, Binder's opponent.

". . . is in a crisis. Our technological infrastructure was fatally wounded when Japan was invaded, as surely as if the Chinese had landed in California. For nearly a decade my opponent has been leading a policy of government inaction. For twenty years our quality of living has been degrading. There are fewer engineers in the United States now than there were at the turn of the century—"

"Sit down." She motioned toward a beige love seat that looked like it could hold him. "I was just about to fix myself a drink. Want one?"

Nohar sat on the love seat and wriggled to get his tail into a comfortable position. "Anything cold, please."

Gardner went on as if he had found a new issue.

". . . space program as an example. It's been four decades since a government program—a program since disbanded for lack of funding—discovered signals that are still widely believed, in the scientific community, to be an artifact of extraterrestrial intelligence. NASA's nuclear rockets have been sitting on the moon ten years, waiting for the launch and we are losing the ability to maintain them. We've lost the ability to maintain cutting edge tech. . ."

Nohar wasn't interested in the political tirade. Instead of listening, he wondered why the pink female was acting so— relaxed wasn't quite the word he was looking for.

Weir walked into the kitchen and Nohar's gaze followed her. He enjoyed the way she moved. No abrupt motions, every move flowed into every other seamlessly. He watched as she stretched to get a glass from a cabinet. The smooth line of muscle in her arm melded into a gentle ripple down her back, became a descending curve toward the back of her knee, and ended in the abrupt bump of her calf.

She said something, and Nohar asked himself what he'd been thinking about.

"What did you say?"

Weir apparently assumed the comm was too loud. She called out, "Pause." Gardner shut up. "I said I've been waiting for you to mention it."

Nohar felt lost. "Mention what?"

She returned with two tumblers and handed one to him. He couldn't read the half-smile on her face. "Well, I'd picture a detective jumping all over me for not being more broken up about Derry."

"I was just trying to be tactful." That was a lie. The fact was, Nohar had been so nervous he hadn't even noticed. He took a drink, hoping it was something strong. It turned out to be some soft drink whose carbonation overwhelmed any taste it might have had. At least it was cold.

"I guess I'm not used to tact." She sat down in an easy chair across from him. He could identify her natural smell now, somewhere between rose and wood smoke. He liked it. "So, let's talk about Derry."

Nohar took another long pull from the glass. It did little for him but give him a chance to think. "Could you describe your relationship with him?"

"We weren't that close. At least, not as close as it was supposed to look. I suppose you've gotten the intended message from all the photo-ops and the social events. All window dressing, really."

"Meaning?"

"Just what I said. It was supposed to look like Derry was hot for me when he could really care less about women. It was all an elaborate game. I was supposed to cover up one of Binder's political liabilities." *Now* Nohar could read her expression. The hard edge in her voice helped.

"Daryl Johnson was gay?"

She nodded. "I got recruited by the Binder campaign right out of Case. Major in statistics, minor in political science. So I can go to parties and look cute. All because Binder is too loyal to fire his chosen, and is too right-wing to accept a homosexual on his staff. Publicly anyway."

That was amazing, even though he had some idea how extreme Binder was. "That attitude's bizarre." He had to restrain himself from adding, "Even for a pink."

"You don't know the man."

"You put up with that?"

That brought a weak smile. "Selling out your principles pays a great deal of money, Mr. Rajasthan. Until he died, anyway."

She noticed they both had empty glasses. She got up. "Can I get you a refill? Something a little stronger this time?"

Nohar nodded. "Please—"

He didn't like questioning good fortune, but he was beginning to wonder why she was so open with him. "What was playing on the comm?"

"One of Gardner's speeches. Sort of self-flagellation."

Odd way to put it. "Are you still *with* Binder organization?"

She stopped on the way to the kitchen and shook her head. "Binder's legendary loyalty doesn't apply to the window dressing. After all I put up with—you know, someone even started a rumor I was a lesbian."

"Are you?"

Weir's knuckles whitened on her glass. Nohar thought she might throw it at him. The smell Nohar was sensing was powerful now, but it was more akin to fear and confusion than anger. The episode was brief. She quickly composed herself. "I'd really rather not talk about that right now."

Nohar wondered what he'd stepped in with that question. Pinks tended to lay social minefields around themselves. Nohar wished had had a map. "Sorry."

She managed a forced smile. "Don't apologize. I shouldn't have snapped at you. I've never been very good around people . . ." She sighed.

Nohar tried to get the conversation back on track. "I'm supposed to be here about Johnson. Not you. What *do* you know about Johnson? What kind of enemies did he have?"

Nohar watched covertly as she walked to the kitchen and went from cabinet to cabinet. "I suppose his only enemies would have been Binder's enemies. He had been with Binder since the state legislature. Straight from college. Loyal to a fault. A big fault considering Binder's attitude toward homosexuals. I never understood it, but I wasn't paid to understand. Young and Johnson were already an organizational fixture when I came on the scene."

"Were they—"

She came back with the drinks. "I really shouldn't talk about it. It's Phil's business. But he shouldn't have snubbed the funeral. After fifteen years, Derry deserved more than Phil worrying about someone figuring out the obvious."

"Could you tell me about what Johnson was doing the week he died?"

"I didn't see him the week he died. I think Young mentioned him seeing some bigwig contributor."

"When was the last time you *did* see him alive?"

"A fund-raiser the previous Saturday. On the end of his arm as usual. He left early, around nine-thirty." She lowered her eyes. "You know what the last thing he said to me was?"

"What?"

"He apologized for consistently ruining all the dates 'an attractive girl' should have had." She lifted her glass. "To the relationships I should have had." She drained it.

The way she was shaking her head made Nohar change the subject. "Can you tell me why Johnson would have three million dollars of campaign funds in his house when he was killed?"

Weir looked back up, her mouth open, and her eyes a little wider. "Oh, Christ, in cash?"

"According to the police report's interpretation of the finance records, yes."

Weir got up from her chair and starting pacing. "Now I'm *glad* they let me go. There's no legitimate reason for having that kind of money in a lump sum—"

"Why would he?"

"Could be anything. Avoiding disclosure, a secret slush fund, illegal contributions, embezzlement—"

"Could this have to do with Binder pressuring the police to stop the investigation?"

"I heard that, too. Sure. That's as good a reason to pressure his old cronies in the council and the police department as any."

Nohar stood up and, after a short debate within himself, held out his hand. "Thank you for your help, Ms. Weir."

Her hand clasped his. It was tiny, naked, and warm, but it gave a strong squeeze. "My pleasure. I needed to talk to someone. And please don't call me Miz Weir."

"Stephanie?"

"I prefer Stephie." Nohar caught a look of what could have been uncertainty cross her face. "Will I see you again?"

Nohar had no idea. "I'm sure we'll need to go over some things later."

She led him to the door and he ducked out into the darkening night. Before the door was completely shut, Nohar turned around. "Can I ask you something?"

"Why stop now?"

"Why are you so relaxed around me?"

She laughed, an innocent little sound. "Should I be nervous?"

"I'm a moreau—"

"Well, Mr. Rajasthan, maybe I'll do better next time." She shut the door before Nohar could answer. After a slight hesitation, he pressed the call button.

"Yes?" said the speaker.

"Call me Nohar."

Nohar sat in the Jerboa and watched the night darken around him. He was parked in front of Daryl Johnson's house, a low-slung ranch, and wondering exactly why he'd acted the way he did with Weir—with Stephie. He really couldn't isolate anything he'd done or said that could be called unprofessional, but he felt like he'd bumbled through the whole interview. Especially the lesbian comment—"I don't want to talk about that right now." Nohar wondered why. She was willing to talk about anything but, even seemed reluctant to let him leave.

The night had faded to monochrome when Nohar climbed out of the convertible. He decided the problem had been Maria. Thinking about that was beginning to affect his work.

Nohar watched a reflection of the full moon ripple in the polymer sheathing that now covered the picture window. The scene was too stark for Shaker Heights. The moon had turned the world black and white, and even the night air tried to convey a chill, more psychic than actual. From somewhere the breeze carried the taint of sewer.

The police tags were gone. The investigation had stopped, here at least. Nohar approached the building, trying to resolve in his mind the contradictions the police report had raised.

He stood in front of the picture window and looked across the street. Five houses stood in line with the window and Daryl Johnson's head. Similar ranch houses, all in well-manicured plots, all well lit. The specs for the sniper's weapon said it weighed 15 kilos unloaded, and it was over two meters long. None of the possible sniper positions offered a bit of cover that would have satisfied Nohar.

Chapter 7

It didn't rain on Friday.

Philip Young still refused to answer his comm, so Nohar donned his suit and went to see the finance chairman in person. Philip Young's address was in the midst of the strip of suburbia between Moreytown and Shaker. It was close enough to home that Nohar decided to walk. By the time he was halfway there, his itching fur made him regret the decision. When he had reached Young's neighborhood, Nohar had his jacket flung over his shoulder, his shirt unbuttoned to his waist, and his tie hung in a loose circle around his neck.

Young's neighborhood was a netherworld of ancient duplexes and brick four-story apartments. The lawns were overgrown. The trees bore the scars of traffic accidents and leaned at odd angles. Less intimidating than Shaker Heights—Moreytown, only with humans. He still received the occasional stare, but he wasn't far enough off the beaten path for the pinks to see him as unusual. Only a few crossed the street to avoid him.

Nohar felt less of the nervousness that made his interview with Stephie Weir such an embarrassment. Nohar was well on his way to convincing himself he might just be able to get Young to give him some insight on that three million dollars. His major worry was exactly how to approach Young about homosexuality. Pinks could be tender on that subject.

Nohar stopped and faced Young's house with the noontime sun burning the back of his neck. Young should be home. The staff had the week off because of Johnson's death.

Gnats were clouding around his head, making his whiskers twitch.

He wondered why the finance chairman—who presumably guided those large sums under the table—lived here. This was a bad neighborhood, and the house wasn't any better off than its neighbors. The second floor windows were sealed behind white plastic sheathing. The siding was gray and pockmarked with dents and scratches. The porch was warped and succumbing to dry rot. It was as much a hellhole as Nohar's apartment.

And the place *smelled* to high heaven. He snorted and rubbed the skin of his broad nose. It was a sour, tinny odor he couldn't place. It irritated his sinuses and prodded him with a nagging familiarity.

Why did Young live here?

Young was an accountant. Perhaps there was a convoluted tax reason behind it.

Nohar walked up to the porch with some trepidation. It didn't look like it could hold him. He walked cautiously, the boards groaning under his weight, and nearly fell through a rotten section when his tail was caught in the crumbling joinery overhanging the front steps. Nohar had to back up and thrash his tail a few times to loosen it. It came free, less a tuft of fur the size of a large marble.

After that, he walked to the door holding his tail so high his lower back ached.

The door possessed a single key lock, and one call button with no sign of an intercom. Both had been painted over a dozen times. Nohar pressed the button until he heard the paint crack, but nothing happened. He knocked loudly, but no one seemed to be around to answer. He had the feeling Young's directory listing was a sham, and Young lived about as much at his "home" as Nohar worked at his "office." He carefully walked across the porch to peer into what he assumed was a living room window. The furnishings consisted of a mattress and a card table.

So much for the straightforward approach.

Nohar undid his tie and wrapped it around his right hand. He cocked back and was about to smash in the window, when he identified the smell.

The tinny smell had been getting worse ever since he had first noticed it. Nohar had assumed it was because he was approaching the source, which was true. However, he had been on the porch a few minutes and the smell kept increasing. What had been a minor annoyance on the sidewalk was now making his eyes water.

The smell was strong enough now for him to identify it. He remembered where he had smelled it before. It had been along time since he'd watched the demolition of the abandoned gas stations at the corner of Mayfield and Coventry, since he had watched them dig up the rusted storage tanks, since had had smelled gasoline.

Instinct made him back away from the window and try to identify where the smell was coming from. His tie slipped from his claws and fell to the porch.

The smell was strongest to the left of the porch. It came from behind the house, up the weed-shot driveway.

The garage—

Carefully, he descended the steps and rounded the porch. He walked up the driveway toward the two-car garage and the smell permeated everything. His eyes watered. His sinuses hurt. The smell was making him dizzy.

The doors on the garage were closed, but he could hear

activity within—splashing, a metal can banging, someone breathing heavily. He slowed his approach and was within five meters of the garage when the noise stopped.

Nohar wished he was carrying a gun.

The door shot up and chunked into place. Fumes washed over Nohar and nearly made him pass out. Philip Young faced him, framed by the garage door. Nohar knew, from the statistics he had read, Young was only in his mid-thirties. The articles had portrayed him as a *Wunderkind* who had engineered the financing of Binder's first congressional upset.

The man that was looking at Nohar wasn't a young genius. He was an emaciated wild man. Young was stripped to the waist, and drenched with sweat and gasoline. Behind him were stacks of wet cardboard boxes, file folders, papers, suitcases. Some still dripped amber fluid. Young's red-shot eyes darted to Nohar and his right shook a black snub-nosed thirty-eight at the moreau.

"You're not going to do me like you did Derry."

Nohar hoped his voice sounded calm. "You don't want to fire that gun."

The gun shook as Young's head darted left and right. "You're with them, aren't you? You're *all* with them."

Young was freaked, and he was going to blow himself, the garage, and Nohar all over the East Side. "Calm down. I'm trying to *find out* who killed Derry."

"*Liar!*" Nohar's mouth dried up when he heard the hammer cock. "You're all with them. I watched one of you kill him."

Young was off his nut, but at least Nohar realized what he must be talking about. "A moreau could have killed Derry and I never would have heard about it. Why don't you put down the gun and we can talk."

Young looked back at the boxes he'd been dousing. "You understand, I can't let anyone find out."

Nohar was lost again. "Sure, I understand."

"Derry didn't know he was helping them—what they were. When he found out, he was going to stop. You realize that."

Young was still looking into the garage, Nohar took the opportunity to take a few steps toward him. "Of course, no one could hold that against him."

Young whipped around, waving the gun. "That's just it!

They'll *blame* Derry. People would say he was *working for them*—"

Young rambled, paying little attention to Nohar. Nohar worked his way a little closer. He could see into the garage better now. His eyes watered and it was hard to read, but he could see some of the boxes of paper were filled with printouts. They looked like payroll records. One suitcase was filed with ramcards.

Young suddenly became aware of him again. "Stop right there."

Young's finger tightened and Nohar froze. "Why did 'they' kill Derry?"

The gun was pointed straight at Nohar as Young spoke. "He found out about them. He went over the finance records and figured it out."

"You're the finance chairman. Why didn't you figure it out first?"

Mistake. Young started shaking and yelling something inarticulate. Nohar turned and dived at the ground.

Young fired.

Young screamed.

Nohar was looking away from the garage when the gun went off. He heard the crack of the revolver, immediately followed by a whoosh that made his eardrums pop. The bullet felt like a hammer blow in his left shoulder. The explosion followed, a burning hand that slammed him into the ground. The acrid smoke made his nose burn. The odor of his own burning fur made him gag.

Young was still screaming.

The explosion gave way to a crackling fire and the rustle of raining debris. Nohar rolled on to his back to put out his burning fur. When he did so, he wrenched his shoulder, sending a dagger of pain straight through his neck.

He blacked out.

The absolute worst smell Nohar could imagine was the smell of hospital disinfectant. As soon as he had gained a slight awareness of his surroundings, that chemical odor awakened him the rest of the way. Before he had even opened his eyes, he could feel his stomach tightening.

"Someone, open a window!" It came out in barely a whisper.

Someone was there and Nohar could hear the window whoosh open. The stale city air let him breathe again. Nohar opened his eyes.

It was what he'd been afraid of. He was in a hospital. It was in the cheap adjustable bed, the awful disinfectant smell, the thin sheets, and the linoleum tile. It was in the odor of blood and shit the chemicals tried to hide. It was in the plastic curtains that pretended to give some privacy to the naked moreys lined up, in their beds, like cattle in a slaughterhouse.

Nohar hated hospitals.

Nohar turned his head and saw, standing next to the window, Detective Irwin Harsk. The pink was as stone-faced as ever.

"Am I under arrest?"

Harsk looked annoyed. "You *are* a paranoid bastard. Young blew up, you're allegedly an innocent bystander. Believe it or not, we found two witnesses that agree on two things in ten. Give me some credit for brains."

"Why *are* you here?"

"I'm here because you're giving me problems downtown. I'm supposed to be some morey expert. They expect me to exercise some control over you. I don't like jurisdictional problems. I don't like the DEA staking out half of my territory. I don't like the Fed. And I don't like outsiders pressuring me to bottle something up. I don't like Binder. I don't like Binder's friends—"

Nohar struggled to get into a sitting position and his shoulder didn't seem to object. "What?"

"A bunch of people who think they're cops are trying to dick me around. They want me to keep you away from Binder's people, or bad things will happen. Like what, I don't know. I'm already as low as you get in this town." Harsk slammed his fist into the side of the window frame. "Hell, Shaker's screwing around the Johnson killing for Binder. They *deserve* you."

Harsk looked like he needed to strangle someone. For once, Nohar was speechless.

"Look," Harsk said, "I'm not going to do their shit-work for them. But you're on your own lookout. I just want to avoid the bullshit and do what someone once laughingly described as my job." Harsk walked to the door and paused.

"One more thing. The DEA has a serious red flag on your ass."

With that, Harsk left.

Nohar watched Harsk weave his way between the moreys, and didn't know what to think. He'd always pictured Harsk as constantly dreaming up new ways to screw him over. Maybe Harsk was right. He *was* paranoid.

He felt his shoulder. The wound didn't seem to be major. The dressing extended to the back of his neck, which felt tender when Nohar pressed it. He pulled back the sheet. There were five or six dressings on his tail. That, and a transparent support bandage on his slightly swollen right knee, was the only visible damage.

Considering how close he was to Young when the nut blew himself up, he'd gotten off light.

"Damn it." Nohar suddenly remembered Cat. He didn't know how long he'd been out, and Cat only had half a day's food in his bowl when Nohar left.

He looked up and down the ward. No doctors, no nurses, not even a janitor. Harsk had been the only pink down here and he had already left. Nohar knew when, or if, hospital administration finally got to him, there would be a few hours of forms to fill out. Just to keep the bureaucracy happy.

To hell with that.

He swung his legs over the edge of the bed and gently started putting pressure on his right leg. It wasn't a bad sprain. It held his weight. He stood up slowly and felt slightly dizzy. He was alarmed until he realized it was still from that damn disinfectant smell. Breathing through his mouth helped.

There was a window between his bed and the next one. The fuzzy nocturnal view—Nohar wished he could kill the lights in the ward so he could see better—of the skyline told him he wasn't far enough down the Midtown Corridor to be at the Clinic. That meant he was at University Hospitals and only a few blocks from Moreytown. He was probably in the new veterinary building.

Lightning flashed on the horizon.

Nohar looked at the bed on the other side of the window. In it was a canine who had an arm shaved naked inside a transparent cast. He—like Nohar, the canine was naked and not covered by a sheet—was watching Nohar's activity with some interest. The canine spoke when he saw he'd caught Nohar's attention.

"You blow up?"

It was hard placing the accent, but defiantly first generation. Probably Southeast Asian. Nohar began looking for exit signs as he answered.

"Yes."

"Pink law's bad news. Best eye yourself, tigerman—"

Nohar was barely listening. He'd located the exit. "Sure. You have the date?"

"Fade side of August two. Saturday is five minutes from nirvana."

Thirty-six hours. He must have been drugged.

That was it. He was leaving.

The canine was still nattering. Nohar thanked him and started toward the exit. Most of the moreys here were asleep, but a few watched him leave. There were a few comments, mostly of the "Skip on pinks" variety. He did get one sexual proposition, but he didn't pause enough to register the species or the gender the offer came from.

He slipped out of the wardroom, the glass doors sliding aside as he passed, and found himself in a carpeted reception area. There was a waiting room, and a nurse's station across from it. No one in sight. The elevators and the stairs were directly across from the doors to the ward. All he needed to do was cross between the station and the waiting room. Once in the stairwell he could make it to the parking garage.

He limped across no-man's-land and nearly made it to the stairwell.

The elevator doors opened without any warning. He was caught right in front of the elevator. If it hadn't been so damn silent, he might have had a chance to duck to the side.

The last person he expected to see in the elevator was Stephie Weir.

As the doors opened, she took a step forward and her motion ceased. Nohar thought he must have looked as surprised as she did. Neither of them moved. They stood there, staring at each other, until the doors started closing again.

Realizing he was about to blow his escape, Nohar jumped into the elevator. He called out, "Down. Garage level," and pressed the button for the garage level just in case the thing didn't have a voice pickup. Nohar hoped no one else in the building would want to use this particular elevator in the next half-minute.

Stephie was staring at him. Nohar waited until he felt the car moving downward, then he asked, "What are *you* doing here?"

The question seemed to break her out of shock. She lifted her gaze. "I want to know what happened to Phil. I was waiting down there two hours until Detective Harsk — Christ, what are you doing with no clothes on?"

That damned pink fetish. "Avoiding bureaucracy."

"What the hell are you talking about? *You're naked!*"

"Not until they shave me."

The doors on the elevator opened and Nohar held his breath. They had made it all the way to the garage. Again, no one in sight.

Nohar turned to Stephie who looked and smelled of confusion. "If you want to talk about what happened, you better come with me."

He stepped out on to the cold concrete. He finally felt comfortable breathing through his nose. The only strong smells down here were the slight ozone smell from the cars, and Stephie's smoky-rose scent.

She choked back a few monosyllables and started walking after him. "Just tell me why, please."

He almost gave her a curt answer, but he decided she deserved something of an explanation. "I need to get back home. Checking out and getting whatever the explosion left of my clothes could take a long while, and they might just decide they want to keep me for a day or two. Besides, I hate filling out forms. They can bill me."

"What's so important?"

"I don't have anyone to feed my cat."

That got her. "You're not kidding, are you?"

Nohar shrugged and started toward the entrance of the parking garage. His claws clicked on the concrete.

She called after him. "Where's your car?"

"I suppose it's still parked outside my office."

"You're going to—" She paused. "Of course you intend to walk home like that. Come back here. At least let me give you a lift so you won't get arrested."

Nohar turned around. He didn't know what to make of the offer. "Can I fit in your car?"

"A Plymouth Antaeus? What it cost, you better fit."

"Sure you want to do this? My neighborhood—"

"Screw your neighborhood. We need to talk about Phil."

Nohar silently agreed they needed to talk about Phil. He allowed himself to be led to the brand-new Antaeus.

Chapter 8

The Antaeus pulled up behind the Jerboa, splashing a deep puddle by the curb. The barriers prevented Stephie from driving any closer to Nohar's apartment.

When Stephie parked, she turned to face Nohar. She seemed to be making an effort to keep her gaze fixed on his face. "It doesn't sound like Phil."

"It's what happened."

"The cops called it a suicide. Detective Harsk said Phil *shot* you."

Nohar reached up and rubbed his left shoulder. "Can *you* explain what happened?"

Stephie turned toward the windshield, shaking her head. She was silent for a few seconds. Finally she said, "He bought that house so he could have a separate address."

So, it *was* a sham. "He lived with Johnson?"

"Five years now." She still looked out the window. A street lamp shone through the cascading rain and carved rippling shadows on her face. She spoke slowly and deliberately. "I can't believe Phil would kill himself."

Nevertheless, that's what Young had done, as surely as if he had pointed the gun at his own head. Nohar could still picture Young saying they all—Nohar presumed Young meant moreys—were with *them.* Nohar suspected *they* were in MLI.

"How'd he feel about moreys?"

"I don't know—" *Very few people do,* thought Nohar. "I didn't talk to him much. I knew him mostly through talking to Derry." She sighed. The sound seemed to catch in her throat.

After an uncomfortable pause, she changed the subject. "I don't think Derry's death *would* make him. . . ."

"What would it take?"

"More, just . . . *more*." Stephie turned and looked Nohar in the eyes. Her expression seemed to show bewilderment and she smelled of fear, nerves, and confusion. "Do you think I'm a bad person?"

What the hell brought that on? "Of course not, why?"

"I feel terrible about what I said about Phil snubbing the funeral—"

Nohar restrained the immediate impulse to ask her why she was telling him that. Instead, he tried a close-lipped smile. "We all say things we end up regretting. It doesn't mean we're thoughtless."

"It's not just that. My whole life has been a hypocrisy—"

"You don't mean—"

"I know exactly what I mean. I never even was a Binder supporter—I despise the man." She sucked in a shuddering breath. "Me, Phil, and Derry—we were all playing the twisted charade. All of us hiding because Binder was signing our paychecks."

"What were you hiding?"

The look in her eyes changed for a moment. Nohar felt like he had let his mouth make a major mistake again. Instead, she smiled, even let out a little laugh.

"I was hiding myself, I guess."

Nohar realized he was only going to get that cryptic comment. He nodded and opened the rear door to let himself out into the rain. The damp soaked into his fur in a matter of seconds.

"Thanks for the ride." Nohar didn't know why he felt obliged, but he added, "I'll give you a call later on, if I find out anything."

Nohar shut the door and she looked like she still couldn't quite believe he was going to walk home without any clothes. "Nohar?"

He paused and looked back into the Antaeus. "Yes?"

"Forget it, never mind . . ."

She shook her head and drove the Antaeus into the darkness without an explanation.

Nohar stood and watched it go for a while, wondering. Moreytown pressed around him. He had three blocks to go, so he started walking. He was safe from the cops here. Moreys were so casual about clothing that trying to enforce pink exposure laws in Moreytown would be impossible. His lack of attire would only be noted because of the rain, and the time of night. Now all he had to worry about were how many eyes had seen him with the pink female.

He nearly made it home—

A ratboy bumped into him.

No, they wouldn't be that stupid.

He was on the wrong side of the street. He was between the abandoned bus and a boarded-up pizzeria. His usual alertness had failed him, and he realized the hospital smell was still clogging his nose.

The familiar-looking ratboy, brown fur and denim cut-offs, rebounded from Nohar's side. "Lookee—"

Now Nohar could catch the rat's musk. The ratboy was flying a wave of excitement, reeked of it. It was Fearless Leader, and he was jacked about as far as a rat could go.

"The stray just ruffled my fur!"

Footsteps, two sets one end of the bus, two at the other. Subordinates. From the look and smell of it, Feareless' boys were jacked worse than he was. Bigboy was there, and he snicked a blade. Nohar should have taken the knife when he had the chance.

Bigboy made a few ineffective waves with his switchblade. "Let's shave the kitty pink."

A chain rattled from the other end of the bus. "Teach some respect for the coat."

Great, they *were* stupid.

So much for the Finger of God.

Fearless Leader pulled a gun, a twenty-two. Fortunately, he wasn't doused in gasoline. "We don't like pink moreys. We goina mark you. You move and we veto your pretty kitty ass."

Nohar always held his fighting instinct under iron control. Both nature and the Indian gene-techs had designed his strain for combat, for hunting, for the spilling of blood. Almost always, that part of his soul was at odds with his conscious mind. Nohar thought of it as The Beast.

When Fearless pulled the gun, Nohar felt a shock of adrenaline. His heart began to pound and he felt the rush in his ears and his temples. There as the anticipatory taste of copper in his mouth. His breath like a blast furnace in the back of his throat.

The Beast wanted out. It was scratching at the mental door Nohar always kept locked.

Nohar opened the door and let The Beast take over.

The night snapped into razor-sharp monochrome. The smells erupted into a vivid melange. He could hear the rat-boy's heartbeat as well as his own. Time crawled.

The Beast roared.

Nohar roared. The sound bore no trace of his speaking voice. It was a scream of rage that tore the skin from his throat. The ratboys hesitated at the sound. Fearless smelled of fear now, fear that told Nohar he had never seen a morey turn wild before.

Nohar's left arm, the one with restricted mobility, shot out toward Fealress' gun hand. Nohar grabbed the weapon and turned it toward the ground. There was a snap of bone before the gun blew a hole in the side of the bus. Fearless Leader had some control. No scream.

Not until Nohar's right hand, sweeping upward with the claws fully extended, caught Fearless between the legs. Nohar didn't simply rake his claws across Fearless' body. His claws came up, point first, and when they bit flesh, jerked up, hooked forward, and partially retracted. Fearless Leader screamed when Nohar lifted him up. Nohar's claws were hooked into the flesh of his groin.

Nohar was jacked higher than the rats now. Fearless Leader's 50 kilos weighed nothing. Fearless slammed into the bus through a broken window. The gun was still in Nohar's left hand. Fealress' hand was still holding it, reaching through the bus window. Nohar yanked the gun away. There was another crack.

Bigboy was now within reach, swinging his knife. Nohar pivoted and the knife missed. Nohar's cupped right hand aimed for the eyes as Bigboy passed. Bigboy slipped in the rain before the claws hit him. Lucky. The claws sank in behind the ear and tore off a flap of skin down the left side of Bigboy's face.

Nohar's left arm blocked a chain coming at his head. It wrapped around his forearm. He pulled that rat toward him and upward. He sank his teeth into the weapon arm. A toss of Nohar's head disarmed his attacker and dropped the rat off to his right. Into the same puddle that had saved Big-boy's eyes.

Two others. They spooked.

Leader in bus. Bigboy huddled in doorway to pizzeria, trying to hold half his face on. Chain trying to stop the bleeding, hand limp, muscle severed. Fight over.

Slowly, Nohar shut the door on The Beast.

The comedown was hard. He began shaking. The rats didn't notice. They had their own problems. That fifteen seconds of savagery had jacked him higher and faster than these ratboys had ever thought of going. The crash would've killed them.

Nohar stumbled across the street and to the door of his building.

When he staggered into his living room, Cat hissed at him. Nohar was covered in rat blood. He wobbled into the kitchen, opened a cabinet, and spilled Cat's food all over the counter.

It would have to do, for now.

Nohar dragged himself into the bathroom and slumped into the shower. He turned on a blast of cold water.

Dipping into his reserve as a bioengineered weapon had its price.

When Nohar woke up, the shower was still going full blast. Cat was asleep on the lid of the john, and the only remains of the night's activity was the taste of blood in his mouth. The bandage on his shoulder fell off the moment he moved. It revealed a puckered red wound where they had dug out Young's bullet. There was a shaved area around it the size of his hand. The flesh was a pale white, contrasting with Nohar's russet-and-black fur. Nohar quickly looked away from it. The skin made him uncomfortable.

The support bandage was still there. At least he hadn't aggravated the injury to his knee. That was good because there was no way he was going to end up in a hospital again.

He stood up, killed the cold water, and hit the dryer. He barely noticed when Cat spooked. Nohar stood under the dryer and shook. He tried to tell himself it was his unsteady knee, but he was too adept at spotting bullshit. He knew it was a reaction to loosing The Beast.

All moreys dealt with The Beast in one form or another.

Some, like Manny, lived with it without it making so much as a ripple in their psyche, the techs having let a basically human brain mute the instincts they weren't particularly interested in. Then there were moreys like Nohar, who bore the legacy of techs playing hob with what nature gave them. This was only the second time he had let out The Beast with no restraint. Nohar was grateful nobody had died.

He had enjoyed it too much.

He saw in himself the potential for becoming another type of morey. The one who gave himself over to The Beast and reveled in the bloodlust. The one like his father—

"No," he said to his reflection as he left the bathroom. To his practiced ears, it sounded like a lie.

Forget the rats, he told himself. He still had a job to do. Even if it cost him two days, his run-in with Young had given him something besides a gunshot wound and a sprained knee. If Young was not totally out of touch with reality—no mean assumption—Nohar now had some idea of how Daryl Johnson was killed, if not why.

First things first—he went to the comm and turned it on. "Load program. Label, 'I lost my damn wallet!' Run program."

"searching...found. program uses half processing capacity and all outside lines for approximately fifteen minutes, continue?"

"Yes." It was going to take him that long just to run through his messages. While his cards and Ids were being canceled and reordered by the computer, he perused the backlog.

There were no phone messages on the comm, but a pile of mail was waiting in memory for him.

It was early in the morning on Sunday the third. Predictably, bills predominated in the mail. He'd have the comm pay them off as soon as it was done with his lost wallet program. There was the usual collection of junk mail. However, for once, there was something more than those two categories in his mail file.

"John Smith," his client, had been true to his word to keep in touch. Two days after their meeting, he had left a voice message for Nohar to meet him in Lakeview Cemetery, for noon on Saturday—when Nohar had been zoned in a ward at University Hospitals. About twelve hours after that little bit of mail, Smith apparently found out what had happened. The slimy voice carried little emotion. "Mr. Rajasthan, I regret this incident with Binder's finance chairman. I am unable to meet with you personally, but I finance your medical expenses when I hear what happens to you—"

"Pause." Nohar was having trouble following the frank's heavy accent. Nohar, living in the middle of Moreytown, had to deal with, and understand, an incredible variety of unusual accents. A Vietnamese dog not only had an Asian accent, but a definite canid pronunciation. The problem with the frank was more subtle. Nohar didn't think it was a South African accent—even if that *was* one of the few countries to have defied the long-standing United Nations ban on engineering humans. Nohar promised himself he'd press the frank a little more closely about his origins next time they met.

"Continue."

"—I hope this does not prevent you from the discovery of Daryl Johnson's murderer. I increase your fee to reflect your current difficulties. I call to set up meeting when you are released from hospital. There you tell me what you discover."

It took Nohar a few seconds to figure out exactly what the frank meant.

The next item in the mail file was from Maria. Nohar was afraid to play it. Then he cursed himself and told the comm to play the damn thing. It was the same husky voice, much calmer this time. Nohar wished he could see her face. "Raj, I thought you deserved a more civilized good-bye. I still can't meet you face-to-face, and for that I apologize. I just want you to know it isn't your fault. We're incompatible. Maybe it would be easier for me to deal with your wholesale contempt for everything if you weren't such a decent and honorable person."

There was a pause as Maria took a long breath. "I am going through with it. You were right about the money— you always are about things like that—but I'm going anyway. California is a lot more tolerant, and the few communities there aren't just glorified slums the humans abandoned. I know you can't appreciate this, but God bless you."

Nohar sat, her voice still ringing in his ears, remembering. He had the comm store the message and sighed.

"instructions unclear."

He had sighed too loudly. "Store mail. Comm. Off."

She had been wrong about one thing. He *could* appreciate the blessing. Especially after their last argument, the night before he had stood her up for that fiasco with Nugoya—

It had started when she suggested they both move to California. Of course, there was no way they could afford it. She brought up God, and Nohar went off. That damned little bit of pink brainwashing infuriated him. Especially when a moreau spouted it. Religion, pink religion, wasn't just a form of mind control, but the primary justification for people like Joseph Binder to consider moreys worse than garbage. Why should a morey believe in God, when people like Binder said they were abomination in His eyes?

Maria was a devout Catholic and Nohar had been drunk enough to think he might be able to talk her out of such stupidity. How could she be secure in her belief when she only had a *soul* by dispensation of some sexagenarian pink in a pointed hat? A decision that had more to do with politics than divine inspiration.

Why couldn't he keep his damn mouth shut?

Worse, all his money problems had evaporated with the ten thousand Smith gave him. Maria's message had come in yesterday. Knowing her, she had left town by now.

Chapter 9

Nohar parked the Jerboa in front of Daryl Johnson's ranch. He stayed in the car. Shaker Heights still made him paranoid about cops. It was early Sunday morning and he suspected the slow-moving bureaucracy at University Hospital was just now discovering him missing. Shortly afterward, the cops would be notified. Nohar didn't know exactly what would happen then. He was a witness to Young's explosion—they *should* want a statement from him. But Binder was pressuring the cops. Binder probably wouldn't want any real close investigation of Young's empty house, or the records Young had destroyed.

At least Nohar's investigation, such as it was, was progressing. He had checked the police records again. The air-conditioning *had* been going full blast when Johnson was blown away.

Nohar yawned and raked his claws across the upholstery of the passenger seat. He spent a few minutes picking foam rubber as he looked at the sheathing covering the picture window. His watch beeped. It was eight, Manny would be answering his comm.

Nohar took the voice phone out of the glove compartment and called him.

"Dr. Gujerat here. Who—" There was a pause as Manny must have read the text on the incoming call. "Nohar? Where in the hell are you? I got to the hospital during nocturnal visiting hours. You were gone—"

Fine, his disappearance had been discovered that much earlier. "Manny, I'm fine. I need to ask you something—"

"Like the percentage of untreated bullet wounds that become gangrenous? Damnit, you weren't in the hospital just to be inconvenienced."

Nohar shook his head. At least Manny wasn't saying, "I told you so." Even though he'd been right about getting involved with pink business.

"I needed to feed Cat."

"Great, just great. I won't even tell you how silly that sounds. You couldn't have gotten me to do that?"

Nohar thought of the ratboys. "No, I couldn't."

Manny sighed and slowed his chittering voice. "I know how you feel about hospitals, but you can't avoid them forever. Things have gotten a lot better. They don't make mistakes like that anymore—" Nohar knew Manny stopped because of the ground he was treading. *Thanks for reminding me,* Nohar thought. He was about to say it, but, for once, he managed to keep his mouth shut.

"You better promise to come over and let me look at that wound. There are a lot more appropriate things to die of."

"Promise."

"I know you didn't just call to say hi. What do you want?"

Nohar caught the dig at him. It was unlike Manny. Manny really was worried about him. "Before I ask you, promise *me* something."

"What?"

"When this is over, we get out together. No business, no corpses."

There was a distinct change in the quality of Manny's voice that made Nohar feel better, "Sure . . ."

Damn, Manny was almost speechless. "I wanted to ask you about the time of death. How accurate can that be?"

Manny found his professional voice. "Depends on a lot of things. The older the corpse, the less accurate. Need a good idea of the ambient temperature and the humidity—"

That's what Nohar wanted to hear. "What if they were wrong about the temperature? Fifteen degrees too high."

"Definitely throw the estimate off."

"How much?"

"Depends on what they thought the temperature was to begin with."

"Thirty-two at least."

Nohar could hear the whistle of air between Manny's front teeth. "Nohar, the time of death could be put back by up to a factor of two. If the humidity was off, maybe more."

"Thanks, Manny."

"You're welcome, I think."

Nohar hung up the phone and looked at the ranch. All the little nagging problems with Johnson's death— And it was so damn simple.

Problem—it took much too long for the local population to notice the gaping hole if it had been shot when Johnson was shot. Solution—the window was shot out long after Johnson was dead. Probably during the thunderstorm that Thursday, so few people would have heard the glass—real glass, expensive—exploding and none would recognize its significance.

It had taken Young to make Nohar think of that. Young said he had seen a morey kill Johnson. "One of you," he said. The only way Young could have seen the killer shoot Johnson was if he, the killer, and Johnson were all more or less in the same place when Johnson died. If the assassin was in the house, he could have offed Johnson with one shot—no need for a shattering window to draw Johnson's attention. Johnson could have remained facing the comm, oblivious enough to be shot dead center in the back of the head.

Because no alarm, no break-in. That meant Johnson let him in.

With a Levitt Mark II? Not likely.

Johnson let in someone else—one of *them*—and that person let in the assassin. Yes, Johnson let in someone. Perhaps to confront the person with whatever he had found in the financial records. Young lived in the ranch with Johnson, but no one was supposed to know that. So Young would be hidden from the guest. Maybe in a darkened bedroom, looking out a crack in the door.

The guest—maybe one of the franks from MLI—talks to Johnson in the study. The frank leaves the door open, so the assassin can sneak into the living room and set up the Levitt. The door to the study must remain closed except for the last minute, to give the assassin a chance to prepare. Young would only see the gun when the frank opens the study door to give the morey killer a field of fire.

The one shot gets Derry Johnson in the back of the head. Young is in shock. The frank and the morey clean up a little and leave.

It must have been Saturday night, after that fundraiser Young and Johnson had departed early. That would explain Johnson's state, and why no one could finger Johnson's location during the week. Young wasn't thinking right. He freaked, packed his stuff, and ran out to his empty house.

The corpse was left in an air-conditioned, climate-controlled environment, until the morey with the Levitt blew away the picture window on Thursday. The storm ruined the traces of the assassin in the living room. The killing became an anonymous sniping. The time of death shifted to Wednesday and nobody got the chance to plumb the inconsistencies because Binder clamped down immediately.

Neat.

But why didn't Young call the cops?

Something had freaked Young. If Stephie was right, something beyond Johnson's death. From the way Young acted, it was something linked to the financial records. Something Johnson saw and Young didn't.

Nohar looked back at the broken window. The police

ballistics report was based entirely on the assumption that both shots came from the same place. Now the second shot, the one that blew the window out, no longer had to be in line with Johnson's head. The field of fire at the picture window was *much* wider. The sniper no longer had to be crouching in one of the security-conscious driveways across the street.

Nohar stood up on the passenger seat of the Jerboa and looked for good fire positions. He scanned the horizon—lots of trees. The Levitt needed a clear field of fire; crashing through a tree could set off the charge in the bullet. Nohar kept turning, looking for a high point, above the houses, behind them, without a tree in the way.

Feeling a growing sense of disillusionment, Nohar parked the Jerboa next to the barrier at the end of the street. He had been pounding pavement and checking buildings for most of the day. Evening was approaching and, while he had found a number of buildings both likely and unlikely to hold a sniper, he was little closer to discovering where the sniper had shot from. He was afraid he might actually cross the path of the gunman and not recognize it.

Fire position number ten was inside Moreytown, which was a plus as far as likelihood was concerned. Nohar figured you could drive a fully loaded surplus tank inside Moreytown and the pink law would give it just a wink and a nod.

The name of the building was Musician's Towers. It was a twenty-story, L-shaped building, supposedly abandoned since the riots. Good spot for a sniper. Hundreds of squatters in the place, but there weren't likely to be any *witnesses*.

There had been a halfhearted effort to seal it up. It'd been condemned ever since a fire took out one wing—as well as the synagogue across the street. Most of the plastic covering the doors and windows had been torn off ages ago.

He slowly approached the doorway, on guard even though it was still daylight. The entrance hall was in the burned-out wing. The hall went through to the other side, looking like someone had fired an artillery round all the way through the base of the building. He had to climb over the pile of crumbled concrete in front of the entrance, debris that came mostly from the facade on the top five floors.

White sky burned through the empty, black-rimmed

windows at the top of the building. That was the place for a sniper.

Above the gaping hole that led into the building some-one had spray-painted, "Welcome to Morey Hilton."

Inside, the heat became oppressive. Nohar was nearly used to the itch under his shirt, but in the sweltering lobby—it might have been because of the still lingering smell of fire—he had to take it off. He leaned against the hulk of a station wagon someone had driven into the lobby, waiting to become acclimated to the heat.

No sign of the squatters yet, but Nohar doubted any lived near the first floor. That would be a little too close to the action. The empty beer bulbs scattered across the floor, the occasional cartridge from an air-hypo, the fresh bullet pockmarks, marked the lobby as a party spot for the gangs. Not to mention "Zipperhead" painted on the side of the station wagon. Hmm, Nohar corrected himself. *Gang*—singular. Lately, the one gang seemed to be it. He didn't know exactly what to make of that. There had been at least five gangs around when he had been running with the Hell-cats. But that was a long time ago—the years before this building burned up—and Nohar really didn't want to think about it.

He decided he had waited long enough and went straight for one of the open stairwells. The winding concrete stairs were swathed in darkness, and Nohar's view became color-less and nocturnal. Here, the heat was even worse, and the smell of fire was overwhelmed by the aromas of rust, mold, and rotting garbage. The stairs were concrete, but every other footstep fell on something soft.

Nohar tried to ignore the garbage and think like a sniper. The face of the burned-out wing was pointed at the target, so the assassin would take a point amidst the wreckage. Few squatters in the remains of the fire—

Nohar hit floor ten and had to pause because he thought he'd come across a corpse. A lepus was curled in a fetal position in the corner of the tenth-floor landing. An acrid odor announced the fact the rabbit had soiled—him, her? Nohar couldn't tell in the dark—itself. As he approached, the rabbit's twitching showed it was still among the living. An air-hypo cartridge lay on the ground.

A jacked rabbit—might have even been funny if it hadn't

been so obvious the rabbit was on flush, and having a bad reaction. Nohar knelt next to the rabbit. She—Nohar could tell now—wasn't wearing anything. Filth covered her dark fur. He felt a wave of anger when he didn't see the hypo. That meant one of two things. Either someone had done her, or had stolen the hypo. In both cases they'd left her on her own like this. Scenes like this made Nohar think the fundamentalists might be right and moreys were an abomination in the eyes of whatever deity.

It was flush, all the classic symptoms. Near catatonia, chills, dehydration, voiding the bowels, rolling up of the eyes, shallow breathing, slight nosebleed. She was lucky. In truly severe reactions, the nervous system went. Then he *would* have found a corpse. She'd been through the worst of it, though. What she needed now was light and water. The darkness tended to perpetuate the hallucinogenic effects of flush. She could be psychologically unable to move long after the physical effects had worn off.

Nohar picked her up. She weighed nothing. She was a small morey to begin with, and she was skinny as well. He hoped the squatters still kept those rain barrels up topside.

On the burned-out wing, with the exception of the concrete facade, the top three floors were gone. Nohar carried the rabbit out of the stairwell and into the open air of the seventeenth floor. Nohar saw the orange plastic barrels immediately. Good, the occupants still collected rainwater. He looked at the shivering rabbit, silently asked himself what he was doing, and lowered her face gently into one of the cleaner barrels.

The moment the water brushed the side of her face, her ears picked up. Good sign. They stayed like that, Nohar holding her face just above the water, the rabbit curled up with her neck resting on the edge of the barrel, for close to fifteen minutes. The only thing keeping Nohar from giving up on her brain-lock was the gradual improvement, and the fact she did seem to be drinking a little.

There had to be a better way to deal with this, Nohar thought. He wasn't a trained medic. He was following the home procedure for a bad flush trip. It was a lot easier with a toilet handy—the running joke was, the comedown in the head was the way the drug got its street name.

A sputtering came from the barrel. Nohar hoped she

wouldn't vomit. "Listen to my voice." Nohar tried to sound reassuring. "It was a bad trip, but you're coming back. It wasn't real. You can relax now. It's important to untense your muscles, slowly—"

After a decade plus, the lines came back with surprising ease. She didn't say anything as he talked her down, and Nohar counted himself lucky she wasn't a screamer.

"*Let go, damnit!*"

A wide foot made a hollow slap on Nohar's chest, announcing the fact she had regained some contact with reality. Nohar didn't think letting go of her was a good idea, but the rabbit had suddenly erupted into thrashing motion from near paralysis. She was saying something in Spanish, and from the tone of her voice, it wasn't very pleasant. Good intentions only went so far. He set her down next to the barrel. She was panting, and a little unsteady on her feet.

Nohar rubbed his shoulder. It was tightening up after the stress of holding the rabbit above the barrel. He knew he was asking for it, but he said it anyway. "Are you all right?"

She looked up. She had a scar on one cheek that turned up her mouth in a quirky smile, as if she enjoyed some private joke at his expense. "Don't do no favors, Kit."

"Name's Nohar." He shrugged and started walking toward the windows on the south wall.

He got to the windows, began looking for Johnson's house, and immediately realized the limitations of his vision. The houses were mere blobs.

Nohar turned back to the rain barrel and saw the rabbit, apparently recovering out of sheer cussedness, doing her best to clean herself off with a rag. Oops, not a rag, he had left his shirt over there. Oh, well, the shirt was too hot anyway.

"Hey, Fluffy—"

She glared at him.

"Better at giving favors than receiving them?"

"Name's Angel. Fuck you."

"You owe me something for that shirt you just wasted."

She looked at the dripping cloth she'd been wiping herself with. "Yeah, you and every Ziphead this side of nirvana."

"Your trip an old debt coming home?"

"Wow, Kit, you have a grasp of the obvious that's worthy of a cop." She stood up—most of the filth now out of her spotted brown fur—walked over to the window and slapped the wet shirt across his midsection.

"Your shirt."

Nohar wrung out the shirt and tied it around his waist. "Thanks, Angel— Can you help? I need someone with better vision than I have."

Angel sighed. "What you want?"

"I need to find a window overlooking a ranch house with a shot-out picture window."

"You say shot?" A real smile overcame the ghost of the scar.

"Yes. I can't pick it out—"

She shook her head. "Kit, I didn't know the cops were hiring—"

"I am not a cop!"

Angel stepped back, still smiling, showing a pair of prominent front teeth. "Sore point? What are you then? What you looking for?"

"I'm a private detective. I'm trying to find a sniper."

She laughed and said, "I can tell you who. What I get?"

It took Nohar half a second to realize she was serious. He closed the distance between them in an instant and grabbed her shoulders. There was a brief adrenaline rush, but he contained it.

"Tell me."

"Not for nothing."

"What do you want?"

"You played the savior, play it all the way. I want protection. You're a big one, Kit. Keep Zipheads from expressing me to nowhere again."

She had him. He'd gone to the trouble of saving her life. Now, he had to make it worth something.

Nohar looked into her eyes and she stopped smiling. "I will, if you tell me two things. First, why are they after you?"

She shrugged. "Made stupid mistake. I tried to keep Stigmata, my gang, going after the Zips moved in. Didn't know then that they were backed from downtown. My clutch didn't fall off the map; so got erased."

Nohar could live with that. "You on flush—or anything else?"

"Do I look stupid?"

He told himself not to answer that.

He might as well play the samaritan while he could. "You get the couch."

Chapter 10

Nohar didn't see any rats when he parked the Jerboa across from his office. He hoped that meant Fearless Leader and his cronies were laying low. Even so, he was nervous, and Angel was more so. He gave her his shirt—it dragged on the ground when she wore it—and had her hold her ears down.

With ears down and her body covered, she could pass for a deformed rat.

It was the longest three blocks Nohar had ever walked.

They got to his apartment, and no ambush was waiting for them. Nohar breathed easier once he managed to un-wedge the warped door and close it behind them.

Cat ran up, as usual, and seemed puzzled to find one of Nohar's shirts moving under its own power. When Angel lowered a hand, Cat shied away and hissed, but the moment she stopped paying attention to him, Cat attacked the end of her foot that struck out from under the edge of the shirt.

"Ouch! Shit, Kit; put a leash on it."

"*His* name is Cat. If you have an argument with his be-havior, you have to take it up with him. He doesn't listen to me."

Cat backed up, crouched, shook his ass back and forth, and pounced on Angel's exposed toes.

Angel jerked her foot up and Cat tumbled back into the living room. She twitched her nose and snorted. "You think that name up by yourself?"

Angel unbuttoned the shirt and took it off. She tossed it so it landed on Cat. Cat found the shirt more absorbing than Angel's toes, and he started rolling across the living room floor buried inside it. Occasionally a paw would come out and swipe at the air. Angel made for the couch. Nohar went into the kitchen and filled a bottle of water. When he returned with it, she took the bottle and started drinking greedily.

By the time she'd finished her first bottle, Nohar had already made the trip for the second one. She drank this one more leisurely, and her story came out.

Angel had seen the sniper on the twenty-fourth, the stormy Thursday. "Ancient history now," she said. Stigmata still had a few loyal holdouts at the time. By then, though, the Zips had confined Stigmata's turf to the tower. War was about to break out all over. Everyone knew that. The Zips were going to vanish the remaining gangs. Only three were left—Babylon, Vixen, and Stigmata. According to Angel, Vixen's last shred of territory was the strip of Mayfield Road between Kenelworth and the concrete barrier, and Babylon was hunkered down in an enclave somewhere on Morey Hill.

Everyone was edgy. There was always someone watching, hidden behind a wall of rubble in the lobby. Angel, and the rest of them, wanted the chance to take some ratboys down with them. The twenty-fourth was her watch and Thursday was the night all hell broke loose. Angel thought Stigmata must've been the first of the mopup because the Zips must've realized there were only six members left.

The Zips weren't subtle about it. They announced their presence by having a burning station wagon rocket into the building. She told him car wrecks were a territorial symbol for the Zips. The wagon was loaded with explosives and went off in the lobby. Not enough to do any major damage, but enough to spook the whole building and knock Angel out before she could get warning upstairs.

She was only out a few minutes, just long enough for her and the ratboys to miss each other. The rats had made their way upstairs and she could hear gunfire and fighting above her. The Zips had left three as rearguard to catch stragglers. Two brown males and a white female hung around the open stairwell. Angel said she wanted to be sure of taking down one particular rodent. They didn't know she was there, the fighting covered her noise and the garbage covered her smell. She aimed her Nicaraguan ten-millimeter at the white one's head. Their leader, Angel said.

She was about to lay a slug right between the white rat's eyes when the canine showed.

"This guy was a chiller, Kit. Should've seen that righteous weapon."

From Angel's description, that "righteous weapon" had to be a Levitt. It was two meters long, with a scope the length and twice the diameter of Angel's forearm. The canine was carrying the weapon in one hand, a tripod in the other.

The newcomer was out of place at the scene of a gang war. The way Angel described him, the genetechs that designed him were at least as advanced as the ones who produced Nohar's stock. That made the canine Pakistani or Afghan.

Nohar had a bad feeling that he had met this canine before.

Angel described a dog with the domestic veneer removed. The canine was lean and had a shaggy gray coat, prominent snout, green eyes. He stood about two meters and massed about 100 kilos. Angel said he looked mean enough to take a bite out of a manhole cover.

"He had a raghead accent. Walked right to Terin—the white one—and asked, 'Is the roof cleared?' Ain't going to forget him. You could smell my people getting whacked up topside, and I smell *him* when he passes me. He was getting off. The blood was turning him on something fierce.

"She calls him Hassan, Hazed, Hazy—something like that."

Damn it, it *was* Hassan. The same morey who offed Nugoya. Nohar shook his head. What the *hell* did a small-time pimp and a gang war have to do with Daryl Johnson and the franks running MLI?

"There's this mother of arguments between Terin and the pooch. The raghead is blowing my shot, standing right in front of me—"

"What were they arguing about?"

"Fuck if I know, Kit. Terin's pissed for some reason, like the dog is treading on her territory. She also rants about her best people being dragged off to the four corners of the country—hell and gone, she said. Dog's frosty, though—think he's got the handle on the Zip's supplier, guns and drugs. Terin can mouth off, but not do much. Pissed her good.

"After blowing off steam, she leads him up. There goes

my shot. I might've written myself off to get Terin, but I wasn't about to give it up for two goons. I laid it low. Not that I wasn't tempted when they tossed Hernandez out a window, but not much I could do. I waited them out, hoping for another shot at Terin. Didn't happen."

Nohar was sitting on the floor across from Angel. Cat, half wrapped in the shirt, had tired of his game and had come to rest by Nohar. Angel was chugging her third liter of water.

"Thy caught up with you."

"Inevitable. They knew all of us. Snatched me by surprise—five to one, they like that kind of odds—up the Midtown Corridor. Wasn't in Moreytown so my guard was off. Was last Thursday—end of the month—the day after Vixen bought it."

Nohar remembered the burning Subaru and the dead foxes, both Wednesday.

Angel was still talking. "Surprised they didn't vanish me then and there. Upset I'd survived, more upset I had been at the tower when the raghead dog showed—someone saw me book outta there an' told the Zips. Terin wanted to know if I had told people, told her to fuck off. Pissed her good. Took me back to the tower an' pumped me with flush. Someone calling the shots said look like an O.D. That really pissed Terin. I could tell she wanted to off me painful. Must've been Friday when they left me. What day is it?"

"Sunday."

Angel yawned and stretched out on the couch. She barely filled a third of it. "Well, I'm getting some real sleep."

She fell asleep instantly.

They should have pumped another into her—but that would have looked like murder—and they were trying to make it look like an O.D.

Why? Because she'd seen the canine?

Again, what the hell did Zipperhead have to do with Daryl Johnson?

Nohar had a nasty thought—another morey uprising?

He shuddered at the idea. He'd been through that once already, when he was in the Hellcats. His own father had been shot, deservedly, by the National Guard.

"Don't let it be a political killing," Nohar whispered to Cat.

*   *   *

The express mail people had left a message for him. He'd have to come pick up his package of ID replacements, they didn't deliver to his neighborhood.

Nohar let Angel sleep when he went out. Once he got most of his wallet replaced, Nohar realized there was nothing for his guest to eat. Nohar did some hasty shopping down by the city end of Mayfield Road, around University Circle.

Then, now that he had a card-key replacement, he stopped at his office.

The Triangle office building was a crumbling brick structure that was still trying to fight off the advancing decay from Moreytown. The brick looked like a patchwork from the many attempts to remove graffiti. It was getting dark, and the timers had yet to turn on the lights inside. There was just enough light to give Nohar a slight purple tint to his vision. He climbed the stairs in the empty darkness. Nobody else was around this late on a Sunday.

His office lived in the darkness at the end of a second floor hallway. It didn't even have a number to distinguish it. The door was simply a fogged-glass rectangle with a basic card-key lock. Nohar ran his key through the lock and the door slid aside with a slight puff of air.

The room was barely big enough to hold Nohar, even though it only contained two items of furniture—a comm that was a few generations out of date, and a file cabinet that was older than the building it lived in. Nohar knelt down and punched the combination on the padlock that held the bottom drawer shut.

"Comm on."

There was a slight change in the quality of light in the room as the screen activated. This comm was mute, the synth chip had burned out a decade ago. He made sure the forwarding list was up to date, and got a bit of a surprise in the mail—a note from Stephie Weir. She'd found his listed number. It had been forwarded to his home comm while he was out. He played her message.

"Nohar, I need to talk to you. Can we meet for lunch tomorrow at noon? I'll be at the *Arabica* down at University Circle."

That was it. At least the joint she picked for the meet wasn't adverse to moreys. Although Nohar wasn't a great fan of coffee or coffeehouses, the college crowd seemed a little more tolerant.

He wondered what she wanted.

Nothing more interesting on the comm, so he opened the file drawer. It was nearly filled by a dented aluminum case, about a meter long by a half wide. The electronic lock on the case had long been broken, and there were scorch marks on that side. There was a painstaking cursive inscription on the lid that contrasted with the ugly functionalism of the box itself. The inscription read, "Datia Rajasthan: Off the Pink."

He pulled his father's case out of the drawer. The lock had been broken for nearly a decade, ever since Datia Rajasthan had been gunned down by a squad of National Guardsmen. Nohar'd gotten it a few weeks later when he split the Hellcats.

Nohar opened it. The seal was still good. The lid opened with a tearing sound as the case sucked in air and released the smell of oil. Nohar looked at the gun. The Indian military had manufactured the Vindhya 12-millimeter especially for their morey infantry. A pink's wrist couldn't handle the recoil. It was made of gray metal and ceramics, surprisingly light for its size—the barrel alone was 70 centimeters long. The magazine held twelve rounds. There were three magazines in the case, all full. A dozen notches marred the composite handgrip.

He held up the gun and cleared it, checked the safety, and slid a full magazine in. The magazine slid home with a satisfying solidity. The Vindhya was in perfect condition, even after ten years of neglect. The weight was seductive in his hand.

Nohar had practice with guns before it was a felony for a morey to own a firearm, but he had never even taken this one out of its case.

There were two holsters in the drawer. He left the combat webbing and removed the worn-leather shoulder holster. Nohar had never worn it, but he tried it on now. It fit well, comfortably, and that disturbed him.

One final item—a file folder containing a sheet of paper and a card for his wallet. Both items were pristine, the card still in its cellophane wrapper. It was the gun's registration and his license to use it. They were still valid, despite the ban on morey firearms. He'd gotten them a year prior to the ban.

He put the card in his wallet, holstered the loaded gun, and, hot as it was, put on his trench. Nohar had brought the trench coat despite the fact there had been little threat of rain. He had brought it to hide the gun. He pocketed the two extra magazines and put the case back in the drawer. As he locked the drawer up again, he told himself he was never going to fire the thing, but he knew, if he'd really believed that, he would have never opened that drawer.

Nohar left the office, the gun an oppressive weight under his shoulder.

Angel was awake again when Nohar returned with the groceries. She began cursing in Spanish the second he opened the door. Nohar had thought he'd get back before she woke up. After an experience like she'd been through, she should have slept like the dead.

"We had a fucking deal, Kit—" More Spanish. "You don't leave me alone like that."

He ducked through the living room and into the kitchen, shucking the trench as he went. Cat followed Nohar, and the food, into the kitchen.

"You listening to me, Kit?"

The dry cat food was still covering the counter where he had spilled it last night. Nohar had forgotten the mess. He set down his bag and picked up Cat's dish. After rinsing it off, he swept about half the spilled food off the counter and into the dish. When he put it down, Cat pounced on the bowl, oblivious to the fact that it was filled with the same stuff that was on the counter.

Nohar decided he could afford the waste and brushed the rest of the spill into the sink and turned on the disposal.

Angel was leaning against the door frame. She looked a lot better. She had taken a shower, returning her dirty brown coat to its original light tan. Her ears had perked up, though even with them she was still over a meter shorter than Nohar.

She was jabbering in Spanish, and Nohar knew she wasn't saying anything nice.

He asked her what she wanted to eat.

She walked into the kitchen and looked into the bag. She

was still angry, Nohar could smell it, but her tone was softening. "And I thought you *weren't* a cop."

"I'm not."

She squatted next to Cat. She was calming down, and Nohar began to realize exactly how scared she must have been when she woke up here alone. Angel was someone who wouldn't like being scared. It would screw with her self-image.

Angel was looking at Nohar's left armpit. "What about the sudden artillery?"

Nohar had forgotten the Vindhya. "Just because I have a gun—"

"That righteous? That fine? Something that worthy goes for 5K at least. Tell me you bought it."

She tried to pet Cat, but Cat was eating and couldn't be bothered. When Cat hissed at her, she stopped.

Nohar began putting away the stuff he'd bought, tossing a half-kilo of burger into the micro for himself. "I didn't *buy* it. My father brought it over from the war. Got it when he died."

She stood up. She wasn't argumentative anymore. She seemed to have gotten it out of her system. "Knew your sire?"

"It's not unheard of."

"Only morey *I* heard of with a set." She intercepted a bag of tomatoes he was putting in the fridge. "Even the rats make kids with a needle, and they're as common as fleas on a Ziphead. How'd two modified *panther tigris* ever get together to make you?"

The micro dinged at him and he pulled out the burger. Angel's nose wrinkled. She was vegetarian.

"Mother and Father were in the same platoon. He led a mass defection. The entire company of tigers, even the medic. Of all the cubs he must've made, I was the only one to track him down afterward."

From her expression he could tell he'd talked too much. "Hot shit, that *is* a Vind twelve. You're talking about the Rajasthan Airlift. You *knew* Datia—"

"Yes, I knew him, I don't want to talk about it."

Nohar took his food and ducked into the living room.

Angel followed, with her tomato. "Datia's a legend, the first real morey leader—"

Oh, that was great. A true leader. Nohar whipped around to face Angel. Cat was there to pounce on a spilled hunk of burger. "Datia Rajasthan was a psychopath. He needed to be gunned down, and if you so much as mention him one more time I am gong to hand-feed you to the Zips one piece at a time."

Angel just stared at him.

Nohar sat on the couch, ate a handful of hamburger, and turned on his comm to the news.

Chapter 11

Monday morning was breaking into a steel-gray dawn when the Jerboa pulled up in front of Young's shadow house. "Wake up, Angel. We're here." The rabbit, who'd looked like an inanimate pile of clothes until Nohar spoke, stirred. "Kit? Time is it?"

"Five after." Nohar stood up and stepped over the nonworking driver's side door. Young's house was the worse for wear. The garage had gone up like a bomb. The only remains of it was a black pile of charred debris at the end of the driveway. The house itself had caught. Nohar supposed some burning debris had landed on the roof.

There was a yawn from behind him that seemed much too large for the rabbit. "Five after what?"

"Six." The fire had gutted the house to the basement. The windows looked in on one large, black, empty, roofless space. The two neighboring buildings—Nohar hoped they had been unoccupied—had caught, too, but had escaped with relatively light damage.

"Six, Kit, this is no sane time to be awake—"

"You said that when I woke you up."

"Could have let me sleep—"

Nohar shook his head. "Not after that tirade yesterday."

Angel hopped over the door. She was dressed in an avalanche of black webbing and terry cloth that used to belong to Maria. The only clothing Nohar had for her. Somehow Angel had gotten the castoffs to fit her with a shoelace and a few strategic knots. The problem was, she smelled like Maria. "Couldn't wait till a decent hour?"

"Quit complaining. If I had a safe place to file you, I'd do it. For now, Your along for the ride."

Angel yawned again. Her mouth opened so wide it seemed to add twenty centimeters to her height. She shook her head and her ears flopped back and forth.

"So, what we doing here?"

Nohar started walking down the driveway. He could smell the gasoline. Even now, after at least one night of rain, there was still no question of arson. "I want to see if anything made it through the fire."

They passed the rear of the house, and the damage was much worse. The entire rear wall of Young's house had collapsed. The siding was sagging and puckered and bowed in the middle. Angel was only a few steps behind him. "Hope you're not talking architecture. This place is worse than the tower."

Nohar wasn't talking about architecture.

There's a difference between a supervised, methodical destruction of a body of records—Nohar was pretty sure Young was trying to torch, judging by the volume, close to everything in the Binder campaign finance records—and the accidental combustion Young had initiated. Something would have survived.

Apparently he hadn't been the only one to think so. He walked up to the spot where the garage used to be. The charred remains were in piles that were much too neat, and it looked like someone had gone through the ashes with a rake. "Damn it."

"What's the prob?"

Nohar waved at the garage, and expanded the gesture to take in the entire backyard. The rear lawn had been turfed by truck tires to the point that no grass was left. "Someone beat me here. Whoever it was, shoveled up everything Young didn't torch."

Nohar wasn't expecting to find *the* piece of evidence, but it would have been nice to find *something*. Angel was walking around the backyard, wide feet slapping in the mud. When he had looked for clothing for her, Nohar couldn't find a damn thing that even resembled a shoe for a rabbit.

"What am I looking for?"

Nohar was surprised Angel wanted to help. He supposed she was bored. "It was mostly paper. Some might have blown to the edges of the property where our trash-pickers missed it."

That was a bit of wishful thinking. The plot was bare of even normal garbage. Nohar supposed the people with the truck had grabbed everything that had even a slight chance of having been part of the records. They had a full weekend to work in. They were very thorough. Nohar wondered if they'd been the cops, or Binder's people, or MLI, or—

Nohar looked up from the edge of the driveway he was examining. "Angel? Do the Zips have any workings with a congressman named Binder?"

Angel's laugh was somewhat condescending. "Must be kidding. Zips and politics? Me becoming president'd happen sooner. All Zips want is a free hand to deal their flush."

Nohar shrugged. A connection seemed unlikely, but he couldn't deny the fact that there was a connection—somewhere. Hassan was involved with the Zips, and it looked like Hassan killed Johnson. But Hassan wasn't working for the Zips. If anything, it looked like the other way around.

"Were the run-ins with the other gangs because of the drugs?"

"Don't know about other folks, but my clutch was into protection—When you do, you have to protect people you charge. Both Zips and flush were pretty dangerous." She sighed. Her ears drooped. "Too dangerous for us."

She turned to face him. Her scar fighting the frown she wore. "Could've used someone like you back then, Kit."

Nohar didn't have a response for that. So he went back to his fruitless search.

By nine they had combed every inch of the property at least twice. The only result was part of a letter-fax Angel had found halfway across the street. It had been written by a gentleman named Wilson Scott, presumably to Binder or someone in the campaign. They only had the bottom half, so Nohar didn't know. It could be totally unrelated.

The letter went into detail on "the late morey violence." It got pretty down on the moreys, talking about moreys offing pinks, moreys taking hostages, morey air terrorism, and other generally alarmist topics.

Sounded like something somebody wrote during the riots. It was dated the tenth of August. Nohar wished he had a year to go with it. He also wished Scott didn't have a habit of writing in sweeping generalities.

With just half a hysterical polemic, the morning seemed to have been a waste of time. They didn't even have an address for Scott.

Nohar took Angel to his office with him. He wanted to make a few phone calls, now that people in the Binder campaign weren't on vacation. He would have liked the less-cramped atmosphere of his apartment. However, he figured the more he kept Angel away from Moreytown, the better off they both would be.

Even with Angel, the office wasn't more cramped. He lifted her up, and she fit on top of the filing cabinet, out of the way—and out of view of the comm . . .

Not that he intended to use the video pickup. He was going to try and bull through to the one living member of the Bowling Green gang of four he had yet to talk to. Edwin Harrison, the legal counsel.

Nohar's funeral picture had him sitting right next to Binder, front row, center. With Daryl Johnson's death, Harrison would be the most powerful man in the Binder organization, after Binder himself. In fact, Nohar remembered news off the comm had him as the current acting campaign manager.

The top, or close to it.

He killed the video pickup and hoped he could reach Harrison before anyone realized who was calling. Nohar also engaged in a slight electronic legerdemain. The outgoing calls he had been placing from his apartment had all been piped through his comm in his office. This was the listed one, his professional voice, so to speak. This was the comm everyone was locking out.

However, the process worked in reverse. He could pipe calls from the office through the unlisted comm at his home. They wouldn't be locking that out—yet.

It turned out to be easier than Nohar had expected. The strained voice and the strained expression on the secretary—from the obvious makeup, and the hair perfect as injection-molded plastic, she would fall into Stephie's category of window dressing—made it obvious she'd been operating the phones too long. Nohar could see lights blinking on the periphery of the screen. She had at least a dozen calls coming in. The way her eyes darted, she had at least four on the screen.

Nohar asked for Harrison. Her only response was, "Hold on, I'll transfer you."

The screen fed him the Binder campaign logo and dry synth music as he waited for Harrison's secretary to pick up the phone. It was a long wait and Nohar had to restrain the urge to claw something.

The call was finally answered, not by a secretary, but by Harrison himself.

Edwin Harrison had to be the same age as Young and Johnson. They had all been contemporaries out of college about the same time. But Nohar knew pink markings well enough to see the graying at the temples and the receding hair as some indication of premature aging. Harrison bore the slight scars of corrective optical surgery—Nohar had a brief wish his rotten day-vision could be corrected as easily—distorting his eyes. Under a nose that had been broken at least once, he had a salt-and-pepper brush of a mustache. There was no real way to estimate height over the comm, but Harrison looked small.

Harrison's shirt was unbuttoned and his face looked damp. The man was rubbing his cheek with one hand. Nohar figured he'd been shaving, a pink concept the moreau didn't understand.

Nohar found his polite voice. "Mr. Harrison—"

Harrison sat down in front of his comm. "Whoever you are, if you want to talk to me, you better turn on your video pickup. I can tell the difference between a voice-only phone and someone with a full comm who just doesn't want to be seen. I have no desire to spend a conversation with a test pattern when you can see me perfectly well."

So much for polite.

Nohar just hoped the guy was too long-winded to hang up immediately. He did as requested.

Harrison's reaction was immediate. In the same, level, conversational tone of voice, he said, "Holy mother of God, it's a hair-job."

Hair-job?

Nohar hadn't heard moreys referred to as hair-jobs in nearly a decade. "Can we talk?"

"Mr. Raghastan, correct?"

Nohar hated it when people mispronounced his name, even if it was only a generic label for that particular generation of tigers. Nohar nodded.

"I am sorry, but I have a very busy schedule. If you could make an appointment—"

So you can ignore me at your leisure, Nohar thought. *Not without a fight.* "I only have a few questions about Johnson and the campaign's financial records."

Harrison seemed to be indecisive about whether he wanted to be evasive or simply hang up. "I am sure you know any financial information that isn't a matter of public record is confidential. I can refer you to our press secretary. I am sure he can—"

—brush me off as well as anyone in the campaign, Nohar thought. "No, you don't understand. I don't want specifics." *A lie,* Nohar thought, *but there's little chance of getting specifics out of you, right? Right.* "I was just wondering how thorough Young was in torching the records."

Harrison looked pained. "I am afraid I can't discuss Young. We are still dealing with the police on that matter."

Probably true. Trying to cover things up, no doubt.

"Your headquarters was closed down last week. I suppose Young just waltzed in and took what he wanted?"

From Harrison's expression, Young *had* just walked in. It also looked like Young had done a lot of damage.

"How many years back, five? Ten ? Fifteen?"

From Harrison's face, fifteen.

"How much were you able to salvage?"

Harrison looked puzzled. "Salvage?"

Binder wasn't the one with the trucks. Nohar supposed there was little harm in telling the lawyer, and it might jar something loose. "I was under the impression you were in charge of the trucks that carted away the remains of the fire."

That got Harrison. "I am sorry. I really must go—"

I bet you must, Nohar thought to himself. He wondered exactly what kind of illegal crap was in those records that could turn Harrison white.

Harrison regained his composure. "I should tell you. Stay out of this—it doesn't involve you, or your kind."

As the connection broke, Nohar said, "But it does. More than you know, you little pink bottom feeder."

If *he* could pick up that much from Harrison's face, Nohar decided the lawyer would never win a jury trial.

There was a snore, and Nohar saw that Angel had fallen asleep on top of the filing cabinet. Instead of waking her up and leaving, he leaned against the wall and thought.

All that talk—well, all *his* talk—about Young had shaken loose a doubt. He was missing something, a big something. Young's motivation.

It just wasn't your standard grief reaction to torch the finance records of your employer. Nohar could, even with Stephie's doubts, believe Young blew himself up over lost love. But why the records?

Slowly, it began to dawn on Nohar that he was missing the obvious.

True, Johnson and Young had been lovers, fifteen years, above average for any relationship, pink or otherwise. Young saw Johnson's killer—the morey canine Nugoya called Hassan—he probably saw Johnson get shot. *But Young never called the cops.*

Not only didn't he call the cops, but Young actually covered for the missing Johnson. Stephie said Young had mentioned Johnson was out with "some bigwig contributor."

Then, after a few weeks, he blows himself up.

Someone very purposefully removed almost every trace of the records Young had torched. If the motive for Johnson's assassination was in those records, the odds were they had been carted away by the people responsible for Johnson's death. There were four ways they could have known what Young had been trying to destroy. Binder's people, Young himself, or the cops could have told them. All unlikely.

Or, they told Young to destroy the records.

"You're not going to do me like you did Derry."

Fear. Young was scared when he said that. He was talking paranoid. "You're *all* with them." Moreys, he was talking moreys and—something else. Franks? MLI? Whoever *they* were, *they* were in charge of Johnson's death—and Young.

Young was afraid of *them*. Young was also pathological about Daryl Johnson taking the fall for something.

"Derry didn't know he was helping *them*—what *they*

were. When he found out he was going to stop.... People will say he was working for *them*."

Why that fear for Johnson's rep? If Young cared that much, why wasn't he at the funeral?

Guilt.

Nohar triggered Young's suicide: "You're the finance chairman. Why didn't you figure it out first?"

Then, blam.

Of course Young knew what was in the finance records. Nohar felt like an idiot for not realizing sooner. *Young* was the one to let in the canine assassin with the Levitt Mark II. Young was in a conspiracy with *them*. Somewhere there was a trail in the records. Johnson had found it and had confronted *Young* with it.

The two of them were close, but Johnson was going to put a stop to it, whatever *it* was. Young couldn't let that happen—no, not quite right, *they* couldn't let that happen. *They* hired the morey. *They* killed Johnson. *They* probably just told Young to turn off the security and leave the door open so *they* could explain things to Johnson. When Young blew up, *they* made sure the records vanished.

No way Young could call the cops. Whoever was handling Young must have forced him to go on, business as usual. Go into work, go back to his shadow house. All the while, guilt ate Young up. He felt responsible for Johnson's death.

The whole charade of blowing out the picture window was to cover *Young's* tracks. To give *Young* an alibi.

It was working so well—up to the point Young torched the records.

That seemed an act of desperation, and not just Young's desperation—

Nohar had a bad thought.

Thomson had mentioned Johnson's executive assistant, Stephie, as having the same access to the financial records as the gang of four. That was obviously just the "official" slant on things. After all, Stephie described herself as window dressing. What if *they* didn't know that?

That worried Nohar.

What if *they* thought Johnson's executive assistant knew something, and just weren't sure enough to go to the lengths they went with Johnson?

What if she was being watched?

Could it be a coincidence Young went ballistic the day after Nohar talked to her?

Could it be a coincidence that the white rat's—Terin's— "Finger of God" seemed to have lifted?

He called Stephie. No answer.

It was ten-thirty, an hour and a half before he was to meet her. Damn. Nohar clutched the filing cabinet and started deep breathing exercises. His concern had triggered the fight-or-flight reflex, the adrenaline was pumping. He wanted to fight something. It was still too soon after those Ziphead rodents behind the bus. Something inside him was responding to the pulse, the adrenaline, the stress—

He fought it off.

Nohar couldn't let his control slip like that.

He had barely brought himself back under control, when the comm buzzed.

Nohar told the comm, "Got it."

The comm responded.

Smith had the video on. He was as eldritch as ever. The glassy eyes still stared out of a flat, expressionless face in the center of a pear-shaped head. Moisture glistened on the rubbery-white skin. On the monitor, Nohar got a chance to examine Smith from a closer perspective than he really wanted to. The pear shape of the frank's head, Nohar now saw, was caused by a massive roll of flesh that drooped over the frank's collar. The roll of fat obscured any neck or chin the frank might have had. The frank was totally hairless, too, no hair at all, anywhere. No pores Nohar could see. The frank could have been a white polyethylene bag filled with silicone lubricant.

The reason the frank didn't blink was because he didn't have any eyelids.

Smith also didn't have any nostrils.

No ears either.

The frank was calling from an unlisted location, and the lighting only picked up the frank's white bulk, nothing of the background. "I am glad I see you mostly unhurt from when you go to Philip Young."

"Thanks." Nohar immediately noticed Smith's weird accent again. It was not Afrikaans. "Your message said you paid the hospital."

"It is a legitimate expense of the investigation."

"You want a progress report."

The frank attempted a nod, sending the flesh of his upper body into unnatural vibration.

Nohar told the frank what he knew and what he thought he knew. How Johnson was killed, who was involved, and, of course, the as yet nebulous why. Nohar had convinced himself, despite Young's unreliability, that the reason lay in the now-destroyed-and-or-missing financial records of the Binder campaign.

"Excellent progress in such a short time."

"Now let me ask *you* a few things." Nohar knew he had jumped into the case prematurely, and what bothered him most wasn't his involvement in a pink murder, or even his involvement with a murder, period. What bothered him was the absence of information on his client and his client's company.

"I render what aid I can."

"First, you're worried about MLI being involved in the killing, and you told me you're an accountant—what's in the campaign records that could have connected back to MLI?"

"Only our heavy financing of the Binder campaign. A connection our board informs me will be severed as of our last payment—the three million Binder is missing and we are not. Our only contact with the Binder campaign is our money and suggestions on appropriate votes to take on the issues before him."

Nohar snorted. Having a bunch of franks telling Binder what to do bordered on the absurd. "You dictated the way he voted in the House?"

"He never votes against us. Our support is based on his closeness to our views."

That *did not* ring true. A frank's views being close to Binder's? Binder was a little to the right of Attila, was for the sterilization of moreys and probably the outright extermination of franks.

However, the finance records *were* the only connection between MLI and Binder. That gave credence to Smith's suspicion someone in MLI was behind the killing. Since the money trail had been sitting tight that long—fifteen years back, the way Harrison acted—if the motive was in the records it was in some incredibly obscure financial tidbit where Johnson never would have seen it in the first place, or it was in those "suggestions on appropriate votes."

"Second, I want to know where you and the other franks at MLI *really* come from."

For the first time Nohar saw what could be the remotest trace of expression on the frank's face. *Close to a nerve.* The bubbling voice seemed just a little strained when Smith responded. "I told you. We come from South Africa—"

"South Africa never signed the U.N.'s human genome experiment ban—but it's just one non-signer of at least two dozen that have the technology. One of a half-dozen that uses it. That isn't an Afrikaans accent."

Smith let out a sound that could have been a sigh. "I do not know if I am glad or not I hire such a perceptive investigator."

"Don't compliment me on noticing the obvious."

"I am afraid this information I cannot give you."

"Oh, great—"

The sigh, it *was* a sigh, came again. "Please, I explain. Our origin must remain private. Just as we must remain unseen ourselves. It is for the company's survival. If MLI has a murderer, or murderers, in its midst, such secrets are public. But my loyalty will not permit such knowledge until I know if the guilt is there. If you can't pursue this without that information, I will let you go with the money you have earned."

Good, you have an out. Nohar stood there, staring. He told himself he was going to say to hell with it. Drop the whole mess then and there. . . .

He thought of Stephie.

He couldn't.

He had never ditched anything in the middle.

"You know you're hobbling me when you withhold information."

"I am sorry."

"I need copies of those 'suggestions.'"

"They're on file. I get them. At ten-thirty Wednesday night we meet in the cemetery."

"Comm off."

What in the hell did he think he was doing?

He should have dumped the case when he had the chance.

Chapter 12

The walk past the city end of Mayfield was nerve-racking for Nohar. His sudden concern for Stephie had hit a few buttons. He was passing Ziphead territory with Angel. He felt the gun was all too obvious under his green windbreaker, even though when he chose the jacket it had seemed up to the job of concealing the Vind.

It felt like there was a target strapped to his back and the weight under his arm didn't really help.

There were no rats around, hadn't been since yesterday. That was becoming suspicious. There were always rodents around in Moreytown, even in daylight.

The streets were bare of them.

There was new graffiti under the bridge that separated Moreytown from the Circle. It was under the sarcastic, "Welcome to Moreytown." It read, "The Zipperhead rules here." The Zip graffiti was becoming too ubiquitous.

Nohar remembered the too-common slogan, "Off the pink," from the riots. A decade later, that slogan—Datia's slogan—had passed into general usage as a stock anti-authoritarian comment.

Nohar wondered if the people who used it habitually were consciously aware it was a call for human genocide.

It felt like he was in the Hellcats again and everything was about to explode into brimstone and shitfire. The feeling didn't leave after they passed the concrete pylons demarking the end of Mayfield Road.

The pink universe of Case Western Reserve University was only a few blocks from the farthest extension of Moreytown. The border was marked by the sudden shift into decent landscaping.

Angel turned toward him. "You feel safe, Kit?"

"No."

"Feel the shit's about to go ballistic?"

"You, too?"

"When the players absent all of a sudden, you know the situation is going to ground zero on you."

Nohar shrugged. "I've got a meeting to go to."

"Right. Whatever it is, it ain't us."

Nohar let it go with an insincere nod. He knew Angel didn't believe that. Neither did he. He didn't believe in coincidence. He thought it pretty damn likely the absence of Zips had a hell of a lot to do with them.

They made the coffeehouse at a little after twelve. The aroma of exotic, rare, and engineered coffees overwhelmed Nohar's sense of smell—at least it removed Maria's ghost-odor from Angel's clothes.

It was a college lunchtime crowd, with only one other morey—at least he and Angel weren't the only ones—a graying red vulpine who was engaged in a chess game with a black pink. Some of the patrons gave the new pair a few stares. Nohar, being a rather singular morey, got more than his share. Nohar was relieved to see Stephie in the back. She had chosen a table with enough room for him to maneuver around.

Nohar walked straight to the table and sat down. Angel hovered a second at the counter, until she seemed to realize she didn't have any money. Stephie was looking at Angel, but she directed her question to Nohar. "Who's your friend?"

"She's a lead from the Johnson killing."

"*She?*"

Sometimes pinks weren't quick on the uptake when it came to morey gender. Nohar supposed it had to do with the lack of prominent breasts.

Angel turned a chair around and sat on it backward. She rested her chin on the back, and scratched the base of her scar—her nose twitched. "Name's Angel, Pinky. Kit here's my bodyguard."

"Ah, hello. My name's Weir, Stephie Weir."

Odd, Nohar thought, now she *was* acting like he'd expect a pink to around morey. It was usually one of three things—fear, condescension, or this vague nervousness that was now spilling off of Stephie in waves.

"You wanted to talk. What about?"

She took her eyes off the rabbit and looked at Nohar. "I've been offered my job back—"

Nohar gave her a close-lipped smile. "Congratulations—"

Stephie interrupted him. "—aren't in order. It was conditional I didn't talk to you. That kind of job security I don't need. I've been let go once, like excess weight on a ballistic shuttle. I'm not going to be blackmailed into helping in a cover-up."

Angel chuckled. "Good for you, Pinky. Fuck the PTB."

Stephie looked confused. "PTB?"

Nohar felt his claws digging into the table. He untensed his hand and tried to stare Angel into shutting up as he explained. "P. T. B. Powers that be. Terminology from the riots— When did you get this offer?"

"After I gave you the lift from the hospital. It was waiting on my comm when I got back home. I never liked Harrison that much." She smiled now. "I called his house the minute I got the message. I got him out of bed at two in the morning to cuss him out and tell him what to do with his offer. He gave me a raise twice. I told him, at this point, not even if I supported Binder."

That nagged at something. The Binder campaign was riddled with that kind of inconsistency. "I want to know why the campaign has people like Thompson, Young, and Johnson in it."

"I never probed too deeply into that. I told you I was just window dressing. It was a money thing. I admit it. I sold out. They needed me for Derry. Anyway, there are precious few women in my age-group that are for Binder. Those that were might have had some principles."

He appreciated the fact she wanted to tell him about Harrison's offer. It also reminded him about his worries earlier today. "Who'd you tell about our meeting?"

Stephie shrugged. "No one, not even Harrison—though I was tempted to tell him he was too late with his little job offer. Just to make him stew."

Angel beat Nohar to the question. "Why not?"

Nohar glared at her as Stephie answered. "It's *my* business. Why should I have told him about it?"

There's the anger again, Nohar thought, *just like that lesbian comment.* It was laced with confusion, too, but less of it. It felt like she had come to some sort of decision.

Oh, well, let Stephie be pissed at the rabbit. "Stephie, you told no one?"

"Right."

"Not boyfriend, girlfriend, family, your mother?"

"I said, no one—" She gave a weak smile. "Not even my nonexistent boyfriend."

Now Nohar had reason to worry. Young's self-destruction and the Zip attack on him had been just too well-timed.

"Someone found out. You're being watched."

"What?"

Nohar glanced at Angel, and gave Stephie the story. Nohar briefly wondered if he should be doing all this exposition in front of Angel, but she *was* involved in this—however tangentially—and she was getting the short end of it as well.

After the brief rundown, Stephie looked thoughtful. "You might be right. I think Phil could handle the strain of losing Derry. But if he thought himself responsible. If he actually *was* responsible. . . "

Stephie shook her head. "But I *do not* understand why you think the black hats from Phil's conspiracy are watching *me*. Of all people, I am—was—the least significant person in the Binder organization."

Angel dived in again. "Pinky, do *they* know that? Overheard your story, and the whole point was to make you look like honcho's squeeze *and* his second. Like, this is what pissed you in the first place, right? You just *looked* highmighty when your *real* job was to make mister rump-ranger look like an upstanding pink hetro."

Angel was crude, but right. Nohar jumped in before Stephie could say something to Angel. "As Johnson's 'executive assistant,' you 'officially' had access to all the finance records Young torched. *They* might not realize your only function was to cover for Johnson's homosexuality. Also, Young started destroying records, not right after the murder, not when the body was found, not even right after the funeral. Young waited till nearly two weeks after the killing—"

Nohar leaned in for emphasis and tapped the claw of his index finger on the table. "He waited until the day after I talked to you."

"I see what you mean—"

"Hey, Kit. You smell something?"

Nohar looked at Angel. He was finally about to tell her to shut up, when he smelled it too. If it wasn't for the coffee, he would have noticed it immediately. Someone was wearing a very distinctive perfume. Nohar remembered the first time he had smelled it—in front of the ATM in Moreytown. It belonged to a female white rat.

Terin.

The Zipheads were here.

Nohar looked to the front. The front door was closing. As it did, the waft of sickening perfume died out. The fox was still the only other morey in evidence inside the coffeehouse.

"Terin?" Nohar asked Angel.

"Terin," she agreed.

The only change in the street was the car parked in front. It was a black ailing Jerboa, like Nohar's. Older and not a convertible. The windows had been painted black on the inside. Nohar heard the door slam on the car, and saw a hunched form run away from the vehicle. Nohar couldn't tell if it was pink, morey, or one of the Ziphead rodents. But Nohar remembered the Zips' trademark.

The driver was running away—

"Stephie, get down!"

Angel had already dived under a table. Nohar didn't wait for Stephie to reach cover on her own. He circled his left arm around her chest and slammed her against the far wall behind the table, putting him between her and the windows. His right hand went for the Vind.

For three seconds, Nohar felt real stupid.

Then the car exploded.

The windows weren't glass. They were some engineered polymer. They didn't shatter so much as tear and disintegrate. Then the air blew in carrying the heat and smoke of the blast. The pinks were yelling and screaming. Thankfully, Stephie wasn't one of them. Her face was buried in the fur of his chest.

The sounds began to fade as Nohar became too aware of his own heartbeat in his ears. He felt his pulse behind his eyeballs and in his temple.

He tried to fight it.

Nohar turned as soon as he realized there wasn't going to be a secondary explosion. He wasn't surprised to see four rodents diving through the now-open windows. The pinks didn't know squat. They had all hit the ground. The members of the gang advanced on the patrons, jumping overturned tables, kicking aside chairs.

Nohar was back in the riots again, watching one of Datia Rajasthan's terror runs on the pinks.

He was breathing heavily. Against his will, he could feel his time sense telescoping. Things were slowing down. His head throbbed as the adrenaline started kicking in.

A black rodent with a sawed-off shotgun was diving straight for their table. The room was hazed with smoke, and his eyes stung and watered, but Nohar knew Blackie was aiming at them. Nohar jumped to the side, hoping to draw Blackie's fire.

Nohar assumed he was the target.

He was wrong.

Blackie kept going straight for Stephie and leveled the shotgun at her.

The Beast kicked the door wide open, roared, and pulled the gun.

The Vind 12 slid out of its holster like it was on greased bearings. His thumb had clicked the safety as it cleared his windbreaker. He leveled the Vind about twelve centimeters away from Blackie's head and pulled the trigger.

The report deafened Nohar.

It did worse to Blackie, who had started to turn when he realized Nohar was armed. The bullet caught Blackie in the face, under the right eye. Datia's bullets weren't the standard Indian military teflon-coated armor-piercers. They were twelve-millimeter dumdums, strictly antipersonnel. The bullet carried away half of Blackie's head out of the back of his skull.

Time was moving incredibly slowly. It seemed there was a full second between each heartbeat, but Nohar knew his heart was running on overdrive and trying to jackhammer out of his rib cage. His nerves were humming like an overloaded high-tension wire.

He had whipped around to face the other Zipheads before Blackie hit the ground. The rodents, who had been about to lay waste to the pink population, were all looking in his direction. One of them had an Uzi nine-millimeter. The rat had been facing the wrong way, and as only now swinging the gun toward Nohar.

The Vind was already pointing in Uzi's direction.

Three shots in rapid succession. One for each heartbeat in the space of a second. Nohar's aim wasn't great. The first shot went high. Nohar corrected and the second went low, taking out Uzi's right knee and knocking the rodent sideways—sending the gun sailing over the counter. Third correction got Uzi right in the chest as the rat was spinning. The shot took Uzi off his feet and slammed him down nearly two meters back toward the smoking window.

There was a pop, it sounded like someone breaking a light bulb. Someone rammed what felt like a white-hot knife into Nohar's right hip. The warmth spread down his leg, soaking into his fur.

The rats were unfreezing.

One had a familiar-looking twenty-two revolver. Wasn't Fearless. As Nohar turned, the popgun fired again. Nohar felt a breeze on his cheek, brushing his whiskers as a supersonic insect grazed his neck. The Vind swung at the rat with the popgun and Nohar saw one of the Zipheads had a forty-four. Forty-four had a nice, expensive Automag. Problem was, the rat must have been used to revolvers. He seemed to have forgotten about the safety.

The Vind stopped on the dangerous one and unloaded four rounds as Twenty-two popped off another shot that missed.

Forty-four got it in the gut twice, once in the neck.

Twenty-two ditched his gun and ran for the window, diving.

Nohar had a perfect shot and three bullets left. He almost pulled the trigger.

The door creaked shut on The Beast. Reluctantly.

The front of the *Arabica* coffeehouse was now obscured by smoke from the burning car. Pinks were making for the exits. Nohar's hearing was coming back and he could hear the fire alarms wailing. The sprinklers came on.

Unlike most everyone in the room, with the exception of Angel, Nohar had been through shit like this before. It wasn't over.

"Angel, you still with us?"

A table turned over and Angel climbed out. "Yeah, Kit."

"Grab Blackie's shotgun, cover our rear."

"Gotcha."

Stephie, like most of the other pinks, had yet to react.

She was still staring at the rodent whose head had done a halfways vanishing act in front of her.

"Stephie, rear exit."

She turned toward Nohar with a blank expression. The crash was already hitting him. He didn't need to deal with this. He grabbed her and shook her a little too hard. "You know this place, where's the back door? They're only hesitating because they didn't expect a gun in the crowd!"

Angel had the shotgun. She was leveling it at the windows. "That Vind ain't a gun, it's a howitzer. Kit, I got two shots—and the way this shotgun's been treated, lucky if it don't blow up."

"Exit!"

Stephie was finally getting a grip on herself. She started back to the rear of the place. Nohar was grateful. She wasn't one of those pinks that suddenly collapse at the sight of blood and violence. And thank whatever deity, she didn't suggest waiting for cops.

"Here."

The rear of the shop was, for the most part, covered with old sacks and bags that used to hold coffee. At this end of the store, the bean smell overrode even the smoke. Stephie pulled aside one of the bags. Behind it was a short hallway with a public comm and restrooms, terminating in a fire exit.

They piled in, Nohar first. For the first time since he had broken free from the adrenaline high, he realized the hole in his right hip was more than minor. The engineered endorphins were wearing off. Felt like someone was holding a hot iron on his leg. "Stephie, you drive here? Where'd you park?"

"Lot behind the building. Were they after *me?*"

Nohar pressed himself against the fire door and peered through the one small pane of cracked yellow glass. "Blackie went straight for you. The Zips are hooked into the Johnson killing."

"If they've been watching, they know my car."

"Pink has a point. Zips are real fond of burning transport." Angel paused because the chaos in the front room had just upped a notch. Nohar thought he could hear the sound of distant sirens. "We best vanish ourselves, quick."

Nohar had been scanning the parking lot, looking for the

Antaeus. The huge Plymouth was hard to miss. Especially with the rat fumbling over the open hood to the power plant. Nohar grunted. His temple was pounding and there were little flashes of color interfering with his peripheral vision. Keeping his concentration focused while he slid the downside ride from that violent high was giving him a migraine.

"Bad news, you're right. They're wiring the car. Angel, cover me and be quiet."

"Gotcha, Kit."

Lucky, lucky. They were lucky because the Mad Bomber didn't quite seem to have a handle on what he was doing. Lucky because there weren't any other rats in the back. Mad Bomber was supposed to be the rearguard. Apparently the Zips gave him too much to do.

Nohar didn't rely on stealth, but Bomber seemed oblivious. Nohar closed the space between him and the rat in five running steps—each lumbering step drove a spike into his hip—and leveled the gun at the back of Bomber's head. By then, the rat knew something was up.

Mad Bomber was in the process of turning around. Nohar cocked the Vind and clucked his tongue at the rat. "Car has a wonderful finish, I wonder if you'll see the brains leave your head in the reflection?"

"Wha?" The wave of fear that floated off the rat was gratifying.

"Undo it, now. Or we're walking and you're on permanent vacation."

"Yeah." The rat started taking things out of the power plant. Too slow, the sirens were getting louder.

"Remember, fifteen seconds and you're going to start the car."

Bomber hurried, ripping other things out of the power plant. Nohar hoped the rat knew the wires he was pulling.

Mad Bomber finally came out with what looked like an Afghani landmine. It had Arabic markings on it.

Bang form behind them.

Angel called back as the smell of cordite and blood drifted over. "Kit, that's one shot. Hurry up, pink law's coming!"

Nohar kept his eye on the rat. It was becoming hard to keep his vision focused. He had all his weight on his left leg.

"You heard the rabbit, hurry up. That sound back there was your backup."

"Done, it's done. . ."

Mad Bomber was shaking now. Nohar could see why he didn't get the job of diving in on the pinks. The rat couldn't handle it. He was going to die. Not from the cops or another gang's guns. He was going to die from his own stupidity—or the gang would kill him itself. Nohar waved the two females over.

"Some advice. Quit the gang before you make a fatal screwup. Take the mine, stand over there."

Nohar motioned with the gun and Mad Bomber did meekly as told. Angel ran up, Stephie in tow, and leveled the shotgun at the rat. "Shell left, let me vanish the ratboy."

At least she asked. "Self-defense, no preemptive strikes." The migraine was getting worse.

"Fine with me, Kit. Saves the ammo."

Stephie eased behind the wheel and Nohar hustled Angel into the passenger side. Bomber was still blubbering under the stare of the Vindhya, but he managed to say something. "You said I would start the car . . "

"I lied."

Nohar dove into the back seat. The fire in his hip totally blacked out his vision when he hit the seat. As Stephie floored the Antaeus, the door slammed shut. Nohar heard the cables tearing out of the metered feed. He hoped they had some jumpers in the trunk or they'd only have one full charge to go on. A car this size didn't go far on one charge.

They were topping sixty klicks per as they jumped the curb on to the Midtown Corridor. Nohar's sight came back a little as he watched the destruction from out the rear window. Smoke billowed out from the car in front of the *Arabica*. Black, brown, and white rodents were bugging out of the place, heading toward Moreytown. All attention was riveted on the coffeehouse, or the flashers coming from the east. Except—

Two moreys in an off-road four-wheeler, the kind of thing you needed to drive into Moreytown past the barriers. With the speed the Antaeus was going and his pain-shot vision he could only make the types. White rodent, grayish canine. Terin and Hassan, had to be. Terin was aiming what had to be military binocs at them.

Nohar gave her the finger.

Stephie called back to him. "Where are we going?"

After telling Angel to make sure they weren't being followed, Nohar gave her an address on the West Side that, in Manny's words, was about as far from Moreytown as you could get.

With luck and a pink driving, they might not get stopped by the cops.

Chapter 13

Nohar woke up somewhere on the Main Avenue bridge. Someone had bandaged his hip. Maria's clothing was pulled tight on his leg and seemed to have stopped the bleeding.

The Antaeus was tailing a three-trailer cargo hauler out the other side of downtown Cleveland. The car was surrounded by the towering structures of the West-Side office complex. The sun glared off the acres of mirrored glass—it felt like they were traveling through a giant microwave. Nohar's eyes hurt. It felt like someone was squeezing them in time to his pulse. Nohar's blackout had lasted nearly fifteen minutes, and his migraine was still sending streaks of color across his field of vision. His hip still throbbed.

He tried to focus out the rear window, but his vision was too blurred to make out any details on the cars behind the Antaeus. He did a self-inventory and found himself in less than ideal shape. He had bled all over the back seat, despite Angel's—at least he hoped Angel had done it, Stephie shouldn't have stopped the car—field dressing. The twenty-two had only grazed his neck, opposite his bad shoulder, but the shot that clipped his right hip felt like it had ripped out a good chunk of meat. It felt like someone was running a drill bit in the joint. Between that and the sprained knee, his right leg was nearly immobile.

He didn't remember doing it, but somewhere along the line he had cleared, safetied, and holstered the Vind. Stephie was still driving. Angel still had the shotgun. Fortunately, Angel wasn't stupid and kept the gun down in the foot-well out of sight of neighboring drivers. Armed moreys usually didn't even get a warning from cops. . . .

Angel was the first to notice him revive. "Kit, how you doing back there?"

"I'll live." Nohar tried to get into a sitting position. His groan got Stephie's attention.

"Nohar, I've been trying to tell Angel here that we've got to get you to a hospital. She stopped the bleeding, but—"

"No pink hospitals."

"Pinky, Kit's in charge. He said West 58th, we do West 58th. You don't break command structure if you wanna live."

"Nohar, you're wounded."

He grunted and finally shoved himself up into a sitting position. He could feel the bones grinding together in his hip. "Don't worry about me. We're going to the house of the best combat medic that was ever in the Afghan theater. Be worried about someone following us."

Angel turned around and wrinkled her nose. "Moreys this far west shine, Kit. We've not been stopped only 'cause Pinky's driving. The off-roader with Terin in it paced us halfway up the Midtown Corridor. Quit when they figured we were headed downtown."

"Stop calling me Pinky."

"Hey, Kit, we got a sensitive one here—"

The byplay was getting on his nerves. "Angel, did anyone ever tell you you don't know when to shut up?" Nohar's vision was still blurred, but the colors weren't washing over as badly. He thought he caught a hint of a smile play around the edge of Stephie's mouth. He wondered exactly what kind of conversation the two of them had been having while he was blacked out.

"Sorry, Pin—I'll quit. What's your name again?"

Stephie made an abrupt lane change that shot them around the left of the cargo hauler. They rocketed out in front of the truck to the blare of its horn. "The name is Stephanie Weir. I would like it if you call me Stephie."

"Sure, Stephie . . ."

The Antaeus pulled off the bridge and on to Detroit Avenue. In the space of one city block the glass monoliths gave over to old brick warehouses with dead windows. Even the few places that were in use were aged black. They passed the first Ohio City marker and they were in Manny's neighborhood.

Nohar pointed to the side of the road, next to a white-washed building that held an unnamed bar that was just opening. "Pull over."

"What?"

"We pull over and wait for our shadows to catch up with us."

"Kit, I told you they pulled—"

"Angel, the Zips aren't the only ones in on this."

Stephie pulled over. "Now what?"

"We hunch down, out of sight."

"If you say so." Stephie crouched in the foot well with Angel. Nohar eased back into a prone position.

Nohar looked back the way they had come. At the height of lunch hour, in this part of town, traffic was dead.

It only took half a minute for their shadow to show up. An unmarked industrial-green Dodge Electroline, programmed or remote-driven, was moving down Detroit. It paused, hazards on, directly across from them and stayed there for nearly a minute. Then it accelerated and took the next right. Nohar figured it was about to perform some sort of search pattern.

Angel shook her head. "What now? And where did that come from?"

"Now, we walk and avoid the pattern that remote is running."

Stephie was pulling herself out of the foot well. "What about your leg?"

"I'll manage—"

Nohar felt a little more warmth ooze down his leg. He pressed the bandage and tried to get adequate pressure on the wound. "Van's from Midwest Lapidary Imports, I think. The company involved in this mess."

He pulled the shirt tight and winced. "Ditch the shotgun, let's go."

He hobbled out and his leg nearly buckled. In the daylight, his leg was soaked from the hip down, and his denim pants were beginning to adhere to his fur. He could put weight on it, but the bloodstains could be seen from a block away. Nohar was getting the feeling any halfway decent search would turn them up. They were too damn conspicuous.

He just hoped nobody called the cops on them.

He led the way through a vacant lot across the street from the bar, down an alley between two warehouses, through someone's cracked-mud backyard, across a narrow brick dead-end street, through a gaping hole in a rusted chain link fence, over the rotting ties that were the only remains of the abandoned train tracks, and finally into an alley that led behind some residential garages.

When he stopped, he had to look down to make sure his leg didn't end in a ragged stump. Angel spoke.

"Lady above, Kit. You know this place better than my runners knew Moreytown. And this place is solid pink—"

Nohar paused a second to catch his breath. "Angel, the divisions aren't clear as they seem to be when you're in Moreytown. I used to *live* up here."

Stephie asked, "Open housing policy?"

Nohar snorted and rubbed his leg. "Call it no housing policy and a relative absence of lethal anti-morey violence. By the way, we're here."

Nohar hooked a thumb at the rear wall of the garage they had stopped behind. Carved in the wall, amid a host of childish doodles and vertical claw marks, was some blocky lettering. "Nohar and Bobby, 2033," The threes were carved in backward.

Stephie was tracing the old carving. "Who was Bobby?"

"First and only pink friend—Let's get inside."

Nohar limped off around the garage. Manny's van was gone. Manny probably wouldn't be back until late afternoon or evening. When Nohar thought about it, he had probably contributed a lot to Manny's current caseload.

The side door was locked—in this neighborhood, predictable. Nohar rang the call button. He was right. Manny wasn't home. Angel and Stephie were rounding the side of the house. He called out to them. "This place has an old key lock, if you check the loose clapboard under the vehicle feed in the garage, you'll find a spare."

Nohar didn't add the "I hope" he felt. It had been nearly fifteen years since he'd had occasion to use the spare key. Luck was with them. Stephie came back with the key in hand.

Nohar let them in.

*   *   *

It was close to seven-thirty and they were all waiting for Manny in his living room .Nohar sat on his windbreaker to avoid leaking blood on the furniture, while Stephie and Angel watched the news off the comm. News wasn't great. The attack on the coffeehouse resulted in three dead—all rodents— and the local news called it a morey gang war. Great.

Even better were the reports of similar, and more deadly, incidents on the fringes of morey communities in New York, Los Angeles, and Houston. All had the car bomb tie-in. All Honduran rats.

Reports were still coming in, they said, about unconfirmed attacks in San Francisco, Denver, and Miami. Everyone made connections back to the "Dark August" of 2042. Eleven year anniversary of the first riots in Moreytown, also on a Monday, August 4. Nohar didn't need the reminder.

What really freaked the pinks was the obvious coordination between all the incidents. Same gang name. Same M.O. The Zips could have done no damage whatsoever, and the pinks would still freak.

The mall in New York was the worst. All four Zips there had automatic weapons, and the car bomb was a bit nastier than most. The vids had panned with loving attention to every body-bag.

Angel had overheard Terin complaining about her best people being dragged to the four corners of the country. While all the attacks were violent and bloody, the news never mentioned more than four rats involved in any one attack. Thirty rats, max. All heavily armed, supplied with explosives, and timed to the minute.

Terrorism staged to be a media event.

The whole situation made Nohar sick to his stomach. "A decade out of the hole, and a bunch of psychopaths push us back in."

Angel stared at the screen. For once, her wiseass attitude was gone. "Kit, hell the Zips trying to do? Why?"

"Wish I knew."

"Binder's moreau control bill is going to make it through the House."

Angel turned toward Stephie. "Huh?"

"The bill shuts down moreau immigration and starts mandatory sterilization."

Nohar shut off the bodies on the comm. "We're on the wrong side of another anti-morey wave. The riots all over again."

Angel let out a nervous laugh. "Come on, Kit. You were there, this ain't nothing like the riots."

Stephie responded for him. "All you need is some media terror and Congress will jump on the bandwagon. It seems almost engineered to push Binder's legislation."

The front door interrupted their conversation. A very tired-looking mongoose entered the living room. Manny glanced at Stephie, then Angel, and finally Nohar. He seemed beyond the ability to register surprise. He was still wearing his lab coat, and a ghostly odor of blood, death, and hospital disinfectant was following him.

"You stupid bastard, why aren't you in a hospital?"

Nohar was still wearing the Vind, but from Manny's attitude, more concerned than angry, Nohar knew Manny hadn't connected him with the rodent attack yet. Guiltily, he didn't explain.

Manny released a whistling sigh from his front teeth. "I wonder what would happen to you if I wasn't a medic. Can you walk?"

"I got here, didn't I?"

"That's not what I asked. How long have you been sitting there?"

Manny had a point.

Nohar tried to get up, but a shivering wave of agony rippled up the entire right side of his body. He collapsed on the floor, pulling the bloody windbreaker after him. Both women underwent a brief panic, but Manny shooed them away as he pulled out a sheet and laid it on the floor. It took all three of them to help roll Nohar on it.

"I hope you've already written off the clothes . . ."

Manny walked out of the living room and into the kitchen where he kept his medical equipment. Manny came back with a loaded air-hypo and a medical bag. He set the hypo down, next to the sheet.

"Introduce me to your friends." Manny started shredding Nohar's jeans with a pair of scissors.

Nohar tried to ignore the pain of the clotted blood tearing out his fur. "Angel, Stephanie Weir, the doctor doing violence to my pants is Manny, Mandvi Gujerat."

Manny nodded. "Pleased, I'm sure."

Angel twitched her facial scar. "You were really a combat medic?"

Manny had laid open Nohar's pants leg and was examining the remains of Maria's shirt that still bound the gunshot wound. "Five years in the Afghan frontier before New Delhi got nuked—You, Stephanie? Hand me those forceps." Stephie removed them from the bag. Manny took the forceps from her and used them to start peeling away the outer layer of the makeshift bandage. "Nohar, if it wasn't for that engineered metabolism of yours—"

Manny shook his head at the mess of Nohar's hip. "No, forget it, I'm not going to get through to you anyway."

Manny stood up. "I'm going to wash up. I've got to do some cutting and stitching on this obstinate lump of stupidity." He looked at Angel. "You know, when this bastard was six, he broke his arm and forced me to set it myself? A compound fracture yet . . ."

Manny left the living room and soon there was the sound of running water from the kitchen. Stephie looked at Nohar. "What is this with you and hospitals?"

Nohar looked down at the gory mess on his right hip and suppressed a shudder. "I don't trust them—"

Manny came back, pulling on a pair of gloves. "Yes, he'd rather trust himself to my floor. Who needs a sterile environment?"

Manny turned to Angel. "Pick up that hypo I brought in here?"

Angel did as she was asked. Manny turned to Stephie. "It's probably a futile gesture, but would you tie on my mask?"

Stephie tied the conical face mask around Manny's muzzle, muffling his voice. "Angel, can you handle that thing?"

Angel nodded and there was a mumble behind Manny's mask that sounded like, "Doesn't surprise me."

In a louder voice trained to be heard from behind a jaw immobilized behind the restrictive mask, Manny told Angel to empty the cartridge into Nohar's arm. Angel rolled up Nohar's right sleeve, there was a slight sting, and the world floated away.

Chapter 14

Nohar had an intense fear he would wake up in a hospital. However, no disinfectant assaulted him when he awoke. He could smell alcohol, a much sharper and cleaner scent. There was also the faint coppery rust smell of his own blood. There was the dry dusty smell of old cloth and paper.

And nearby was the smell of roses and wood smoke.

Nohar opened his eyes.

He was in the attic. His old room still had no air-conditioning, and should have been hotter than Hades — but the omnipresent rumble and the breeze through his whiskers told Nohar the old ventilation fan still worked, pulling a crosswind through this two–room insulated oven. His eyes quickly shifted into nocturnal monochrome.

Her scent had betrayed her presence. Stephie Weir was asleep in a claw-scarred recliner across from Nohar's bed.

He gave the room a brief scan and was thankful Manny wasn't overly sentimental. The chair and the bed were the only remains of his old furniture. The attic was now a haven for boxes, old luggage, and older clothes.

Nohar's gaze lit on the small end table that jutted out the side of the antique headboard. After a decade and a half, the table was still familiar. Nohar remembered the scratches that marked its surface. His name and idle crosshatches had clawed through five layers of paint to reveal the black finish underneath. The desk lamp was still clamped to it, still with three or four knots of electrical tape holding the cord together.

Orai's picture was still in its cheap gold-plated frame, cocked at an obsessively perfect forty-five degree angle toward the bed. Its lower edge rested in a groove worn in the last two layers of paint. The gold was flaking and rust spots dotted the gray metal beneath. The glass was hazy with dust and, in the dark, Nohar could barely make out the picture.

Nohar sat up on the edge of the bed—his hip objected, but only slightly—and turned on the desk lamp which, to his surprise, still worked. Now he could see the picture. In it, Orai was in her combat harness, but unarmed. She was center frame and holding up one end of an American flag. The other end was being held by some friend from her unit. In the background he could see the Statue of Liberty and part of the Manhattan skyline. Orai and her friend, both tigers, were smiling, totally oblivious to the show of teeth. Orai was already beginning to show her pregnancy. The writing on the old picture was faded a bit, though the picture itself was still in good shape. It read, "Rajasthan Airlift—March 2027."

Nohar sighed.

He realized Stephie was awake now. She was leaning forward in the recliner, probably trying to get a glimpse of the picture. Nohar didn't know what to feel about that. It was a personal part of his life. But Stephie was just sitting there. She seemed to know it was his decision to tell her. She didn't ask.

Nohar realized he liked this pink woman.

He handed her his childhood icon. "She's the one on the left."

Stephie took the picture. "Who is she?"

"My mother. She was already pregnant when the company defected. Her name was Orai."

Stephie's eyes raised from the picture. "You used the past tense."

Nohar was about to evade the question, but why shouldn't she know? He cleared his throat. "Died when I was five, just old enough to remember. She'd gotten inseminated, wanted to give me a little brother or sister. She'd saved for the procedure since getting to the States. Things went fine. Then, three months in, she went for a prenatal checkup—" Nohar sucked in a breath. "Those *damn* idiots at the Clinic—do you know what Pakistani gene-techs had done with feline leukemia?"

Stephie shook her head. The color drained from her face.

Nohar went on. "Those doctors didn't know either. They misdiagnosed a Jaguar, put him in with the other felines, including Orai." Nohar's voice cracked a bit. He brought it under control. "They *could've* quarantined the Jaguar. But they don't give moreys private rooms. Every feline in the ward started dying. *Then* they knew. She was near to term. She died miscarrying two cubs—"

Nohar fell silent. There wasn't much left to say. He closed his eyes and tried to remember when he had told anyone that story in full. No one came to mind. Not even Manny, though Manny knew the story well enough.

The smell of smoky rose was suddenly very close, and Nohar felt a tiny naked hand on his cheek, brushing his whiskers. He opened his eyes and saw Stephie's face, close to his own. Her breath was warm on the skin of his nose. Her eyes were liquid green nothing like the eyes of a cat— visible whites, tiny round pupils.

Nohar had never realized how alien human eyes were.

Her lips parted in a whisper. "Lord, how you must hate humans."

Nohar shook his head. "No, no hate. Not for people."

The hand left and Stephie replaced the picture, in its groove and at its forty-five degree angle. She did it in one fluid motion, stretching across Nohar to replace the picture. Again Nohar found himself admiring her muscle tone and her economy of movement.

She sat down next to him on the bed. The springs barely noticed her weight. Her nervousness was back. Just like at the table at the *Arabica*. She shook her head and looked up at him. Nohar wished once again that he was better at reading human expression.

"Nohar, would you tell me, who's Angel?"

Back to business. "I told you, she's a lead. She saw the sniper—"

Stephie was shaking her head again. "Not what I meant. I want to know who she is *to you*."

Huh? Maybe not. "What? Only met her yesterday— We sure as *hell* aren't lovers. If that's what you mean."

Stephie turned a bright red. She clenched a fist that made her knuckles whiten. "I'm sorry, forgive me. I didn't mean to offend—"

Nohar got a sensation he often got when talking with humans. There were two different conversations here. Stephie was, he felt, about to bolt off somewhere and cry. He didn't want to be responsible for that, even if he didn't understand what was going on. He placed his hands on her shoulder. Nohar didn't know how to do this gracefully, so he just told her the truth. "I *wasn't* offended. But the idea of having relations with that little twitch is ludicrous."

Nohar could tell Stephie almost laughed. She was still flushed.

"Why ask?"

Nohar could sense a slight tensing of her muscles under his hand. "Angel was bragging all the time while you were unconscious. I just wondered, you're such different . . ."

Ah. "Different species? I'd admit, me and her, it would be unusual, but not unheard of."

"Isn't that bestiality? Would it be possible?"

"Some human taboos, like nudity, can't wash with moreys for practical reasons."

Stephie was still looking up at him, and Nohar realized he'd only answered half the question. "And, uh, some morey characteristics came out the other end of the labs remarkably similar. I think it might be linked to bipedal . . ." He trailed off.

Great, no *he* was getting embarrassed.

Stephie had a questioning look in her eyes. The flush was fading. "Who *do* you have, Nohar?"

Nohar thought of Maria. "No one, anymore."

"You're lonely, aren't you?"

He would have objected, but he had trouble lying to people he felt something for. He nodded. "You?"

They faced each other, on the bed. He was feeling her breath on his nose again. No longer warm, hot. Beads of perspiration were forming on her forehead. Her voice was a whisper. "My nonexistent boyfriend." She tried to laugh, but it died. "No girlfriend either."

"Why did you get so upset when I asked if you were a lesbian?"

"Too close to what I was feeling."

They were very close now. He could feel her pulse under the hand that still rested on her shoulder. It was incredibly rapid, like her heart belonged to a kitten or a small bird. His heartbeat was racing to catch up with hers. Her sweat was beginning to lend a tang to the air that was alien to him, one he liked. What was going on had dawned on him gradually, and a small part of his mind was screaming at him, asking him what the hell he was doing. It wasn't the time for that question.

Her alien—human—eyes were staring deep into his own. "You saved my life. Have you ever heard of Chinese obligation?"

Nohar had. "I'm responsible for you now."

She sucked in a shuddering breath, and her lips touched his. He had seen kisses in human videos—but a feline skull and lips didn't move the right way for it. Even so, he tried. He let her small lips part his mouth and felt her amazingly smooth tongue alight on his own, caress one of his canines, and withdraw, to be felt, briefly, under his nose. When her eyes opened, the nervousness was gone.

Nohar, what are you doing? He ignored the questioning voice because he needed her, human or not. He moved his hand up from her shoulder and undid the bonds that were keeping her hair in a ponytail. He nuzzled the top of her head, thankful not to smell any heavy chemicals, and began to groom her hair. The taste and texture of her human hair was different from Maria's fur. The ritual perhaps seemed as strange to Stephie as kisses did to Nohar.

When Nohar had cleaned her hair, he began to move to her ears and the back of her neck. He expected the taste and feel of naked skin to repulse, but it was quite the opposite. The sweet acidic taste of her sweat and the smooth surface of her walnut-colored skin was beginning to excite him.

The questioning voice shut up.

By the time he had reached her shoulders, he realized she did have fur, of a sort. Tiny, downy hairs were scattered over her arms and her back. Somewhere along the line, he didn't know where, her blouse had disappeared.

They both reclined on the bed as Nohar worked his way down her body. He groomed both her arms. Her skin broke into a burning flush under his tongue. He cleaned the small puddle of perspiration that pooled between those odd human breasts. When he cleaned her breasts, she began to moan loudly. Nohar thought he was too rough, so he lightened the pressure. Stephie immediately responded by locking her hands in the fur on either side of his head and pulling his face back down.

He worked his way down her abdomen. She continued to urge him lower with her hands—

Humans kept their hair in the strangest places.

When Nohar could no longer restrain himself he rolled over on his back, ignoring the pain in his hip, and pulled her on top of him. She drew him in and shuddered, arching her back.

Nohar added his voice to hers.

It took them a long time to expend each other.

Nohar awoke.

He could still smell Stephie—between them they had drenched the bed with their scent—and he realized it wasn't a dream. Now was the time to ask the question. He opened his eyes and whispered, "Nohar, what the hell are you doing?"

The desk lamp was still on. The small fluorescent tube was now overwhelmed by the morning light. Stephie was curled up next to him. Her head rested on his chest, spilling her black hair across his upper body. It contrasted with the areas where his russet stripes faded to near-white. In the sunlight, where his color vision reached its optimum, he could appreciate the similarity of their coloring. Her black hair and golden-tan skin formed a near-perfect match to the shading of his stripes. They both had green eyes—

He had been perfectly prepared to blame last night on the emotional pit he had fallen into. But when he considered the way he was watching the light from the window curve its shadows around her tailless rear, he couldn't blame that night on any temporary condition.

Stephie stirred, and turned to face him. "Morning."

"Do you realize how much this complicates things?"

He could feel her twisting the tip of his tail between her toes as she spoke. "You're as romantic as five lanes of new blacktop."

"Please, I'm serious."

Her foot was going up and down the undamaged length of his tail. "I know." She rolled over and sat up, looking down at him. "Is this going to be it?"

Nohar tried to answer the question, but his thinking process was a mess. "Damn, I don't know how I feel about it. What prompted you to—with a morey—why *me*?"

Nohar damned his mouth, it was still running away with him. At the worst times. He'd just parroted one of the five stupidest questions anyone had ever uttered in any situation.

Stephie closed her eyes. "Don't ask that. I don't know *why*. Until I met you, I didn't think I could care for anyone—male *or* female."

She exhaled. Nohar didn't interrupt her. She was quiet for a few seconds. Then she opened her eyes and looked at him. "You've asked me twice, I might as well tell you. I *was* a lesbian—for about four months at Case Western I was the most radical bull-dyke feminist lesbian you could want. It didn't do a damn thing about my inability to have a relationship with another human being. I was posing as much as Phil and Derry ever were."

She idly ran her fingers through the fur on his abdomen. "Then I met you. I was set to be lonely for the rest of my life, and you screw everything up. After I met you the first time, I couldn't wait to see you again. All during that drive from the hospital I desperately wished you were human. Last night I decided I didn't care."

Nohar knew the kind of repulsion most humans held for moreys. Stephie had to be feeling even more confused than he did. He didn't know what to say. "I *should* dump you. For your own good."

There was a hopeful note in her voice. "Why don't you?"

Nohar thought about Maria. "I may be stupid and self-destructive, but I'm *not* going to do that to you."

Stephie gave him a hug that made him forget moreys weren't supposed to get involved with pinks.

He left Stephie to clean herself up and hobbled down to breakfast. As loud as they had been with each other, there was no question Manny and Angel knew what had gone on with him and Stephie last night. They didn't mention it.

He walked into the kitchen and found Angel watching Manny with rapt attention. Manny was involved in one of his passions, cooking. Angel actually seemed interested in Manny's omelete-making procedure. She wasn't even wrinkling her nose as Manny started adding raw hamburger to the cooked sausage. They both seemed to avoid watching his entrance.

"Found a disciple, Manny?"

Manny added the sausage/hamburger mixture to the omelette in the large skillet and folded the eggs over perfectly. "Don't make fun of an appreciation of good food, even if she's never heard of olive oil."

Manny got out a platter and let the omelette slide out on to it. Angel was trying to act spellbound. "Doc, how you keep the eggs from sticking?"

"You just have to remember to start with a—"

Stephie came down, interrupting what might have been an endless speech—Nohar had always seen Manny's cooking as obsessive. Nohar noticed, with some pleasure, Stephie wasn't put off by the lack of clothing on him and Angel. Stephie, however, was fully clothed, and she'd worn the outfit long enough that it was beginning to broadcast her scent on its own, even over the sausage.

Manny cut his omelette speech short. "What will you have? We have a vegetarian and a carnivorous version."

"Could you do both?"

"No problem—"

Nohar and Angel had the same reaction. "In the same omelette?"

Chapter 15

Stephie sat on the recliner as Nohar searched the boxes in the attic for something to wear. Nohar's mind had drifted back to MLI, Binder, Hassan, and the Zipheads. Somehow they were connected and he still had no easy way of fitting the pieces together.

"The answer has to be in those financial records."

Stephie sighed. "I know. That's the third time you said that."

Nohar pulled out a relic of his gang days, from before he'd left school—and Manny. It was an old denim Hellcats jacket. It still fit and it was big enough to hide the Vind when he wore it. "Are you sure that you never saw or heard anything that would help me?"

She shook her head. "I don't care what they wrote down

on my job description. They never let anyone near those records. It was a tight little group, the five of them. Even though Derry trusted me, no one got into the inner circle who wasn't there back in '40."

"Trusted you?"

"Yes, not to screw up the campaign machine. He knew me from my radical phase at Case. It's a right little community, even for the ones who are still in the closet. I managed to convince myself that I was helping him out. Found out it was Binder's idea much later. By then I was used to the lifestyle."

"Why didn't Binder just let Johnson go?" The potential for a media explosion was even worse with Johnson in the campaign, than if he left under a cloud.

"I don't know. Derry never expressed any great love of Binder, but he also never gave any indication of ever being willing to resign. Believe me, I tried to talk to him about it. He was always evasive about why he stayed."

"What about Young and Thomson?"

"Young was never willing to talk about anything but business. I think he resented me. Thomson, I don't know, he's slick and never says an ill word about Binder or the campaign—but he acts like he knows some joke the rest of the world doesn't."

Still batting zero for hard information.

Nohar pulled out a T-shirt. It was the only black one, but it had a yellow smile-face on it. Stephie repressed a giggle.

Nohar frowned as he pulled out the most intact set of jeans. They'd still been using the human model for morey clothes when they'd made it. The seams on the legs were split so his legs could move, and there was a slit in the ass for his tail. He pulled them on. "And nobody ever discussed Midwest Lapidary, or morey gangs?"

"You must be kidding." Stephie had reached over and pulled the Hellcats jacket off of the bed. The denim covered her legs like a blanket, and she ran her fingers over the embroidery. "How come you get to ask all the questions?"

Nohar pulled the shirt over his head. It ended up twenty centimeters short of his waist. "What do you want to know?"

Stephie looked up. Her fingers traveled over the demonic feline form that graced the back of the jacket. "Well, you called Bobby your first and only pink—"

Nohar felt like he'd gotten blindsided by a baseball bat. "No. That's not—I mean . . ."

She laughed. "I'm sorry. I didn't want to sound accusatory." Stephie stood up, leaving the jacket on the chair. "I was just wondering who Bobby was."

Nohar was still recovering. "Bobby, Bobby Dittrich. I met him when I was trying to make it through high school We were both sort of misfits—Though as we got older, he fit in more and more, and I fit in less and less . . ."

He lapsed into silence.

Stephie walked up and put her hand on his arm. "Are you okay? Did I hit another bad memory?"

He shook his head. "No, not at all."

He grabbed the jacket and hobbled down the stairs. He was wondering why he hadn't thought of it sooner. Stephie was following, "Where are you going?"

"I have to call Bobby."

"Are you sure it's the time to look up old friends—"

Nohar didn't answer until he got down to the comm. "I think he might be able to help me."

He switched off the news. "Move it, Angel—"

Angel said something unkind in Spanish as she moved off the couch. "Damnit, Kit, you *could* ask."

She stalked off to the kitchen, probably to take out her aggression on some poor vegetable. Nohar ignored her as he called the number for Robert Dittrich. It buzzed once, then he got a test pattern as the home comm forwarded the call.

"Budget Surplus, can I help—" Bobby displayed a rapidly growing smile of recognition.

Nohar was happy to see a friendly face.

"Christ, what's going on with you? The Fed is looking for you—"

"I need your help as a prime hacker."

"You *know* I *never* engage in illegal activity—" Bobby winked.

"Can you help?"

"Come down, we'll talk."

Stephie's car was out of the question. Everyone—the cops, the Zips, MLI—would know it on sight. Nohar called a cab.

Angel didn't object when Nohar left. She seemed a little resentful. Nohar supposed he'd been a little too curt with her, but he had other things on his mind.

The cab that showed up in front of Manny's house was an anachronism. It was a prewar Nissan Tory. The thing was almost as big as the Antaeus, but the huge hood covered batteries and a power plant that took up nearly half the car's volume. Nohar got into the back of the cab before he realized it had a driver.

A black human woman, her hair dyed red and strung into dreadlocks, was staring at Nohar with a wide-eyed expression. Nohar decided it had been too much to ask them to send a remote into this neighborhood.

"Shee-it." She was articulate, too.

"Don't tell me, you've never given a ride to a morey before."

"Dispatch didn't tell me no—"

Nohar slipped his bank card into the meter and tapped out his ID on the keypad. In addition, he typed in one hell of a tip. He could afford it. "Welll, I didn't tell *them*. Is there a problem?"

She saw the numbers come on her display. She spent a few seconds composing herself. "Sorry *Mr.* Rajasthan, didn't 'spect someone like you 'sall. Where you going?"

Money was a great equalizer.

Budget Surplus was a dirty little marble-fronted warehouse that hugged a nook between—really under—the Main Avenue bridge, and one of the more obnoxious mirror-fronted towers of the West Side office complex. It took more than a little creativity to find the grubby dead-end street that was the only access to the building.

The cab pulled up and Nohar typed in a hundred, on top of the tip. "Will waiting for me be a problem?"

The cabbie shook her head. "No problem at all. Take your time."

Nohar stepped out of the yellow Tory and felt like he'd been abandoned at the bottom of a well. One side was the warehouse, one side the black-dirt underside of the bridge, the other two sides flat sheets of concrete forming the foundation of the office building—whose doors would open on more wholesome scenery.

When Nohar entered the building, it no longer seemed

small. The interior was one huge room. Windows made from dozens of little square panels let in shafts of bright sunlight. Despite the sun, the corners of the building were covered in darkness. Standing in the light, Nohar found the shadows impenetrable. Endless ranks of metal shelving dominated the space, tall enough to barely give clearance to the slowly rotating fans hanging from the corrugated ceiling.

Nohar heard the slight whine of an electric motor. Then Bobby's wheelchair made a sudden appearance through a gap in the shelving that was invisible from Nohar's vantage point. The shelf Bobby rounded held nothing but oscilloscopes ranging in age from the obsolete to the archaic. Bobby wheeled forward and thrust his hand in Nohar's direction. Nohar clasped it.

He released Nohar's hand and maneuvered the chair around. "Let's talk in my office."

Nohar followed the chair as it wove its way through the acres of shelving. He smelled the omnipresent odor of old electronics—a combination of static dust, ozone, transformers, and old insulation. Shelves held dead picture tubes, keyboards, voice telephones, spools of cable—optical and otherwise—and rows and rows of nothing but old circuit boards. Mainframes were stacked against the walls like old footlockers filled with chips and wire.

Bobby's office was defined by four shelves that met at right angles with a single gap in one corner that would have been difficult to detect if Nohar wasn't looking for it. The shelves of electronics tended to camouflage themselves, any open space looking over more of the same. The illusion was of endless parallel rows, when the reality—demonstrated by their erratic maneuvering—was anything but.

His suspicions of the eccentric layout were confirmed by a rank of four monitors behind Bobby's desk. The monitors were connected to security cameras looking down on the floor. The arrangement of shelves resembled nothing so much as a hedge maze.

Bobby whirred behind his desk—a rusty cabinet trailing optical cable, it had the Sony logo on it—and motioned to a chair that was another chunk of technoflotsam. Nohar sat down. It was hard to get comfortable, buttons in the armrests dug into his elbows.

"We shouldn't be bothered here. Now you can tell me what's going on."

Nohar told Bobby what was going on.

An hour later, Bobby leaned back in his wheelchair and shook his head. "I thought the shit had hit the fan with Nugoya. I guess there's shit, and then there's *shit*."

Nohar had almost forgotten about his run-in with Nugoya.

"You picked the right politico to involve in this." Bobby whirred around the desk toward one of the shelves. The shelf he picked was dominated by a large bell jar-looking thing; it sat on a sleek black box. Nohar recognized the box as an industrial card-reader. "Even though all politicians are slime."

"Why the right one?"

Bobby parked himself next to the bell jar, and drew a metal cart from another invisible gap in the shelving. Three different processor boxes rested on the cart. There was an ancient Sony that was held together with duct tape. On top of it was a more compact Tunja 2000. On a shelf, by itself, was a huge homemade box. Frozen rainbows of ribbon-cable snaked from box to box.

"Can't get more right than Binder—" Bobby snickered. "Hate Binder. Wish you were investigating *his* absence from the mortal coil."

"Why?" Nohar could understand Bobby's dislike for Binder. But Nohar had never heard him express a political view on anything before. Legislation had always been irrelevant to Bobby.

"Need a license to hate a politician? Give you just an example—last session in the House, he led a vote to scuttle NASA's deep-probe project."

Ah, the space program.

Bobby pulled a small blue device from a shelf. Nohar got up and walked over. The device had AT&T markings on it, a pair of LCD displays, and a standard keypad. It could have been a voice phone, but there was no handset. Instead it had five or six different jacks for optical cable. "Those probes have been sitting on the moon—would you plug this in?"

Bobby handed him the end of a coil of optical cable and indicated a small plate on the floor. The plate had old East-

Ohio Gas company markings. Nohar reached down and lifted it. Under the plate was a ragged hole in the concrete. Half a meter down was a section of PVC pipe running under the concrete floor of the warehouse. A hacksaw had cut a diamond-shaped hole in the pipe, and a female jack had been planted amidst the snaking optical cable. Nohar knelt down and made the connection.

Something Bobby was working on, probably the blue AT&T box, made a satisfied beep.

"Thanks, I have trouble getting down there myself. Where was I? Oh, yeah, Binder's shortsightedness. His group of budget nimrods in the House have been stalling the launch for nine-ten years. Finally decided maintenance was too expensive, so they're going to dismantle the project. Forget the fact they would have *saved* money in the long run by launching on schedule, *and* we would be getting pictures back from Alpha Centauri by now, and the Sirius probe would have started transmitting already—"

Nohar shrugged. "My concerns lie closer to home."

"Yeah. My friend, the pragmatic tiger." Bobby snapped a few more connections. "Worst bit is, he started as a liberal."

"You're kidding."

"Nope, kept running for the state legislature as a civil libertarian, government-for-the-people type guy. Lost. Kept losing until he shifted to the far right and got elected. Never looked back. Children—can we say 'hypocrite'?

"Enough of that—*The Digital Avenger* is now online."

Bobby flipped a switch and a new rank of monitors came to life with displays of scrolling text. Inside the bell jar, lasers were carving the air into a latticework of green, yellow, and red light. "Now what kind of system do we want to run our sticky little fingers through?"

First things first. "Any information on MLI you can dig up."

"As you wish—" Bobby pulled out a keyboard and rested it across the arms of his wheelchair.

He paused for a moment. "Another thing about Binder. With just a little tweak of government finances, we might have caught up to the technology that got wasted with the Japs—"

"I thought you were an anarchist."

"Don't throw my principles at me when I'm drooling over biointerfaces nobody this side of the Pacific knows how to install. Besides, the engineering shortage is degrading the quality of my stock."

There was hypnotic movement in the bell jar as the holographic green web distorted and a blue trail started to snake through the mass. Bobby noted his interest. "Like the display? You ever hear a hacker refer to the net? That's it. My image of it, anyway. The green lines are optical data tracks, the yellow's a satellite uplink or an RF channel, red's a proprietary channel—government or commercial—the few white ones are what I and the software can't figure out   whoops, close there, someone's watching that one." The blue line took a right angle away from a sudden pixel glowing red. "Nodes are computers, junction and switch boxes, satellites, office buildings, etcetera. Jackpot!"

Bobby smiled. "Anyone ever tell you credit records are the easiest things in the world to access?"

The blue line had stopped at a node, which was now glowing blue and pulsing lightly. Text was scrolling across three screens as Bobby's smile began leaving his face. "You gave me the right name?"

"Midwest Lapidary Imports."

Bobby sighed. "Never as easy as it looks." He typed madly for a minute or so, then he typed a command that faded the blue line back to the neutral green. Bobby shook his head. "MLI doesn't exist."

"What are you talking about?"

"No credit records—"

"Check *my* credit. Someone is making deposits to my account."

More mad typing and colored lights. Bobby ended with a whistle. "You want to loan me some money?"

"Did you find anything?"

"Just daily cash deposits to your account, untraceable. Thirty kilobucks, plus . . ."

Nohar was speechless. He hadn't had the time, lately, to check the balance on his account. After a while, he said, "Check somewhere else."

"If you say so. I have an in at the County Auditor's mainframe." The blue trail snaked out again, and headed straight for a small nexus of red pixels and lines in a corner of the bell jar. Just before the blue line hit the nexus, it turned red itself. "Isn't that neat? But I am telling you, you *can't* have a company without a credit record. Economically impossible. Even the most phony setup in the world is going to be in debt to someone, you can't—"

Bobby paused as the new red line pulsed and text scrolled across one of the screens. "Okay, I'm wrong, you can."

"What?"

"I just downloaded the tax info on MLI." The scrolling continued. "Shit."

Bobby remained silent and the scrolling eventually stopped. The new red line faded. Bobby hit the keyboard again and numbers scrolled across another screen, and stopped. Bobby was looking at the display with his jaw open. Nohar looked at the screen. No more than columns of numbers to him. "What're you looking at?"

"The third line. The net assets they reported to the County."

"Eighty thousand and change, what's so great about—"

"Those figures are in *millions*."

Time for Nohar's jaw to drop. Eight—no, *eighty*—billion dollars in assets. Bobby started scrolling through the information. "And forty thousand mega-bucks in sales and revenue— With no credit record? Someone is playing games here."

These guys were having billion-dollar turnovers from gemstones? Maybe he was in the wrong line of work. This was one set of rich franks.

"And Christ is alive and selling swampland in Florida— these guys have never been audited."

"So they play by the rules."

Bobby shook his head. "You dense furball. That has nothing to do with it. The Fed assigns auditors for anything approaching this size. And those auditors aren't paid to sit on their hands. They're paid to dig up dirt—"

"So why hasn't MLI been audited?"

"Beats me." Bobby studied the screen. "It ain't normal. For some reason, MLI hasn't raised a single flag in the IRS computers. They don't pay too little, or too much—and that is damn hard to do. They even have this little subsidiary, NuFood, to dump money into so they can smooth out their losses. Know what I think?"

"What?"

"It's all a fake and they have a contact in the Fed telling them what their tax returns should look like."

Nohar shrugged. "So what are they spending their money on?"

"I can give you a list of real estate from the property taxes." This was accompanied by a few keyboard clicks and scrolling text on one screen. "There's records of withholding, I can give you a list of employees and approximate salaries." More clicks, another scrolling list, "That and a few odd bits of equipment they depreciate. Not much else, sorry."

Nohar was looking at the names scrolling across one of the screens. He was hoping he might glimpse a name he'd know. No luck on that score.

"The main thing I want to know is how they were paying Binder—"

Bobby shrugged. "Public database at the Board of Elections, no sweat. But there's a solid limit on the amount of individual and corporate contributions, even for a Senate race. I can't itemize the public record, but all the illegal shit ain't gonna be there."

The blue rail began snaking its way through the net.

Bobby had just raised another question in Nohar's mind. The cops had at least one look at the finance records that told them that the three million was in Johnson's possession. However, Smith said all the money was from MLI—and that wasn't legal. Nothing in the police report he'd read had mentioned it. From the campaign end of things, the money had to have looked legitimate—to the cops at least.

More names were scrolling past Nohar on the last screen. Again, Nohar watched it for names he knew—and, suddenly, he got lucky. Nohar stared in widening fascination at the scroll. It was almost too fast to read at all. He was only picking up about every tenth name, but that was enough.

Except for the label on it, he was looking at a copy of MLI's employee list.

Bobby stopped clicking and in the periphery of Nohar's vision, the blue line faded. The room was silent for a moment. The only noises were the slow creaking of the ceiling fans, the buzz from the holographic bell jar, and the high-frequency wine of the monitors.

"What do you see?"

Nohar was smiling. "Can you cross-reference the MLI employee list with the Binder contributors?"

"Sure thing, compare and hold the intersection." Tap, tap, tap.

"Why don't you have a voice interface on this thing?"

"Silly waste of memory. My terminal smokes about twenty megahertz faster than anything else because I don't bother with the voice. Besides, some of the shit I pull with this thing is best conducted in silence— Bingo!"

A third list was scrolling by on the last monitor. "Hell, I missed that. Good thing you were paying attention. The intersection set is the entire MLI payroll. Every single one of MLI's employees made a contribution close to the limit . . ."

Bobby had stopped talking. Nohar was beginning to smell anger off his friend. "What is it?"

"The contributions from Midwest Lapidary cover sixty-five percent of Binder's treasury. These guys *own* Binder. I knew he was corrupt, but *this*—"

Now it made sense. Binder's finance records held the key—but it now made even less sense for MLI to be behind the killing. Their investment in Binder was incredible. MLI was probably going to lose all that hard-bought influence.

Then, Nohar remembered what Smith had said—MLI's connection with Binder was to be *severed*. That was right before the attempt on Stephie. He still didn't believe in coincidence, and sever was a sinister verb. Nohar wondered if the other people in the Binder campaign were all right.

"You've got a rat's nest of innuendo here."

Nohar looked at the three lists. Only the last portion of each was shown on their screens. On the left was the list from the public contribution records. In the center was the withholding list from the County Auditor. To the right was the list of the names that intersected the two other lists. Something bothered him—

"How many people are on the withholding list?"

"Eight thousand, one hundred, and ninety-two."

The employee list had finished with an endless list of T's— Tracy, Trapman, Trevor, Troy, Trumbull, Trust, Tsoravitch . . .

"This is alphabetical?"

"Yes, you seeing something?"

"There's something about this list of names. It seems un-natural somehow. I can't put my finger on it."

Bobby hit the keys again. "Perhaps if I ran some pattern-analysis software on it—"

A brief summary replaced the list on the screen. Bobby read a couple of times. "Blow my mind! There are—get this—exactly 512 names for sixteen letters of the alphabet. 512 starting with A, 512 starting with B, same thing for C, D, E, F, but no G's, 512 H's, 512 I's, no J's or K's. There's L, M, N, O, P, no Q's, R through T, then nothing till the end of the alphabet. Talk about unnatural patterns—"

"It's all fake."

Chapter 16

Nohar stayed with Bobby until it was nearly noon. After Bobby had found those unnatural patterns, he had started dumping tax and credit info on individual employees. All the employees they had checked had no credit record and overpaid their taxes. None of them took more than the standard deduction, no investments, no losses, no dependents. The credit record was an anomaly, since the employees they had checked had all been homeowners without a single mortgage among them.

One of MLI's employees was named Kathy Tsoravitch. She allegedly lived in Shaker Heights. Her address gave Nohar something to check, to see just how phony the MLI employee list was.

The Tory was still waiting for him when he left Budget Surplus. The cabby had been leaning back and listening to the news, looked like it was going to be a profitable day for her. Nohar got in the back.

" 'Kay, where to now? Back to the 'hio city?"

"No, Shaker—"

She shrugged and started off east. She was a talker, and started going off on recent news events. The Ziphead attacks, a bomb on the Shoreway, and so on. Nohar let her, all her passengers probably got the same treatment.

When they pulled up outside an empty-looking one-family brick house, there was still thirty dollars left on the meter. Nohar added another twenty and told her to wait.

Nohar got out and quickly walked up the driveway to get away from immediate observation. He wasn't dressed for the neighborhood. The clothes made him look like a hood.

The back of the house was as closed up as the front. Shades were pulled at every window. There wasn't the ubiquitous ozone smell by the empty garage. It hadn't been used in a while. The backyard had withered in the summer sun. It was too yellow for Shaker Heights.

Nohar stood in front of the back door of the house. The lock was a clunky one with a non-optical keypad. The door probably led to the kitchen, but he couldn't tell because a set of venetian blinds blocked his view. He tried the door. It was locked.

He stepped back and raised his foot to kick it in, and he had an inspiration. He lowered his foot and typed in zeros—five of them, enough to fill the display—and the enter key. The keys were full-traverse and a little reluctant to move, but Nohar managed to force them to register.

In response to the dipshit combination, the deadbolt chunked home.

It made a perverse sort of sense that someone on the MLI payroll never bothered to reprogram the deadbolt combination when it came from the factory.

He opened the door and went inside Kathy Tsoravitch's house.

The door *did* lead to the kitchen—a pretty damn empty kitchen. He let the door close behind him as he surveyed the nearly empty room. No furniture except the counters, no stove, no micro, no fridge, not even light spots on the linoleum tile floor to show where they should be. The only appliance was a dishwasher built into the base cabinets. He turned on the lights and the overhead fluorescent pinged a dozen times before coming on full.

He walked over to the sink and his left foot slipped. He looked down and saw that one of the linoleum tiles—some faded abstract geometric pattern on it—had come loose from the floor in a small cloud of dust, the adhesive no more than crumbling yellow powder. He slid it across the floor with his foot and it hit in the corner of the room, shattering into a half-dozen brittle pieces.

He stopped at the sink. Its stainless steel was covered with a thin layer of dust. He turned on the water. There was a banshee scream from the plumbing, and a hard knocking shook the faucet. It sputtered twice, splattering rust-red water speckled with black muck, and settled into a shuddering stream. Nohar killed it.

He opened drawers, but there wasn't much to see. One drawer held a five-centimeter-long mummified body—a mouse or a bat.

The house was empty. The place had the same smell as the boxes in Manny's attic—dry and dusty. Any odor with texture to it had faded long ago to a nothing-smell. Even the little mouse corpse smelled only of dust.

There was a newspaper—a real newspaper, not a fax— lining a drawer. He pulled out the sheet. The date on the paper was January 12th, 2038, fifteen years ago. The headline was ironic, considering Bobby's view on recent events. According to the paper, NASA had just gotten appropriations to test the nuclear engines for its deep-probe project. The original plan was to have a dozen probes going to all the near star systems. Now, fifteen years later, Congress was going to scuttle the project before the first one was even launched.

The end of the Pan-Asian war was news, even two years after the fact. The paper had a rundown on the latest Chinese atrocities in occupied Japan. It also contained the latest 2038 reshuffling of the boundaries within a balkanized India. The Saudis had finally killed off their last oil fire, and found their market gone along with the internal-combustion engine. Even the sheikhs were driving electric. Israel hadn't yet been driven into the sea, but most of the occupied territory was now radioactive. Russia signed peace treaties with Turkmen and Azerbaidzhan—finally. And the INS released new figures on annual morey immigration. In 2037, it topped at one-point-eight million. Putting the new, 2038 moreau population at over ten million. The United States had the largest moreau population in the world—with the possible exception of China from which no figures were available.

A candidate for the state senate named Binder was adding his voice to the growing concern about moreau immigration. Bobby was right about Binder's radical shift. Binder spoke before the Cleveland City Club about the moral imperative to allow moreau refugees across the border. Poor tired huddled masses and all that. Five years later, Moreytown would explode into an orgy of violence, and Binder would be in the House as the congressman from the 12th district of Ohio with promises to ban moreau immigration altogether.

He balled up the depressing paper. It crinkled and disintegrated like an old brown leaf. He dropped the remains and kicked the pieces away as he entered the living room.

The living room had wall-to-wall carpeting, an old comm, nothing else. Nohar walked to the comm, kicking up dust and loose pieces of carpet. Worth a try. "Comm on."

It must have heard him. He could hear a click from inside the machine. Nohar looked over the relic as it began to warm up. It was a Sony and that meant old, at least five years older than the paper. Probably came with the house.

The picture was wavy, and the "message waiting" signal had carved a ghost image into the phosphor. The voice the comm used was obviously synthetic. It tried to sound human, but it sounded more fake than Nohar's own comm. "Comm is on."

At least the commands were standardized. He asked it for messages, and there were one hundred and twenty-eight of them. The comm's memory was filled, and had been for quite some time. Each new message was erasing an older one—stupid system, Nohar's home com erased anything more than a month old to avoid memory problems.

Nohar wondered what kind of messages were waiting on the comm. It was clear now the intended recipient didn't exist.

"Play."

Static, then a digital low-resolution picture with every tenth pixel gone to volatile memory heaven. "Kathy Tsoravitch, I with—bzzt—in person. Even so I wish to give my personal—bzzt—for your generous contribution—bzzt—"

Hell, it was Binder. Saturday, July 29th. The last night Stephie had seen Johnson alive.

Nohar smiled. She had last seen Johnson at a fundraiser—that Saturday. On that same night, Binder was thanking the nonexistent Kathy Tsoravitch for her generous contribution. A contribution that must form part of that missing/not-missing three million dollars.

Now he had something to play with. He wondered how well Thomson or Harrison could stonewall if he threw this in their faces.

However, this was only one message. He played the next one. "Play."

"My dear friend, K—bzzt—Tsoravitch. Even though I am unable to thank you in—bzzt—I am giving you my personal promise that I will jus—bzzt—your confid—bzzt—I intend to fulfill my promises of law and order—bzzt—waste in government, and humane laws to promote huma—bzzt— and I am glad there are still people like you in this—bzzt—"

Someone named Henry Davis in Washington D.C. Nohar didn't believe in coincidence. The first two messages were thanks for political contributions—

"Play."

Berthold Maelger from Little Rock, Arkansas, a month ago. Thanks for helping his run for the Senate, appreciating the fact transplanted natives still took an interest in Arkansas politics. He promised his best to try and eliminate pork-barrel politics and to legislate the Hot Springs federal moreau community out of existence.

"Play."

Prentice Charvat, Jackson, Mississippi, same week as Maelger. Running for the Senate. Nohar knew him. The vids portrayed him as the most abrasive and vocal anti-morey congressman in the House. He let it be known he wouldn't stop at sterilization. He wanted to deport moreys—by force if necessary.

Nohar played every single message. With a few exceptions for junk calls and wrong numbers, the entire message queue consisted of thankful politicians. The queue went back for nearly two years. Even with the repeats, Nohar must have counted ninety different congressmen—only two or three Senators—that owed Kathy Tsoravitch thanks for her contributions.

Between taxes and donations, it was a good thing Kathy didn't exist. Her salary barely covered her expenses.

Nohar walked back to the cab, dazed. He let himself in the back and sat in silence for a few minutes. The cabby didn't seem to mind, though after a while she asked, "We gonna sit here, or you got somewhere else in mind?"

"Get on the Midtown Corridor, go to the end of Mayfield. There's a parking garage behind the Triangle office building."

She nodded and started gabbing again as the Tory left Shaker. Nohar was ignoring her. Zips or not, cops or not, he had to empty his apartment. There were things he needed to wipe off his comm, there was the remaining ammo for his gun, and, of course, there was his cat. He was going to have to take Cat over to Manny's since he didn't know when, or if, he'd get back to his apartment again.

Fortunately, there was more than one way in.

They rounded the Triangle and Nohar saw his Jerboa. His car was now a burned-out effigy at the base of the pylons under the old railroad bridge. He thought he caught some movement around the abandoned bus, but his vision wasn't good enough to make it out.

The parking garage was a block away and behind the Triangle. It had its own street. Two-lane blacktop ran under a bridge straight to it. Nohar's office cardkey let them in. He told her to go to the fourth level and park. There, he put forty dollars on the meter. "Wait for me until that runs out."

"Sure thing."

Nohar got out of the cab and walked to the barrier at the edge of the fourth floor and looked out. The garage was a relatively new addition to the Triangle, but it was old enough to predate the expansion of Moreytown into what used to be Little Italy. Now, Moreytown surrounded the garage on three sides. For four floors, the openings in the sides of the structure were covered by chain link and barbed wire. However, years had atrophied security, and one corner of the chain link on the fourth floor had been pulled away from the concrete.

Nohar looked out of the hole now. No sign of the Zips yet. A meter away and down was the tar roof of a neighboring apartment building. The piercing smell of the tar made his sinuses ache. The building blocked his view of the street, which was good. It meant anyone on street level couldn't see him.

Nohar straddled the lip and ducked under the gap in the security fence. He reached over with his good left leg. His left foot hit the tar roof and slid a little. The tar was melting in the heat. He was glad for the boots he'd found at Manny's, tar'd be impossible to get out of his fur.

Nohar eased himself across the gap, trying to be gentle to his injured leg. He brought his right foot down on a clay tile on the lip of the roof. The tile was loose and his leg slipped. His foot followed the tile into the narrow gap between the building and the garage. He managed to hook his claws into the fence to avoid falling.

The tile exploded on top of a green trash bin below him. The sound was like a rifle shot.

For a moment Nohar could sense a target strapped to the back of his head. Once it was clear no one was going to appear at the sound, he could move again. Staying to the rear, to avoid being seen from Mayfield, Nohar crossed the connecting roofs to reach his own building, which was a floor taller than its neighbors. Five windows with wrought-iron bars stared across the roof at Nohar. He made for the rearmost one.

The bars were connected to iron cross-members that were bolted to the brick wall. However, security maintenance was even more lax here. The bolts were resting in holes of crumbling masonry and the whole iron construction came loose with a slight pull on Nohar's part.

The window was painted shut, the glass was missing, and a black-painted sheet of plywood had been nailed over it from the inside. He stood up on a wobbly right leg and kicked in the plywood with his left foot. The plywood gave too easily and Nohar had to catch himself on the window frame. It almost broke off in his claws. Tight fit, but he managed to lower himself through the opening he made. He briefly considered replacing things, but if cops or Zips were around, he might need to leave in a hurry.

He was in a broom closet at the end of the fourth-floor hallway. The sheet of plywood had landed on a double-basin sink and Nohar had used it as a step to get down from the window. The sink was now at a forty-five-degree angle from the horizontal, and rusty water was beginning to pool across the hexagonal tiles on the floor.

Nohar made for the stairs.

As he descended, the odor of tar receded. He became aware of a familiar perfume—

The Vind came out. Nohar backed toward the wall and crept down the steps. He rounded the landing, sliding under the window to the street, and pointed the gun down toward the third floor. No one. There was the ghost smell of blood—

He was getting a sick feeling.

Bottom of the stairs, nobody in the third-floor hallway. Three meters away, his door was ajar. The frame was splintered, proving Nohar's belief in the uselessness of an armored door in a wooden door frame.

No sounds. The perfume was still ghostlike, but the blood was stronger. Nohar flattened himself against the right side of the door frame and pointed the Vind through the opening as he pushed the door open with his foot. Blood, feces, the burning smell of terror filled his apartment—

Nohar covered all the rooms in record time, but the bastards were gone.

They had left Cat in the shower. Nohar found his pet, strips of skin removed from the back and chest, lying in a pool of blood, urine, and feces. They'd hadn't even the decency to kill the animal before they left it. Cat had bled to death, limping around the stainless-steel pit.

Shaving is a different thing to a morey than it is to a human. To a morey it is a gesture of hatred and contempt. Removal of hair is still the basis of it, but the skin is often removed as well. Survival is rare.

The Zips couldn't find Nohar, so they had shaved Cat.

They left a message on the mirror for him, in Cat's blood. "You next, pretty kitty."

Nohar put his fist through it.

Chapter 17

Nohar wanted to kill something. It was an effort for him not to listen to the adrenaline and finish trashing the apartment. What was worse, every time he thought of Cat, he couldn't help picturing Stephie—

He tried to calm himself by making a methodical inventory of the damage. The Zips had wrecked his comm, along with most of his apartment. They had shredded his clothes out of spite. The couch was dead; it had been ailing to begin with. The kitchen was a disaster. It looked like the Zips had been trying to burn down the building.

But they had missed the two extra magazines for the Vind. Those were where Nohar had left them, on top of the cabinets in the kitchen. The rats weren't particularly thorough, just violent.

Once he made sure the ammo was the only thing he could salvage, he took a sheet—one they had shredded—and wrapped Cat's stiffening body in it. The blood soaked through immediately, and Nohar wrapped him in another sheet, and finally stuffed him into a pillowcase. He didn't know what he was going to do with the corpse, but he couldn't leave it here.

On the way back to the cab, Nohar had the gun out. He hoped Zips would show themselves, but the way was clear through to the garage. He holstered the gun as he closed in on the cab.

The cabbie interrupted him before he could get in the back. "What hit your hand? No, don't want to know—stop right there."

Now what?

"No shit, piss, or blood in the back of my cab. They lemme drive, but I clean it up." She got out of the cab and walked around to the back and popped the trunk. She pulled out a first aid kit. " 'Spect one hell of a tip for this. Come 'ere."

Nohar hadn't bothered dressing his right hand. It hadn't seemed important. There were several deep cuts on the back of it, from punching the mirror.

The cabbie cleaned off the wound and tied it up.

"There—what's in the bag?"

"A dead cat."

"Won't ask if that's a joke. Put it in the trunk."

What now? Nohar got in the back of the cab and tried to think clearly, putting his head in his hands.

"Where to now?"

"Sit tight for a minute. We're still running off the forty bucks I gave you."

"Sure 'nuff."

Damn good thing Angel didn't want to be left alone in the apartment.

Should have ditched things when he had the chance. Now he was waist-deep in shit river no matter what he did. Ziphead had a serious in for him. *Guess the limit for rodents in this towns topped off at six—*

He shook his head. That kind of thinking didn't help. He wanted to claw the upholstery, but it wasn't his car.

The Zips had trashed his comm, that was bad. If Terin knew what she was doing, she would have dumped the call record and read or copied the ramcards before her muscle scragged them. The Zips would have his Binder database. That was public info, not too bad. They had all his photographs. Again, something he could live without.

But now they had the forensic database, and that was bad. Nohar didn't want to think what could happen if they figured he had a contact in the Medical Examiner's office.

Worst of all, he had no idea what messages had been waiting for him.

Nohar cursed under his breath. He was looking out the cab's window, across the garage and the bridge. He was looking at the Triangle office building—

Wait a minute. He had another comm! It the calls were being forwarded—and most of them were—there would be a copy on the comm in his office. Did the Zips know about that? Were they watching his office? Did the gang even know he had an office?

"So, you want a big tip?"

She turned around and gave him a look ranking that as a stupid question.

"Like to make a quick hundred?"

"Nothing illegal?"

"No." Nohar pulled out his card-key to the Triangle. "You just go to my office and pick up my messages."

The cabbie only took a few seconds to make up her mind. She took his key and left the garage.

She took her own sweet time getting back. It gave Nohar some more time to think. As Angel would say, things were beginning to look like they were going to ground zero on him.

The Zips' nationwide spree of violence made things loom large. MLI's pet congressmen were as ominous, and scared him more than the Zips—especially if MLI was as reactionary as Binder. He wished Smith wanted to have the meet tonight. Nohar didn't want to wait for tomorrow.

The cabbie came back with a ramcard and sat back behind the wheel. "Like you, but I'm nearly off shift. Last ride, where to?"

Nohar told her to drop him off downtown, near East Side. He was going to pay press secretary Thomson a visit.

He had the cabby drop him off next to the lake.

Nohar walked out on a pier, carrying Cat. He picked a chunk of crumbling asphalt and placed it into the pillowcase. After making sure the knot was tight, Nohar picked up the bundle and looked at it. It was a shapeless mass, but blood had seeped through and the outline of Cat's body was becoming visible in red. "Good-bye, you little missing link."

He walked up to the end of the pier and looked over Lake Erie. There was an overwhelming organic stink from the reclamation algae that hugged the shore. He spared a glance to the light-green plants that shimmered slightly in the evening sun light. Then he tossed his package over the water like an ungainly shotput. Cat hit the water about five meters out, splattering algae. He watched as the pillowcase ballooned up with trapped air, then slowly sank with the weight of the asphalt, pulling the algae in behind it to cover the surface of the water again.

He looked back behind him.

A few blocks away were the massive East-Side condos. On top of one lived Desmond Thomson, Binder's press secretary. Nohar was angry enough about recent events to not even consider how the pinks would react to him. He needed to take this out on someone.

Thomson would be a convenient target.

Nohar started walking toward the condos. The sun was setting, coating the windows of the buildings in molten orange. As Nohar walked toward the building, he amused himself by picturing Thomson's reaction when he unfolded the conspiracy MLI represented, and how deeply the Binder campaign was involved. It wasn't something you could hide, once someone knew what to look for.

Nohar smiled. When this got out, the vids would have a field day. Bobby had been right, Binder *was* the congressman to involve in this.

As Nohar walked into the valley between the ritzy condominiums, reality set in. These were security buildings. How did he think he was going to get in to talk to Thomson in the first place? Bad enough, being a morey. But he was dressed like a gang member and he was armed.

If he walked into one of these lobbies, he'd be lucky if security didn't shoot him and claim self-defense. Nohar got as far as the front door to Thomson's condo before he realized his chances of talking to Binder's press secretary was somewhere between slim and none.

For one of the few times in his life, Nohar wished he wasn't a morey.

He was sitting on the biggest political scandal of the century and he couldn't even confront someone with it. He felt positively useless. What now, he asked himself. Sit here all night and wait for the guy to leave for work? Go back to Manny's?

He thought of Stephie waiting back there and decided to call it a day.

He turned away from the door and smelled something.

Pink blood, and canine musk. Nohar turned back to the door and looked through the glass, into the lobby. There was a guard station in a modern setting of black enamel, chrome and white carpeting. Nobody was behind the desk. That wasn't procedure. The whole idea of security in ritzy places like this was to be high-profile. There should be a pink guard there.

Nohar tried the door. Locked.

He tried to buzz the desk. A guard wouldn't let him in once he saw him, but the guard would have to come to the desk to see who was buzzing. Nobody showed.

Nohar looked deeper into the lobby because he thought he saw some movement. It was an elevator door. It was opening and closing, opening and closing, again and again.

The doors were blocked by a blue-shirted arm on the ground, extending out from the inside of the elevator. The arm belonged to a pink, and in its hand it held a large automatic.

"Shit." Nohar could barely produce a whisper.

There was the echoing squeal of tires from his right. Nohar turned that way and faced the exit of the condo's underground parking garage. A green remote Dodge Electroline shot out and bore to the right so hard it jumped the curb and almost ran Nohar down. Nohar jumped and his back hit the lobby door with a dull thud.

The van shot by him, accelerating, going east.

It made no sense to do so, but Nohar drew his Vind and started chasing the van. Five seconds after he started running his limp had gotten bad to the point where he was in danger of toppling over. There was no way he was going to catch the van anyway. Not unless he shot out the inductor or a tire—and that would be pointless when he didn't know who was inside the vehicle.

Nohar holstered the Vind and began massaging his hip.

Something behind him exploded. A tearing blast that made Nohar immediately turn around, jerking his wounded leg. The shot of pain he felt was forgotten when he saw what had happened.

The top of Thompson's building had erupted a ball of flame that was being quickly followed by rolling black smoke. Nohar felt a hot breeze on his cheek as he heard the distant bell-like tinkle of cascading glass. There was a secondary explosion and the floor below belched black smoke through shattering windows.

Nohar had chased the van three or four blocks away from the condos. He still backed away involuntarily. Within seconds, the top of the cylindrical building was totally obscured by thick black smoke. Nohar was starting to smell the blaze.

It was the choking smell of melting synthetics and burning gasoline.

Nohar was stunned. He stared at the burning building until, a few minutes later, five screaming fire engines blared by him. By then, the entire top three floors were belching out smoke like a trash can that had caught on fire. Nohar backed into an alley. Cops would be arriving soon, and he didn't want to be questioned.

Nohar found a vantage point on a fire escape. At that point, a dozen fire vehicles surrounded the condo, twice that many cop cars. The vids had showed, like a flock of carrion birds. Three helicopters arrived in tight formation and aimed foam-cannons at the top of the building.

The copters pulled a tight turn, carrying them over Nohar. They were flying low and the loud chopping of the rotors made his molars ache. More smells hit him, ozone exhaust from the choppers, the dry-fuzzy smell of the foam—it made him want to sneeze—above it all, the choking, nauseating smell of the burning building. Up there, with all the synthetics, the smoke was probably toxic.

Streams of foam from the cannons cut through the air in precise formation. Three thin bands of white flew from the copters in parallel ballistic arcs, expanding as they went, until all three hit the building as one stream. Nohar watched the foam hit the east side of the building and smash through a window on the top floor. The stream displaced volumes of smoke, and after a short pause, white foam began cascading out windows, dripping down the sides of the building.

Desmond Thomson, MBA, press secretary for the Binder campaign, had lived on the top floor.

Nohar doubted Thomson lived anywhere anymore.

Chapter 18

Nohar waited for the chaos at Thomson's condo to die down before he walked out on the street again. Harsk had called him a paranoid bastard, but he didn't want to deal with cops. Being this close to blatant arson, Nohar doubted he'd be let alone. Nohar had the feeling if he got too close to the cops now, he'd be hung out to dry.

He hung by a public comm, painfully aware of Angel's comment, "Moreys this far west *shine*." He was glad rush hour was long over. The pinks had abandoned downtown Cleveland for another day, and the cops were involved elsewhere. The only pink Nohar had to worry about was an oriental rent-a-cop staring at him from the lobby of the Turkmen International Bank. The pink's suspicion was ironic. The pink was probably a Japanese refugee—during the Pan-Asian war Japan and India would have been on the same side, and both had been nuked into a similar fate.

Species before nationality, Nohar guessed.

The cab pulled up. This time, better neighborhood, the cab company sent a remote Chrysler Areobus. Nohar got into it, to the visible relief of the pink rent-a-cop. The van was brand new. Nohar could still smell the factory scent form the upholstery. No one had pissed in this one yet.

"Welcome to Cleveland Autocab. Please state your destination clearly."

The computer started repeating itself in Spanish, Japanese, Arabic—

Detroit and West—" not too close to Manny, just in case— "63rd. Ohio City."

"Five point seven five kilometers from present location—" Nohar would have walked if not for his leg and the neighborhood. "ETA ten minutes. Please deposit twenty dollars. Change will be refunded to your account."

Nohar slipped the computer his card, punched in his ID, and deducted the twenty dollars. There was a slightly overlong pause while the computer read his card.

"Thank you, Mr. Rajasthan."

The cab rolled out onto the Midtown Corridor, passed through downtown, and got on the Main Avenue bridge, heading west. Night had wrapped itself around the West-Side office complex. The buildings had shifted from chrome to onyx. Traffic was dead with the exception of Nohar's cab and the endlessly running cargo-haulers.

The cab reached the Detroit Avenue off-ramp—

The cab passed it, still doing 90 klicks an hour.

What the hell? "You missed the exit."

The computer was mute. Nohar tried typing on the keyboard provided for passengers. It was dead. So was the voice phone sitting next to it. Nohar began to worry about that pause over his card.

The cab passed the Detroit on-ramp, and two cars pulled off the ramp to follow it. Even in the dark, with his vision, he knew their make. Late-model Dodge Havier sedans.

Unmarked police cars were always Dodge Haviers.

Stupid. Of course the cops would put a flag on his card. They were probably going to have Autocab dispatch send the cab straight to police headquarters.

As if the cab was reading his mind, once it had picked up the shadows it took the next off-ramp, circled around under the bridge, and got back on the bridge—going east, cops in tow.

If he was going to do something, he'd better do it quick.

Now he wasn't so glad he'd gotten a new cab. An older cab

would have been fitted with a seat and controls for a driver. This cab's interior was totally filled with pseudo-luxury passenger space. Nohar had little chance to override the controls.

He got down on one knee and felt around the carpet between the forward two seats and the passenger console. When he found the edge, he clawed it up. There had to be a maintenance panel in here. The cab had no hood, and the design people didn't have hatches on the outside to mar the plastic-sleek lines of the vehicle. The only other place for a maint panel would be under the damn cab, and if that was the case, Nohar would be in trouble.

Nohar held his breath until he saw the maint panel under the carpet. It had a keypad, and a red flashing light. A breach would alert the cab's dispatcher. Nohar looked back at the two Haviers behind him. Alerting dispatch wouldn't be a very big problem.

Nohar unholstered the Vind, wishing for the standard teflon-coated rounds, and fired a point-blank shot at the keypad. The gun bucked in his hand and the keypad exploded under him. Little plastic squares with numbers on them went everywhere in the van. It set off the car alarm. He looked back at the cops and saw them activate their flashers.

Where the keypad had been was now a smoking rectangular hole. The sour odor of burning insulation filled the cab. The magnetic lock had only been on the maint panel for the deterrence value. The dumdum had scragged it. Nohar hooked his hand into the remains of the keypad and pulled out the panel.

From the light of the flashers, he could tell the cops were pulling up next to him. He kept low. If the cops had heard the shot, they wouldn't hesitate to blow his head off.

Under the maint panel were the electronic guts of the computerized driver. Now he had to think fast. The sky was suddenly visible out the side windows. He was passing over the Cuyahoga River. The three cars were hitting downtown Cleveland, and soon after would be at police headquarters.

The circuit boards were labeled and color-coded. Nohar pulled the one labeled "RF Comm." That should cut signals from dispatch—he hoped.

The Haviers were pacing the cab, one on each side of the center lane. The second the three cars hit downtown, the cab pulled a hard left—against the light. There was a skidding crunch as it clipped one of the Haviers on the inside of its turn. Nohar was thrown against the right wall. He grunted as the impact reawakened the wound in his hip.

It seemed he'd done two things in addition to cutting contact with the Autocab dispatcher. He had activated a homing program—the cab was no longer heading to police headquarters. It was probably returning to Autocab itself—and the collision with the Havier showed that he had cut the cab's ability to pick up the transponders of other cars.

He heard the long blare of horns and the screeching of brakes—

Fuck the cover—the sides of the cab wouldn't stop a bullet anyway. Nohar sat up so he could see what was gong on. The cab had run a red light without stopping. The cab wasn't picking up on transmissions from the lights anymore. Or the street signs—it was accelerating. Nohar had blinded the robot cab as well as deafening it. It was following the streets from its memory.

Nohar looked behind him. Only one Havier was following—the one the cab had violently cut off wasn't in sight. The cop had to slow to weave through the chaos the cab had left in the previous intersection.

More horns, another crunch. Nohar was thrown flat on his back. Now his hip sent a crashing wave of pain that made his eyes water. Somehow, he managed to keep hold of the circuit board. He saw the front windshield split in half and fall out onto the road. Nohar staggered up and looked out the back. The cab had plowed through the front end of a slow-moving Volkswagon Luce. The Luce spun out and almost hit the pursuing cop.

The cab must have been moving over a hundred klicks an hour now. He was actually losing the cop. Even so, he wondered if pulling the circuit board had been a good idea.

He turned around to see where he was going. Down the road was a row of sawhorses dotted with yellow flashers. The city was digging up another chunk of road—

The cab's brain had no idea the flashers were there. They were topping one-twenty. . . .

Nohar slammed the circuit board back home and dived for one of the rear chairs, trying to get a seatbelt around himself. The cab suddenly knew what was ahead of it and how fast it was going. The brakes activated, almost in time.

Whack, one sawhorse hit the front. The flasher exploded into yellow plastic shrapnel. The rest of the sawhorse flipped over the top of the cab. There was an incredible bump, thrusting Nohar into the seat belt. The belt cut into his mid-section as the nose of the cab jerked downward. The front-right corner of the cab slammed something in the hole, and the rear of the van swung to the left. The left rear wheel lost pavement and the van tumbled into the hole. It rocked once and stopped on its side.

The seat belt and the brakes had saved his life. The cab had hit the hole only going thirty or thirty-five klicks an hour. Nohar was lying on the left side of the van, which was now the floor. Nohar was still for a moment, letting the fires in his right leg fade to a dull ache.

After the cops were done with him, Autocab would probably want his balls for breakfast. Hell, it was their own fault—a remote that gets disabled like that ought to stop.

Nohar unbuckled himself and smelled the dry ozone reek that announced the inductors had cracked open and melted. The cab was dead. Nohar stumbled out the remains of the windshield. Outside was knee-deep mud that smelled of sewer and reclamation algae. Nohar faced the round, three-meter-diameter, concrete mouth of a storm sewer buried in the wall of the hole. He didn't hesitate. He knew providence when he saw it.

He limped into the echoing darkness under the streets.

It seemed like an eternity in the colorless dark, slogging through the algae, listening to the echo of his own breathing, unable to smell anything but the sour odor of the water. The only redeeming feature of his slog through the storm sewers was the fact the air was cool. The water itself was cold, and after a while his feet had numbed to a dull throbbing ache that matched the pulse in his hip.

For once he was worried about Manny's admonitions about infection.

The one big problem he was facing now was that not only had he lost the cops in the sewers, he had also lost himself. From the Hellcats, he knew every inch of the storm sewers under Moreytown. But, of course, he had no idea where the storm sewers were under downtown Cleveland. He had lost his sense of direction a while ago, so he was going upstream—had to be away from the river or Lake Erie. The direction was somewhere between east and south. Eventually he would find an inlet and get his bearings.

The few times he was tempted to go into a smaller branch off of the main trunk he was following, he decided against it. While the trunk was arrow-straight, and an obvious subterranean highway for the cops to follow, he would have plenty of warning before pursuit caught up with him. The slight phosphorescence from the algae was enough light for him to see a couple meters in any direction, the pinks would need a flashlight—that would give them away a hundred meters before they ever saw him.

It was also the only route that gave him enough clearance to stand upright.

Nohar's time sense was screwed. He'd gone for what seemed like hours without sign of pursuit. He kept glancing at his wrist, but his watch was still with whatever Young's explosion had left of his clothes at University Hospitals.

After an interminable period, the world began to lighten. At first Nohar thought it was pink cops with flashlights. However, even though the light let some blue back into his monochrome world, it was much too dim for pink eyes.

He drew the Vind and slowed his approach to the light ahead. It wasn't an inlet. It was a line of holes, large and small, that had been drilled through the concrete wall of the storm sewer. He ducked under a small one that was halfway up the wall, and crept up on a large ragged hole he might fit through.

A glance through the hole only showed him a metal-framework scaffold that was draped in opaque plastic from the other side. The tiled floor outside came to Nohar's waist. Under the scaffold he saw a jackhammer, a small remote forklift, a portable air compressor, and someone's hard hat hung up on one of the struts forming the scaffold. Nohar holstered the Vind and hauled himself up with his good arm.

He climbed in, crouching under the scaffold. He paused and looked back over his shoulder. He sensed something was wrong, even though he didn't hear or smell anything. He turned around, kneeling on his good knee, and leaned slightly back out the hole. He was waiting the split second for his eyes to readjust to the darkness beyond.

He heard a splash and his hand went for the Vind. A

hand shot out of the darkness, much too fast, and grabbed a handful of T-shirt and fur, while a shoulder hit him in the right thigh. He wasn't well balanced and the way his leg was, it buckled immediately.

Things were going too quickly. He barely had time to recognize the arm belonged to a pink. Nohar tumbled through the darkness and splashed into the green algae water. His hand had only gotten halfway to the Vind.

His head went under for a moment . . .

Nohar came up sputtering. His eyes had adjusted to the darkness. Facing him, and pointing his own Vindhya at him, was a pink female. She had short, dark hair—black as the jumpsuit she wore. She was only 160 centimeters or so, *maybe* 50 kilos. Despite her size, the way the cords stood out on her wrists as she held the 12 millimeter told Nohar she was prepared to take the massive recoil of the weapon.

"FBI." One hand left the gun, whipped a pair of cuffs at him, and was back bracing the Vind before Nohar could react. "I am placing you under arrest. You have the right to remain silent . . ."

The cuffs fit.

As she mirandized him, he noticed something. Her eyes, pupils dilated all the way, were reflecting light back at him. Her pupils glowed at him. He hadn't noticed at first, since a lot of morey eyes did that.

Pink's eyes did not have the catlike reflection.

She was a frank.

He stared at this small woman who held the Vind like it was a Saturday night special, and he realized he was scared shitless.

Chapter 19

Nohar didn't know much about human standards for such things, but he was pretty sure that this frank agent was the "babe" the Fed sent to Bobby. He went with the agent quietly. He had no desire to test her capabilities. Despite a probable resisting arrest charge, he could claim he'd pulled the circuit because he'd thought they were Zipheads out to kill him. Wouldn't convince the cops, but it was enough to keep the charges down to reckless endangerment, discharging a firearm, and whatever Autocab wanted to lay on him.

She called in on her throat-mike and wasted no time getting him to the surface. Despite the long walk alone with the agent, Nohar smelled nothing from her that made him think she was worried about him escaping. He noticed she put on a pair of chrome sunglasses as soon as they left the underground. They didn't seem to affect her vision at all, even though it was close to midnight. They came out by the shore of the Cuyahoga River, in the Flats close to *Zero's*. There was still a ghostly smell of carnage to the place.

The pink law was there, in force. A few dozen uniforms had scrambled down to the shore and taken up positions covering the exit from the tunnel. They seemed almost disappointed when Nohar didn't come out, gun blazing.

She led him up the rise next to the river, toward the congregation of parked black-and-whites. The pink cops gave her a wide birth and Nohar detected a slight odor of fear from them. He wondered if the uniforms knew the agent wasn't quite human.

She ignored the uniforms and headed right for the one puke-green Havier. Harsk was sitting on the hood, drinking a cup of coffee that smelled synthetic. She smiled, first time her face showed something other than a hard, expressionless mask. It stopped short of being a sneer.

"Detective Harsk, when I say I have the target in custody—the target's in custody. I was assigned to this for a reason."

Harsk grunted and got to his feet. "Isham, don't dick me around. I don't tell the Fed how to blow its nose. Don't tell me how to wipe my ass."

So her name was Isham. Nohar had thought he detected a slight Israeli accent.

"These men would be of better use elsewhere."

Harsk was steaming. Isham's smile was widening. Nohar wouldn't be surprised if she could smell Harsk's irritation herself. Harsk grabbed Nohar by his good arm and addressed Isham in a tone of forced civility. "I appreciate you helping us with your expertise." That was a blatant lie, Nohar could tell. "But I am still going to do things by the numbers. Especially with moreys. Especially after yesterday."

For a brief moment they were both hanging on to his arm. Harsk had a firm grip. He was strong for a pink. But Isham's hand felt like a steel band. When her hand left—it didn't release his arm so much as vanish—there was an ache where it had been. He suspected she had left a deep bruise there.

Harsk squeezed him into the back of the unmarked Havier, algae and all, and slammed the door shut. Soon Nohar was headed to police headquarters.

The two DEA pinks had fallen into a good-cop, bad-cop routine and didn't seem to realize they were stuck in the middle of a cliché. The bad cop was the fat one. His name was McIntyre. Good cop was a cadaverous black man named Conrad. From every indication, both their first names were "Agent."

Nohar had already gone through the numbers with Harsk, who was, if not civil, at least businesslike and professional about things. These two acted like they were going for first prize at the annual asshole convention.

McIntyre was into rant number five. "We got you by the short-hairs, you morey fuck. There's over thirty grand in *cash* deposits to your account. You expect us to believe it ain't morey drug money? You suddenly get that kind of *cash*, in the middle of the burg with the biggest flush manufacturing center we've found to date—*and* you show up in a firefight with the biggest distributors. Tell us what's going down, tiger, because we're going to trace those bills no matter how well you laundered them."

So far, Nohar had gotten more information from the pinks than they'd gotten from him. Apparently, somewhere in Cleveland was a major flush industry. Somewhere, the DEA didn't know where, was the lab, or labs, that manufactured the flush for the drug trade throughout the center of the country. The Zips were the major dealers of flush on the street level.

Conrad was doing his variation on being reasonable. "We don't want you. We want the labs. Tell us where they are, or give us some names, we can work with. We can intervene with local judicial system, make it easy for you."

He had already protested his ignorance. So he ignored them and studied the acoustic tiles, silently counting the holes that formed abstract patterns in the white rust-stained fiberglass. He wanted to go home, forget about Zips, Binder, MLI. Worse, he was beginning to worry about Stephie. Someone torched Thomson. Of the people with access to the finance records, that only left Stephie and Harrison.

It was going to be a long night. At least he knew McIntyre was blowing smoke out his ass about the cash. If the money was dirty, they'd know by now, and he wouldn't be in an interrogation room at police headquarters. He'd be in a cell in the federal building. As it was, all they had was the fact any morey with that much cash had to be guilty of something.

When Nohar didn't respond, rant number six was on the horizon. McIntyre never got to deliver on the steaming invective he must have been considering. Harsk opened the off-white metal door and let in Isham, who was still wearing her mirror-shades. Harsk smelled angry. He pointed at the agents and hooked his thumb out the door. "McIntyre, Conrad, get out here. I have to talk to you."

McIntyre wasn't impressed. "We aren't done here."

"Out, *now!*" Harsk was pissed. The DEA pinks obviously didn't expect this from someone they saw as a local functionary. They collected their recording equipment and left.

That left him alone in the room with Isham. She skidded a key ring at him across the formica table. It came to a stop right in front of him. She indicated his handcuffs.

"Take those off."

She didn't wait for him. She turned around to face the large mirror on the wall opposite Nohar. She took off her sunglasses, knocked on it twice, and pointed back toward the door. "I'm waiting."

The comment wasn't addressed to him.

Nohar didn't want to be alone in a room with this woman.

He thought he heard a door open out in the hall. she had just dismissed the cops stationed behind the one-way mirror. By the way her head nodded and moved, he could tell she was watching the cops leave.

"Now we can talk in private." She turned around to face

him and smiled. He finally saw her eyes in the light. They looked like pink's eyes at first, with round irises and visible whites. But there were few, if any, pinks with yellow irises, and none with slitted pupils.

"Aren't you going to remove those?"

He had forgotten about the cuffs. He picked up the keys and fumbled them off. "What's a frank doing working for the FBI?"

She put her sunglasses back on. Now there was no visual cue to her nature. But she was still not a pink. For one thing, she didn't have a scent. For another, her breathing was silent. This woman could be behind him and he would never know she was there.

She paused a moment before she spoke. "The executive isn't as picky about humanity as some people would like. If it wasn't for the domestic ban on macro gene engineering, they'd build their own agents."

Nohar slid the cuffs and the keys back across the table. He tried not to let his nervousness show, but she could probably smell it as well as he could. "So they pick up whatever trickles over the border?"

"Let's get down to business. I want information."

Nohar sighed. "I told the DEA I knew jack—"

That evil smile widened. If she had been a morey, the display of teeth would make him fear for his life. "Those schmucks never dealt with moreys before. They're convinced all moreaus know each other *and* are involved in the drug trade."

She reached into a pocket and tossed a grainy green-tinted picture on the table. It showed a shaggy gray canine in desert camouflage. It had been taken with a light enhancer.

Even with the rotten resolution, there was no question it was Hassan.

"I am searching for a canine calling himself Hassan Sabah. Contract assassin, specializes in political killings. Started in the Afghan occupation of North India. Works for every extremist cause you can name. Japanese nationalists, Irish republicans, South African white supremacists, Shining Path social humanists in Peru—"

Every group she mentioned was punctuated by a picture dropped on the table: the car bomb that took out the Chinese political director in Yokohama; the hotel fire that killed three UK cabinet ministers in Belfast; the half-dozen Zulu party leaders hacked apart by machetes in Pretoria; the barracks of lepus-derived infantry taken out by a remote truck filled with explosives in Cajamarca . . .

"Hassan smuggled himself into the country last year with the Honduran boatlift. The Fed didn't know he was in the country until a native of Belfast living in Cleveland recognized this canine." Isham tapped Hassan's picture with one of her slightly-pointed nails. "He's in the country, and he's involved with the Zipperheads."

"Why aren't you talking to your tip?" Nohar had an idea why. A morey from Belfast meant a fox.

Isham flipped out another picture, confirming Nohar's suspicion. The picture showed a morey vulpine, very dead. The fox had a small-caliber gunshot wound, close range, right eye.

"She was our witness. Whelp fox from North Ireland. Had the bad luck to be in a street gang that called itself Vixen—I see you know what happened to Vixen. Never got the chance to contact her."

She leaned back and glanced, over her sunglasses, at the one-way mirror. Then, satisfied, she went on. "The Fed only has suspicions of what Hassan is doing. But it scares Washington. Joseph Binder's Senate campaign seems to be his latest target. The Fed thinks a radical morey organization is operating out of Cleveland. The terror attacks by the Zipperhead gang give credibility to the suspicion."

"You want information on Hassan."

"We put you and Hassan in the same area on at least three separate occasions. When Hassan killed a local pimp named Tisaki Nugoya. During the attempted assassination of Stephanie Weir, former assistant to the late Daryl Johnson. And the arson attack that killed Desmond Thomson."

"Hassan was there?"

"One of the security guards lived long enough to give us a tentative ID."

Maybe he could bargain. "What do I get for talking to you?"

Isham took off her glasses and looked at Nohar as if she was examining a corpse to determine the cause of death. "You'll get my good will."

The smile was gone. "Nohar, you are going to walk. Make me happy."

Nohar scratched his claws across the linoleum and decided he didn't want Isham as an enemy. "I'll tell you, but it's mostly second-hand . . ." He gave her the story, as he saw it, leaving out the MLI angle in deference to client confidentiality. Saturday the 19th, Young had let Hassan into Johnson's house. Johnson gets whacked by Hassan's Levitt. Thursday the 24th, while Stigmata is being wiped up by the Zipheads, Hassan takes position up on Musician's Towers during a thunderstorm and blows Johnson's picture window. Thursday the 31st, Young empties the Binder finance records, torches them, and himself, on the 1st. Monday the 4th, the Zips attack the coffeehouse. Hassan and Terin are together in the four-wheeler.

She completed the list. "Today, Desmond Thomson is a victim of a firebomb in his condo and Edwin Harrison's BMW explodes on the Shoreway—"

"Harrison's dead?"

"Haven't you followed the news?" Nohar remembered the cabbie mentioning something about a bomb on the Shoreway. "Him and twelve other commuters during the morning rush hour. So far, because of you, Weir is the only one to survive an attempt by Hassan. Do know where she is?"

"No." He didn't want to lie. He didn't know how far he could push Isham, but he didn't want to get Manny involved with this. "She gave me a lift to my old neighborhood. I don't know where she and the rabbit went after that."

Isham seemed to know it was a lie. "I want to know if you find out where she's hiding out. The Fed would like to put her under protection—"

The conversation stopped because a muffled yell was coming from the hall. It was McIntyre. "*What?*"

The room was supposed to be soundproof, but Nohar could hear the conversation if he concentrated. From the pause in Isham's speech, she was eavesdropping as well.

"I said," Harsk's voice, "the tiger walks. Your own fault. Screwed your own collar, if there *was* a collar to begin with. Acted worse than a couple of rookies."

"You can't talk like—"

"Maybe if I put it like this. *Fuck* you, *fuck* your little proprietary DEA investigation, and *fuck* inter-agency co-operation if you're going to fuck up like this around here!"

"Detective Harsk—" That was Conrad.

"Shut the fuck up! DA sent the word. No prosecution on the coffeehouse, self-defense. None on the gun. Check your files, he's had a license since 2043. As far as recklessness is concerned, *you're* the glorified dimwits that stormed into Autocab dispatch and not only disabled the override comm, but the emergency shutoff as well. DA's position is, since you didn't identify yourself, and the emergency shutoff was disabled, Rajasthan was justified."

"You don't understand," Conrad again, "this is our first lead—"

"The charges from Autocab—"

Harsk almost sounded pleased. "*You* don't understand. You have shit. Autocab *is* going to press charges—*against you two.* It might come as a surprise, but not everybody likes to have the DEA walk in and take over. Not to mention the fact the Transportation Safety Board is upset with you. Cutting the override on a remote vehicle is a felony. Because you two goobers couldn't identify yourself to the suspect, the cab goes flying blind into traffic. You're lucky you don't face kidnapping charges. You're not too far from assault with intent."

"You don't really believe he thought it was the Zips—"

"*You unbelievable shits!* Just because it's a morey, doesn't mean you can forget all that bothersome civil rights crap. The collar *still* has to fly in court. You blew it. Now get the hell out of my station and back to your stakeout in Morey-town—or better, back to the rock you crawled out from."

"Your superiors are going to hear about this."

"What a coincidence, your superiors already have. A district chief named Robinson would really like a word with you two."

That ended the conversation. Nohar turned back to Isham. He was confused. "If DEA started this, why were you the arresting officer?"

"Only one with experience tracking moreaus. Trained by Israeli intelligence." The evil smile was back.

Harsk burst into the room. "Agent Isham, where the hell you get off dismissing the observing officers? It's against operating procedure for an officer to be left alone with a suspect—"

"I'm not one of your officers, and Rajasthan is no longer a suspect."

"Christ, woman, are you pulling this shit just to piss me off? Nohar, you're walking. The DEA guys are fucked worse than a ten-dollar whore, and the DA doesn't want to press charges."

Nohar stood up. "Thanks."

"Don't thank me yet. Because of you, and Binder, I got internal affairs clamping down on my ass—even if it was those Shaker cronies of Binder's that dicked around the Johnson murder. This Ziphead crap has got City Hall in a panic, the vids are having a field day—And I got suspicions it's all because you stuck your nose where it don't belong. If it was my choice, I'd lock you up and never let you go."

"As it is." He turned to Isham. "If the special agent would kindly leave me and the tiger alone. Nohar, we have things to discuss, in private."

Harsk led him out of the interrogation room.

Chapter 20

Harsk's office was in the basement of police headquarters. It smelled of paper, dust, and mildew. When Harsk led him in, Nohar had to duck the pipes that snaked along the ceiling. There were two chairs opposite the rust-dotted green desk. They were water-stained chrome pipe with red-vinyl seats that were held together with silver-gray duct tape. Neither one looked like it'd survive him, so Nohar stood.

Harsk took a seat behind the desk. He picked up a cup of old coffee that had been sitting on one corner of the desk. It was one of many cups that occupied various open spaces in the room. Harsk took a sip, grimaced, and finished it.

"So, Nohar, you think you just walked out of all that crap because of a clean lifestyle and goodness of heart—"

Nohar wrinkled his nose. He thought he saw something floating in the coffee Harsk was drinking. "You're about to tell me otherwise?"

The left corner of Harsk's mouth pulled up. The closest the pink cop would ever come to a smile. He drained the cup and tossed it in the corner of the room, near a wastepaper basket that was awash in a tide of old papers. "Good. Your bullshit detector is working. I'm going to tell you *why* you're walking. It has little to do with the DEA's incompetence—"

Harsk opened a drawer and took out the Vindhya. "How many people know who your father is?"

That was the last thing Nohar expected to hear from Harsk. "What has that go to do—"

Harsk started taking out the magazines for the Vind. He arranged it all on the desk in front of him. "Everything, Nohar. If you don't see that, you're dumber than most people give moreys credit for. Do you realize what the Fed, much less those dimwits at the DEA, would do if they knew you were your father's son?"

"It isn't my fault who my father is."

Harsk gave Nohar a withering stare. "If that ain't a load of bullshit, I don't know what is. There's a good chance that half the tigers descended from the Rajasthan Airlift were sired by him. You're the fool that had to track down your paternity. There's a few hundred Rajasthans out there that left well enough alone. You brought Datia's history on to yourself. Now you got to deal with it."

Nohar wished he had a good argument for that. He didn't. "What do you mean, if the Fed knew?"

"They don't, yet. I'll answer my first question for you. Perhaps a half-dozen people in the department know that Nohar is Datia's son. The DA's one. I'm another. All of us were at that last showdown at Musician's Towers. He held off a SWAT team with that gun." He motioned to that Vind. "When the Guard showed up, they torched the building to get him out."

Nohar didn't want to hear this. He was grateful that Harsk was a pink and couldn't smell the emotions off him.

"Datia was a dyed in the wool psycho who left about half his mind in Afghanistan. A lot of humans don't understand why hundreds of moreys followed the bullshit he spouted.

Datia, at the end, didn't believe it either. Could've been anyone, though, That August was too tense, too hot, too unstable. Moreytown was primed, anyone could have touched the spark—A lot like it's been lately."

There was silence in the room. It stretched out for a long time. "What are you getting at, Harsk?"

Harsk shook his head. "You blind SOB. Do I need to spell it out for you? Six people in the department and two National Guardsmen were with your dad when he croaked. He mentioned you. His ramblings are in the official transcripts. It's just that no one has cross referenced them yet. It is only a matter of time before someone in the Fed is going to see how closely this Ziphead thing was engineered to look like the riots, and look up your dad. Poof, all hell breaks loose."

Harsk stood up. "Does the word scapegoat mean anything to you? What you think McIntyre and Conrad would do if they knew this?"

Nohar felt the world slipping away from him. "They'd think I was . . ."

"—running the show, you shithead. It's damn lucky me and the DA know different. Though, if it wasn't for two things, I'd lock you up just to be on the safe side."

"What two things?"

Harsk sat back down. "Me and the DA think you'd make a great martyr. If you get locked up, or shot, or anything, and word got out of your parentage, that could be the spark that blows everything up again. Right now, we have to deal with the rats—that's enough."

Nohar could feel his own past bearing down on him. It felt like he had spent a decade running away from his own tail. "You said, 'two things.' "

Harsk turned the chair away from Nohar. "The other reason is your typical interagency departmental screwup. Agent Isham seized your weapon and didn't turn it over to property. Somehow the Vind got lost in the shuffle and never got tagged as evidence. You can't have a weapons charge without a weapon—"

Nohar looked at his gun, laid out on the table. He didn't need more of a hint. He holstered the Vind and pocketed the magazines. "Is that it?"

"Fucking enough, ain't it? Do me a favor and stop being one of my problems."

Nohar left Harsk's office.

When Nohar got to the lobby, dawn was breaking across a slate-gray sky. He was glad that they didn't make people pass through the weapons detectors on their way out.

The public comms in the lobby of police headquarters were in better than average condition—which meant maintenance spent at least one day a week cleaning off the piss and graffiti.

He called Manny collect, hoping to catch him before he left for work.

Angel answered the phone. "Fuck you be, Kit?"

"What the hell are you doing answering the phone? Nobody's supposed to know you're there—"

"Chill, Kit." Angel looked chastened. "Whafuck happen to you? Pinky's been up all night—" Nohar felt guilty for the way his spirit lifted when he heard Stephie was worried about him. "—and Doc's been riding a pisser ever since he got back last—Speak of the devil."

Manny came on the comm, pushing Angel aside. "Do you have any idea how lucky you are? I told myself I shouldn't ask where that hole in your hip came from—I was just about out the door to do more autopsies on rodents you shot—"

"Sorry, only place I could go."

Manny sighed. "I know, and I can't well turn you away. I hear that no one is pressing charges."

"It *was* self-defense."

"Next time would you go through the process? Where are you? You look like hell."

"Is that a professional diagnosis?" Nohar was still coated with algae. He probably smelled like the pit, but his nose had long ago gotten used to it.

"When am I going to get the full story on what's going on?"

"You don't want to know if you like to sleep nights. How's Stephie?"

Manny shrugged. "Better than most humans around a group of moreaus. She's been asking me a lot of questions about you mostly." Manny looked off to the side of the screen and lowered his voice. "Stupid question, but did you—"

"Yes." And he'd do it again in a minute. Manny took a few seconds to respond.

"Damn." There were a few more seconds of silence while Manny recovered. "Well, did you know that they've re-opened the Daryl Johnson murder investigation? Internal Affairs got wind that the Shaker division dropped the ball on purpose. Congressman Binder might get called before the House Ethics committee. Half the cops involved rolled over on him. It's all over the vids."

"I got some idea of that from Harsk."

"My office is pissed. They've been given a court order to exhume Johnson's body, even it if wasn't the autopsy that got fugged."

They talked for about ten more minutes. The rest of the conversation consisted mostly of Nohar's stories of the DEA, and Manny's inquirers after his injuries. Neither of them raised the subject of Stephie Weir again.

Then Nohar called for a cab. He specified one with a driver.

Fifteen minutes later, a familiar Nissan Tory pulled up in front of the building. Same driver as yesterday—Autocab probably only had one.

" 'Spected it was you."

Nohar climbed in the back and slipped his card into the meter. She pulled the cab away and started west toward the Main Avenue bridge. "Busy night. Clocked in this mornin' and, whoa, the rumors. Narcs bust into dispatch and take over a remote. They ain't no drivers. They trash the van with some poor fool inside it. Never trust those remotes . . ."

The patter went on and Nohar dozed off.

She woke him up when they got there, probably after copping a few dollars from the timer. He didn't begrudge her and gave her a fifty dollar tip. "Thanks. Any time you call you can ask for me special. Tell 'em you want Ruby. Shit, you're not bad—for a moreau."

Nohar stood in front of the whitewashed bar with no name and watched the Tory go. The heat was beginning to bake the early morning pavement, as well as the algae caked in his fur. But, for once—though clouds threatened—things were dry. He paused a moment where they had parked the Antaeus. The only trace of the car was one of his own bloody footprints on the asphalt.

He walked to Manny's and had barely limped up to the door when Stephie yanked him inside. Nohar followed, stumbling slightly. He could smell fear and excitement as she pulled him into the living room. Angel was there. Manny had already left for work.

Stephie was breathless. "They started broadcasting it five minutes ago. It's on all the stations. All over the comm—"

Angel pushed her away from in front of the comm. "Shhh—"

Nohar watched the newscast. There was a pink commentator standing in front of the video feed. "We are now going to see exclusive footage of the disaster. Tad Updike, our Channel-N weatherman for the Cleveland area was on the scene. We now give you the uncut video as we received it."

The commentator faded, leaving Tad Updike there, in a safari jacket. He *looked* like a weatherman, slick black hair, insincere smile. He seemed to be standing on top of one of the terminal buildings at Hopkins International Airport, on the far west side of Cleveland.

"—it promises to be another record scorcher. Today, a high close to 33, and the National Weather Service is announcing the third UV hazard warning this sum—*cut it.*" A plane was approaching, rendering Updike nearly inaudible "[bleep] damn planes, didn't anyone look at the flight schedu—"

The cameraman had panned to the plane, over Updike's right shoulder. It was a 747 retrofit, the huge electric turbofans clung to the reinforced wing like goiters. Something streaked up from the ground and hit the plane, behind the front landing gear—

A cherry-red ball of flame engulfed the lower front quarter of the aircraft. It was still over a hundred meters in the air. The nose of the 747 was briefly engulfed in a cloud of inky-black smoke. The right wing dipped and the camera started shaking as the cameraman tried to follow the plane. Updike was screaming. "*My God, someone shot it! Someone shot the plane—*"

The wing crumpled into the runway, pulling the nose of the plane into the ground. It skidded like that for a half-second and the camera lost the plane off the right of the screen. The cameraman overcompensated and swept the picture back to the right, losing the tumbling plane off to the left.

The picture caught the plane center frame again. The focus was fading in and out. In the meantime, the plane was skidding on its side down the runway. The left wing pointed straight up, reflecting the sun back at the camera. The image briefly resembled a chromed shark. The camera followed the plane as it twisted and started to roll. The left wing crumpled and the tail section separated, letting the body roll twice before it broke in two as well. The nose kept going the longest.

Updike's voice-over was useless, so the commentator took over for him as the camera panned over the trail of wreckage and bodies that was scattered over the length of the runway. "Casualty estimates are still coming in, but there are at least one hundred dead. It has been confirmed that among the dead is Ohio Congressman Joseph Binder—"

Nohar felt like someone just kicked him in the stomach.

"—Binder was returning to Cleveland from Columbus, where he was reorganizing his Senate campaign which has been in chaos ever since the assassination of campaign manager Daryl Johnson. Also, sources say Binder's return was to answer allegations that there was a cover-up involving the Shaker Heights police investigation of Johnson's death.

"The FAA will not comment on the possibility that a surface-to-air missile was involved in the crash . . ."

Nohar slowly sat down. Someone, it had to be Hassan, had killed a few hundred people just to kill Binder. Nohar could feel that events had steamrollered way past him. Everyone who had any connection with the Binder finance records was dead now—

With one exception. Nohar reached out for Stephie, and pulled her into his arms. They watched the plane explode a few dozen more times.

Nohar turned off the water in the shower. He had finally gotten the baked algae out of his fur. He stepped out and unkinked his neck. Stephie was sitting on the john and drying her hair.

Nohar faced her, dripping, and asked, "What do you mean, I've been 'too hard on Angel'?"

Stephie looked down, shaking her head. Nohar cold tell she was smiling. She picked up a washcloth and cleaned off a steak of algae on the inside of her thigh that her shower had missed.

Nohar was getting impatient. "Come on—"

Stephie handed him a towel. "I just think you haven't seen how bad this has all been for her."

Nohar started squeezing the water out of his fur, wishing for a dryer. "Stephie, this whole business has been bad for everyone."

"I know. But she's taking it hard. I know she puts on a brave face—" *You mean an irritating, obnoxious one,* Nohar thought. "But she's scared, Nohar. Scared and alone." She stood up and helped him towel off. "She has nightmares."

"Look, she should have known better than to answer Manny's comm. And I'm sorry if her wiseass attitude gets on my nerves."

"She's only fourteen."

Nohar sighed. "Stephie, for a morey, that's adult."

"Physically adult. She's still just a kid. How do you think you'd handle her situation if you were her age?"

That hit close to home. When he was that age, he was still with the Hellcats. Back then he was probably worse than Angel—

"What do you want me to do?" He mentally added, *fuck her?* He congratulated himself on not actually saying that.

"I think she needs some respect. She needs someone to show some confidence in her, reassure her. Most of all—" Stephie looked up at him, her hands knotted in a towel resting on his chest. "I think she needs you to like her."

"I do like her, sort of."

"She needs to know that."

Nohar shook his head. He supposed he had been treating Angel like a liability. Angel didn't deserve that. He changed the subject. "Stephie, I think we better get both you and Angel out of town."

She cocked her head to one side. "Is that necessary?"

"You're not safe in Cleveland. You're the only one left from the campaign that could have seen those records. Hassan blew that plane just to take out Binder. God help you if

Hassan, or the people he works for, finds out where you are."

"Thought you were an atheist."

Huh? Nohar mentally ran through what he'd just said. "Figure of speech. Anyway, we can't have you anywhere near me until this is over. I'll have Bobby reserve a car rental and a motel room somewhere. He can fudge the records so no one will see your name—"

"Why me *and* Angel?"

Nohar put his arm around her. "I want someone to be around to keep an eye out for you when I'm not there. Also, you pointed out, Angel needs a friend. You fit the bill better than I do."

"When do I leave?"

"Soon as possible. Sorry."

She turned around and started wiping the condensation from the mirror. "Why is Hassan killing everyone in the campaign?"

Nohar saw the two of them together in the mirror. She was so damn small. "I still think it's the campaign finance records—the Fed thinks some radical morey group is behind the killing. The *target* makes sense, but I'm not convinced."

"Why?"

"Daryl Johnson wasn't a terror hit. It was precise, to the point, with no collateral damage. Doesn't fit. There's a motive for Johnson's death beyond some ideology."

Stephie shrugged. "You're the detective. You talk to Bobby and I'll try and see if any of Manny's clothes fit me—"

She walked out of the bathroom, leaving behind the pile of her old clothes. He watched her naked back recede down the hallway and realized that she *was* adjusting well to living with a bunch of moreaus.

Nohar limped downstairs and headed for the comm. Angel was still stationed in front of it. She seemed to have a growing addiction to the news channels. She was flipping through the stations with the keyboard.

Morey this, morey that ... The nonhuman population was getting top billing everywhere across the board. It wasn't just the Zipheads either now. Harsk was right about the summer being explosive. There were already reports of retaliatory human-morey violence from New York. A Bensheim clinic in the Bronx had been firebombed, killing three doctors and three pregnant moreaus.

He thought about what Stephie had said about being curt with Angel. "Angel, I need to use the comm."

Angel turned around, like she hadn't heard him approach. She looked a little surprised. "Sure, Kit."

Angel got up and Nohar slid in and started calling Bobby.

"Nohar?"

She called him Nohar? He turned around and Angel was looking at him, "What?"

"Do you mind when I call you Kit?"

Huh? "No, go right ahead—"

The comm spoke up, "Budget Surplus."

From behind Nohar heard Angel. "Thanks for not minding."

Angel left him alone with Bobby. Nohar watched her leave.

"What do you want, Nohar?"

Nohar turned to face Bobby and explained his problem. After he was done, Bobby nodded. "Simple enough. I'll get back to you in a few hours with some specific instructions. By the way—"

"What?"

"Are you ever going to want that data on Nugoya? It took a little effort to dig up . . ."

Nohar had totally forgotten about that. "What could I possibly want out of that now? He's dead."

"Well, Daryl Johnson's name pops up in it."

Nohar sat bolt upright, ignoring the protests of his hip. "*What?*"

Bobby displayed his evilest smile. "I *knew* that would get your attention."

Chapter 21

The wait while Bobby's electronic gears whirred into motion gave Nohar a chance to think. For the most part he thought about Daryl Johnson. He now had a connection, however tenuous, between Johnson and the Zipheads.

But then, there was so much junk in Johnson's system when he died, he had to be hooked on something. It was too bad flush addiction didn't show up on an autopsy unless they looked for it. That's what it must mean—had to be flush.

Bobby had traced one of Nugoya's financial threads and it led back to, of all people, Johnson. There were only two reasons why Nugoya would be receiving money from Johnson. Since Nugoya only pimped female morey ass. it probably wasn't sex.

Nugoya was offed for reselling the flush he got from the Zips.

Johnson was buying that flush.

Was he? Nohar wondered. If he was, Young had taken all trace of that drug from Johnson's ranch. Bobby had only found three weekly payments—if it was the sign of an addict, it was a recent one.

Blackmail? No, the deposits were much too small for Nugoya's taste had he known anything damaging. There was plenty of information that was damaging. . . .

It was another piece of the puzzle that didn't quite fit.

The comm beeped. It was time for Bobby's ride to show up.

A familiar Nissan Tory pulled in front of Manny's house, Ruby again. It would be a long time before Nohar would trust a remote van. Nohar opened the front door and waved at the cab. Then he turned to Angel and Stephie. Stephie had somehow made some of Manny's clean clothes fit her even when the proportions were all wrong.

She still looked good in them.

"You both know what you're supposed to do?"

"Sure, Kit, no prob."

Nohar shook his head. He was trusting the rabbit, but he wanted to be sure she got it right. "Let me hear it."

Stephie and Angel looked at each other. Stephie cocked her head and motioned with the palm of her hand, Angel first. "Right, Kit, um, we go to the Hertz counter at the airport—"

"Hopkins."

"Lady above, I know that. There's a prepaid '51, ah—"

"Maduro, it's a black, General Motors Maduro sports coupe." Stephie gave him a critical look and Nohar reined himself in.

Angel rolled her eyes so the whites could be seen.

"Lemme finish the rundown, Kit. Paid for with Pink— Stephie's—new name." The little scar pulled into a smile at Stephie's expense. Stephie didn't seem to mind.

The name was Bobby's doing. He had programmed a shell identity over Stephie's card. It wouldn't fool a real close scrutiny. However, it would run up false data trail on any casual ID scan. It was a total software construct— Bobby didn't even need to see the card. The software would self-delete when its usefulness was expired.

"—then we blow to the other end of the country, and shack up together across the line in Geauga—she drives so pink law don't stop us. Woodstar Motel is in Chesterland, off highway 322."

"Good enough. I'll get word down as soon as the shit clears."

Nohar smiled at the rabbit, and, to his surprise, he got a full smile back.

He piled them into the Tory and paid Ruby. The cabby must have been getting used to moreys. She didn't even comment on Angel, who was buried in one of Nohar's old concert T-shirts.

Stephie mouthed, "I'll miss you," out the window as Nohar shut the door.

The cab drove west, toward the airport. Nohar was left alone in front of Manny's house. He kept looking down the road long after the Tory had passed from view.

He yawned, walked back into the house, and planted

himself next to the comm. The chair still smelled of his blood.

Tonight was the meeting with Smith. He'd pretty much decided he was going to tell that blob of flesh to go straight to hell if he didn't get the full story on MLI. Things were too dangerous now to cater to his client's sense of secrecy. Smith's lockjaw might have already cost a few hundred people their lives.

He stretched and tried to make sense out of it all.

Johnson's death had an air of precision and forethought about it.

Staring with the 4th, the deaths in the Binder campaign were loud, messy, and seemed to fit into a nationwide spree of violence by the Zipheads. Violence that seemed engineered to resonate with the riots of eleven years ago. Up to and including starting the violence on the generally accepted anniversary date, August 4th. It was a coordinated effort by the Zips to scare the pinks shitless.

Nohar raked his claws across the armrest of the chair. The upholstery ripped.

The Zips weren't making sense. The Zipperheads were drug dealers, not terrorists. What kind of profit would there be in encouraging the pinks to clamp down? If there's a new wave of morey riots, nobody wins.

Somehow, it also seemed MLI was involved with the Zips. That made little sense either. It was also hard to deny. The rats'd kept showing up, ever since he'd discovered Hassan. He wouldn't be surprised if MLI was using those green remote vans to smuggle the rats back and forth. Especially after he saw that van shooting out of Thomson's building. There was also no denying that there was some higher authority than the Zips, represented by Hassan. From Angel it sounded like Terin was under somebody's thumb—her supplier?

Was it MLI?

And, even embedded in a wave of rodent terrorism, the deaths were going to focus everyone's attention on the Binder campaign. If there was some information buried in the campaign *they*— Young's nebulous *them*—were trying to cover up, this would be counterproductive—wouldn't it?

Nohar fell asleep feeling like he had forgotten something.

*   *   *

Manny woke Nohar up. He was home early.

"Where are the girls?"

Nohar yawned and sat up. "I sent them to a motel out of town, out of harm's way—"

"As opposed to you . . . and me."

Nohar was stung by that. "I've been trying to keep you out of this. That's why I sent them—"

Manny sighed and sat down on the couch, across from him. Manny formed his engineered surgeon's hands into a peak before the tip of his nose. "Has it ever occurred to you that I don't want to be left out?"

Nohar didn't respond.

"Why do you think I told you you could come here if things got rough? Why do you think I help you with all those missing persons investigations? Why do you think I took that slug out of your hip? Manny shook his head. "When you left home and disappeared with that gang, I knew there was no way I would ever talk sense to you. But I have the right to know what you get mixed-up in. I promised Orai I'd keep an eye on you."

Manny stopped talking. The only sounds now were the faint buzz of a fluorescent and Nohar's own breathing.

"I've already involved you in enough to lose your job—"

Manny cast a glance out the window, toward the driveway where the van was parked. "I was trained to save lives. Today, we had an emergency, the 747. So damn many bodies to identify. We need all the help we could get. *They dismissed me from the scene because there weren't any more dead.* You think I really care about conflict of interest?"

Manny deserved to know.

Nohar told him everything, including the money, the frank, Hassan—everything. Manny didn't interrupt, didn't ask for elaboration. He just sat and listened. Nodded a few times. Fidgeted a little with his hands. Otherwise he let Nohar explain the last week—

By the time Nohar was done, the sky outside had turned blood-red.

Manny seemed to weigh his response before he said anything. When he spoke, it was in the even tones of his professional voice, as if he was describing a corpse he had dissected. "You're right. Your frank is not from South Africa. All their franks have been cataloged since the coup d'état in Pretoria. What you describe isn't anything *they* came up with, and it doesn't sound Israeli or Japanese. On the other hand, the way you describe Isham, it's pretty clear she's a Mossad assassin strain, something they co-opted after the invasion of Jordan. Hassan's Afghani, a strain they abandoned after the war, likes killing too much—

Manny put his hand to his forehead and stopped talking. "I knew this would be bad. You should have seen that 747—"

"Are you all right?"

"I'll be fine, it's nine-thirty, you better read your messages if you want to meet your client on time. I'll drive you to Lakeview."

Nohar had forgotten about the messages he'd had the cabbie fetch for him. So much had happened since—

He turned on the comm and got the ramcard out of his wallet. He put it in the card-reader. He called up the messages. There was a predictable—and out of date—message from Harsk about how, if he turned himself in, things would go easier for him. In retrospect, Harsk wasn't lying. Then there was a message from the late Desmond Thomson, the press secretary.

Thomson's face was sunken. His skin looked hollowed out and the vid anchorman's voice had turned into the voice of a jazz musician who smoked too much. "I have no idea what your interest in this is. Whatever you've uncovered, I am supposed to request that you refrain from making it public until Congressman Binder's press conference tomorrow."

Damn, if Terin copied this message some time Tuesday night, when they wrecked his home comm . . .

He played the next message. It was John Smith, the frank, in the same unidentifiable location.

Light was glistening off the frank's pale polyethylene skin. The glassy eyes stared straight ahead. A pale, mittened hand adjusted the comm. Manny stared at the screen, fascinated by the figure of Smith.

"It is worse than I think before. We meet in Lakeview and we must go public. I discover it is not one individual responsible. The whole company is involved and condones the violence. I cannot let them do this, the organization is not supposed to physically intervene. MLI is corrupted and we must make it known who they are and what they do here. I bring all the evidence I can carry to the meeting to-morrow."

Nohar sat back. It looked like he didn't have to threaten the guy to get the full story.

Manny was looking at him now. "Didn't you say these Zipperheads had probably copied your messages off your home comm?"

Oh shit, Terin had that message! They knew the meeting was at Lakeview, *today*. They blew a 747 to get Binder. They'd certainly be willing to ambush the frank—if MLI hadn't dealt with him already.

"Manny, we got to get to Lakeview now!"

The green Medical Examiner's van sped down the Midtown Corridor. Manny drove.

Manny had wanted in. He was in, and God help him— Nohar caught the thought and told himself what he had told Stephie, figure of speech.

He almost missed telling Manny where to take the turn. It was the opposite side of Lakeview that he was used to using. Nohar yelled, and Manny skidded the van into the driveway of the Corridor gate. There was an immediate problem in that this was the Pink entrance, so the gate was closed and chained shut. Nohar's normal entrance was the gate on the Jewish section, which was rusted open.

It was ten-fifteen. They didn't have time to circle around East Cleveland to get to the right gate.

In a pinch, Manny's van could double as a rescue vehicle— a half-assed rescue vehicle, but a rescue vehicle—so, it had its share of equipment to deal with these situations. Nohar pulled a pair of bolt cutters and got out of the van. He walked up to the wrought iron gate and looked through.

No pinks, no security, nothing but darkness, graves, and the surreal image of a tarnished-green bronze statue of a natural buck deer. It stared at the gate. Nohar cut the chain. They had twelve minutes to beat the frank. He pushed the gate open and waved Manny into the cemetery. The head-lights targeted the statue, and for a moment it looked like luminescent jade.

Nohar jumped into the passenger seat—pain shot through his right leg—and started yelling directions at Manny.

Lakeview was a large place, and it was a good thing Nohar knew its layout by heart. They were racing through at the maximum safe speed, and it felt to Nohar as if they were crawling up the hill that formed Lakeview's geography. When they crested the bluff where President James A. Garfield resided in his cylindrical medieval tomb, it was ten-twenty.

They rounded the turn on the other side of the concrete barrier on the Mayfield-Kenelworth gate, and Nohar saw a familiar green van in the distance. *The bastard was early.*

Chapter 22

Smith's remote was pulling up to Eliza's marker, and the damn headlights were fucking with Nohar's night-vision.

"Manny—kill the lights."

There were still the lights on the remote, but they were pointed away from them. Nohar could start making things out in the gloom, like the pneumatic doors opening on the frank's van. The frank stepped out carrying a briefcase. Almost immediately, the remote drove away.

"Stop here." Nohar had a slight hope, maybe they'd be lucky and there wouldn't be an ambush. "Radio the cops."

Nohar got out and limped up to the frank.

Smith stood alone, clutching a briefcase to his flabby chest. Now that Nohar saw him standing upright, Nohar realized he was looking at a creature that wasn't designed for bipedal motion. The frank's mass seemed to slide downward, reinforcing the basic pear shape. He still smelled like raw sewer, but in the open air, Nohar could make an effort to ignore it.

Nohar stared into the frank's blank, glass eyes. "If I'm going to help you, Smith, you have to tell me everything, *now.*"

"Please, let us move. We tell everything to media. We must—"

Nohar put his hand on the frank's shoulder. Even under the jacket, a jacket much too heavy for the weather, Nohar could feel his hand sink in and the flesh ripple underneath. "You're going to tell me first. You've been using me, withholding information—if you'd told me about MLI up front, that 747 might not have been shot down."

Smith said something that must have been in his native language. It was low, liquid, and sounded like a dirge. Then he went on. "Do not say that!" There was the first real trace of emotion in the frank's voice, even if it didn't register on his face or in his odor. "They do not let me know what they do. You must understand, violence is anathema. Murder is unforgivable. They do this without me—"

Nohar shook his head. "What are they doing, and why are you out of the loop?"

"We must go—"

"Look, the cops will be here any minute. So calm down and tell me why you set me up in this mess."

"No, I do not intend, you do not understand—" More words in that odd sounding language. "When authorities find out what goes on, they will not let us go public. You must make this public." Smith handed Nohar the briefcase. "It is mostly in there. I tell you what is not."

Smith loosened his tie. and the roll of fat around his neck flowed downward. The frank was trembling, as if he was in pain. "You know our purpose is to support politicians. We do so fifteen years for the benefit of our homeland. I am not just an accountant, I am—" The frank let out a word that sounded like a harsh belch. "Perhaps the right term is political officer. I enforce our laws not to physically intervene. We do not engage in violent acts. To do so will prelude a war."

The frank sounded despairing. "Fifteen years in a foreign land is too long to do such work. Laws from so far away become less binding. I am supposed to prevent this. I fail. An operation has left its controls. They try to isolate me and accelerate things beyond safe limits.

The frank pulled a letter out of his pocket and handed it to Nohar. "This is the proof I find when I search our files. It is a filing mistake. I am supposed to handle the letters, but they cannot let me see this. The files are not their job and they make an error filing this paper too early. I do not know what other mistakes they make by keeping this from me—"

It was a letter from Wilson Scott. The same letter Angel

had found at Young's. Only, this copy was intact. It went on mentioning moreys offing pinks, moreys taking hostages, morey air terrorism. It was dated August tenth—

This year.

"Oh, shit."

"English is a difficult language for us. We compose letters months in advance. But I am the one who is to deal with the outside world. I conduct the business. I handle the money. Without me it becomes easy for them to make mistakes of sending letters too early."

"They are telling the Zips what to do?"

"Yes. They do not pay in money, to avoid me."

Flush. Nohar shook his head. "But why?"

"They are impatient. They feel control progresses too slowly. They want our men in the Senate, and they can't wait—"

Nohar could see now. "They want to panic the pinks so antimorey candidates like Binder get elect—"

He shifted the briefcase and the letter to his left hand. He had heard something moving out in the darkness. He started drawing the Vind. "Smith, there's a van right behind me. Get to it."

"But I have to tell you where—"

"Move!" Nohar could smell canine musk in the air now. Something was approaching, fast. Smith started running. The poor frank bastard seemed to have trouble moving. He was wobbling on rubbery legs. Why the hell would someone engineer something like that?

The bulk of the frank was moving toward the van when Nohar heard the rustle of some leaves above them.

It was no louder than the crickets or the gravel crunching under his feet, Nohar could smell a rank canine odor now—a wave of musk that overwhelmed the frank's sewer smell. The canine was riding a wave of excitement sexual in its intensity.

The smell hit Nohar too late, because the canine, Hassan, was already in the air, falling out of a tree and on to the frank.

Hassan landed on the frank. Nohar whipped around, aiming the Vind at the canine, but his knee and bad hip fought him. Smith hit the ground, his flesh rippling. The canine sank his right knee into the frank's chest and he was jabbing a rodlike weapon deep into the folds of flesh where the frank's neck should be.

Nohar fired. A hole appeared in the chest of Hassan's jacket. The slug carried the canine over a monument—Eliza's monument—to collapse behind it. Nohar ran up to the marker. The air near it was now ripe with the odor of burnt flesh as well as the frank's sewer smell. Nohar glanced at Smith, who lay on Eliza's grave, unmoving, eyes staring upward. There was a circular purple discoloration on the frank's neck.

Nohar rounded the monument, and Hassan wasn't there. He whipped around, dropping the briefcase to brace the Vind with both hands, and a foot came out of nowhere and hit his right hand. The Vind tumbled out into the darkness. Nohar kept turning to face Hassan. Hassan's jacket hung open now. He was wearing a kevlar vest. The dumdum had only knocked the dog over.

Nohar dived at the canine. Hassan spun sideways, letting Nohar pass over and slam into the ground. Nohar's right knee hit a low-lying monument and spasmed with an excruciating wave of pain, blurring his vision. He could hear and smell the canine approach. He dodged blind.

He went through a line of hedges and started to roll down a steep hill. He caught himself before he rolled all the way down.

Hassan hunched low, tongue lolling. He leapt over the hedge and started bounding over the monuments that dotted the hillside. Nohar knew he couldn't move that fast, even with a good leg. He braced himself defensively to receive the canine's charge. Hassan didn't seem to have a gun. Hand to hand, he had a chance to take the assassin.

Nohar felt his heartbeat accelerating. The adrenaline was kicking in.

Hassan passed him and Nohar tried to pivot to follow him. Nohar wasn't quick enough. He felt a kick slam into his lower back, above the base of his tail. He tried to roll with it, but the blow still sent him to his knees.

The Beast was roaring—

"Time for death, cat." A shaggy canine arm hooked around his neck, and there was a fiery tingle under his left armpit. He smelled his own fur burning.

He could feel the rush as The Beast was triggered. But

he couldn't move. Hassan was using a stun rod—Nohar was paralyzed. When Hassan pivoted Nohar's body around on his bad knee, pain fogged his sight again. When he could see again, he was propped in front of an open grave. The canine arm began to choke him.

"Your final reward. Make your peace, cat."

Why didn't the sick bastard just shoot him and get it over with?

Manny said they were exhuming Johnson's grave. Apparently, they had. The open grave he was looking into was Daryl Johnson's less-than-final resting place. Lack of oxygen was making him begin to black out. The effects of the stunner were beginning to wear off, but his muscles felt like mush. He didn't want to have to smell Hassan's musk when he died.

Suddenly, there was a bright light. Nohar saw something—a bullet?—ricochet off Johnson's marker. They were both bathed in white light, their shadows extending forward into infinity. Hassan was quick, and the arm around Nohar's neck disappeared. Hassan's shadow jumped out of the light to the sound of another bullet.

Nohar's muscles weren't under his control. He tumbled forward, into the grave.

He splashed facedown in an inch-deep layer of black mud. His whole body cramped up on him. The stunner had been military-style, not a street or a cop version. His muscles had been through a blender and felt predigested.

It took an interminable time for him to recover. As he fought to get his body under control, he could hear sirens in the distance. It certainly took them long enough. By the time he could get up on his hands and knees and look up, the grave was surrounded by Manny and three nervous pink medics. All backlit by red and blue flashers. They were about to climb down into the rectangular hole. Nohar waved them away and stood up. His right knee nearly buckled, and from the loose way it felt, the support bandage had torn off.

Standing, he could reach the lip. It wasn't a good idea in his condition, but be damned if he was going to a hospital. He grabbed the edge, buried his left boot in the side of the grave, and hoisted himself up. His bad shoulder protested and he nearly slid back into the hole—but he clawed his way out.

There was some fear from the medic, but the strongest smell was coming from Manny. He was worried. Nohar tried to allay Manny's worries by walking—without any help—back up the hill, to where all the cops were. Manny followed. "Are you all right? What did he hit you with?"

Nohar answered through gritted teeth. The walk up the hill was sending daggers of pain through his knee and his hip. "I'm fine. Hassan was using a stun rod—" Nohar noticed a bandage around Manny's right hand. "What happened to you?"

Manny handed Nohar the Vind. "This thing has one hell of a kick."

Nohar stopped. "Oh, hell, Manny, your hand. You broke your fucking hand to shoot—"

"Calm down, it isn't like anyone's going to die from it."

Manny, Nohar thought, *your hands are your life.* "How's Smith?"

"Smith's dead."

They passed the broken hedge Nohar had fallen through and were on level ground again. "*Dead?* He only got hit with a stunner, I saw it."

Manny shrugged. "Then that's what killed him—"

There were a half-dozen black-and-whites parked around Eliza Wilkins' grave. There was also Manny's van, an ambulance, the predictable unmarked Havier, and, of all things, a black Porsche. The frank was still there, looking like an inert lump of flesh only vaguely molded into a humanoid form. Cops were all over, planting evidence tags and yellow warning strips. Harsk was yelling into a radio, alternately cussing someone out for losing Hassan, and trying to hurry the forensics guys. The only nonhumans were Nohar, Manny, the frank—and Agent Isham, FBI, who left the Porsche and walked toward him and Manny.

She still wore the shades. "Doctor Gujerat, I've cleared it with your office. We want you to make a field ID of the deceased."

Manny nodded. "No promises with just the equipment in the van—"

"Do it."

Manny gave an undulating shrug and walked toward the van. Nohar started to follow, but Isham grabbed his arm.

"We talk, Mr. Rajasthan. Sit down, your knee will appreciate it."

Nohar found himself sitting on one of the cold granite
monuments. She was right—taking the weight off his leg
was a relief. It had been in constant pain. Isham pointed to
the dead form of Smith. "So, who has Hassan killed this
time?"

He didn't have any reason left to be recalcitrant. "He
called himself John Smith. He's an accountant for a company called Midwest Lapidary Imports. Apparently the
board of directors consisted of franks like him. Claim to be
from South Africa, but they aren't."

Isham nodded. "Not South Africa. The frank's much too
xenomorphic. Doubt his type is anywhere in the catalogs.
Why did Hassan hit him?"

Client confidentiality was irrelevant now. "Until the killings started, MLI was a quiet little covert operation buying
influence in Washington. The company has over eight thousand false identities they funnel the money through to
avoid the limits on individual campaign contributions. The
amount runs into the billions. Smith hired me to find out if
someone in MLI was behind the Johnson killing."

"Was there?"

Nohar waved at the dead form of Smith. "The papers in
the briefcase are evidence with which he wanted to go public. The MLI organization seems to have slipped out of the
control of whatever government was backing them. They're
in direct control of the Zips."

Isham lowered her sunglasses. "What government?"

"Hassan showed up before Smith told me. He implied
that information isn't in those paper—"

Nohar turned to face the corpse. She was already watching. Manny had come out of the van with a large hypodermic needle. He was trying to take a fluid sample and do a
field genetic analysis. He was kneeling over the body, removing the needle from the frank's doughy chest. As
Manny withdrew the needle, odors erupted from the
corpse—evil bile and ammonia smells. A few cops covered
their mouths and retreated into the darkness. From somewhere behind him, Nohar heard the sound of retching.
While the cops backed away, he, Manny, and Isham watched

in horrified fascination as fluid began leaking from the hole Manny's needle had made.

Manny had ripped the frank's shirt open to get at the chest, and now, cloudy liquid was seeping from a tear in the otherwise featureless skin. The tear was widening with the pressure of the escaping liquid—Manny seemed to realize what was happening. He ran back to the van. Fluid was now pouring from the frank. The smell had driven back all the pinks, and Nohar's nose was numbing. The frank's clothes were soaked with the cloudy liquid, and there was a growing dark spot on the yellow lawn. Nohar thought he could see steam rising from the corpse.

The rip was no longer tearing open. The edges seemed to be dissolving. Manny was racing back with an armload of evidence jars. He was barely in time. The frank had already spilled half its mass on to the ground, and the pace of the dissolution was accelerating. Manny began shoving jars through the hole in the frank's chest— Harsk's eyes widened and he turned around, falling to his knees. Manny got three of the specimen jars into the body before holes began spontaneously erupting in the frank's skin. The skin dissolved like an ice cube in boiling water. Manny tried to get a solid piece of the frank's skin into one of the empty jars. He scooped it up, and it melted into more of the cloudy white fluid.

The body was gone. It left only a pile of clothes, a pair of pink dentures, and a pair of fake plastic eyes.

"Holy Christ." One of the cops was crossing himself.

Manny looked at the puddle surrounding the clothes where John Smith had been, and said, in a tone of epic understatement, "This wasn't normal frank."

Isham walked over to Harsk. She seemed to be listening to her earplug. "The Fed's taking this over, Harsk. National security."

Chapter 23

The trip to Metro General, down the Midtown Corridor and I-90, was a convoy. Nohar didn't want to go to the hospital. In fact, just the idea of it made him nauseous. But Isham was clamping down and the Fed was going to keep all the principals in one place. Manny's van was led by Isham's Porsche. The black-and-whites followed, and downtown they were joined by a group of five dark-blue Haviers.

The convoy converged on Metro General. The cops were shunted into quarantine, Isham shouting down Harsk's objections with talk about waiting for a delegation from the Center for Disease Control. Isham had most of the cops believing the frank was some bio-weapon delivery system.

Isham knew it was a crock, Nohar could tell, but it gave her a convenient excuse to lock up the local law enforcement. It was her show now. Nohar decided she could have it.

She didn't quarantine him. She wanted the cops isolated, and she didn't want him telling them about international conspiracies to control the U.S. government. She took him and Manny to the brand-new genetics lab on the fifth floor of the new Metro wing. The floor was dotted with her agents, and Manny was given lab assistants who were not on the normal hospital payroll. The Fed had dived in with both feet.

Isham spent a half hour in someone's day office, poring over the documents in the briefcase. She had Nohar sit across from her, getting graveyard mud all over some poor doctor's leather couch.

Occasionally Isham would shoot a question at Nohar. The questions were instructive in themselves. A hundred and fifty members of Congress had received MLI's money. Over seventy had been supported enough to have a massive conflict of interest. Thirty-seven congressmen had received enough money to owe their careers to MLI. Half of these people MLI bought had made it into the various House committees. Three of them held chairs—including the chair of Ethics committee. There were records of outright bribes to dozens of people in the executive.

And all of this had been done indirectly.

MLI's money *did* come from wholesale dealing in gemstones—massive dealings. They moved so many rocks that the whole lapidary industry was suffering a depression. The devaluation of diamonds and lesser stones didn't seem to bother MLI's balance sheet. They simply moved more rocks to compensate. There was no sign of where their inventory came from, but its volume justified the eighty billion in assets MLI claimed.

In with the accounting information was a collection of letters.

Isham asked about a few of them. None came from MLI itself. They were all forgeries from the hands of MLI's nonexistent employees.

A Jack Brodie from South Euclid, Ohio, wrote to ask a California legislator to consider helping to eliminate federal morey housing in that state. Just a simple request from someone who contributed twenty-five grand to his campaign.

Diane Colson, allegedly living in Parma, Ohio, "informed" a committee member on House Appropriations of all the waste in the federal budget. In the military and NASA in particular.

There was that August 10th letter—Wilson Scott from Cleveland was urging support for Binder's moreau control package, "in view of the recent violence." The smoking gun as far as the Zips were concerned. The proof the violence was engineered to get certain people elected Senate.

Isham dispensed with most of this with a few questions. She seemed to be in a hurry to assimilate the information. She only slowed once, over a letter from the familiar name Kathy Tsoravitch, written to Joseph Binder back in the Fall of 2043.

Isham looked up at Nohar. Her sunglasses were off and her retinas cast an orange reflection back at him. "What's NuFood?"

Nohar shrugged. "A little R&D enterprise MLI bought

out. My friend with the computer thinks it's only there to smooth out the loss column of their taxes. Some sort of diet food."

"Why a food company?"

Nohar really didn't care. It wasn't his problem any more. "Diversification?"

To his surprise, Isham actually laughed a little. Her laugh was as silent as her breathing. "They went to a bit of trouble to get this particular company—"

Isham slid the letter across the desk and Nohar glanced it over. Kathy was positively adamant Binder prevent Nu-Food's enterprise from being approved by the FDA. If he remembered correctly, MLI bought out NuFood only a few months after this letter.

Isham riffled through the papers. "NuFood's ten million in assets is barely a ripple in MLI's finances. The patents are nearly worthless. It doesn't seem to have an income at all."

"I told you it was a tax dodge. A money pit the IRS would buy."

Isham looked at length of computer printout. She seemed to be talking to herself. "Then why would they be piping money into it *before* it failed?"

The comm rang. Even though it wasn't her office, Isham didn't hesitate. "Got it."

When the comm lit up, only showing black, she said, "Bald Eagle here. This isn't a secure line."

An electronically modified voice came back. "We have the go."

The caller hung up.

Isham smiled and gathered up the papers. "Well, I'll ask these franks about NuFood when we have them in custody."

She locked the case and gestured to the door as she put on her mirrored sunglasses. When Nohar stood up, his knee began throbbing again. He had to grab the door frame to help himself move outside. Isham walked by him and started down the hall. She paused to turn and say to him, "I'm afraid we're going to have to keep a close eye on you until this clears. You're probably going to be stuck here for a while."

"I don't have anything better to do at the moment."

Nohar hobbled down the corridor and collapsed in a chair in a waiting room across from the lab where Manny was working. Isham passed him, going toward the stairs. She looked at the red-haired FBI agent who was sitting across from Nohar. She pointed at Nohar and the agent nodded.

It seemed Nohar now had his own personal pet FBI agent. The agent didn't wear shades, a normal human—

Even with the pet FBI guy, for once, Nohar was thankful for the Fed. With all this, MLI was blown open. There'd be nothing left for them to cover up. The violence should be over. He was sorry for Smith, but Nohar was glad *his* part had ended.

The agent looked vaguely uncomfortable. Nohar wondered whether it was because he was guarding a morey, because the morey he was guarding was still covered with graveyard mud, or because FBI agents were trained to look constipated as a matter of course. Nohar yawned and struggled his wounded leg up on a table.

Manny came out of the lab across from the lounge, trailing another agent. He carried a black bag in his good left hand. "Seems to be my eternal duty to patch you up. Let me see that knee while the lab techs troubleshoot the chemical analyzer."

Nohar's agent walked up so the two FBI guys framed Manny like human bookends. Manny was ignoring the agents as he felt along Nohar's right leg. Nohar tried not to wince, but Manny knew when he got to the tender area. "Damn it, you should have gone to the emergency room."

"And make the Fed divide their forces?"

"Very funny." Manny slit the pants around the knee, which was swollen a good fifty percent. Even under the mud and the fun, Nohar could see the discoloration. "You need an orthopedic surgeon. You may have done yourself some permanent damage."

Manny reached into the bag and got out an air-hypo and slipped in a capsule. "This is a local—" Manny shot the hypo into the leg and the pain left Nohar's knee, leaving no feeling at all. Then Manny pulled out a hypodermic needle, a large one. Manny found the needle impossible to maneuver with his bandaged right hand and shifted it to his left. When he did, the color leeched from the face of Nohar's agent. "I'm going to drain this and put another support bandage around it. And if you don't see a specialist about this,

I swear I will hunt you down, trank you, and drag you there myself."

Manny slid the needle home. Nohar only felt a slight pressure under his kneecap. Nohar's agent, however, began to look ill. The guy got worse when Manny started withdrawing blood-colored fluid from Nohar's knee. Manny filled the hypo, put it in a plastic bag, and repeated the process with another hypo. The agent turned away, looking out the window at the hospital's parking garage.

Manny sponged off Nohar's knee with alcohol and a strong-smelling disinfectant that made Nohar want to retch. As Manny scrubbed, Nohar tried to get his mind off the smell. "What's with the analyzer?"

"Every new piece of equipment has some bugs—" Manny sounded like he didn't quite believe it. He looked up at the agent who'd accompanied him. The guy stayed expressionless. "Your client was one weird frank. If frank is even the right term—nothing to indicate the gene structure even has a remote basis on the human model. It looks like it was engineered from scratch. I don't know what we got here. There was no cellular differentiation in the samples I salvaged. Through and through this guy was made of the same stuff."

Manny pulled out a bandage, a white plastic roll this time, not clear. As he wrapped it tightly around Nohar's leg, he continued, "No organs, nerves, skeletal system . . . all I can think of to explain it is all the constituent cells are multifunctional, able to do duty as anything the body needs as it needs it."

That was just plain weird. "No organs? Nerves? It—he had to have a brain. He was intelligent. He talked to me—"

"His identity, his 'mind,' would be distributed in electrical signals over his entire body. Just as all the other functions would be diffused within the creature. Eating, excreting—probably reproduces by binary fission."

Manny stood up and watched the bandage fuse and contract in response to Nohar's body heat. Nohar was still having trouble accepting what Manny was telling him. "Smith was just a huge amoeba?"

"In essence. Though a multicellular one. Just looking at the little sample we have is fascinating. The gene-techs that built this thing were geniuses."

"Great— *Why* would someone build something like that?"

Manny produced his undulating shrug again. "I'm only making inferences from a limited sample. But these things would be incredibly tough. Having all their vital function distributed throughout their mass, there's very little you could do to hurt them. Fire, acid maybe—"

"So how the hell did he die?"

"Electricity. The stunner is intended to temporarily paralyze a normal nervous system. Neural paralysis to *this* creature rendered the entire mass inert. Once that happened, the mass dissolved, from the inside out."

Manny closed up the black bag and picked up the used hypos. "They have a set of showers here for the staff, use one. I left you some hospital greens that might fit you. I better see if they've 'fixed' the analyzer yet." He turned and started trailing his agent back to the lab.

As Manny started back down the hall Nohar called after him. "What's wrong with the thing anyway?"

"Nothing much." Manny sounded like it was pretty major. "We'd just started to catalog amino acids and the display keeps coming up backward."

Once Manny had disappeared back into the lab Nohar waved at his redheaded agent, who still looked a little queasy. "You heard. Doctor's orders—shower."

As Nohar limped toward the showers, he tried to talk to his agent. "So, what do you think of Agent Isham?"

He answer in a voice as colorless as he was. "She's a good agent."

Talk about your stock answers. "So where is she now?"

"I've been encouraged not to speculate."

"Loosen up. You sound like the voice-over for a hemorrhoid commercial."

That got him. Nohar could swear he got a ghost of a smile from the guy. He looked down at the agent who was afraid of needles. "You bothered by guarding a morey?"

The agent shook his head. "I've worked with moreaus before. It's what our division is trained for."

Nohar stopped in front of the doors to the changing area. "That's not what I asked you."

Now there was a smile. A small one. "I suppose not. perhaps I'm bothered, a little. This is my first assignment, and all the moreaus I've trained with were federal recruits. Mostly Latin American—"

"Never prepared you for a tiger?"

"They can't train you to deal with everything. I apologize if I've seemed remote. You're an important witness, not a suspect—"

"My *name's* Nohar Rajasthan. What do I call you?"

The agent held out his hand. "Agen—Patrick Shaunassy."

Nohar gripped it and decided there was hope for him. "Pleased to meet you."

Shaunassy gave Nohar's hand a healthy shake. "Ditto. You're going to be taking a shower here?"

"Like I said, doctor's orders . . ."

Shaunassy opened the door. "Well, once I secure the area why don't I go back to the vending machines and get us some coffee?"

Nohar usually detested coffee, but he was feeling the lack of sleep catching up with him. "Do that, I could use a few cups."

They entered the changing area and Shaunassy stopped him at the door. Shaunassy made an economical search of the room and the shower stalls as he spoke. "Sugar, cream?"

"Both."

He checked the toilet stalls. "Anything to eat?"

"Hate hospital food."

He returned to the door and made sure it had a lock. "Lock this until I come back. Shouldn't be more than ten minutes. If you're in the shower, I'll wait."

Shaunassy left and Nohar locked the door as requested. Amazing, scratch an FBI agent and there might be a person underneath.

The changing area was a study in white. White plastic lockers with recessed keypads, white fiberglass squares in the ceiling, white tile on the floor, white fluorescents—the only things in the room that weren't white were the greens Manny had left folded on the bench, and the chromed fixtures in the showers. The glare was irritating, so Nohar killed the lights, letting his eyes adjust to the darkness.

The disinfectant was bad here. It was killing his sense of smell. He wished there was a window in here he could open.

He breathed through his mouth as he removed the latest set of clothes he had destroyed.

He got into a shower, turned on a blast of cold water, and let the mud melt off his body. He found himself thinking, not of the FBI or the whole MLI business, but of Stephie Weir. All he wanted, right now, was to be in that motel room in Geauga. He was exhausted and had had enough of this bullshit. He just wanted to hold somebody—her—and get some sleep.

There was thirty grand in his account. He wondered if it was worth it.

He killed the shower and stood there, dripping, listening to the drain gurgle and wondering why he had taken the case in the first place. Did he really, subconsciously, want to go to California after Maria? Did he just want enough money to leave this burg? And where was that coffee?

He stepped over to the dryer—he was going to be done before Shaunassy got back—and slapped the large button with the back of his hand. He was enveloped in a nearly silent column of warm air. His abused muscles appreciated it.

Nohar nodded off a bit.

He slipped against the cold tiles and woke up. He shook the sleep from his head and walked out to the changing room. He spared a glance out the little rectangular windows into the hall. He hoped Shaunassy didn't see the lights off and assume he'd left already. He decided he wasn't going to wait behind a locked door just for Shaunassy to get back. The disinfectant smell in here was getting to him.

He unfolded the bottom of the greens and pulled them on. They fit around his waist, and they came down to a dozen centimeters past his knees. Nohar still had to split the seam on the bottom of the right leg to fit around the swelling.

The top that went with the pants—came short above the waistline and both arms—looked just plain silly. Nohar left it. While the boots he had been wearing were still intact, he left them. His feet needed to air out and it felt good to give the claws on his feet a chance to stretch.

Still no coffee, damn it.

Nohar opened the door and was no longer immersed in the disinfectant smell. Now he could smell fresh coffee, the same synthetic-smelling stuff Harsk drank.

Nohar also smelled blood.

He grabbed his Vind from the pile of his clothes and

ran—limped, really, the drug Manny had shot into him was keeping him from feeling his knee, but didn't make it work any better—down toward the vending machines, the waiting area, the labs. The first corner he rounded brought him to the vending machines—

Shaunassy was dead.

He had slid halfway down the wall between the micro and the coffee dispenser. His right hand had knocked over a brown plastic tray, scattering small bulbs of cream and packets of sugar into the widening pool of blood. Three cups of coffee had spilled on the linoleum tile floor. The edges of the spill mixed with Shaunassy's blood, pulling swirls of red to mix with the tan—

Nohar's heartbeat was thudding dully in his ears.

Nohar pulled him away from the wall. Shaunassy hit the ground with a boneless splat. His throat hung open and his shirt was drenched with red. He was still warm.

The canine's musk hung in the air.

Hassan had done this. Probably with a straight razor.

Nohar kept up his limping run to the genetics lab, his breath a furnace in his throat. Why? Why was Hassan doing this?

The hall smelled like an abattoir. The smell of blood seemed to adhere to the back of Nohar's sinuses.

Nohar passed another agent. This one was crumpled in the middle of the hall. Hassan had sawed through the windpipe and had held the throat open. Blood had splattered halfway up the walls. Nohar stepped over the body, and his left foot slipped in the agent's blood. He ignored it and kept running, his foot making little tearing sounds each time he pulled it away from the linoleum.

He took the safety off the Vind and cocked it. The blood smell was getting worse. There was no question in Nohar's mind that Hassan was heading for the lab.

Nohar took in a deep breath, sucking in the smell of blood. His heart hammered in his ears, his head, and neck. Nohar raised his left hand to his mouth and tasted Shaunassy's blood.

For the first time, Nohar willingly invited The Beast into his soul.

The Beast came out and sniffed the air. Blood, it smelled human blood from at least five different people. It smelled the discharge of someone's gun. It smelled an excited canine. It smelled blood from a morey—

From Manny.

Nohar would have roared, but he was stalking now. Hassan didn't know he was here. The canine had passed by the changing area and the room had looked empty, the disinfectant had covered Nohar's smell. Nohar closed on the lab. It formed a T-intersection at the end of the hall. Ahead were a pair of fire doors, an agent crumpled against them, one arm hooked through one of the crash bars. To Nohar's right was the lounge. An agent was sprawled across the table. To Nohar's left were the swinging doors to the genetic lab. He could hear someone moving in there. He could smell Manny's blood.

Things slowed down as the adrenaline kicked in. One of the doors was half open. And this time Nohar recognized the smell of gasoline—

He crept up on the open door and listened, smelled the air. Hassan was in the rear of the room, to his right—

He burst through the door. Hassan turned, very quickly. Not quickly enough. Nohar's first shot hit him. Hassan's right shoulder exploded into a shower of blood. The canine dropped the package he was carrying and spun off to the left. Nohar, still moving toward the rear of the room, followed with another shot. That one missed and hit a large piece of equipment—probably the chemical analyzer—the impact exploded a picture tube and caused the body of a dead tech to roll off it and hit the floor.

The third shot followed Hassan, missed again, and slammed into a stainless steel sink. Water shot up in a minigeyser.

Nohar was moving slowly, dreamlike. Hassan took cover behind a large, stainless steel object, an oven or an autoclave. Hassan was drawing a gun. Apparently the need for the stealth of a razor was over. Hassan took too long to aim, and Nohar's fourth shot hit his cover. A white jet of steam blew from the side of the machine, hitting his gun arm. Hassan's wild shot hit the ceiling, taking out a light fixture, and his gun sailed into the middle of the room.

The gun slid and came to rest next to the corpse of another FBI agent, sprawled facedown in a pool of blood in the center of the room. Nohar looked up and Hassan was hidden behind something—a cabinet, the chromed oven, or the other lab-tech, who was slumped over a cart, giving some cover.

Nohar covered the door and backed toward the corner where Hassan had started. His foot stepped on something soft—

Manny.

Manny was facedown on the ground. The slashing wounds on his throat were multiple, violent.

Nohar roared. He screamed rage as he advanced on Hassan's cover—

"Cat—"

Where did that voice come from? Behind the lab cart?

Nohar pumped four shots at Hassan, through the corpse of the lab-tech. Blood sprayed the white lab coat and the cart rolled across the floor with the impact, bottles rattling. There was scrambling, perhaps the smell of canine blood.

Nohar walked up and kicked over the cart. The tech thudded on the ground and the glass bottles shattered. The smell of alcohol filled the room. Hassan had moved behind a counter, closer to the exit. "Cat, thirty seconds and the place goes up. We both go. Still time to leave."

Nohar replied by pumping a shot into the base of the counter. Cabinet doors under the sink splintered.

The canine bolted for the door. Nohar bolted after him, firing. He missed and hit the light switch. The fluorescents winked out as a few anemic sparks leapt from the wall. Next shot was an almost. He could see the shell slam into Hassan's back, pushing him through the door—But the bastard wore a vest. The third shot slammed into the door, blowing a perfectly circular hole in it.

Nohar slammed through the door after the canine. Hassan was still picking himself up from the impact in his back. He had rolled into the lounge. Three shots in rapid succession—

Hassan would be dead if the gun wasn't empty.

Hassan stood up and backed toward a window. He started to open it. "Ten seconds, cat. You can make it down the hall—"

Hassan warded off Nohar with a blood-soaked straight razor in his left hand. His right was trying to fumble open the window in time . . .

The Beast didn't give up that easily, and Nohar wasn't going to stop it this time.

Nohar shifted the weight off his bad knee and leapt at Hassan, claws extended, roaring. Hassan cocked back with the razor to slash at Nohar's neck, but he was wounded, using his off-hand, and he was trying to do too many things at once. In peak condition, he might have hit Nohar. Instead, his forearm hit ineffectively against Nohar's right shoulder. Nohar grabbed Hassan's neck with his teeth as the window gave way before his weight.

Hassan's blood was the sweetest thing he had ever tasted.

The lab exploded.

Chapter 24

The window was blown apart by the explosion. They fell onto the top floor of the adjoining parking garage.

Hassan's back slammed into a car below them. The fiberglass underneath them gave and Nohar felt his knee sink into Hassan's chest. Something inside it broke. The canine coughed up blood.

Hassan cocked back with the razor again. Nohar responded with a back hand slash. The fully-extended claws of his right hand hit Hassan's left arm, slicing open Hassan's wrist. The razor went tumbling into the darkness.

Nohar's teeth were still buried in the flesh of Hassan's neck and canine blood spilled into his mouth.

Hassan jerked underneath him. The canine's flesh ripped out of his mouth, and Nohar heard a collarbone snap. Hassan spilled out on the concrete drive and backed away, toward the end of the garage.

Somewhere a pink screamed.

Debris from above began to rain down on them.

"...cat." Hassan spat a gob of bloody phlegm at the pavement. He seemed to be laboring to breathe and his voice had a breathy, bubbling quality to it. Nohar thought a rib must have punctured a lung. "Too bad, you didn't go ..."

Hassan paused to get his breath as Nohar jumped from the car and advanced. "To Geauga with everyone else . . ."

Nohar was barely a meter from the canine and Hassan actually smiled. How—no, he couldn't have. There wasn't enough time.

But where had the Zipheads been when Smith got hit at Lakeview? Where were they now?

Hassan had backed all the way to the railing. Behind him was only space.

Nohar—The Beast—roared and swung his right hand. He aimed at the soft part of the skin under Hassan's lower jaw. The claws, and his fingers, dug in through the skin under Hassan's muzzle. Nohar's claws pierced the skin and crushed Hassan's tongue against the inside of the jaw. Hassan's eyes went wide with shock. Warm blood streamed out of the wound, soaking Nohar's arm.

Nohar put his whole body into the follow-through. He grabbed hold of Hassan's jaw from inside the mouth and his arm continued the swing. Hassan's weight barely slowed it. The swing carried the canine out over the edge of the roof. He was actually thrown upward before he started falling. Hassan slid off of Nohar's hand and followed a near-perfect ballistic arc to the ground.

Hassan crashed into an ambulance that was in the process of pulling out of the driveway below. The roof caved in with his weight, and the siren and flashers—for some reason—kicked in. The ambulance slowed to a stop and a pair of medics piled out to see what the hell had happened.

The Beast retreated but didn't leave. Nohar was shaking as he ran through Metro General's parking garage. No one stopped him as he made his way down, even though his arm and his face were streaked with Hassan's blood—or perhaps because of it. Good thing. Nohar was in a dangerous state of mind. Even an innocent bystander who got in his way would find himself in trouble.

Manny's van was still where they had parked it less than an hour ago. It cut diagonally across three parking spaces and was surrounded by a flock of dark-blue Haviers. One of the Haviers' doors hung open. The agents from it must have rounded the building to see Hassan's splat.

Manny had never bothered to hide the van's combination from Nohar. Nohar punched it in, opened the door, and got in the driver's seat. The feed ripped out as he floored the van out of the Metro lot.

He could still taste Hassan's blood and it didn't do a damn bit of good. Manny was dead, pointlessly.

"WHY?"

MLI was finished. It was all blown open. *Why?*

Nohar smelled Manny off the driver's seat and he wished the Indian techs had made his strain able to cry.

He was already pushing the van at one-twenty klicks an hour when he hit the I-90 ramp. He was dodging slower-moving cars when he remembered this van had a siren. He found the switch and turned it on. He stopped dodging. The other cars were pulling to the side.

He maxed it out at one-fifty as he shot through the exit on to the Midtown Corridor.

Even blowing down the Corridor, going twice the speed limit, gave him time to think, time he didn't want. He didn't want to know Manny was dead. He wanted The Beast to handle it. That's what it was for, damnit.

However, invoking his bioengineered combat-mode didn't help him a bit when it came to dealing with the death of the closest thing to a father he had ever had.

He needed to hit Mayfield, and fuck the barriers. He put on the seat belt.

He shot past the city end of Mayfield and took a right toward the Triangle parking garage. Between the bridge over Mayfield and the one over the driveway, there was a small hill that sloped toward the tracks. Nohar left the driveway and shot the van over the mostly dead lawn, up the hill, and over the dead tracks. A Dodge Electroline wasn't intended to take that kind of grade, but the velocity carried it over. The van started spilling over the other side of the hill, only going seventy now, headed for the side of an apartment building.

Siren still going, Nohar skidded the van to the right. The rear left corner clipped the building as he bumped on to the crumbling Moreytown section of Mayfield. The van rolled to a near stop, scattering the nocturnal population off of the street.

Nohar floored it again, feeling the uneven road in his kidneys.

After the first block, he was going eighty.

He passed the abandoned bus going a hundred.

Third block, he was going one-twenty—

Three concrete pylons blocked the road ahead of him, each three meters tall. The hulk of the dead Subaru was still wrapped around the center pillar.

He pulled the van all the way to the left, on to the sidewalk. On one side was now a concrete wall to Lakeview, and coming up on the right, one of the pylons. Nohar hoped the gap was big enough.

The front end screeched and the van bucked forward with a crunch—

He was through.

He'd made it. There was now a wobble on the front left tire, and he'd left both front fenders behind him. But now he was shooting east down Mayfield.

He was back to going one-fifty when he passed by Coventry. The cop on the riot watch only took three seconds to decide to give chase. Good for him. Nohar saw the first 322 marker when he passed the minimum-security prison. So far, the cop was the only shadow.

As long as the cop didn't try to stop him.

The vibration from the front wheel was getting worse, but he didn't slow. Malls and suburbia shot by him, a ghostly gray blur under the streetlights. His headlights had been taken out by his squeeze through the barrier. He drove by his night-vision and the infrequent streetlights.

Some shithead going through an intersection didn't get out of the way. Nohar wove a tight arc around the vehicle without hitting the brakes, and raked the side of the van across the rear end of the new BMW. It spun out and hit a light pole.

Suburbia vanished in a wave of trees. The Cleveland cop was still the only shadow, and they were now three suburbs out of his jurisdiction. The streetlights vanished with the malls and the split-levels. The only light now was the van's red flashers, turning the world ahead into a surrealistic image in pulsing-red monochrome.

He hit the county line and could see the blurred lights of the motel coming up on his right. Bobby had chosen a fifty-year-old relic to stash the girls—all tarnished chrome and flickering neon. Nohar saw the lights when he was about a klick away from the hotel and cut the siren as he slowed the van.

When he passed the entrance, he spun the van into the

parking lot. The van was going seventy. The first thing he saw in the parking lot was a Ziphead with a submachine gun. The rat was standing guard outside a familiar-looking remote van. Nohar aimed his vehicle at him.

The ratboy's reaction time was just too slow. He jumped to the side too late to avoid being hit. Nohar heard a burst of ineffective gunfire as the wobbly front tire bumped up over the rat.

The front end of Manny's van plowed into the side of the remote. The remote tumbled forward like it had been jerked on a cable, the sudden deceleration throwing Nohar against the seat belt.

There was the sound of shattering glass. Then more gunfire. He felt a wave of shots strafe the rear of the van. He heard more gunfire, not aimed at the van.

Where the hell was his Vind?

Nohar felt the bottom fall out of his world when he realized he had lost it somewhere in the fight with Hassan.

Something inside him smelled the rat-blood under the van and told him it didn't matter. He was the hunter, they were prey—

And Stephie was in there.

He loosed a subliminal growl as he popped the seat belt and tumbled out the driver's side door, away from the motel. When he hit the ground he shuddered in pain. He was beginning to feel his knee again. He let the pain jack up the adrenaline.

He took cover behind the van—most of the shots were coming from the hotel. He looked at where the shots seemed to be going and saw the Cleveland cop car. The cop was huddling down behind the front fender. The flashers were going, but a bullet had taken out the plastic covering them—the flashers were now giving off a stark white searchlight glare. The cop looked like he had taken a hit or two. Nohar recognized him. He was the pink cop who had looked so scared when he and Manny had passed him—the night all this shit started.

The whelp had better've called backup.

The ratboy who'd guarded the remote was a smear on the pavement. When he looked at the corpse, he could feel his time sense telescoping. The rest of the Zips were holed up in the motel. The Zips weren't paying attention to him yet. The cop must've rounded into the parking lot just after he had plowed in.

The wreck of the remote offered him some more cover. Nohar hunkered down and ran along the side of the wreck on all fours, right leg barely touching the ground.

The motel was simply a line of rooms facing the parking lot. The nose of the remote was only a meter in front of a door—the room next to the Zips. Nohar tackled the door, and the cheap molding splintered. He kept going, tumbling onto a twin bed. The legs on the bed snapped off and spilled Nohar onto a synthetic rug that smelled of moth-balls, rug shampoo, and old cigarette smoke. The room was empty.

Nohar could hear the gunfire and the Zip's chittering Spanish through the thin drywall. He stood up and looked for a weapon.

The room's comm was bolted to its own table. His shoulder protested as he lifted it. The cable connection ripped out of the wall, taking a wall plate and ripping a hole up the drywall for nearly a meter before it snapped free. Knee shaking, he lifted the comm over his head—it had to weigh thirty kilos—and listened to the Zips.

One was near the wall. It sounded like he had a nine-millimeter. Nohar aimed the comm at that one—

The comm and attached table flew in an arc that inter-sected the wall. It hit dead center at a fake painting—some anonymous landscape—and crashed through the drywall separating the two rooms. The mylar wallpaper tore away in sheets, following the comm through the hole.

Perfect hit on the rat—bandage on the face marked this guy as Bigboy—the side of the comm hit the rat in the face and the picture tube imploded, adding a small cloud of phosphor powder to the plaster dust.

The comm kept going, knocking away a table another rat was using for cover. The rat—dressing on his arm marked him as the one with the chain—turned to face Nohar. That was a stupid mistake. The cop was still covering the picture window from behind the cop car.

The cop put a .38 slug through the rat's neck before the ratboy realized he had lost his cover.

The hole in the wall was a meter square.

Nohar jumped through without any hesitation. He aimed

at the third rat, who was hiding behind a set of dresser drawers.

For a moment Nohar bared his entire flank to the cop, the kid had a perfect shot through the long-ago-vaporized picture window. Nohar didn't care.

Nohar landed on the third rodent, Fearless Leader. Leader had a revolver, a forty-four. An old gun but powerful. He tried to turn it on Nohar, but Nohar grabbed the ratboy's wrist—it was in a cast—and slammed it into one of the open drawers of the dresser. Then he crunched the drawer shut with his entire weight. The gun went off inside the dresser, blasting chunks of particleboard over the rat the cop had shot.

Fearless was looking at Nohar with wide eyes, going into shock. Somewhere, under the growling, Nohar found his voice. "So, 'pretty kitty's' next?" The rat tried to shake his head.

Nohar slashed Fearless Leader's throat open with his claws, opened the drawer, and removed the gun from the sputtering rodent.

The gunfire had ceased.

He could smell perfume coming from the bathroom, over the cordite. Nohar could also smell blood that didn't come from a rat. He gave the cop a great shot at his back as he bolted for the bathroom door at the rear of the motel room.

Somewhere, where his rational mind was hiding, he prayed to Maria's God he wasn't too late.

He kicked the door open, sending a piercing dagger of pain through his right leg. Terin turned toward him. She was picking up a nasty looking assault rifle. It looked too big for her. It was certainly too big for the small bathroom. Terin couldn't sweep it to cover the door.

There was a bloody knife sitting on the sink. Something small and blood-covered was hanging in the shower—

"I'll give you the fucking Finger of God."

The first shot hit her in the chest, slamming the rat into the white tile wall.

The second got her in the face.

The third clicked on an empty chamber.

There was a weak sound from the shower ". . . way to go, Kit . . ."

Chapter 25

Angel's voice brought him back. The Beast didn't go back to its mental closet—the closet didn't seem to be there any-more—but it did let his rational mind take over. For the first time Nohar felt the full impact of what he had put his body through. Glass had been ground into his left foot. The falls and the leaping had strained his back. His knee couldn't hold his weight anymore. Any pressure on it was agonizing—

He grabbed the sink and pulled himself into the bath-room. He looked into the shower. Angel's hands were tied to the showerhead. Her feet didn't touch the floor. She was still conscious, and her face was recognizable. Terin had been working from the bottom up. Terin was experienced at shaving moreys—the process was supposed to be long, painful, and the victim was supposed to live up to and, hopefully, a little past the end.

Angel's legs had become strips of bleeding meat.

"Kit, you look like hell . . ."

Nohar gritted his teeth and knelt slowly to examine the damage. It was bad, Angel was probably in shock. He dropped the forty-four in the toilet and grabbed Terin's knife. He stood on his left leg and circled his right arm around, under Angel's armpits, as he cut the bonds on her hands. Her weight nearly toppled him over. He pulled him-self along, out of the bathroom, with his left hand. The three rodents that had been covering the picture window didn't move. Every half-second the room was bathed in the searchlight glare of the cop's flashers. Nohar wondered where the cop was.

He laid Angel out on one of the twin beds. Her legs be-gan to stain the white sheet. "I'm calling an ambulance—"

Her head was cocked toward the front of the room. "Only one?"

Nohar went to this room's comm, it was intact. He called emergency. "I need a half-dozen ambulances, Woodstar Motel off route 322 in Chesterland, humans and moreys—cops, too, some of these people are dead—"

The dispatch cop nodded. "What's the problem there?"

He didn't bother to hang up. He turned to Angel. Somewhere along the way he had screwed up, badly. "Where's Stephie?" He almost didn't get the words out. He was too afraid of the answer.

"Back in our room, last in line. Talked about having a hostage. Left a Zip with her . . ."

Oh, shit. If a ratboy was left with her, the bastard would probably kill her once he saw how the fight went. Nohar hobbled over to the picture window; still no sign of the cop. He reached and turned Bigboy over. The rat had been using an Uzi. Nohar grabbed the gun and crawled out the window. Once outside, he saw the cop. Fearless had got off one well placed shot. The cop was unconscious or dead.

Because of his knee, he had to advance on Stephie's room while leaning against the wall. His progress was agonizingly slow. He passed the wreck of the remote and the door he had busted in. He passed an unoccupied room. Slowly, he came upon the last in the line, the black GM Maduro parked in front.

He checked the clip on the Uzi. Good thing Bigboy wasn't spraying the cop. There were a few shots left. He hit the ground and scrambled under the picture window—the right knee was beginning to make popping sounds every time he moved—and rolled in front of the door.

With the feeling this was going to be it for him, he shouldered the door open and covered the room with the Uzi.

And there was Mister Mad bomber, looking like he was about to wet his pants. The rat's twenty-two thumped on the carpet.

Stephie was alive, and apparently unhurt. She had been stripped naked and tied to the bed. She turned her head toward the door when it burst open. She had never smelled so good to him.

The Beast wanted Nohar to shoot the rat. To Nohar's surprise, he still had control. Even though the mental door was no longer there.

"Kid, second chances are rare, use yours. Get out of here."

The rat carefully approached the door, where Nohar was still half-sitting, stepped over him, and ran into the night. Stephie's eyes were wide as she watched Nohar pull himself into the room and on to the bed. Nohar didn't waste time. He bit through the rope.

As soon as Stephie was free, Nohar found himself on the receiving end of an embrace that smeared her with blood. "God, what's happened to you—where's Angel?"

"Angel, I called an ambulance for her—and everyone else. They killed Manny—"

Stephie broke off the hug. "Oh, Christ, I'm sorry—"

"Can you find me something to use as a cane?"

The curtain rod was stainless steel, and not as cheap as everything else in the motel. It made a halfway decent cane. Stephie found a robe and followed him out to the parking lot. He asked aloud the question that had gnawed at him ever since he had smelled Shaunassy's blood—

"Damn it, why?"

He hobbled to the wreck of the remote. The power plant was still alive. The wheels were trying to drive it away despite the broken axle. He walked up to the vehicle. Green, just like Smith's van. Hell, it could *be* Smith's van. "The whole thing was *blown*. The Fed has *everything*."

He slammed his left fist at one of the dangling pneumatic doors. There was a slow hiss, and the door slid aside with the smell of leaking hydraulic fluid. There were guns and a dozen white plastic crates in back. Most of the crates had burst open. Little vials of red liquid rolled out the rear of the van. Hypo cartridges—flush, a few million dollars' worth.

The DEA would be happy.

Nohar leaned in and looked at the crates more closely. They were labeled. "NuFood Inc. dietary supplements— MirrorProtein(tm)"

MLI was using NuFood as a drug lab.

There had to be another reason for NuFood. The Zips had only come on the scene recently. MLI had been dealing with NuFood ever since MLI's inception.

MirrorProtein?

What was it Manny said about the chemical analyzer? They had been cataloging amino acids and the display was reversed. Nohar had thought the picture had been coming up backward.

What if it was the amino acids themselves that were coming up reversed?

"Stephie, do you know any biochemistry?"

Stephie was already at the Zips' room checking on Angel. "*What?*"

Nohar hobbled after her. His thoughts were flying, trying to remember things, put them into place. "This is important. Really important. Biochemistry, proteins, amino acids, what do you know?"

"Next to nothing." She had her hand on Angel's neck. "She's still alive—What the hell are you talking about?"

"I need to remember if we're based on levo or dextro amino acids . . ."

"Derry was the chemistry major. Where the hell are you getting this from?" Stephie was looking worried, as if she thought he had gone over the edge.

Far from it. Things were making sense. "I don't know if you'll understand this." He was racing to get it all out. "I lived most of my childhood with Manny—a doctor and an expert on moreaus. I got a biology lesson every time I asked a question like, 'Why am I different from the other kids?' "

Even to him he sounded like he was rambling. He slowed down. "You can't live like that and not pick up on biological trivia. Like the fact our amino acids all have their mirror image versions." He finally remembered. "Almost all the life in this world is based on levo amino acids—"

"So?"

Nohar shook his head. "Just tell the cops when they get here. You have to talk to an FBI agent—Isham. Tell her the franks aren't at MLI's office building. It's just a front, like everything else. If they're anywhere, they're at NuFood's R&D facility. Tell her the MLI franks are based on a *dextro* amino acid biology. Got that?"

"Yes, but—"

Nohar was hobbling back to the Maduro. He stopped at the remote. An Uzi wouldn't do much to one of the things Manny described. He looked in among the crates of flush and saw a pump shotgun. He'd take that, and hope.

He was beginning to hear sirens in the distance. Stephie ran after him. "Where are you going?"

"NuFood. This isn't over—"

He slumped up next to the car. "Did they wire the car?"

"No—"

"What's the combination?"

"Nohar, you can't! You're in no condition . . ."

"*The damn combination!*"

Stephie backed up a bit at Nohar's growled command. Nohar shook his head. "*Please,* God damn it."

Stephie heard the sirens now as well.

She stepped up and punched the combination on the driver's door. Nohar watched the numbers. She looked up at him afterward. She was crying. "You are not going to die on me."

Nohar hugged her with his good arm. "I don't intend to."

The Maduro had pulled out of the parking lot and was going down Mayfield by the time a convoy—Chersterland and Cleveland local cops, sheriffs from Cuyahoga and Geauga, six ambulances, two police wreckers, a fire rescue vehicle, and three Haviers—shot by going in the opposite direction. Everything but the National Guard.

Nohar drove by them going a sedate sixty klicks an hour. He was squeezed in the sports car, but the gentle ride of the undamaged suspension made up for it.

Everything came together for him when he saw that Nu-Food label. He had been right along. Despite the hyped violence, the morey terrorism, the Johnson killing came down to one little piece of information in Binder's financial records.

The precognitive letter from Wilson Scott was only part of it. That only proved MLI had a hand in planning the Zipheads' terrorism. MLI was trying to hide something else.

Their origin.

Johnson used to be a chemistry major. It made sense he would figure this mess out.

It had all started thirteen years ago. Midwest Lapidary would have approached Young, Binder's new finance chairman. It would have been a very tempting offer. Young took the offer, and the bucks poured into the campaign.

And Binder's position became more and more reactionary.

Over the next few years, other, similarly unpopular candidates had made some sort of deal with the shadowy diamond merchants working out of Cleveland—candidates that weren't supposed to win. Their positions would evolve as well.

Then, in 2042, morey communities across the country exploded into a week of riots and burning that took the National Guard to control. Led by the psychopathic rhetoric of a morey tiger named Datia Rajasthan.

The violence created a convenient wave of anti-moreau sentiment that catapulted most of MLI's candidates to office.

MLI had about seventy hard-core puppets in the House now, all incumbents. They only had a few men in the Senate, though, and a large percentage of their men, including Binder, wanted to be Senators.

The rogue agents in MLI, without Smith's knowledge, recruited the Zipheads to step in to create their own "Dark August." The Zipheads were happy to comply, considering the profits they made on flush on the street level.

Daryl Johnson knew or suspected all of this. At first he must have condoned it. You couldn't keep that kind of conspiracy secret from the campaign manager. The whole Binder inner circle must have known about the illegal financing. That's why it was so tight. Harrison, Thomson, Johnson, and Young stuck with Binder through his radical shift to the right. They *all* had been bought.

Johnson was the first to have second thoughts. Nohar suspected that it would probably have originated with the whole duplicitous situation with Stephie. It must have grated badly. He stewed for years. Even tried to drug himself out of an untenable situation.

MLI must have thought they had him under control because he was hooked on flush that they supplied—though indirectly. If he did anything to break the silence, his supply would be cut.

Three weeks before his death Johnson found a new supplier. Nugoya.

That wasn't what got him killed. The flush still came from MLI, they still controlled his supply even though Johnson didn't know that. What killed Johnson was *why* he was trying to get out from under the thumb of his supplier. Johnson's problem was curiosity. He thought too much.

He had thought too much about NuFood.

He thought too much about Kathy Tsoravitch's letter.

Johnson made the mistake of wondering, as Isham had just a few hours ago, why MLI would be interested in preventing NuFood from succeeding. Tsoravitch lobbied to prevent FDA approval. Denial of that approval bankrupted NuFood.

Whereupon, MLI bought out the company, and the patents. Why?

The question must have nagged Johnson for years. Especially when MLI simply sat on the company. He might even have realized that MLI was using NuFood as its flush lab. A very expensive drug lab.

He finally figured out the real reason. When he did, he made his second, and last, mistake. He told Young. And Young had told the creatures running MLI—

That's when the shit went ballistic. That's why Young was so scared, as well as guilty. He *knew* MLI's secret—they would have killed him once he had served his purpose, ID-ing the people in the campaign whom Johnson had talked to, those who read the letter.

But Young toasted himself, so MLI had to use their agents— Hassan and the Zipheads—to waste anyone who could have read that letter.

All from Kathy Tsoravitch's letter, and her pleading that the FDA reject NuFood's application to mass market their dietary supplements. Supplements that were based on synthetic proteins derived from the mirror image dextro amino acids. Proteins a creature based on a levo amino acid biology—like the fat pinks at whom the food would be targeted—couldn't metabolize.

Johnson had looked too closely at MLI's agenda. He saw NuFood, moreys as a hot issue to be counted on to get MLI's people elected, and the budget. And the letters about government waste always mentioned NASA.

Johnson must have seen the creatures running MLI— the humanoid things that could only be franks. Otherwise, Nohar doubted Johnson would have come to the conclusion he must have. Because the truth was quite a leap.

Nohar's Maduro had glided into the suburbs again. He began watching the left side of Mayfield. NuFood's R&D complex was at 3700 Mayfield, near the minimum security prison he had passed earlier. NuFood's plot was cheap property, little-traveled.

The conclusion was simple, if hard to accept. Johnson must have asked himself the same question as Nohar did when Smith told him MLI supported Binder.

Why were a bunch of franks backing right-wingers like Binder?

They weren't franks.

Why the hell were they involved with something like NuFood?

Johnson must have inferred what Nohar had told Stephie. These things were based on a dextro amino acid biology. Manny had discovered that from Smith's remains. Manny had known, but he had never gotten the chance to double-check the results. He never got the chance to make sure the analyzer wasn't broken.

That was what MLI had to cover up.

The prison came up on the left.

Nohar pulled the Maduro over and parked on the sidewalk across from it. NuFood was next to the prison's barbed wire topped chain link. It sat in the midst of a grove of trees and bushes that nearly hid the two lab buildings from sight.

They couldn't let anyone know they were based on a mirror image biology. It was because of that *they* needed NuFood. *They* literally couldn't live without it. Normal living things couldn't metabolize NuFood's products, but the converse was true. NuFood's production was the only thing *they* could eat.

No gene-tech, even as an experiment, would give their work such a bizarre handicap. Johnson would know that. It left one conclusion.

These things *weren't* bioengineered.

They had evolved naturally.

It was a fifty-fifty chance life on Earth ended up stabilizing around the one type of amino acid. Life elsewhere, if it evolved as it had on Earth, would end up stabilizing around one form or the other, dextro or levo. Same chance, fifty-fifty. Even odds. It was just bad luck, for everyone concerned, that these guys came from a planet that was based on the wrong type.

They were aliens.

Nohar hobbled across the street.

Chapter 26

The storm that had been threatening all night finally came as Nohar crossed Mayfield. It was a sudden deluge that washed some of the blood off of him. His makeshift cane was thumping an erratic counterpoint to the click of his claws. It was slow progress, but it was nearly three in the morning and there wasn't any traffic. The street was dead.

He made it across. To his right was the prison hiding behind its electrified chain link. Its yard was bathed in arc lights.

To his left was a line of shrubs and trees that almost hid an old, low slung, office complex from the street. Ahead of him, between the overgrown shrubs and the five-meter tall electric chain link, was a dirty-gravel driveway. It looked like a landscaping afterthought.

He began worrying about the pink guards at the prison. They weren't involved in this, but it wouldn't be good if they noticed a morey with a shotgun skulking just outside their grounds.

He limped a dozen meters down the gravel path, all the while cursing his knee and wishing he could move faster. He made it to a point where the hedges got sickly. He turned away from the prison and pushed through a small gap between the bushes. He immediately tripped over a rusted "No Trespassing" sign. He managed to land on his left side, but the fall still hurt his knee.

He was sprawled on a shaggy, uncut lawn, looking across at a parking lot of broken asphalt. The only light came from the arcs of the prison behind him. Half the NuFood complex was wrapped in glaring blue light, the other half in the matte-black shadows of the surrounding trees.

Two remote vans were parked in the lot, the only vehicles there. There were two buildings in NuFood's complex, both old two-story studies in metal, glass, and dark tile. The tiles had been falling off in clumps, helped by ill-looking ivy. The glass was sealed shut from the inside. A few panes were cracked and broken—real glass—allowing Nohar a good look at the white plastic that covered the windows from the inside.

Between the two buildings were an overgrown lawn and a crumbling driveway. A fountain was choked by an advancing rose-bush—and even in the rain, he could smell the stagnant water filling it.

These guys weren't big on maintenance.

Nohar pushed himself up and got unsteadily to his feet. The makeshift cane sank about half a meter into the sod when he put his weight on it. He squished to the asphalt parking lot.

The remotes were parked next to each other. Nohar hobbled between them. He decided if the guards back a the prison started hearing gunfire, the worst thing they could do was call the cops.

He eased himself down on the ground and looked under the chassis of one of the vans. The inductor housing was nestled in front of the rear axle. Nohar leveled the shotgun at it, the barrel a few centimeters from the housing. He turned his face away, closed his eyes, and pulled the trigger.

The blast popped the pressurized housing, and the air was filled with the smell of freon, ozone, and the dust from a shattered ceramic superconductor. There was a wave of heat as the housing sparked and began to melt.

He did the same to the other one.

There went their transport. If *they* were still here, they'd *stay* here.

The guards back at the prison had heard the gunfire. Sirens began sounding behind him.

Nohar hauled himself upright and limped up the circular driveway to the first NuFood building. The door was glass and black enamel. Gold leaf on the glass announced this was indeed NuFood. Its slick modern logo was flaking off. A chain was padlocked around the handle, the one thing that looked new and well maintained.

Locks on glass doors made about as much sense as an armored door in a wooden door frame.

Nohar hunched up against the wall for support and

raised the curtain rod. He put the end of the rod through the logo, shattering the glass—real glass again. There was another plastic sheet sealing the window. It tore away from the frame, loosing the bile-ammonia smell Nohar associated with Smith.

Bingo.

There was a crash bar on the inside of the door, halfway up. The plastic caught and bent over it. Nohar had to lean the curtain rod up next to the doorjamb so he had a hand free to knock the plastic out of the way. In response to Nohar's break-in, an alarm inside the building did an anemic imitation of the sirens at the prison.

Because of his leg, Nohar put down the shotgun and scrambled under the crash bar on both hands and his good leg. He sliced open his right palm on a stray piece of glass.

Once he pulled the cane and the gun after him, he pushed himself up to a standing position.

Inside, the place was much better maintained—and strange. He could smell *their* odor, as well as the odors of chemicals—there was a strong hint of sulfur and sulfur dioxide—and disinfectant that had a fake pine odor. The hall he was in was brightly lit with sodium lamps. They cast an unnatural yellow glow over the hallway. There were filters on the lamps that seemed to increase the effect. The floor he was hobbling along had been stripped to the concrete. It had been polished and felt slightly moist under his feet. Not water. It was damp with something more viscous that made it hard to keep his footing.

The first door to his right was open. He looked in and saw a storage area. The room must have filled half the building, both floors. It was stacked with white plastic delivery crates. It was lit with normal fluorescents, and to the rear was a rolling metal door that must open onto a truck-loading bay. Nohar could smell the flush—even through the packaging, there was so much of it—a rotten, artificial fruit smell, like spoiled cherries.

Nohar continued to limp down the hallway. The doors he passed on his left were new, solid, air lock doors. He looked through the round porthole windows, and saw clean rooms containing glass laboratory equipment filled with bubbling fluids. Here was the damn flush lab the DEA wanted. Nice sterile environment. The stuff must be real pure.

He kept walking, following the ammonia smell. *They* were here. He could feel it. He kept going down the corridor. It took a right turn near the far wall. More labs, older, not behind air lock doors. Nohar noticed familiar items that matched the genetics lab at Metro General. Especially the hulking form of the chemical analyzer. This had to be part of the food production, R&D anyway. Any real volume processing must happen in the other building.

Nohar rounded the corner and faced a stairwell, up and down. Same slick polished concrete. The sulfur and the ammonia were worse going down. That's where he went.

The steps went slowly, one at a time. Each step felt like he was going to slip and break his neck. As he descended, the atmosphere became thicker, denser. The sodium lights faded to a dusky red, and Nohar was beginning to feel the heat—the temperature down here must be around 35 or 40. The atmosphere was heavy with moisture that clung to his fur.

The heat and the heavy atmosphere were making his head throb.

He could feel his pulse in his temple.

Down, he was in the basement. Here, there was no pretense at normal construction. The hall was concrete that had been polished to a marblelike sheen. All the right angles had been filled in and polished smooth, giving an ovoid cross section. The walls were weeping moisture that had the viscosity of silicone lubricant.

There were pipes and other basement equipment, but all had been molded into the walls. Nohar looked up and saw a length of white PVC pipe just above his head. Concrete had been molded around the ends where it came in through the wall so the wall's lines melded smoothly with the length of pipe. It looked like some organic growth. Nohar looked at one wall, and from the discoloration he could make out where the lines of the old cinder block wall used to be.

There was only one way to go. He followed the hall. He hobbled down and left the last of the yellow sodium lights, and entered the world of green-tinted red. The ammonia smell was very close now.

He rounded a very gradual turn in the hall. It felt like he was hobbling through a wormhole in the bowels of the earth. He completed the turn, and saw a perfectly round door. Out the door was pouring an evil bluish-green light and that bile-ammonia smell.

Nohar stumbled through the opening and covered the room with a shotgun held, clumsily, in his left hand. He didn't realize the floor was a half-meter lower than the floor in the hall until it was too late. His good foot slipped away. He tried to catch himself with the cane in his right hand, but the pipe was slick with blood from his palm and slid off into the room, beyond his reach. He slid down a steep concrete curve sitting on his bad leg. He heard a crack. A shiver of agony told him he was not going to walk again for a long time.

He did manage to keep a grip on the shotgun.

Through his pain-blurred vision, he realized that if there had been any doubt Smith wasn't the product of some pink engineer, one look at this room put all doubts to rest. The room was a squashed sphere nearly ten meters in diameter. Eight evenly spaced round holes were in the walls, doors like the one he had come through. In the center of the room was a two-meter-tall cone, molded of concrete, shooting up a jet of blue-green flame. From it came most of the oppressive heat in the room, and the smell of burning methane.

The wall had niches carved into it. Hundreds of them, all the same size, a meter long by half a meter high. They were concave, oval pits that angled down into the wall slightly. From nearly half of them came the glitter of MLI's wealth, diamonds, rubies, emeralds. Thousands, perhaps hundreds of thousands, of stones—

And, of course, there were Smith's kinsmen. The creatures that ran Midwest Lapidary. Four, in all, were facing him. They were wearing pink clothing, like Smith had. They all had the same blubbery white humanoid form that Smith wore.

"That's why," Nohar managed through gritted teeth. "The hit in Lakeview. Couldn't tell who he *was* over the comm ..."

One of them addressed him in Smith's blubbery voice. "We do not do such things lightly. We must be certain of the right when we do such irrevocable acts. A waste you must be here—"

The pain in his leg was making him dizzy. He was beginning to feel cold, clammy. In this heat? He must be going into shock. *"Right?"* It was a yell of pain as much as an accusation. "I talked to Smith." Nohar caught his breath. "You were breaking your own rules when you cut him out of the loop." Nohar wished he had one of Manny's air-hypos.

"He is a traitor. He knows not that the mission is paramount. He clings to propriety as if we are in—" A word in the alien's language. "And not in this violent sewer."

Another one continued. "We do not allow ourselves to perform physical violence. The traitor does not understand our circumstance is dire and requires an exception."

Nohar was beginning to have trouble feeling his leg. The dizziness was getting worse. "End justifies the means?"

A third one, near the cone, spoke. "It is a waste. The tiger understands."

The first one—perhaps the leader, but Nohar was having trouble keeping track of these similar creatures—continued. "The traitor, perhaps, understands or suspects our plans when he hires you. It is intended you lead the new unrest—"

The one by the cone, "—like your father leads the convenient rebellion eleven years ago. The traitor anticipates us and hires you against us—"

"The traitor," one of them went on, "knows what kind of resonance there is when he hires you—"

"—Datia is a useful charismatic figure to keep unrest going, Datia's son is useful as well. A waste the traitor talks to you before us—"

The one by the cone bent—no, oozed—over to turn a valve that was recessed in a concave depression near its base. The flame sputtered out. "It doesn't matter. We go, take our supplies and begin elsewhere. We have done well to prepare for the time the plan is uncovered—"

Nohar shook his head too quickly. He felt faint.

He couldn't tell them apart. They all looked like Smith, all smelled like Smith, talked like Smith. "You guys blew it—"

"Who are you to judge? We achieve our end—"

"It was the vote to scuttle the NASA deep-probe project, wasn't it? It will hit the Senate after the election and you just couldn't wait . . ."

All the *things* stopped moving. They didn't say anything, didn't move. Nohar slowly raised the shotgun.

"Enough of your pet congressmen were supposed to win

Senate seats to tip the scales on the vote. Then the shit hits the fan and MLI falls apart. You designed the whole thing to be uncovered eventually. The phony identities are just *too* damn phony. You want the scandal and the indictments that would follow to throw the Congress into chaos—"

Nohar paused to catch his breath. He couldn't feel his leg at all anymore.

They were regrouping to face him. He still had the shotgun covering them, and he hoped desperately it would do some good. "The Fed was about to follow up all your false trails. The DEA was about to find its flush manufacturing center. But you blew it. Forensics was not supposed to get to Smith's body that fast. There wasn't supposed to *be* a body. You tried to have Hassan erase that mistake. It was too late. I know, and now, the Fed knows."

That got them. They were looking at each other. One spoke, "Then we must end it—"

"End us—"

One of them headed back for the cone while another addressed Nohar. "We complete our original mission. We end ourselves. Nothing is left but speculation and pieces of paper. Without physical evidence, no probes are sent. Your violent races will not contaminate our star systems. We need those new worlds, you will not take them away—"

Nohar was leveling the shotgun at the one that was at the cone. "No, you're not getting off that easy. No suicides. And you call us violent. How many people have you managed to kill because of those probes? A tac-nuke on the moon would have done the same thing, and not killed anyone—"

"Law requires we act indirectly in covert activity."

Nohar gagged on that one. "*Law?* You screwed-up bastards—no wonder the only one of you with a shred of morality ended up a 'traitor.'"

It kept moving. They were going to flood the room with methane. Nohar pumped the shotgun and shot the creature. Bile and ammonia filled the air, and the creature was knocked back to the far wall. A chunk of the creature's translucent flesh splattered against the wall. But it didn't bleed, didn't even leak. The shot had passed right through it.

It stood up, none the worse for wear.

"Unnecessary display, such things do not hurt our kind. Useless since we end now anyway."

The thing went back to the valve and started turning. "You, and others, may know we originate from a different biology. But without us to examine, your ethnocentric culture never accepts the idea of an extraterrestrial culture."

Nohar lowered the shotgun.

What were they going to do, asphyxiate or ignite? Didn't matter, he was dead either way—his leg wouldn't let him move.

Chapter 27

The one at the valve had finished his job, and Nohar could hear the hiss of the methane.

The creature had half-turned toward him when Nohar heard a soft "phut" from the hole behind him. A small tube had planted itself in the folds under the creature's chin. There was a bubbling groan from the creature, and it raised a flabby white arm to the tube stuck in its neck.

Three more "phuts" and similar tubes embedded themselves in the other aliens. There was a shuddering moan from the first one. Its arm had stopped halfway to its neck. There was a tearing sound as the pink clothes gave way and the thing collapsed into a shapeless white mass. There was a clatter as its eyes, fake plastic orbs, rolled off the mound of shuddering flesh. A pair of pink dentures followed.

The others collapsed as well.

They weren't dead, so much as reverted to some natural state. They still moved, though in a shuddering, rhythmic fashion—occasionally throwing out a multitentacled pseudo-pod from their mass, only to be reabsorbed into the mound of flesh a moment later. They now *looked* like the amoebic form of life Manny had described.

Isham came through the hole behind Nohar and went to the valve on the cone, shut it off. She was talking to herself. "... cave dwellers, lots of heat vents and volcanic activity. Dim red-yellow sun, thick atmosphere, probably high gravity. They could survive very heavy acceleration. Could have ridden in on a nuclear rocket not much more advanced than our own. Gems are probably synthetic . . ."

Nohar hadn't realized how tightly he was holding the shotgun until he tried to drop it. His hands didn't want to move. "Damn it, Isham. Where did you come from, and what took you so long?"

Isham squatted and was looking at one of the quivering mounds of alien flesh. She poked it with the end of an air rifle she was carrying. The white flesh rippled like a water balloon. "We were staked out at Midwest Lapidary 'headquarters.' NuFood seemed too small to rate notice. Our team got word from the DEA. McIntyre and Conrad have been two steps behind the Zipperheads all night, ever since the rats jumped a cabbie at the airport. They radioed your message, and my team had to scramble all the way from downtown. I was point, got here about two minutes after you did—"

"What?" Nohar had spoken too loudly. He was suddenly out of breath and felt faint.

She activated her throat-mike. "Aerie, this is Bald Eagle—nest is clear, send the Vultures in with the cleanup. We need a local ambulance, with our own medics. Out."

She stood up and looked into one of the niches in the wall. She reached in and took out a diamond. It glinted red facets of light.

"I had to tape them just in case the drug killed them. Otherwise, their rapid decomposition would be hard to explain to Washington—"

"You were there." Nohar was fighting alternating waves of pain and nausea. "All that time?"

She tapped a lens hanging off her belt with the diamond and dropped the gem back in the niche. "Two meters behind you. All the way through the building."

Nohar sighed.

"That D amino acid information was vital. But you threw the tac-squad for a loop. We had stunners, but we wanted the 'franks' alive. And because of you, we discovered the trank we were using wouldn't have worked right on their biology—"

Nohar looked at the pulsing forms of the aliens. "What'd you use?"

"The only thing I had access to, flush. It's a symmetrical molecule. Probably use the same stuff, wherever they come from."

Talk about poetic justice. "What happens now?"

"The cleanup crew'll be here in about three minutes. They'll pack these things up. The Fed will take over the processing plant here, keep them alive. If we're lucky, these will lead us to any more covert cells these guys have set up in the country. You *do* understand this is a national security matter. These *are not* aliens. This didn't happen."

The Fed and its passion for secrets. It was becoming difficult to remain conscious. "What about the Zipperheads, and the politicians?"

"The DEA has the Zipperheads. They can have them. The MLI plot was designed to unravel, so we'll let it unravel. We've done extensive computer searches into MLI's background, much more thorough than your hacker friend. These things seeded a money trail that leads back to the CIA. It's going to look to the vids, and everyone else, like this was just another rogue Agency operation—"

Nohar sucked in a breath. "You're not really FBI, are you?"

Isham smiled. It didn't look like a grimace this time. "Only on loan."

"Just let the CIA take the heat for this?"

"That's what it's for. The CIA's designed to take the heat for the NSA, the NRO, and a half-dozen other organizations in the intelligence community. We'll gladly let them fall to the wolves to keep this bottled up. Justice will prosecute a good percentage of Congress, Congress gets to flay open the CIA. Executive hits Legislative, Legislative gets back at the Executive—"

Nohar leaned back on the curved concrete, ignoring the sudden dagger of pain that erupted from his leg. It was just too much effort to stay upright. "Checks and balances, right?"

"The way it works in practice anyway."

"What about NASA's deep-probe project?"

"Congress will scuttle them. The NSA will black-budget them, launch, and eventually, we'll find out where these things come from."

Nohar closed his eyes. It felt like he was losing consciousness. "We're going to do the same thing to them, aren't we?"

"Not my decision . . ."

Figured . . .

Nohar slipped into the darkness.

It was Friday, the 26th of August, and the weather was deigning to cool down a little. That, and it looked to be the first week of August with no rainfall. Nohar had just closed the deal on Manny's house, and he was feeling emotionally exhausted.

He sat down on a box in the center of the empty living room and looked at the comm. He wanted to call Stephie, ask her to go with him. However, he couldn't muster the courage—he'd been avoiding her ever since he made the decision to leave this burg. He knew if she said no, he wouldn't leave. And staying in this town would kill him. Too many memories.

He sat on the box in the middle of Manny's living room, realizing he was going to do to Stephie the same thing Maria had done to him. That decided it. He *was* going to call her.

He had just reached for the comm when someone at the front door rang the call button.

Their timing sucked.

Nohar grabbed a crutch and hoisted himself up to his feet. He was getting good at maneuvering with the cast. He managed to get all the way to the door without bashing it into anything. He didn't bother with the intercom. He just threw the door open.

There she was, carrying a huge handbag, smelling of roses and wood smoke.

Nohar fell into the cliché before he could stop himself. "I was just going to call you."

There was a half-smile on her face. "Oh, you were? I've been looking for you ever since you left the hospital. You moved out of your apartment—"

"Transferred the lease to Angel—"

Stephie nodded and patted him on the shoulder—the left one where the fur had come back in white. "You going to let me in?"

Nohar stepped aside and let her through. She surveyed

the empty living room and sighed. It echoed through the house. "So you're moving out of here, too—how is Angel, anyway?"

"She's lucky rabbits are common. They had skin cultures to match her. The fur on her legs is white now, but she can walk. She got a job."

The concept seemed to shock Stephie. "As what?"

"Cocktail waitress at the *Watership Down*. A bar on Coventry—"

She pulled up a box and they sat down, facing each other.

"So how are you taking things?"

Nohar slapped his cast. "They had to weave some carbon fiber into the tendons, but the cast comes off in a month, and with a few months of exercise—"

She shook her head. "That's not what I mean and you know it. You're still blaming yourself for Manny, aren't you?"

That hit home. "If—"

Stephie put her finger on his lips. "I talked to Manny a lot about you. He was your father for five years, and because of school you ran away to Moreytown and joined a street gang. When your gang got involved with the riots and you found out what your real father was, you ran away from them. Now you're going to run away from this life, right?"

Nohar shook his head. "I can't live here anymore . . ."

"I suppose not. But you aren't going to run away from me. I won't let you."

They sat, looking at each other.

"I suppose not."

She smiled and shook her head. "At least he doesn't object. Well, I got myself a new job, demographics for Nielsen."

Nohar had a sinking feeling. He forced a smile. "Great. Where?"

"Santa Monica."

Nohar was speechless for a moment, and she seemed to enjoy his reaction. "You *knew* I was going to California?"

"'California is a lot more tolerant,'" she quoted.

"Where did you hear that?"

"Those rodents had more than drugs and guns at that motel. The white one left this on the comm." She reached into the overlarge bag and pulled out a ramcard. Nohar noticed the bag kept moving when she took her hand out of it. The bag emitted a slightly familiar smell. "Seems to be a copy of whatever you had on permanent storage on your comm. I *was* going to give this to you when you got out of the hospital. But you slipped out without telling me. So I played it."

Nohar took the card wordlessly.

"That Maria is one stupid cat for walking out on you."

"No, she isn't."

The handbag was still moving. Nohar couldn't hold it in anymore. "What the hell do you have in the bag?"

Stephie broke into a wide grin. "I still remember that line you gave me in the parking garage, about your cat."

Another thing Nohar wanted to forget. He sighed. "Yes?"

Stephie reached in the bag and pulled out a small, gray-and-black tabby kitten and handed it to Nohar. Nohar had to collect himself enough to cup his hands under the little creature. It barely fit on his palm. Nohar watched as it stumbled a little, disoriented, and circled around. Then, finding the new perch satisfactory, it curled up, closed its eyes, and began to purr.

Nohar stared at the little thing in his hands. "Damn it, Stephie. that isn't playing fair."

"I know."

She began scratching the little thing behind the ears.

FEARFUL
SYMMETRIES

Dedication:

This book is dedicated to the Cajun Sushi Hamsters, who saw the first one.

Acknowledgments

I would like to thank the members of the Cleveland SF Writer's workshop who looked over this: John; Jerry; Geoff; Maureen; Charlie; Becky; Mary. I would like to stress that nothing in this book is their fault.

Chapter 1

Nohar Rajasthan stood still, the stand of pines giving him partial cover from the clearing about thirty meters away. His breathing was slow and deep despite the adrenaline that was tightening his perception. He could smell the musk of the deer in the clearing, and from the way the deer stood—taut, alert—Nohar could tell that the animal was beginning to smell a predator in the vicinity.

The bewildered animal had not yet figured out where the smell was coming from. Nohar moved deliberately so that when it knew, the knowledge would be too late to help it.

The wind was in Nohar's face, bringing a light dust of February snow to his fur. He could feel his age in his joints as he raised the bow to be level with his shoulder. His arm was steady despite the ache that shot through his right knee and his left shoulder.

He could feel his pulse, as his aging metabolism sensed the proximity of combat and blood. He sighted through the bow, focusing on the unmoving buck. The scene through the eyepiece had the contrast artificially heightened to compensate for his poor day vision. Nohar placed the crosshairs over a vital spot, and drew back on the bow. A small digital readout in the corner of the eyepiece started reading off the kilos of tension he put on the composite bowstring.

The small green numbers had just crossed three hundred when the buck moved. The movement snapped the animal into focus and Nohar loosed the arrow slightly early.

The shaft plunged deep into the front of the buck's chest. The impact dropped it to its knees and nearly knocked it over. It let out a bellow and struggled to its feet. The wind carried the ferric scent of blood to Nohar.

The smell lit up his nerves like a high-tension wire. The universe shrank down to just him, his prey, and the thirty meters between them. The buck struggled to run, even with its mortal injury. Nohar dropped the bow, springing after the animal.

Nohar's adrenaline-fueled attack closed with the buck before it had reached the edge of the clearing. Like his genetic ancestors, he attacked the neck. He sank his fangs into the soft flesh of the throat, his powerful arms—claws fully extended—crushed the vertebrae, and his one fully functional leg kicked at the buck's abdomen, slicing it open from sternum to groin.

It was dead in less than a minute.

When the buck ceased moving, Nohar rolled off of it, exhausted. He lay next to the body, sucking in breath after burning breath while snow swirled in the pines above him.

In every part of his body, he felt his age. His fifteen-year-old knee injury flared as if he'd just recently torn apart every tendon and ligament. His hands ached with arthritis as the claws slowly tried to retract. The small of his back ached, as if someone was trying to knee him in the spine, right above his tail.

Beneath him, pine needles itched, and were sticking to the blood in his fur.

Over and over, in his mind ran the words, *Too old, way too old.*

When he'd retired to the woods, escaping human and morey alike, hunting wasn't a difficulty. Back then, he'd even occasionally hunted without a bow.

Now, with the bow, he could barely manage it. His forty-year-old body was telling him that his days as a hunter were numbered. Soon he was going to have to either go into town for his food supply or violate the local firearms restrictions.

Doing either was too much like admitting defeat. As far as he was concerned, self-sufficiency was all he had going for him. Someone whose genetic code was engineered for combat, and whose ancestors included Siberian and Bengal tigers, should certainly be able to feed himself.

Nohar winced as the claws in his hands finally retracted. *It'd be easier if the gene-techs didn't always fuck up the hands.*

Nohar's bloody confrontation had lasted less than two minutes, but he lay next to his kill for nearly half an hour. Between that, and the several hours he'd spent lying in wait, it was late afternoon before he tied up the body and started carrying it home.

A year ago he would have hung the meat out in a tree and gone for another kill. Today, though, he felt all of his forty years. Today, he would just return to his cabin, wash up, and sleep.

The mountain snow stopped as he made his way through the pine forest toward the clearing where his cabin was. As the trees thinned, Nohar could catch occasional glimpses of where the Sierra Nevadas merged with the sky. His eyes weren't keen enough to resolve details on the neighboring mountains, but they were a constant, a cloud bank that never moved.

He was so swamped in the aroma of musk, blood, and his own exertion that he was almost in sight of his cabin before he smelled the car. The scent drew him up short. There was strict regulation of vehicles this close to the park, especially in the homestead areas.

Nohar stopped at the base of a bluff that was between him and the cabin. He could smell a human now, which meant that being covered in blood and stinking to high heaven might not have betrayed his presence to the stranger.

Nohar knew it was a stranger, no one he had ever met before. That meant that it was unlikely that it was a ranger. He knew all of the humans that worked the forest around here.

Nohar had been avoiding people for so long that he seriously considered simply waiting out his visitor. Eventually the pink would leave, and he could go back to his life. When the thought made itself concrete, Nohar felt disgusted with himself.

He would deal with the stranger, whoever it was.

He tossed the buck over the bluff, ahead of him. He pulled himself up after it. His shoulder protested, but he swallowed his discomfort. He didn't know who was watching, but there was no reason for him to advertise how difficult this day felt.

The front of Nohar's cabin angled toward the bluff, and his visitor had been sitting on the cinder blocks that made the makeshift front steps. He stood up as Nohar cleared the bluff, took a step forward, and stopped.

The guy got high marks for not shying away. Nohar was old, but he still towered over the man, 260 centimeters worth, and right now his fur was matted with blood. Nohar smiled, but politely, without showing any teeth. "Can I help you?" he asked.

The man did not belong in the woods. He wore a black suit and tie, and his vehicle was a silver Jaguar aircar. The man belonged at a board meeting somewhere. In contrast, Nohar's appearance stopped just short of feral—and then only because of the bow and utility belt he wore.

"Nohar Rajasthan?" The man asked.

"You are?" Nohar asked, picking up his kill. Now that he saw the man, he didn't feel any threat from him. He'd smelled hostility off of a lot of pinks; he wasn't getting any from his man. If anything, Nohar smelled fear—which made sense considering the situation. Precious few pinks ventured into the homestead areas.

As Nohar carried his kill to the back of the cabin, his visitor followed at a careful distance. "My name's Charles Royd. I'm a lawyer from Los Angeles."

Nohar made a noise halfway between a snort and a growl. He didn't like lawyers, and he liked Los Angeles even less. It had been nearly a decade since the National Guard razed almost all the moreau neighborhoods in LA. Nohar had been there when it happened. Ten years was not enough time to wash the taste out of his mouth.

"It's been difficult finding you—"

Nohar nodded. "That's intentional." He hung up his kill on an iron hook attached to the back wall of the cabin.

"I would like to talk with you."

"Come inside, then."

Nohar's cabin was an ancient building made of local wood. There was no electricity, and water came from a rusty hand pump in the corner. The furniture was limited to a bed, a table, a few rough chairs big enough to support Nohar's 300 kilos, and a footlocker. He hung his bow on a peg in the wall and began pumping water into a plastic bucket.

As the handle made screeching protests, Nohar said, "So what does an LA lawyer want with me?"

There was a hesitation in the lawyer's voice as he looked around the sparse room. Nohar didn't prod the man, he simply finished topping off the bucket. Then he brought out a scrub brush and began attacking the blood matted in the fur of his leg. Within a few moments the water had turned the color of rust.

"You're Nohar Rajasthan, the private investigator. You do missing persons work."

From the man's expression, and his confused smell, Nohar could tell that he was having trouble reconciling the rustic surroundings with the moreau he was looking for.

Nohar scrubbed his legs and said, "No."

For a moment he thought to leave it like that and let the crestfallen lawyer leave disappointed. But Nohar knew if he did that, the man would be back. "Once, but not anymore. I'm retired."

The man stepped forward and extended his hand. "I represent a client who wishes to hire you."

Nohar looked from the hand to the man's face, then back again. He didn't take it. He returned to grooming the blood off of his other leg. "I'm retired."

After a moment, the lawyer dropped his hand and said, "Hear me out. My client was adamant that I hire you. I can offer fifty thousand for this job in advance."

Nohar looked up at the man with narrowed eyes. He was starting to distrust him. Pinks bearing large sums of money usually meant trouble. The last time anyone offered him nearly that amount, he'd been beaten, shot, had his best friend killed, and was eventually driven out of his hometown.

"I don't handle human cases."

"This isn't a human case. I'm just an intermediary. My client desperately wants this person found." He took a small folder from his pocket and removed a high-res picture of a feline moreau. "His name is Manuel. He disappeared from his job a week and a half ago." He placed the picture on the rough-hewn table. The picture was obviously from some state or federal ID. Manuel didn't look as if he liked having his picture taken. Nohar didn't reach for the picture, but he did examine it. Broad nose, broader than Nohar's in proportion to the face. The fur was glossy black for the most part, but there were bands of russet in it, sculpting the outlines of a snarl that didn't quite show teeth. The ears were laid back, so Nohar couldn't make out any markings.

"Species?" Nohar asked, though he expected the answer already.

"He's a crossbreed between two large felines."

Mule, he means. Nohar felt a wave of sympathy for the kid in the picture. How old was he—ten, thirteen? Physically mature, but still young enough to take the pain of the world's prejudice personally. Bad enough to be nonhuman and young, but to be a mule as well? That was the worst curse Nohar could wish on anyone, to be an outcast from both worlds, human and nonhuman. The genetics of mules were always a crap shoot. No two moreys had their genes fiddled in quite the same way, and with a mule the engineered and nonengineered chromosomes decided to link up mostly at random. A mule could turn out nearly pink, or—more likely—like a defective beast only slightly out of the jungle. Perhaps worst were the mules that got the engineered body, and whose brain reverted to an animal nature. Manuel looked lucky, humanoid—and the fact he held a job somewhere meant that his intelligence wasn't too adversely affected.

Most moreaus nowadays were born as the result of artificial insemination. Manuel was an exception. Two feline species had merged in him—two parents who probably never expected their union might result in offspring.

In every case, a mule was a minority of one. Even Nohar had the knowledge that there were, somewhere, other tigers descended from the same genetic stock as he. Manuel was different, unique. That uniqueness would forever prevent him from being fully accepted into the moreau community, such as it was.

Almost better to be a frank.

The pink lawyer was still talking. "He was last seen at his job, at the Compton Bensheim Clinic."

There's still a Compton left? Nohar thought.

There was an irony having a mule work at a Bensheim Clinic, where the point was to allow the thousands of moreau species to breed with their own genetic material. There were so many strains that even a couple who looked exactly alike needed genetic testing to see if they could breed true. Nine times out of ten, they couldn't. Two moreaus not only had to have the same genetic ancestors, they had to've been engineered out of the same lot in the same lab. There were probably twenty-five hundred species of moreau rat alone. Add to that the fact that a lot of gene-techs had fiddled with the reproduction instinct in their creations—the idea was to keep a constant supply back during the war—a lot of moreys *had* to breed. It was a problem that the Bensheim Clinics were designed to solve.

From the folder, the lawyer brought out two ramcards and laid them on the table. The little plastic rectangles shimmered rainbow colors, masses of optically-encoded data fracturing the light. He tapped one and said, "This is your fee, to be credited to any account you prefer. The other is a comprehensive data file on Manuel."

"Did I say I'd take the case?"

"Take some time to think it over—"

"Who's trying to hire me?"

"My client has requested anonymity."

Any inclination Nohar had to get involved with the lawyer's offer evaporated at that point. He stared at the man and said quietly, "Leave."

"But—"

"I'm retired," Nohar said with a growl under his voice. "And I don't work for people who hide behind lawyers."

"My client assures me that when you hear the details you'll want to take this job—"

Nohar stood. The scrub brush in his hand sprayed droplets of bloody water across the table and Manuel's picture. "Take your money and leave. Take that sports car and find some Culver City pink who doesn't ask questions."

The man backed up and then reached over, taking the ramcard that was to be Nohar's payment. "I'll take this. But I'm leaving the picture and the file. When you read it, you might change your mind." He put the ramcard back in the folder, and put it away. He then took another shiny card, paper this time, and placed it on the table. "This is my card. Call me if you change your mind."

"I won't."

Nohar stood, towering over the man until he'd retreated from the cabin, and he didn't sit until he heard the fans of the Jaguar aircar engage. As the lawyer flew away, Nohar finally sat. He spared one ironic glance at the ramcard the man had left, the file on Manuel. The thing was worse than useless to Nohar. He didn't have a comm to read the damn thing.

He gave Manuel a last look, wondering why the curve of his dark-furred cheek seemed familiar. Then he returned to the business of washing the blood from his hands.

Chapter 2

Nohar woke up to monochrome night and was instantly alert. He didn't immediately know what had awakened him, but he felt an unease in his gut that he translated into threat. He tensed, unmoving, focusing on what he could perceive.

The wrongness quickly coalesced into a series of rapid realizations. He heard nothing, the forest had fallen into a silence that was unnatural. Something had startled the nearby insects and night birds into quiescence. Large predator, probably human. The second impression came rapidly upon the first, a smell that was alien to the woods. Petroleum-based, it made his nose itch.

The smell had him moving even before the final impression reached his conscious awareness. He rolled off the bed to take cover on the floor even as he realized that the shadow that the front window cast on the wall had acquired a new bulge at the base of the frame, as if someone had gently set something on the sill.

Something that contained a lot of petroleum-based hydrocarbons.

Something that exploded three seconds after Nohar hit the floor.

Nohar hugged the floor, curling up to expose as little of himself to the wash of heat as possible. He felt debris from the window scatter itself on his back like hot coals. He could smell the acrid scent of burning hair, then it became too painful to breathe through his nose.

The moment the explosion was over, he rolled, putting out half a dozen small fires on his back. Adrenaline was already coursing through his veins, awakening ancient programmed combat reflexes. The flames engulfing the ceiling took on an unnatural clarity. They seemed to roll from the front of the cabin like breakers on hell's own ocean.

Nohar heard another explosion. There was little concussion, but he could taste the chemicals in the air. Another firebomb.

The blast from the front window had knocked his bow from the wall. He rolled across the floor, not daring to stand, and grabbed it and the two arrows that hadn't spilled from its attached quiver.

Nohar's cabin had turned into an oven, and he knew that in a few seconds it would become a crematorium. The doors and windows were useless for escape, engulfed in orange fire.

Nohar slammed his fist into the floor. The blow was partly martial art, partly adrenaline, and mostly desperation. Luck was with him. The board under his fist gave with an anemic crack and a puff of dry rot. He dropped the bow and grabbed the boards to either side, pulling up and out with all the strength his aged muscles could manage.

The boards came up with a squeal of protesting nails. Even so, it was almost too late. The air was searing his lungs, and he could smell his fur burning again.

Nohar grabbed the bow and dove through the hole, landing face first in the soft earth under the cabin. There was barely room for him to roll and put out his smoldering fur.

Nohar twisted away from the hole he'd made—he could feel it sucking air from underneath the cabin. He knew he'd only gained himself a few moments. Now that the dry wood of the cabin had caught, it had become a bomb itself. In a minute or two the heat would make the whole building combust into a fireball worse than any of the arsonist's explosions.

Nohar looked around for an escape route. He didn't have much choice. The cabin sat on four cinder-block posts, but the ground was sloped so that the rear and the left sides of the building were too close to the ground for him to wiggle out from. The front of the building was a mass of fire where debris had fallen.

That left one way out. Nohar crawled toward the right side of the building. When he reached the point where he could emerge, his brain finally caught up with events and asked, *Who's done this? Why?*

And, most important to his current survival, *Are they still out there?*

Someone wanted him dead, and if they wanted it badly enough to torch his cabin, they probably wanted him dead enough to have a sniper watch the building for escapees. Luckily for him, the right side of the cabin was the route that offered the most cover. There were less than three meters between him and the lip of the bluff that curved around the clearing in front of his cabin.

It could just as well be thirty if a sniper had a bead on him.

Nohar pulled his bow out in front of him. It was awkward, but the sight had an infrared setting. He looked out at the woods, squinting through the IR noise that the fire was pumping out. Above him, the structure of the cabin groaned, as if it were in pain.

There was someone. A humanoid figure crouched on the crown of the bluff down toward the front of the house. He had a rifle, at the ready, pointed too close to Nohar's location.

Then, above him, Nohar heard the sound of his cabin reaching its flashpoint, a roar that shook the ground beneath him. Nohar had no time for planning, his reflexes took over.

He rolled away from his house, across the three meters of exposure, dropping over the bluff and into the wooded area. He felt dirt spray him as shots from the woods missed him, thudding into the ground.

Even in the woods, he was way too exposed. The exploding fire lit everything like a spotlight and the bluff's shadow was still rosily lit by reflected light.

He rose with an arrow fully taut in the bow. In a single fluid motion, he raised the bow to position, loosed the arrow, and began a scramble along the bluff toward the sniper's position.

His action assumed that his arrow would find the gunman.

The assumption was valid.

He heard other gunshots, but none connected with him. They were coming from places that weren't covering his escape route, and the distraction of the cabin blowing up gave him a little leeway as he ran along the cover of the bluff.

He landed next to the rifleman. The man had taken a header backward after being struck by the arrow. An arm and a leg were bent at ugly angles. The rifle had spilled another four or five meters down the slope.

Nohar stopped next to him. He was human, dressed in black combat gear. He'd been wearing night-vision equipment that the fall had knocked askew. He wore an armored vest, from which Nohar's arrow pointed up at the sky. While the armor might have prevented impalement, the man didn't seem much better off. He was gasping for breath, and his lips were flecked with blood.

Nohar bent over the man, intending to shake some answers from him, find out why this attack was happening. But a look at the man's face told Nohar it was hopeless. The man's eyes didn't track, and the pupils were fixed. There was no reaction when Nohar leaned over him.

"Shit," Nohar whispered, the first time he'd spoken since awakening. The word tasted like smoke.

Even as he bent over his would-be assassin, Nohar began sensing movement in the woods. They moved quietly, but not quietly enough. Whatever was going on wasn't over yet.

Nohar dropped his bow and sidestepped to pick up the fallen man's rifle. It wasn't designed for hands his size, but it was manageable. He kept moving, quietly and low to the ground.

They were getting too close. The first time he'd had surprise going for him. Now, if these bastards got a clean shot at him, he was dead. He could hear them in front of him, closing. Between the light coming from the fire, and these guys' night-vision equipment, Nohar gave it a minute or less before someone had that clean shot.

Nohar put a tree between him and the sounds, putting his back to it. He checked the rifle over. It was a Colt Special Operations rifle—Nohar had heard the thing called the "Black Widow." It was American military issue, designed for covert operations. It was matte black, light, fired caseless ten-millimeter rifle ammo. It was made mostly of composite carbon fiber, and carried a combination silencer/flash suppressor that was built into a barrel that was almost as thick as the body of the gun. Even with the silencer, its shots could punch through the bad guy's body armor as if it were balsa wood.

It had a digital scope with a night-vision setting. Nohar adjusted the sight, and flipped the Widow from single-shot to full auto.

He took a deep breath, and when he felt ready, he dove, flattening upon a bed of pine needles as he brought the rifle to bear.

Someone saw something, because Nohar could hear bullets whizzing through the trees above him. The silencer-muffled gunshots sounded like a fist slamming into wet concrete.

There were two of them, their motion—lit by the fire—was unmistakable to Nohar's eye. Despite the flash suppressors, to the scope, every shot was an obvious flare. Nohar let go with two bursts.

He got up and ran toward the hole he'd made in the encircling enemy. He stayed low, using as much of the cover as he could. He avoided firing again because any more shots would be a signal flare to the Bad Guys, and he could hear the others closing on his location.

The world became a blood-tinted chaos as his engineered reflexes took over. Somehow he made it through the hole before the others closed on him. He jumped over the corpse of one human in a commando outfit and didn't pause.

He could feel the presence of others in the woods around him, but he couldn't stop to determine where they were. Instinct told him that if he ever stopped moving he was dead. He dodged tree after tree as the slope steepened on its way downward.

The forest floor was covered with pine needles that slid as he ran. Soon the slope was difficult enough that every third step was a near stumble down the side of the hill. In the distance he heard the humans, their pretense at silence gone. He heard their radios, their running steps through the woods, and eventually he heard the fans and smelled the ozone exhaust of an aircar somewhere above.

The aircar was unlit, and eventually it left Nohar's hearing. If he was lucky, that meant that the canopy was too thick for whatever video equipment that was installed on it.

He ran for miles down the mountain, adrenaline fueling exertion far beyond what his body should have to endure. It was shortly after the aircar left his awareness that Nohar realized that he no longer felt the pursuit of the heavily armed humans.

He slowed, the panic fueling his muscles draining away with every step. The beast the genetic engineers had designed into him, the instinctual combat machine, confused his sense of time; minutes could be hours, or vice versa. It was sinking into him that what had seemed like a few minutes of panicked escape had been a run down the side of the mountain. The sky above him was lightening, and the slope was flattening out.

He could feel it in every muscle in his body. He looked at the weapon in his hand, the rifle he'd taken. It was empty. Somewhere during his escape he'd emptied the thing. He didn't quite remember, the whole episode was a blood-tinged blur in his memory.

Who the hell are these people? Nohar thought. *What the hell do they want with me?*

Empty, the Widow was useless to him, so when he passed a fairly deep creek, he ditched it.

Nohar stumbled down the rest of the way to the highway. He didn't leave the cover of the woods when he finally reached the roadway; a naked moreau would attract too much unwanted attention. Enough people were giving him that kind of attention.

After dawn had passed, and Nohar was walking in full daylight, he came in sight of a small rest stop off of the highway. There was little there but a scenic overlook and a set of restrooms, but what attracted Nohar's attention was a public comm box.

He crouched in the woods across the highway from the rest stop. There was one blue Plymouth Ariel minivan sitting in the parking lot. Nohar stayed crouching, fatigue dripping from every pore of his body. Every muscle ached, all the way down to the base of his tail. He felt as if all his muscles had been torn off of his body and then reattached at random.

Staying awake was a major effort, but he kept his attention focused on the little family van. Eventually its little family returned. Two adults and a pair of kids. As he watched them, Nohar felt an irrational wave of enmity toward them, the two middle-class pinks and their children.

The parents were probably his age, but with nearly half their lives in front of them. Their kids, happy, smiling, safe. . . .

Nohar felt sick watching them, sicker at his own reaction.

Eventually the Plymouth and its family drove off, leaving the rest stop deserted. Once the car had disappeared around a bend in the road, Nohar dashed across the street to the comm box.

He hoped Stephie was still willing to talk to him.

Chapter 3

The comm box was in working order, which was a plus. It was off to the side of the rest area, boxed in what tried to look like a tiny log cabin with one side open to the outside. The roof was nearly half a meter shorter than he was. There was a bench, but it was way too narrow. Nohar had to crouch, half outside, putting more strain on his bad knee.

He spent ten minutes keying in old account numbers, hoping they were still valid. Most belched out error messages at him, and one telcomm company that he used to use seemed to have gone out of business.

In the end he had to try calling collect and hope that his ex-wife would accept the charges.

The screen fuzzed and went blank after he keyed in Stephie's old apartment. The blackness lasted a long time, and Nohar began to fear that either Stephie had seen his face on her comm and disconnected, or that she'd moved and some poor pink was looking at the ragged moreau on their screen wondering what the hell was going on.

After a few long moments, Stephie's face came on the comm. Nohar saw an office in the background, and he realized that the call had been forwarded. It must be a weekday.

"Nohar?" Her lips mouthed the words almost soundlessly. She was still the same person he remembered. The same golden skin, same lithe neck, same raven hair.

Nohar realized he must look like hell. "I've got a problem," Nohar said, "Do you still have the keys to my locker?"

Anything that might have been tenderness leaked out of Stephie's expression. "Still as curt as ever, aren't you?"

"Something happened—"

"God forbid you just want to talk to me."

"You wanted me to leave," Nohar said quietly.

They stared at each other through the video screen for a few long moments. Nohar thought he saw her green eyes moisten, but it could have been a trick of the light.

"Seven years," she said finally. "That's a long time."

"I know."

Stephie looked at him and shook her head as if she was disgusted with herself. "Of course I still have it. I still have your damn cat. What happened to you? You look like hell."

"Someone tried to kill me."

"I wonder why." After a pause, "I suppose you don't have any way back to the city . . . ?"

Standing, partially hidden at the edge of the scenic overlook, Nohar began to realize exactly how alone he was. What would he have done if Stephie hadn't been willing to help him? She had all the right in the world to tell him to fuck off.

A part of his mind, the same part that hunted in the mountains above him, told him that he would have managed, he was a survivor. There was another part of him, the part that had married a woman named Stephanie Weir, which seemed ominously silent on the subject.

It took two hours for her to arrive. There were two false alarms during that time. One when an old Antaeus started turning into the rest area, and when Nohar stepped out of the woods, it accelerated out of the lot leaving the smell of rubber behind it. The other when an old pickup truck, the back filled with morey rodents, the cab belching Spanish music, stopped by long enough for half a dozen rats to gather at the rail and piss over the side of the overlook. The truck left a dozen empty beer bulbs in its wake.

Stephie finally drove up in a metallic-gray Mercedes. The windows were tinted, so Nohar didn't know it was her until the car rolled to a stop and she opened the door.

When he saw her standing next to the new car, he felt an impulse to stay hidden. He ignored it and stepped around, in sight of the parking lot. As soon as she saw him, standing there naked, she shook her head and muttered, "I *knew* it."

As he walked up, Stephie reached in and tossed him a bundle.

Nohar caught it as Stephie said, "I don't know what it is with you and clothes, but you're going to put those on before you get in my car."

The bundle was a pair of sweat pants and a matching sweater. The sweater had the logo of the Earthquakes, the Frisco morey-league football team. Nohar was surprised to find the sweats cut for a morey, and one his size. The pants even accommodated his tail and digitigrade feet.

The clothes still had the receipt tags on them. Nohar tore them off with his index claw.

"Come on," Stephie said. She looked impatient. "I'd like to get this done and get back to work."

Nohar nodded and walked around to the other side of the Mercedes. He touched the gray surface, seeing the reflection of his hand as if it were some dim pool. "Nice car," he said.

"Yes, damn it," she said. "I did manage to get a life for myself after you left."

After you asked me to leave. Nohar resisted the urge to voice the thought.

The door opened for him and he slipped into the passenger seat. There was a hydraulic whine as built-in motors began adjusting the seat to his weight and height. It actually accommodated him without making him hunch over his knees.

Stephie slipped back into the car and slammed the door. She slid a cardkey into the dash and the windshield lit up with a soft green headsup display overlay on the scene outside.

Nohar was silent for a while as she drove the car back out on the road. It had been a long time since Nohar had been in any vehicle. He had never been claustrophobic. But there seemed to be a dull fear in his gut, now that he was thrust back into the world he left seven years ago.

He didn't know if it was the Mercedes, or the fact that Stephie's familiar smoky smell was dredging up unpleasant memories.

"What do you do now?" Nohar asked.

She stared at the windshield, avoiding any eye contact with him. "I work for Pacific Rim Media." On the windshield, lines of green light sketched their speed, the charge in the engine, and the route they were traveling. Nohar looked at Stephie's profile and realized that she didn't want to talk anymore. They fell into a sullen silence.

She pulled up next to a small warehouselike structure on the edge of what used to be an airport. She popped the locks, tossed him a cardkey, and said, "Get out."

Nohar took the key and slid out of the car. The passenger seat underwent another series of hydraulic gyrations while it settled into its default configuration.

Something made Nohar ask, "Why?"

She looked at him and he could smell a cold anger wafting up from her. "Why bother with you at all, you mean?"

Nohar nodded.

"Because I was naive enough to think seeing you might help me get over it. I was wrong." She pulled the car door shut with a slam. "I don't think we'll see each other again," Nohar heard her say through the door. He didn't know if she intended him to hear it.

The Mercedes pulled away, leaving him across the street from the dull cinder-block complex.

A dented, rusty sign stood above the front gate, saying "Saf-Stor." It sported at least five bullet holes. The gate was rusty chain-link and opened into a parking lot of cracked, weedy asphalt. A dull-gray metal box stood next to the gate, while above it a dented security camera panned across the empty driveway.

Nohar slid the cardkey into the dented box and hoped that both the reader and the card still worked. The reader made a grinding noise and spat out his card. After a few seconds, the gate began sliding aside for him.

When he stepped through, ducking under a bar that said "Clearance 2.5 Meters," a buzzer sounded. As he crossed the path of an electric eye, the gate began rattling shut behind him.

Saf-Stor wasn't the epitome of security storage lockers, but it had allowed long-term storage and had been willing to do business with him. The latter was always a rarity, no matter how enlightened things were supposed to be.

The place was fully automated, and from the empty parking lot, he was the only one here. He looked back through the chain-link and out at the decrepit turn-of-the-century neighborhood. The streets were lined with boarded-up storefronts, many with unrepaired earthquake or fire damage. The only movement came from the cars shooting by on the street between him and the buildings. The only noise was the electric whine of the motors as they passed by.

That was Los Angeles, an empty shell populated by automobiles.

Nohar passed a series of outbuildings, video cameras tracking him from every corner. The buildings were low, one-story cinder-block structures that smelled of concrete dust, stagnant water, and mildew. On each one, two opposing sides held ranks of rolling steel doors; the remaining walls were covered by huge painted letters, black against flaking yellow—A through G.

Nohar's locker was in E.

It had been dry lately, and each step Nohar took kicked dust off the broken asphalt and deposited grit under the claws of his feet. He hadn't worn shoes in ages, but the city made him want some.

Nohar stopped in front of building E, identical to its siblings except for the painted wall, and looked for his locker. It was four doors down. The seams of the steel door had rusted, little trails of rust descended from every bolt. At its base, small piles of windblown debris had gathered against the frame. It looked as if the door hadn't been opened in years.

It hadn't. Nohar had not come here since he and Stephie had separated. In here was everything else he had left behind. His entire material world.

He slid the card into a box next to the door. This one sounded worse than the one by the entrance. This time it didn't spit out Nohar's key.

Above the door, an old grime-covered light flashed red. Inside, Nohar could hear the strain of a motor, and smell electricity and burned insulation. The door began to shake as the motor tried to pull it open. Nohar could hear the tension in the mechanism, until something gave way with the sound of shearing metal. The door shot up about a meter and a half and stuck there. Nohar could hear the motor inside suddenly rev and he heard the sound of a chain striking something.

The motor stopped running, and the grime-streaked light changed from red to green. The box spat Nohar's card back.

The door stayed frozen in place. Nohar shook his head and ducked under it and into the darkness beyond.

The place smelled of rotting paper and rat droppings — thankfully, nonengineered rats. Over all was the smell of scorched machinery. Nohar could hear the ticking of overheated metal.

He fumbled around for a light switch in the dark, and after a few minutes the fluorescents above came on with a buzz. The first thing Nohar noticed was the drive-chain for the door. It dangled from the ceiling, still swinging gently back and forth. The links looked fused together, and when Nohar reached to stop its swinging, it was still warm to the touch.

Nohar shook his head again and looked over the locker. It was a near-cubical room of unpainted cinder block, a bit larger than three meters square. The ceiling was corrugated steel, from which a half-dozen unshaded, fly-specked fluorescents dangled. Half of them were lit, and half of those were flickering.

Wire shelves ran from floor to ceiling on three walls. The shelves held stacks of boxes and a few suitcases. In the center of the floor, three filing cabinets and an old comm unit stood sentinel over a squat, black fire safe.

Neglect had taken its toll. A whole stack of boxes had collapsed off of one of the rear shelves, and rats had nested in the spilled clothes and papers. Leaks in that side of the roof had stained most of the boxes in that corner of the room, and the smell made Nohar write off that corner entirely.

Nohar felt unmoved looking at the damage. Clothing and records from his years as a PI. Nothing truly important. It was as if the things here weren't really his.

He walked over to the wall opposite the one with the leak and started peeling boxes open. He needed some changes of clothes. If he was going to deal with the pink world again, he needed some protective coloration. He found an old military surplus duffel bag and began throwing things into it. Two salvageable changes of clothes and one suit went into it.

In other boxes he dug out some old equipment. He recovered an expensive set of binoculars with a built-in digital camera. They needed recharging. He also uncovered his clunky palmtop comm, which needed recharging and its account renewed.

Then he keyed in the combination of his fire safe. It opened with a sucking sound as the air pressure equalized. He pulled out a leather wallet that lay on top of everything. He checked it. It held a half-dozen ramcards, a few that would still have money on them. There was also about three hundred in cash.

Beneath the wallet, still in its holster, was Nohar's Vindhya 12-millimeter. Nohar drew the automatic out of the holster, cleared it, and checked the action. It was metal and composite ceramics, all with a utilitarian gray finish. Deadly, efficient, and it still worked perfectly.

Nohar looked at the 70-centimeter-long barrel, and felt a premonition that something nasty was going to happen.

He made sure that the Vind was fully loaded before he put on the shoulder holster over the sweater Stephie had given him. He threw on a red wind-breaker—stiff with age but baggy enough to hide the gun from casual inspection—then he filled his pockets with every magazine that was in the safe.

He put on a pair of old stale sneakers, and left, the broken door hanging open on his past.

Chapter 4

Nohar had to call three taxi companies before he found one that would service the neighborhood he was in. After nearly half an hour, a black-and-white van rolled to a stop next to the public comm Nohar'd been using. It was a dented Chrysler Aerobus that ran on remote.

Nohar stepped inside as the door opened for him. A

camera watched him from behind a metal mesh screen. The floor was littered with disposable air-hypos, beer bulbs, and used condoms. It smelled like the lid of a garbage can.

Nohar felt claustrophobic again as the door shut on the cab.

A tinny-sounding speaker in the ceiling said, "State your destination clearly," in a half-dozen different languages.

Nohar gave it the name of an intersection in Compton. He ran one of his cards through the deposit slot before the cab could jabber any further to him. Compton was a long ride down the clogged LA freeways, but Compton was morey territory, and he knew the area. At least he *had* known it, seven years ago. He was confident enough that he could find a motel to hole up in while he tried to piece together what had happened.

The cab drove south down the Hollywood and Harbor Freeways, never managing more than forty klicks an hour for all the traffic. Nohar had a lot of time to sit in the wretched-smelling taxi and look out at the LA skyline. There wasn't much for him to see; it was all a blur of glass and concrete at the extremity of his vision. All he really could focus on was the movement of maniac-driven cars cutting off the taxi, and the debris that collected in the breakdown lanes.

He smelled Compton before he reached it. It was a smoky smell of fires long since dead. It drifted through the taxi's air filters—if it had any—as if they weren't there, overwhelming the ozone smell of the traffic around him.

Compton was in the southern portion of a swath of destruction the National Guard had cut through the second-largest Moreytown in the United States. The riots had burned through a diagonal strip of the Greater Los Angeles area, extending from Compton through to East LA. At one point the area had been devastated worse than the Bronx.

As the cab took the off ramp, the first thing that Nohar noticed were the vacant lots. There were hundreds of them. Places where the city, or the National Guard, had bulldozed the abandoned buildings and spread dirt over the rubble. Tawny grass grew high in ragged patches throughout the lots, and the ground was uneven where erosion had uncovered the remains of the buried wreckage. Each lot was littered with trash and abandoned vehicles, as if the town had become one huge landfill.

The autocab stopped at the intersection of Rosecrans and Alameda, the door opening before Nohar realized that he had reached his destination.

He stepped out on the broken concrete. Behind him, the cab raced off as if it didn't like the neighborhood. Nohar started walking south on Alameda, following the overgrown set of train tracks.

Other moreys walked by, usually on the other side of the street. Mostly young-looking rodents who talked to each other in a combined Spanish-English slang that Nohar couldn't understand. Many of them gave him looks that seemed to say, "You don't belong here."

They were the shortest lived of all the morey breeds. In the seven years Nohar had been in his self-imposed exile, two generations of rats had been born and reached maturity. They had been designed for fast reproduction, and it was only the short life span that kept the engineered *Rattis* from overwhelming every other species.

When they stared at Nohar, he felt something alien. There was a gulf behind the glossy blackness of their eyes that had more than species behind it. Most moreys had been engineered around the same time, in the decades surrounding the Pan-Asian War. Nohar himself was only a single generation removed from the labs. The rats who walked around him, staring and chattering high-speed Spanish, were generations removed from the labs in Central and South America where their kind had been born. In Nohar's lifetime, ten generations of rats had come, and mostly gone.

The rats weren't the only moreys out on the streets, though they were the most numerous. There were other South American breeds, rabbits and other rodents that were harder to identify. There were a few canines, and one or two felines, though none as large as Nohar.

In fact, Nohar stood out in Compton as badly as he would have in Culver City. He towered over everyone else, and even if that hadn't been the case, his dress marked him as an outsider. Everyone else on the street here seemed to have adopted the same dress, almost like a uniform. They wore blousy pants with large vertical slashes through the material, leaving them so much strips of cloth. If they wore anything on top, it was little more than an abbreviated vest. Maybe they would wear a silk scarf or bandanna around the neck.

The clothing was in every material Nohar could think of, from denim to polyester, but the style was almost universal. He saw a few other moreys wearing other things, but they looked as out of place as he did.

One thing made him agree with the rats' accusing stares, agree he didn't belong here anymore—he thought the clothes looked ridiculous.

Nohar found a motel. Its sign was rusted, the neon smelled of a short circuit, and the parking lot was weed-shot and had one rusted hulk of a vehicle that seemed to have been resident ever since they stopped using petroleum.

Nohar ducked in one graffiti-swathed door and stepped up to the desk. The musk smell of a dozen species layered the lobby, making it an easy guess what the rooms here were used for. There wasn't anyone there. Nohar dropped his bag and leaned on the desk. There was a button screwed to the desktop and Nohar pressed it. Deep in the bowels of the building, he heard a buzzer go off.

He scanned the place while he waited. The area behind the desk was a narrow mirror of the lobby. Rusty acoustical tile, scab-colored carpet, and plastic plants that smelled of dust. One thing on the desk caught Nohar's attention and made him feel more of an outsider than ever.

A box of condoms sat on the desk with a little sticker saying "$2.80 ea." The condoms weren't that noticeable at first, and with his bad vision he would have missed the crucial part if he wasn't leaning over them.

They weren't the regular pink-designed condoms, but half a dozen varieties, each color-coded and labeled with a two-letter code. Under the box, attached to the desk beneath a sheet of plastic, a large index listed the species the codes went with. Blue went with mostly canines, red went with rodents—in particular, a "Blue AX" would fit a Qandahar Afghani, though Nohar doubted that any of that particular attack strain would have use for a condom.

Then again, he never had either. Almost all morey relationships were sterile unless you found a mate of *exactly* the same species. Mules, while undesirable, were too rare for most of Nohar's contemporaries to worry about. Looking at the box, Nohar wondered about species-jumping diseases.

"Looking for a little party, are we, good sir?" The voice drifted in on the odor of curry and incense. Nohar looked up and saw a morey of a kind he'd never seen before. That was enough to give him pause.

He had a short muzzle, and wide golden eyes. His limbs were long and thin, the fingers even longer. He wore a kimono that hung loosely on his body, as if he was only a wide-eyed head propped up on a stick. His sinuous movement and long fingers made him think of an old friend named Manny—

Nohar pushed the thought away. "I want a room," he said.

"Good, yes." He hissed the words. "I can provide you with any manner of companionship."

Nohar shook his head. "Just a room, and a bed for the night."

The manager nodded, and it seemed that his head nodded around those huge golden eyes, whose gaze remained fixed on him. Nohar suspected that he was looking at someone whose ancestors were intended for night recon work. "This is fine, and any time of night you change your mind—"

"I'll be sure to call you," Nohar said.

"Yes." The manager held out a hand that was longer than Nohar's. Nohar fished the cash out of his wallet and paid for the room. The manager did not complain about the cash, and didn't ask him for an ID.

"Room 300," he told Nohar, sliding a cardkey across the desk. Nohar turned to go and he heard the manager say, "Rajasthan?"

Nohar stopped, frozen at the mention of his name. He looked over his shoulder, suddenly nervous. "What?"

"Yes, I see, you are Rajasthan '20 or maybe '23." He held out something. Nohar took it. It was a yellow foil wrapper with the letters XT on it. "The only one of those left, you see. On the house. Don't want you contracting the Drips, do we?"

Nohar nodded. He felt more out of place than ever. Not just the condom, or the fact that he'd never heard of "The Drips," but the fact that he was one of a generation named for his species. He knew that his name, by itself, was enough to mark him as from another age.

He put the condom in his wallet and walked out to his room.

Behind him, the manager said, "You call me when you want some diversion, yes?"

Room 300 was a dull gray anonymous hole at the opposite end of the broken parking lot. When Nohar closed the door behind him, he collapsed on a bed that was much too small for him and felt fatigue and pain drip from every pore. It felt as if he had just run down a whole herd of deer by himself, without the bow.

His mind was awake and alert, but every muscle in his body screamed fatigue. He'd been able to hold off the crash long enough to get somewhere relatively safe, but now he paid for it. He stayed immobile, panting, staring at his collapsed body in the mirror on the ceiling. The reflection resembled a crime-scene holo, with him as the shooting victim.

Staring into his own green eyes, it came home to him how close to death he'd been this morning. He had been shot at before, and it wasn't even the first time he had been that close to an explosion. But something about the attack gave him a sick feeling of his own mortality.

"Age . . ." he whispered to himself between burning breaths.

Who wanted him dead? The only answers that came were that they were human, and well-equipped, and they weren't cops. Why they wanted him dead was easier—it had been triggered by the lawyer's visit. There was absolutely nothing else in his last seven years that Nohar believed could have sparked anyone's interest.

The attack had to be related to Charles Royd's visit, and the job he'd pitched. But Nohar couldn't figure out if the attack was because he'd refused the job, or because the attackers thought he'd taken it.

Nohar thought of the picture of Manuel and the ramcard that had burned in the fire. Right now he wished he knew what was on that ramcard. He was going to have to track down Royd and find out who he was working for, and why. . . .

After a half hour lying still on the bed, Nohar began to snore.

Nohar awoke with a start.

The light had gone from the windows, leaving the room in monochrome darkness. The room stank of his own left-over exertion. What parts of his body didn't ache, itched. Nohar sat up slowly, annoyed at himself for falling asleep. Even though his body was designed to grant him short bursts of supernormal activity, the cost was a deep lethargy. Nohar knew he must have slept for hours, and he *still* felt tired.

Old pain from his bad knee and shoulder prodded him awake the rest of the way. Sitting on the edge of the bed, he massaged his right knee and thought of exactly what it was he was going to do.

His cabin had been burned to the ground. The cabin and the small plot of land had been part of a government home-stead grant, an attempt to de-urbanize the moreau popula-tion after the riots. It had cost him nothing, and he never had any insurance on the building. He'd never be able to afford to rebuild.

Even if he found out who had tried to kill him, he had nothing left. He'd been four years on the waiting list for that cabin, and he probably didn't have another four years.

Part of the cheap wooden bed frame gave under his hand. His fingers ached with his claws extending to bite the wood.

Anger began burning in his gut, all of it focused on Royd. It was the pink lawyer's fault, that was a certainty. Whatever the end reason was for the attack on him, Nohar knew that it would never have happened if that human bastard had just left him alone.

After a lifetime of dreams and desires, that was the only one that remained: to be left alone. Royd had taken that away from him.

Royd was going to pay for that.

Chapter 5

Nohar plugged in the palmtop comm he'd liberated from his locker, and the binocular camera, letting them charge while he washed himself off in this place's excuse for a bathroom. Nohar could only do a halfassed job of washing himself off, and when he was done, he could still smell Los Angeles in his fur.

When he came out of the bathroom, his comm was glowing at the head of the bed. The motel had a comm setup, but Nohar suspected that it charged by the minute, and probably didn't have an outside line.

His comm supposedly had a lifetime telcomm usage attached to it that billed one of his accounts monthly for the time he spent on-line. He hoped that the telcomm account was still good.

He sat on the bed, fur still drying, and picked up the little device. He hadn't touched it in years, and it showed. There was an ugly violet tint to the screen, and the letters on the boot screen carried ghosts of themselves on their backs.

He extended a claw and tapped the screen a few times, pulling down menus and finally grabbing a city directory. The lawyer had done a good job of keeping his home address unlisted, but it wasn't difficult to find his office. It was in Beverly Hills.

Nohar snorted. What was this guy doing talking to him? The guy probably made more an hour than Nohar had seen in the past three years.

Charles Royd's home address was supposed to be unlisted. All that meant was that Nohar had to spend half an hour finessing the database—and half that time was spent refamiliarizing himself with what he was doing. Royd wasn't in the public city directory, but he was in the records of every place from the FAA, for that aircar, to the Department of Water and Power. Given his name, and the make of car, it was child's play to lift his address from his vehicle registration.

Beverly Hills again.

Nohar shook his head. Even though Royd had been driving an expensive aircar, Nohar had him pegged as small-time. Mostly because Royd was dealing with moreaus, and only small-timers dealt with moreaus. Back in his cabin, Nohar had been as small-time as he could get.

Nohar keyed the screen until he got a too-purple GTE test pattern, and tried to place a call through to Royd's house. Royd's comm picked up instead, and asked for a message. Nohar disconnected before it was finished asking. He looked out the louvered windows of the motel, and saw the first rose glow of dawn filtering through the dust.

Royd might be making an early day of it. It was just after seven.

Nohar keyed in Royd's office.

Again he got the comm asking for his voice-mail.

Royd could be on the comm with someone else. Nohar didn't want to leave a message, though. Nohar wanted to see Royd's eyes when he called him. If Royd was behind the attack, he would give something away the first time he saw Nohar again. That was the theory anyway.

Nohar spent the next few minutes doing a trick that an old hacker friend had taught him. He built a little script program into his comm's memory to keep calling Royd's numbers and to alert Nohar when something other than a comm answered the line.

That accomplished, he needed a car. There wasn't any way to exist in Los Angeles without a groundcar at the least. While he waited for contact from Royd, he started calling rental agencies.

There weren't any rental agencies in the area, and getting a rental car delivered to Compton was like trying to invite some deer for dinner at his cabin. Nohar eventually had to settle for a little no-name rental company that charged an exorbitant delivery fee and insisted on three times the normal liability insurance.

Nohar figured he had to get to Royd in person. He got himself ready, grooming himself and putting on the old suit he had liberated from his locker. The suit was conservative, black, and itched like hell.

He looked even more out of his element now. But he hoped that he was ready for a trip into the pinkest part of Los Angeles.

He was dressed by the time the car showed up. His comm had yet to get through to Royd.

He heard the horn blare a few times. Nohar took the gun, the comm, and the binoculars and went out to the waiting car. He walked out and saw a nervous-looking pink looking back and forth as he reached in the driver's side and laid on the horn. He stopped when he saw Nohar come out of the motel.

The guy stared at Nohar as he walked up and held out his hand.

He kept staring.

"Keys?" Nohar asked.

The guy shook his head, as if to clear it. "Mr. Rajasthan?"

"Who else?"

He seemed too young to Nohar, barely half his own age. That seemed even younger on a human. He was blond, tan, and smelled as if he expected to die. He handed a cardkey to Nohar. His hand was shaking.

Nohar felt sorry for the guy. "You need a ride back?"

He shook his head vigorously and pointed his thumb back to the street, where a sleek-looking Chrysler Tempest idled by the mouth of the motel's parking lot. Even the car gave the impression that it would spring into a hasty retreat at any moment.

Nohar looked at the waiting car. "Better go, then."

The kid nodded and almost ran back to the waiting Tempest.

Nohar looked at the car he had rented, and quietly sighed. A Tempest it wasn't. The car was an old GM Maduro sedan—which would have been a luxury car five years ago. But the vehicle showed its age with a dented body, threadbare interior, and the smell of decaying ceramic inductors.

Probably the worst part of it, aside from the smell, was the fact that it had been repainted a matte-finish lime green. Nohar thought it the color of dried phlegm.

Fortunately he'd called for a large car, and that's what he

got. It took him a few tries to force the driver's door open, but he managed to slip inside. He pushed his seat all the way back, almost off the rails, so he could drive comfortably.

It took a few more times to close the door. And a few more to disentangle himself from the too-tight automatic safety belt that tried to strangle him. Eventually, he was on his way.

The comm in his pocket had yet to contact Royd.

Rush hour was just starting, and it took Nohar nearly an hour to drive through to Wilshire Boulevard. All the time he had a death grip on the steering wheel. The traffic got to him, the traffic and the feeling that he was sinking in a quicksand of urban landscape. He felt trapped.

He tried to get some music on the Maduro's comm, but the speakers were shot. So he sat behind the crawling traffic in silence, the news feed scrolling across the screen between the two front seats.

The major news item was the launching of the *America*. It had spent nearly twelve months in transit past Jupiter's orbit, and it had just test-fired the main drive within the past few days. In a few more weeks it would start a twenty-five-year journey to Tau Ceti. The news made a lot of the fact that the crew of the *America* had a high percentage of moreaus.

Getting their trash off the planet, Nohar thought.

The sad thing about the *America* was that the Americans had precious little to do with it. It was all a U.N. project now, and had been since the first completed ship, the *Pacific,* was taken over by Japanese Nationalist terrorists. That takeover was the last media news event that Nohar remembered being aware of, back in '63, just before he exiled himself.

Back then, the manned interstellar project was run by VanDyne International and the U.S. Government. Since then, the U.N. had taken over all seven starships, finished construction on four, and launched three. *Pacific* was halfway to Alpha Centauri, *Atlantic* was heading toward Sirius, and *Europa* was on its way to Procyon.

A lot had happened in seven years.

Nohar wondered what it would be like to be on one of those ships. Strapped in a can going half the speed of light.

The next story that Nohar noticed scrolling across the

screen was about the alien containment facility on Alcatraz.
It caught Nohar's eye during a spasm of paralysis in the
traffic. He caught the words ". . . search for survivors . . ."
and pressed the "back" button on the screen.

Nohar shook his head as the story replayed.

Someone had blown up the dome on Alcatraz. The place
had been leveled, destroying the entire habitat. The explosion had killed off a good fraction of the alien population
of the dome, and nearly a hundred of the scientists that
studied the aliens. That had been the single repository of all
the extraterrestrials on the planet, if the government and
the U.N. were to be believed.

A car honked at him, and Nohar shut the news feed off.

He had met an alien once—soft and blubbery, like half-
formed, bad-smelling, white Jello. They didn't think like humans, and they were inscrutably hostile. They'd been at war
with Earth, on this planet, for years before anyone caught
on. Nohar had been one of the first few to catch on, but it
got him precious little.

Nohar suspected that the starships were military mis-
sions, whatever the U.N. said about exploration and the
broadening of humanity's horizons.

Probably some moreau infantry would have their horizons broadened, too—just like their ancestors had in Asia,
getting their guts blown out in a war the humans were running.

Nohar followed Wilshire up to a point just a few blocks
short of Santa Monica, then turned north. In a few blocks
he came to Royd's office, a new polished building set back
from the street. The place was gated, but the gate hung open
on a driveway that tried to look like gravel.

The Asian influence on the structure wasn't subtle at all.
The drive was flanked by statues of Oriental lions—or drag-
ons, they were too stylized for Nohar to tell—and the small
grounds were landscaped into stasis, as if every plant was as
much inanimate sculpture as the lions.

The building itself was a set of green marble cubes, the
roof turned up at the corners to suggest a pagoda. Nohar
pulled the Maduro into the parking lot. It looked out of
place between a BMW and a Mercedes. The cars were all
late-model luxury cars, and all of them seemed to be pastel

shades of red, green, or blue. Nohar felt the same way looking at the cars as he did when he looked at the clothing on
the streets in Compton—here was the style for this year,
and he felt it looked ridiculous.

The place even smells contrived, Nohar thought as he
stepped out of the car. He stood there a moment, looking at
the building, noticing the too-heavy scent of flowers, and
thought of security that was in place. There had to be cameras around here, and the garden smell could be covering
the more subtle smells of the guards themselves.

No reason to make anyone more nervous than they had
to be. Nohar leaned back into the Maduro, slipped the Vind
out of its holster, and slid it under the passenger seat.

Nohar straightened his tie and walked up to the front of
the building. He noticed a metal detector set into the door.
It was well-hidden, but his natural paranoia was returning,
helping him pick up details like that.

The door fed into a lobby that was wrapped in another
Asian-themed mosaic. Nohar walked across a giant wheel
filled with figures that appeared vaguely Tibetan. At the top
of the wheel sat a round desk behind which sat a human
who fulfilled all the connotations of the slang term "pink."
The moreys used the term referring to humans' general
hairlessness. This human was bald, soft, and white. He
looked pink.

"Can I help you?" he said as Nohar walked up. The
guard didn't look up from the screen he was watching, and
Nohar didn't smell any nervousness on the man. In fact, he
didn't smell much of anything from him.

"Here to see Charles Royd," Nohar prepared himself to
do some convincing to get himself in to see Royd. He didn't
have any proof that Royd had even come to see him, and if
Royd had anything to do with the attack he doubted that
the lawyer'd admit to being there.

To his surprise, the guard punched a button, said, "Visitor for Royd," hooked a thumb at one of the corridors out
of the lobby, and told Nohar, "Down there, up the stairs,
first door on your right."

Nohar stared at the guard a moment.

The guard finally raised his head and looked at Nohar.
"Anything else?"

The guard's expression didn't change. Nohar, however,

was startled and hid it by shaking his head and heading for the corridor. The guard's face remained etched in Nohar's mind. The eyes had been gloss-black, the nose hadn't existed except for two vertical slits that had flexed when the guard breathed.

The guard was a gene-engineered human, a frank.

Nohar didn't know what to make of that. Whatever the pink world felt about moreaus, they were an order of magnitude more twitchy about people messing with the human genome. U.N. treaties had banned human genetic engineering for decades. Which was why the moreaus existed—since it was fine with the U.N. if you gene-engineered a soldier, as long as it wasn't human.

Of course, there were a lot of leftovers when the wars were over.

Nohar walked into the outer office where Royd worked. He got another subtle shock. Royd had plastered the walls with etchings of newsfaxes and static holos that apparently showed high points of his career.

The first holo that grabbed Nohar's attention was a picture of Charles Royd with Father Alvarez de Collor. The spotted Brazilian feline was half a head taller than Royd. Nohar knew the jaguar because he was the only ordained Catholic priest on the West Coast who also happened to be a moreau.

Letting the moreaus into the Church had caused a near schism back when Nohar was ten years old. Father Collor was one of the first morey priests in the States. What was Royd doing with him?

A newsfax nearby had the headline, "Beverly Hills Lawyer Aids Homesteaders," and was all about a fight Royd had with the government to allow a number of nonhumans—franks, in fact, not moreaus—to take advantage of the homestead project.

There were other stories lining the walls—Royd defending moreys arrested during the explosive riots a decade ago. Royd bring class-action suits against a number of employers for awful working conditions. Royd fighting against the continued separation of hospital facilities between human and nonhuman. Royd had even once represented the aliens held at Alcatraz.

Royd was neither small-time, nor a typical pink lawyer.

Looking at all the stories lining the walls, Nohar felt that he would have known who Royd was if he had watched anything on the comm in the past seven years.

Now it made sense that Royd was hiring someone to find a lost morey. The guy made a living out of morey cases. He was high-profile enough that any nonhuman with a problem would come to him.

The question wasn't why Royd was looking for a morey named Manuel—the question was why Royd had sought Nohar out to look for him.

"Can I help you?" came a voice from behind him.

From the husky overtone of the voice, and from the scent, Nohar knew that it was a vulpine moreau before he turned around.

He turned around and looked down on the upturned muzzle of a short female fox.

"My name's Nohar Rajasthan, I'm here to see Charles Royd."

"Of course you are," she said. She extended a black-furred arm. "My name's Sara Henderson, I'm one of Mr. Royd's assistants. Maybe I can help you?"

It was odd hearing a Southern California accent coming from a vulpine mouth. This was the first fox he'd ever met who bore no trace of the ancestral English accent. It was also odd seeing a moreau in a dress. Female moreaus weren't built like human women, and human-designed clothing would hang wrong. All the females Nohar knew had worn male clothing, and as little as possible.

Sara wore a dress, though, and one that seemed to be designed for her frame. It was black, businesslike, and most of all, it fit—even around the problem areas for human clothing on a moreau, the chest, where a moreau didn't have breasts to speak of, and the rear where the large human ass was replaced by a tail.

While he'd been gone, someone had started manufacturing moreau clothing.

"Mr. Rajasthan?" Sara Henderson repeated.

Nohar shook the offered hand and said, "I'm afraid I really need to see Mr. Royd himself."

The corners of Sara's mouth turned in a frown. A lot of moreaus couldn't do facial expressions very well, but this one carried just the right amount of annoyance.

"He is very busy. Do you have an appointment?"

You know damn well I don't. Nohar shook his head. "I don't think so. Mr. Royd visited me and made a business proposition. I want to talk to him about it."

Sara stared at him, her black nose pointing at the knot of his tie.

"I was—am—a private investigator."

The fur fluffed out a little on her face when she smiled. Nohar saw a brief flash of a canine tooth. "That's where I've heard that name before." She shook her head. "You were, like, the only mo—" she caught herself as Southern California was on the verge of completely taking over her voice, "—Nonhuman detective in LA for the longest time. Weren't you?"

"A dubious distinction."

"Didn't you retire?"

"Apparently not."

Sara nodded, as if everything made perfect sense now. "Well, I'm sorry but Mr. Royd was called out of town on an emergency."

You have to be kidding. "Do you know how to get a hold of him?"

Sara shook her head, "I wish I did." She looked back toward the office. "All we received was a short memo from his comm saying he'd be gone for a week. We have to shuffle his caseload onto an already overworked staff—In fact, I really should get back to work myself."

"How do I get hold of Royd?"

"Wait till he comes back," Sara said, taking his arm and gently maneuvering him toward the door.

As the door shut behind him, Nohar couldn't help thinking, *What kind of lawyer leaves town without telling the firm how to contact him?*

Nohar answered himself, *Maybe a very scared lawyer.*

Chapter 6

Against his better judgment, Nohar found himself driving farther west, across Santa Monica, into the residential area of Beverly Hills. He drove the green Maduro past twenty-million-dollar homes, feeling as if a signal flare followed him down the street.

Pedestrians, joggers, dogwalkers—all turned to look. Nohar couldn't tell if the stares were for him, or for the car. He passed a number of walled estates that didn't even have access to the street, aircars were the only way in or out.

Royd wasn't in a mansion, for which Nohar was thankful. He lived in a more subdued neo-Tudor building whose most ostentatious feature was the oval driveway and the multicar garage.

Even so, the location probably cost him five mil.

Nohar pulled straight into the driveway. He had thought about this on the way here and had decided he was going to go through with it, despite the fact that this was probably the pinkest neighborhood on the planet. Nohar was gambling that with Royd's association with moreaus, the neighbors wouldn't have the automatic reflex reaction and call the cops because a morey was in the driveway.

If anyone was watching him—and he was certain they were—the suit probably bought him some slack. Since he had no hope of going unnoticed, his only possible tack was to be unashamedly blatant and look as if he knew exactly what he was doing here.

He killed the engine and felt a sudden unease that was more than just the neighborhood. He tried to shake it, but he had a sick feeling in the pit of his stomach. Nohar felt the urge to gun the engine and head for Mexico.

Instead, he quietly took the Vind from under the seat and slipped it back into his holster. Then he stepped out of the car and strode up to the front door.

Nohar could feel all the houses watching him.

His first thought was to try the call button, and if that failed, do a survey of the security on the door and try forcing it as quickly and quietly as possible.

He didn't have to.

The call button was on the door, and when Nohar reached up to press it, the door swung open. The bad feeling came back, magnified.

Beyond the door was a small foyer. A draft came past Nohar carrying the scent of blood. Human blood.

Nohar stepped in, drawing his gun, letting the door swing shut behind him.

The house was thick with blood smell. Nohar ran through the rooms in the house, tracking down the carnage he smelled. He passed through a living room, a den, a dining room. . . .

They had done him in the kitchen.

Nohar lowered the gun and stared through the door into Royd's kitchen. Royd was taped into an antique chair someone had dragged in from the dining room. Nohar could see the scuffs on the kitchen tile. They had propped him up against the wall next to a huge stainless-steel cooktop. More than the blood now, Nohar smelled burned flesh.

Who did you piss off?

Nohar took a few tentative steps into the kitchen. The sink was filled with expensive cutlery, most showing rainbow-burnished edges where someone had heated them red hot. A few dish towels sat in the sink too, stained red. The water in the bottom of the sink was colored a translucent pink.

Nohar looked at Royd. He hadn't seen anything as bad since the last time he had seen a victim of "shaving," a nasty ritual practiced by morey gangs when they thought one of their fellows was getting too close to the pinks. . . .

When they shaved someone, they took off most of the top layer of skin. Only most, since the victim usually died halfway through the procedure.

What had been done to Royd was worse. They—whoever *they* were—had systematically removed bits of flesh from Royd's arms, torso, and face, cauterizing the wounds so they wouldn't bleed. When they were finished, they had just slit his throat and let his life drain away.

From the smell, Royd had been here since before the attack on Nohar. The poor bastard hadn't called out the hit. Which begged the question, who did?

It was beginning to look like the only answers he would get would be from this missing kid, Manuel, and the person who hired Royd to find him.

Nohar backed up and holstered his weapon. He had no desire to contaminate a crime scene with his DNA.

As if the thought were a premonition, outside he began to hear sirens.

He backed out of the kitchen. *This was great.* Someone *did* call the cops on him, and with a body in the house. He wasn't worried so much as annoyed. Dealing with the police was one huge waste of time. He knew that he could look forward to a few hours of interrogation until they discovered that his gun hadn't been fired, and that Royd had died long before he showed up, then he'd face a few more hours as they grilled him about the arson of his cabin and why he didn't call it in to anyone. . . .

Nohar really disliked cops. The only species of pink he disliked worse were Fed agents.

He let his breath out in a sigh that was more like a growl. There was no way around it at this point. He headed toward the front door. The sirens were almost on him when he stepped into the foyer. He could hear car doors slamming as he stepped outside.

Nohar began spreading his arms as he stepped outside, showing he was unarmed.

Someone fired.

Instinct had Nohar diving back through the open doorway before it fully registered that the cops were shooting at him. Above him, chunks of Royd's front door began splintering as slugs tore through the even, vat-grown wood.

When did cops start blowing away unarmed moreys on a disturbance call?

Nohar scrambled backward along the floor as he heard glass breaking inside the house. Adrenaline began pushing him, and he felt the urge to draw his gun and return fire. He suppressed the urge. Escape was his only real option. Escape, and figure out what triggered the goddamn cops.

More glass broke to either side of him. Then, for the moment, the cops stopped shooting. Nohar took the opportunity to get to his feet and head toward the rear of Royd's house. He ran back toward the dining room.

He smelled the ozone before he saw it, and was diving for cover before it started firing. Thirty-two caliber slugs tore into the walls of the dining room, blowing a china cabinet into shards of glass and porcelain. Hovering above the table was a police drone. It was a tiny remote-controlled helicopter that carried a multispectrum video camera and a built-in submachine gun. With its ovoid body, and dual offset rotors, it looked like a flying rat face, the camera one eye, the gun the other, the rotors its ears.

It didn't stop firing, and the gun was swinging back toward Nohar.

He did the only thing he could, diving under the dining room table, directly beneath it. He heard it buzz as it tried to reacquire him. He rolled on his back, drew the Vind, and fired three shots—a quarter of the clip—through the table, straight up. The room echoed with the triple explosion from the twelve-millimeter handgun, and the smell of powder-burned wood drifted down from the holes punched through the table.

Nohar also smelled the odor of fried electronics.

That's it, then. Nohar thought. *I've nuked one of their toys, there's no talking to them now.*

He rolled out from under the table, and he heard more gunfire from the police. He had really pissed them off.

On the dining room table, the drone had fallen cockeyed, dormant, pointing toward the windows it had crashed through. Ozone smoke leaked from the shattered camera, and its twin counter-rotating rotors were still slowly turning.

Nohar heard the buzz of another drone under the sound of gunfire. It was coming from the den and the living room, toward him.

Nohar kept his gun out as he dove through the kitchen door. The second drone banked into the dining room after him. Nohar dove around the door for cover. He heard it closing on him as he hugged the wall.

The thing was less than a meter square and cleared the doorframe as it entered the kitchen. It started to sweep the room, looking for him, but it stopped when its camera locked on Royd's body. Nohar was hoping for that. There was still a human operating the thing, as susceptible to surprise as anyone.

Nohar leveled the Vind at the backside of the drone's chassis and let go with two more shots. The camera exploded and the thing tumbled, slamming into the side of the sink and falling upended at Royd's feet.

The firing outside stopped again.

Nohar heard the sound of something whistling through the air—Multiple somethings. Either tear gas, trying to drive him out, or concussion grenades to stun him while they took the building. Neither one was something he wanted to stick around for.

The kitchen had a doorway into the garage. He made for it, past Royd, little worried about stray hairs or DNA at this point. He reached the door as he heard multiple hissing explosions throughout the house, and the first acid touch of the gas hit his eyes and nose.

He made it into the garage and slammed the door.

He hadn't run from the cops since he was fourteen. It always caused more trouble than it solved. But the cops here seemed hell-bent on killing him. Cooperating with authority only went so far.

It was getting hard to see, even in the garage. His eyes watered, and he began coughing. The gas was leaking from the house, through the cracks around the door. Inside it had to be intolerable.

He held a hand over his nose and mouth and looked around the garage. There was only one other way out, the doors pointed out on the driveway, straight at the cops. There wasn't anywhere else to go.

There were two cars here, the Jaguar aircar and a sleek back BMW with tinted windows. Neither looked bulletproof. . . .

But the tinted windows gave him an idea.

It took Nohar a few agonizing minutes to short out the lock and get into the BMW. By that time the alarms were going off and the car's computer was already calling the police— as if that mattered. Once in, he hacked the auto-navigation feature and jacked up the minimum speed to sixty klicks an hour.

Nohar could barely see through his stinging and watering eyes as he got the Jaguar open. By then, he felt he didn't have much time left. He ducked into the BMW, engaged it in drive, and let the navigation computer take over. Nohar took cover in the Jaguar as the garage door began opening.

The cops began strafing the garage, Nohar could hear the Jaguar taking hits. He could smell melted composites. But he also heard the BMW's engine rev up. Heard it accelerate out toward the cops. The gunfire got a little more frantic.

While he heard all this going on, Nohar desperately worked on the dash, trying to get the Jaguar moving. He ripped panels covering the control circuits, found the security system, and pulled that card out. He tore a wire from the comm to jump the power connection that had run through the card. With his big hands it took him five times with his claws fully extended to get the jumper in place.

When he did, he heard the flywheel engage and the fans start up.

About then he also heard the sound of something going smash out in the street. Nohar risked a look out the windshield. The Jaguar's windshield was pock-marked with bulletholes, and through the spider cracks he saw that the BMW had taken a full header into one of the copcars. The Patrol cars were the traditional Dodge Haviers, but the BMW was a luxury car, heavier, and probably had twice as much metal in it. The nav computer was still driving, pushing the T-boned Havier slowly down the street with it. The police were pouring lead into it as if they were the Islamic Axis and the BMW was the entire state of Israel.

He had a chance to get out while the cops were distracted. Nohar set the attitude on the fans near forty-five degrees, and maxed the accelerator.

The Jaguar shot out of the garage like it was a ballistic shuttle on too low an arc. It skimmed over the driveway, barely gaining enough altitude to clear the flashers on top of the cop cars. Gunfire followed the aircar, but most of the shots went wild.

Nohar didn't have any attention to spare for the cops anyway. He was shooting straight at an old ranch house across the street, and not gaining enough altitude to clear it. He banked, barely clearing the right side of the roof. The sound of breaking glass followed the whine of the aircar's engines. Nohar didn't know if it'd been a wild shot from the cops, or if he had hit something.

He shot out from between a pair of houses, over a

swimming pool. The backwash from the Jaguar's fans splashed chlorinated water through someone's garden.

Nohar hit the headsup, and the windscreen lit with fragmented navigation displays. The one thing that showed clearly on the shattered windscreen was the speedometer. With the aircar's thrust mostly going forward, he was topping one-forty klicks an hour.

He started dodging palms as he sped over someone's estate.

The headsup display flashed facets of red at him. It was a warning, probably that he was flying illegally low over Beverly Hills. Nohar checked the rear video and saw two police helicopters on his tail.

Two?

The Beverly cops probably only *had* two helicopters. Ten to one that the copters meant that it was the LAPD after him. . . .

Which meant that this was some sort of special operation, not just a neighbor calling the cops.

There was little chance he could escape the airborne pursuit. The Jaguar's computers were screaming for the cops, its transponder a gigantic red flare on LA's air traffic control screens. He couldn't gain any altitude, because as soon as he was clear of civilians, the copters riding his ass would probably frag him.

Pretty damn soon he'd be surrounded by police aircars. He had to ditch this thing quickly, somewhere he could get out from under the copters' eyes.

He began to turn west toward the mountains, away from where most of the cops would be coming. He was inviting fire from the bastards tailing him, but he was going to have to risk it. He hugged the hillside as he followed the slope of the Santa Monica Mountains. The copters didn't shoot.

Nohar hoped that meant they were unarmed. What it *probably* meant was that they didn't want to start a brush fire.

The aircar cleared a line of trees, and he saw what he was looking for. The algae-slick surface of a reservoir glistened in the midst of the woods.

Nohar aimed the Jaguar straight for it.

Chapter 7

The Jaguar sliced into the water like an arrow. It slammed to a stop under the surface, blowing an air bag across Nohar's face. The inductors blew with a hydraulic explosion that twisted the Jaguar on its side as water shot into the cabin from the bullet holes in the windshield.

Nohar tore the air bag from in front of him.

The aircar was tumbling, the air in the cabin not anywhere near enough to keep the fans afloat. Nohar scrambled as the aircar turned completely upside down, the cabin already half-filled with water. He took a few deep gasps of what remained of the air, and kicked at the windshield.

With the car upside down, the windshield was already completely underwater, and it gave with a single kick. Nohar ducked and pushed himself out the window just as the Jaguar nosed into the mud at the bottom of the reservoir.

Nohar swam blindly, the water dark and blurred with sediment. His head throbbed with the dull sound of machinery. He pushed himself to clear as much distance between him and the wreck as possible. He stayed under until his lungs burned with lack of air, then he pushed through the inch-thick scum of algae on the surface.

When his head hit the air, he sucked in several deep breaths as he spun around to see the nearest harvesting pylon. He dove under again, heading for the pylon. He had to break the surface twice more before he reached it. The second time he broke the surface right in the path of one of the pylon's three-meter-wide skimming arms; he had to dive under as the rotating boom swept over his head.

Then he made it to the side of the pylon and held himself against it, his head barely above the surface. The shafts of the swimming arms didn't descend below the surface this close to the pylon, but they swept by only centimeters above him. He sucked in deep breaths and watched the sky.

The copters ran a search pattern over the water. They hadn't seen him yet. Nohar hoped that they wouldn't. The machinery running the pylon he clung to should hide his own heat, as should the water and the algae. He held on, his arms going numb and his head throbbing with the rhythm of the pylon as the twenty-meter arms swept a circle in the algae.

They flew low enough for the rotors to ripple holes in the algae, incidentally hiding the scars he'd made when he'd broken the surface. One buzzed the harvesting pylons, the rotor's backwash spilling green water over him. He was sure that they had him then, but the copter kept flying down the line of pylons, oblivious.

The helicopters searched for what seemed like hours. Long enough for Nohar to get a good look at both of them. One was an LAPD chopper, the other was completely unmarked.

Little question it was a Fed helicopter.

Fed involvement meant the situation was screwed beyond belief. It could have been a Fed black-ops unit that attacked him in the cabin. The whole scene at Royd's could have been a setup. They knew he wasn't taken at the cabin, all they'd need to do was stake out Royd's corpse and wait for their lost morey to show. . . .

What had Royd stepped in?

Both copters eventually stopped the search pattern and hovered over opposite ends of the reservoir. They were waiting for a search party. They weren't about to give him any breaks. He was going to have to get to shore under the cover of the harvesting pylons.

Nohar unclenched his arms from the side of the pylon and reached up, grabbing the swimming boom as it passed overhead. As it spun, pulling him in circles around the pylon, he pulled himself hand over hand through the foaming muck the arm pushed ahead of itself. The handholds were slick, and once he was a few meters away from the pylon itself, the arm's mechanism opened up a gaping maw in front of him. Algae foam rose above his head, and slipped past his body into the screens built into the harvesting arm. He tried to get a foothold on the underwater portion of the arm. He had to kick off his shoes, so he could grip with his claws.

It would be easier, and safer, if he grabbed on the trailing end. But the froth on the leading edge offered more cover than the arm's wake.

Nohar made it all the way to the edge of the arm, three meters away from the arc of the neighboring pylon. Then he let go, dived, and came up in front of the rushing wall of foam at the edge of the next pylon. The impact stunned him, and he had to grip for two rotations before he felt up to doing it again. Then he had to spin around once more so he could pick out the pylon closest to shore and farthest from the helicopters.

Somehow he managed to make it all the way to the shoreline without alerting the helicopters. He had hitched a ride on three or four of the skimming booms, and his nose had gone numb from the smell of engineered algae. He had turned a color somewhere between shit brown and bile green from the algae stuck to him and his suit. During his ride to shore, some government boys had shown up. He saw them working the shoreline near where the Jaguar had gone down.

He ducked into the woods in the opposite direction. Once out of sight he ran, getting himself as deep in the woods as he could. Living in this kind of terrain for the past seven years made it easy. He kept moving until the sun had gone out of the sky and his body refused to go on anymore.

Sometime after dark he collapsed against a tree and went through his pockets. The Vind had survived. He did his best to clean it. Out of the extra magazines he carried, he was able to find five shells that were dry enough to be trusted to reload the thing. When he was done, he set it down next to him.

His portable comm was a total loss, which didn't really matter, since the Fed could trace his movements using that comm's account. It was better off fried.

The binocular camera came with its own case, and seemed to have fared better. He set it aside with his wallet to dry.

He had no clue what the hell he was going to do now.

As he stared at his algae-sodden wallet, fatigue claimed him with iron claws, dragging him into unconsciousness.

The itch of algae being sun-dried onto his body finally woke him up. Nohar could feel the dried slime caking his fur in clumps all over his body. His tail had fallen asleep and had stuck to the outside of his right thigh. He had to reach up and help his eyelids to open against the gunk holding them together. Even that little movement sent aches up and down his arm.

He wiped his nose as his eyes focused, trying to get the smell of algae out of it. He stopped because he realized he was being watched. Nohar saw the dog before he heard or smelled it, and that made it sink in exactly how close he'd been driving himself. It stood about four meters away, a gray mutt that looked for all the world like a natural un-engineered canine. It sat on its haunches, looking at Nohar and panting.

The fact that it could get that close without waking him made Nohar very nervous.

The dog noticed Nohar move, and it let loose an odd staccato yip. When Nohar had been an LA native, he had heard stories about the feral dogs that populated the Holly-wood hills, especially around the old reservoirs. He'd never really thought that much about it, until now—

He never thought of a dog as a potential threat. But as he stared at the gray dog, he realized that dogs were natu-rally pack hunters, and in his state he'd probably have trou-ble with *one* fifty-kilo animal. He couldn't even tell how many were out there. His sense of smell was still over-whelmed by algae.

He did his best not to make any sudden moves.

From the woods around him, he heard more staccato barking. Two, three, four, five others at least. Nohar nodded, doing his best not to show teeth as he forced his engineered lips into a facsimile of a smile.

"Nice dog," Nohar said as he slowly reached over to where he had placed the Vind.

It wasn't there.

Nohar heard a low growl next to him. He turned to face it and saw a black dog, somewhere between a Doberman and a Rottweiler, about three meters away from his out-stretched arm. Its forepaws were placed squarely on top of Nohar's gun.

Nohar looked from Blackie to Gray, and back again. Gray was still yipping, the rhythm of it much more complex than normal. Nohar began to look at the structure of the dogs' skulls. It was hard to notice at first, since the proportions were similar to any other dog's skull, but the forehead was slightly higher, the skull slightly wider, and the whole head larger in proportion to the body.

These weren't natural specimens of *canis familiaris.*

The first moreaus, the first examples of macro gene-engineering that were used for warfare, were a species of dogs with enhanced intelligence designed by the South during the war of Korean unification. Almost all of the moreaus since were based in part from those Korean Dogs. Since the U.N. banned the use of the human genome after the Korean Dogs were designed, the countries that built intelligent moreaus all started with the specs from those enhanced dog brains rather than the human—

Which was a bit of hypocrisy, since the Koreans unabashedly used human genes in the creation of their dogs.

That was all history to Nohar. As far as he knew, all those first efforts were destroyed in the labs of the gene-techs or died in the war once the Chinese-backed North overwhelmed the South.

Nohar stared at Blackie and felt as if he was staring into the eyes of his own past.

"Your move," Nohar said.

Blackie kept growling, but didn't move.

The tableau remained like that as Nohar tried to get an impression of how many canines were out in the woods beyond where he sat. His senses were too dull at the moment to give a specific number, but he began to realize that there were a lot of them.

From beyond a tree a few meters in front of him, Nohar heard an electronic monotone ask, "what is your name."

Nohar sat up, causing Gray to retreat and Blackie to growl louder. He hadn't expected a response.

As he sat up, a large brown dog walked out of the woods and cocked its head at him. Around its neck it wore a collar, and an electronic device was attached to the collar with silvery-gray duct tape. The electronic voice came from the device. "who are you. why are you here."

"My aircar crashed," Nohar said.

The brown dog paced in front of him, close enough that Nohar could finally make out the smell of agitation and fear off of him. The box spoke without emotion, but everything in the dog's posture carried tension that the words didn't contain. "men follow you here. men look for you. why."

Nohar looked around him. He was surrounded. Canine eyes seemed to peer from around every tree, every rock, every bush. He could sense that he was just one move shy of a deadly confrontation. He couldn't do anything to spook them.

Nohar decided to rein in his own tension, and tell the truth, If they sensed him relaxing, the whole situation might calm down a few notches. . . .

If his story didn't fire them up.

Nohar sucked in a breath and said, "They think I killed someone."

Brown stopped pacing and looked at him. One eye was clouded, and Nohar finally realized how old Brown was. He could see scars on his side, and one of his ears was ragged.

"did you kill someone," Brown's electronic box asked as he stared at Nohar with his one good eye.

Nohar shook his head. "No."

"why do you carry a weapon."

"Someone is trying to kill me."

"who."

"I don't know."

The pack around him erupted in a chorus of the odd staccato barking. Nohar realized that they had to be talking to each other. He was at a disadvantage. They could understand him, but the only one he could understand was the one-eyed leader with the salvaged electronic voicebox.

Even without understanding them, Nohar could pretty much figure out what they were debating. They were arguing whether or not to kill him.

Of all the groups to have a run-in with after the cops.

Nohar looked at the barking crowd and had an uncomfortable realization. Most of these dogs were sick. Many had crusts around their eyes and noses, many seemed unsteady on their feet.

"we should give you to the men. you are a man problem."

Slightly better than voting to kill him off and bury him in the woods, but not by much. "I could help you out."

"why would you help us." The old dog with the electronic voicebox stared at him. When he blinked, Nohar noticed with a little unease that the eyelid on the leader's clouded eye traveled more slowly than the other.

Nohar slowly pushed himself to his feet. There were a chorus of barks. This time Nohar noticed that a few seemed weak. Blackie growled at him and pulled the Vind farther away. "I don't want to see those pink bastards again."

The old dog's gaze followed him. When Nohar was fully upright, the old dog was dwarfed, despite being large for his species. The dog's posture didn't change, even as he tilted up so his good eye could follow Nohar's movement. "a deal."

"A deal," Nohar said. He turned around slowly. A fine dust of dried algae drifted off of him as he moved. It made him want to sneeze. "How many of you are sick? Half?"

Around him came a chorus of agitated barking. It was as if the woods around him had suddenly come alive. From the sound, he had struck a nerve. The barking went on while the canines debated. Nohar kept moving slowly, trying to look nonthreatening. He stretched overused muscles, and tried to work the stiffness out of his bad knee and shoulder.

"what do our problems matter." For once, the old dog's posture matched the fatalism of the electronic monotone.

"I could bring back a doctor—"

The barking became loud, aggressive. Nohar stopped moving. He had struck another nerve. "no men. no doctors. if that is the help you offer, it is no help."

Nohar swore quietly under his breath. He had no love of doctors and hospitals himself, but the canine pack around him looked at him as if he had suggested mass euthanasia.

"Okay, no doctors. But I could bring you medicine."

"what kind of medicine."

Nohar was tempted to say he'd cure all of them if they let him go. But he doubted they were that gullible, or that he could pull off that kind of fabrication. "I'm not a doctor," he said. "I don't know what's the matter. But I could bring back antibiotics, antivirals, at the very least something to help with the symptoms—decongestants, aspirin."

Nohar spread his arms and tried to look friendly.

More barking, subdued this time. Nohar hoped that they were considering this seriously. Looking at them, he could tell that they did a lot of scavenging. Some of them wore jury-rigged backpacks across their backs. A few wore collars with items hooked or taped to them. Nohar even saw a watch strapped to a dog's foreleg.

But pharmaceuticals weren't things you could easily scavenge.

"what is your name."

Nohar realized he had never answered the first question. "Nohar."

"no-har." The hesitation over the syllable was the first time there'd been a disruption in the voicebox's smooth monotone. "we survive here because men do not know of us. if we make this deal with you, you must tell no one of us, of where we live. no men. no doctors."

Nohar nodded.

"i am elijah. we will accept your help."

Nohar felt a weight lift from his chest. He looked down at himself and said, "Can I clean up somewhere?" Walking into a pharmacy covered in algae was probably going to attract attention.

Elijah stepped in front of Nohar and said, "you will help. you will be followed. do not betray the trust we give you."

Nohar nodded.

"we will return your possessions when you do what you've said."

As Elijah's voicebox spoke, Blackie picked up the Vind in his mouth and slipped it into a neighboring canine's backpack. That answered a nagging question that had been bothering Nohar, how these dogs could get along without hands. He supposed it was only natural, especially in a pack, for the dogs to team together to do things like loading a backpack, or even putting one on.

The busted comm and the camera followed the Vind.

They were about to do the same to his wallet. "Wait, I'll need that to get your medicine."

Elijah shook his head in a gesture the humans seemed to have bequeathed on all their engineered brethren. "we will return your possessions when you do what you've said."

The dogs began to leave him in twos and threes. In a few moments only Elijah was left facing him.

"prepare as you wish. but return with what you've gathered before the sky darkens. you will be watched. you will be followed." Somehow, the one-eyed pack leader managed to instill the toneless voice with a sense of threat.

With that, Elijah left him as well.

Fuck.

Nohar walked down out of the hills.

He wasn't alone. A fluctuating number of canines paced him on the way out of the woods. They stayed out of sight, but Nohar could smell them, and occasionally hear them.

He did get his chance to clean up. He passed a small creek on his way down toward Hollywood where he managed to wash most of the algae out of his fur and out of his clothes. He continued the remainder of his journey toward Hollywood dripping wet.

He was still trying to figure out how he was going to keep his promise to the dogs. He was tempted just to skip, letting them keep his gun and his wallet—

Nohar doubted he'd get far pulling that. However he matched up one on one, he wasn't about to win a fight with a whole pack of angry, engineered canines. And when it came down to it, they could have overpowered him, could have fed him to the cops and whatever Fed agency wanted his hide. He was going to keep his promise.

Besides, he couldn't get into any *more* trouble than he was in already.

He got his bearings when he saw the Hollywood Freeway. He stopped next to it, standing amidst the trash that heaped next to the road. He hunted in the midst of car parts and rubbish until he found what he was looking for, a length of old blackened PVC pipe about one-and-a-half meters long.

Carrying the pipe, dripping wet, his suit wrinkled, streaked with green, and smelling of dead plants, Nohar walked into Hollywood.

The dirty streets had a few moreys in the midst of the prostitutes and hustlers, but even they stepped aside to let Nohar by. The pinks turned away from him and tried to fade into doorways or behind lamp-posts. Nohar didn't pay much attention. He was keeping his eyes out for cops.

He stopped at the first pharmacy he came to. It was an automated storefront, open twenty-four hours a day. Behind a thick window, a large holo displayed an image of a smiling, white-coated druggist, and in front stood a small kiosk where someone could place an order for whatever they needed.

Nohar ducked into a trash-strewn alley next to the store. The drugstore had a few windows back here, set into the looming brick wall. They were small and covered by a steel latticework set into the wall as a security measure. There also was a side door to the pharmacy, armored, flat, featureless, and locked with a cardkey panel.

Nohar was looking for a weak point, and after a moment of looking, he found it. The doorframe was old, contemporary with the century-old building. Above the new armored door was a flat panel where an old-fashioned air-conditioning unit would have fitted. That area was only so much plywood.

Nohar rammed his pipe at the flat space above the door. The plywood splintered, bowing inward. Nohar withdrew the pipe and rammed the panel again. The pipe hit with a crack, breaking the plywood almost in half. When he withdrew the pipe this time, he had to step back as the panel fell from the wall, revealing a small opening above the door.

Nohar could see another security grate over the hole, on the other side. He rammed it with the pipe a few times, and it clattered to the floor inside the building.

Nohar looked around a few times, and when he was sure no one was watching from the street, he tossed the pipe through the hole and heaved himself up and through. His suit caught and tore on splintered wood, but Nohar didn't pay it much attention.

He fell to the floor on top of the bent security grate.

The rear hallway was dark, but he was almost certain to be on someone's security video. All sorts of alarms were going off right now. He had five minutes, ten at the most.

He raced through the narrow hallway until he found a storage area. It was through an open doorway at the end of the hall. Motion sensors turned on the lights as soon as he stepped through the threshold. In the cavernous room, boxes sat on plastic shipping pallets, waiting for the owners to come feed the items into the automated bowels of the store.

A rancid chemical smell permeated the place. It reminded Nohar uncomfortably of a hospital.

He stripped off his jacket and started going from pallet to pallet, looking for what he needed. When he saw a label that indicated an antibiotic or antiviral drug, he tore into the top with his claws and grabbed two handfuls, tossing them into his jacket.

He went from pallet to pallet, tearing open boxes until he felt he had pushed the limit of his time here. He ran back to the rear door as he began hearing sirens in the distance. He tied his jacket in a bundle and tossed it through the opening above the door. Then he raised his foot and kicked at the crash bar on the door, twice. It didn't want to give, but on the second kick something in the mechanism gave and the door swung outward into the alley.

Nohar ducked through the broken door to retrieve his jacket and his booty—

The jacket wasn't there. Instead, lying on the ground in front of the door, was his wallet, the comm, the camera, and his Vind. Elijah had been as good as his word, the dogs had followed him all the way, watching his every move. Nohar found it disconcerting that he didn't know where the dogs were, worse was the thought that he had missed them when they were right outside the door. He never knew how close they'd been.

He must be getting old.

Nohar gathered his possessions and ran to find the other end of the alley before the cops arrived.

Chapter 8

Nohar waited in the dark, a few blocks north of Wilshire and a few blocks east of Santa Monica, trying to figure out another option. There was no way he should be here. He was too exposed. It was only a matter of time before the Beverly cops found him. He didn't dare get within a block of Royd's offices; they were almost certainly watched. Just like Royd's house had to have been watched.

Evening had fallen, and Nohar was crouched in the cover provided by a small park that nestled at one end of the street that held Royd's offices. The other end of the street was a cul-de-sac, so all traffic from Royd's building would pass through the intersection in front of Nohar.

Like when he hunted, he was crouched, absolutely still. He held the binocular camera. He watched through it, looking at a night-enhanced monochrome view of the entrance to the parking lot of Royd's building.

Occasionally, he would hit the zoom button to get a close-up view of a car leaving, and its occupants.

By now he had gotten a pretty good idea where the watchers were. A Chrysler Mirador with tinted windows hadn't moved from its parking spot since Nohar had found his hiding space. It was a luxury sedan, but in Beverly Hills it was anonymous enough to be unnoticed, where an unmarked police car would draw attention to itself.

Though Nohar wondered if they were police.

After waiting for two hours, he started to wonder if he had missed her. Just as he was about to give up and consider what the hell he'd do next, Sara Henderson walked out of Royd's building.

He watched her slim vulpine form walk through the parking lot, through the too-manicured garden. Now was the hard part. He needed her to help him discover what Royd had been up to with him and the missing morey, Manuel—but he doubted that convincing her would be easy.

Nohar took a few deep breaths and prepared to move. He was going to catch her car as it stopped at the intersection in front of him. He was only going to have a few minutes to get down there, and somehow get into her car. He was still trying to figure out how to do that without making it look like an attempted kidnapping.

Henderson got into a jet-black BMW and pulled out of the parking lot. Just before Nohar lowered the camera, the Mirador started up. It pulled out just as Henderson's BMW reached the first statue lining the drive.

The Mirador never turned on its headlamps.

Nohar didn't know what to make of what was going on, but he headed toward the intersection anyway, a heavy feeling in his gut. He reached the edge of the park just as Henderson's BMW came to a stop at the intersection.

The Mirador didn't.

It screeched past the BMW and angled itself across the BMW's path. Nohar's instincts told him that Henderson had to peel out in reverse, *now*.

Henderson didn't have his instincts. Three humans

erupted from the Mirador before it had come to a complete stop. Nohar had a horrid sense of dejá vù. They wore the same black paramilitary gear as the men who had attacked his cabin. Two of them carried Black Widows. The third was already smashing in the window of Henderson's car.

Nohar whipped the Vind out of his holster before he heard Henderson scream.

Twenty meters separated him from the Mirador. He started running to clear the distance before the combat team knew he was there. The unarmed pink was dragging Henderson from behind the wheel, while the two gunmen were turning, realizing something was wrong.

Nohar's nerves sang with the high-tension hum of genes primed for combat. The night snapped into monochrome clarity, and everything slowed to the rhythm of a ballet.

His pulse thudded in his ears as he ran, and he hesitated to aim, almost too long. He could smell the adrenaline of the men, and the fear of Henderson. The first gunman had started firing, the silencer thudding on his weapon, before Nohar got off his first shot.

He was halfway there, and the Vind spoke in a resonating explosion that shook Nohar's jawbone. The shot landed in the gunman's upper chest. The armor he wore didn't slow the twelve millimeter slug much. Nohar saw blood as the man folded backward over the hood of the Mirador.

Gunman Two saw his partner go down and started firing as he tried to dive for cover behind the Mirador. At the same time, the third pink had pulled Henderson out the broken window and was raising his head at the sound of the gunshot.

Nohar was only five meters away when the Vind spoke again.

Glass exploded as the shot blew through the Mirador's rear passenger window, through the Mirador's rear window, and finally through the right shoulder of Gunman Number Two. He spilled to the ground behind the Mirador, his gun flying from his grasp.

The Mirador's driver gunned the engine, jerking the car forward so Gunman One rolled off of the hood.

The guy with Henderson was reaching for a holster. By now everything was razor-sharp. The gene-engineered beast had taken over. Nohar's instincts had overrun his thoughts by about five times, and he had taken the shot before he could think if it was worth the risk.

The bullet landed in the center of the pink's face, spraying Henderson with blood and clumps of brain tissue. She scrambled away, her look of horror unmistakable.

The Mirador pulled out, aiming for him. Nohar ducked aside, but the car still clipped the side of his leg, knocking him spinning. He landed in a crouch as the Mirador turfed the lawn of the neighboring park in an effort to come around at him again.

Nohar leveled the Vind at the car and pumped five shots into the windshield. At least one hit the driver. The car stopped accelerating, slid by Nohar, and crashed into a light pole by the side of the road.

"What's happening?" Henderson pleaded. She was looking down at the guy who'd dragged her out of the car. His face had been obliterated. In his hand he held a Baretta nine-millimeter halfway out of its holster.

Nohar ran to the BMW, reached in the broken window, and unlocked the car. It was still running.

He pulled Henderson into the car and got into the driver's seat. It wasn't until then he holstered his weapon. He put the BMW in drive and pulled away from the intersection. A navigation display rolled by the windshield, one corner flashing red, telling him that one of the windows had been broken.

He kept accelerating until he hit Wilshire, then he turned left, away from Beverly Hills.

"You killed them." There was a hollow sound in Henderson's voice. For a moment she sounded as emotionless as Elijah's voicebox.

"Two of them," Nohar corrected automatically. The Beast was still running his neurochemistry. He was holding on to the knife-edge of battle with ragged mental claws—he couldn't let himself crash now, not when he was going a hundred klicks an hour down Wilshire Boulevard, not in Beverly Hills, not within a few miles of the commandos who had tried to take Henderson.

Henderson was looking down at her dress. It was another black one, with a slightly different cut. She was staring at the flecks of skull and brain that still adhered to it. "I never saw someone die before."

Nohar didn't have a response for that. He maneuvered the car left, to start heading for the Santa Monica Freeway. He felt as if every cop in Beverly Hills was about to appear behind him and start shooting.

Henderson turned to look at Nohar. "Are you going to kill me?"

"What a stu—" Nohar shook his head. "I just saved your life."

She shook her head, and Nohar saw her fatalistic expression out of the corner of his eye. "You killed him."

Nohar was about to say something about nuts with guns when he realized she was talking about Royd. "No," Nohar said, "I didn't."

"The police came to the office, and it's been on the news."

Wonderful, let's try and keep a low profile now; when half the city thinks you killed Royd. . . .

Nohar shook his head. "You work for a law firm. You think the cops are always right? They never jump to conclusions when a morey's involved?"

Nohar looked across at Henderson and saw her eyes glisten. He turned away. His own tear ducts weren't engineered to be triggered emotionally. Like facial expression, it was something the gene-techs often left out when they were building their warriors. He couldn't stand to see moreaus cry. It brought back a memory of something he didn't want to relive. Especially now, when he had a lot of other problems he needed to deal with, in the present.

"He was the best man I ever knew. He was putting me through law school—" She sniffed, wrinkling her muzzle, and looked at Nohar accusingly. "You didn't kill him, like they said?"

"No," Nohar said flatly.

"Why should I believe you?"

"Because I saved you?"

She looked out the front windshield. The reflection of the headsup brought out odd highlights in her fur, making it look like slightly tarnished copper. "What from?" She was staring at the gore on her dress again.

"From the same guys who killed your boss."

"Who are they? What's going on?"

"I'm trying to answer both." Nohar pulled the BMW on

to the Santa Monica Freeway. As soon as he merged with the nighttime traffic, he began to relax a little. He also began to feel the crushing aftereffects of what he'd just gone through. They sat in silence as the BMW carried them into the heart of downtown Los Angeles.

"I want to go home." Henderson's voice sounded weak.

"Not a good idea."

She turned to look at him, but Nohar kept his eyes fixed on the road ahead. "They're probably watching your place."

"They?"

"They're heavily armed and know what they're doing." Nohar looked down at the dash of the BMW. "We've got to ditch this car—"

"What?"

"Tracking devices. Too small for us to find."

"This is insane."

"Do you have a change of clothes in this car?" She looked at him, his green-stained shirt and torn pants, and said, "For you?"

"No. You."

"Maybe in the trunk."

Nohar pulled the BMW into the first parking garage he came to. He parked the car in a spot as far from the entrance as he could. He stepped out and stripped off his shoulder holster and his shirt. "Find something to change into. We can get lost on the subway."

In a few hours, Nohar found himself and Henderson at an all-night Mexican diner on the fringes of East LA. The moreys here were of South or Central American stock, mostly rodents of various types, with the occasional Brazilian oddity.

He and Henderson stood out even without the way they were dressed. Henderson wore a blue sweater, faded and with grease stains, over a pair of ragged cutoff jeans that looked as if they had never really fit. Nohar still wore his suit pants, and the stained shirt which he now wore billowing open so he could hide the holster, somewhat, underneath it. It didn't really work, but they hadn't run into any cops, and no one else bothered them about it.

Nohar had blown most of his remaining cash on dinner. He hadn't eaten in a long time, and his body was screaming for food. He ordered three carnivore burritos—mostly raw ground meat wrapped in a warm tortilla.

Henderson just had a glass of water, which she spent most of her time staring into.

"I should go to the police."

Nohar bit into his burrito and nodded. "That may be an option for you. Not me."

"Why not?"

"Ask the cops who tried to blow me away." Between bites, Nohar told Henderson what had happened, from Royd's visit, until he had come gunning down her assailants.

"These guys figured I'd head for Royd, and set themselves up for me. They were watching for me when I entered the house, then called in the Beverly cops—probably with some story about moreau terrorism, something to push their buttons—prime them to shoot at anything."

"But why?" Henderson shook her head. "Charles Royd was a good man. Why would someone do this to him?"

Nohar shook his head. Henderson seemed awfully naive for someone who worked in the legal profession. "I doubt they were pissed at him personally. They were trying to get information." Nohar picked up a burrito. "Something they didn't expect me to know, something they didn't get."

"How do you know that?"

"If they thought I had what they wanted, they wouldn't have tried to barbecue me. If they'd gotten what they wanted from Royd, they wouldn't come after you." Nohar shook his head slowly. He felt a nagging frustration because he couldn't put a finger on exactly what was happening. "This all stemmed from Royd trying to hire me. This all has some connection to a missing crossbreed named Manuel."

Henderson looked up and said, "What has that got to do with anything?"

"That's the only connection I have with Royd. His anonymous client insisted that he hire me to find this Manuel. He apparently worked at—"

"The Compton Bendsheim Clinic." Henderson finished for him. She was staring at him, and he smelled something like terror coming off of her. "No, this can't be Manuel—Oh, God," Henderson buried her face in her hands.

Nohar bent over and placed a hand on Henderson's shoulder. She was shaking.

He heard her whisper, "It's all my fault. God, I didn't know he was hiring *you* . . . !"

"You're Royd's client?"

She shook her head and stood up. "No. No. But it's all my fault. Christ, do you think they've killed Manuel, too?"

Nohar just stared at her, trying to read her shifting emotions, fear, anger, agitation, confusion—a lot of the latter mirroring his own. "If you didn't—"

"I have to call someone. God, I hope she's all right." She ran off to the front of the restaurant, where a public comm stood.

Maybe the Bad Guys were looking for the same thing he was, the identity of Royd's client. Nohar watched Henderson at the comm. She obviously knew about Manuel.

When Henderson got a connection and started nodding, Nohar stood up and started walking to the comm. It was a good bet that the person Henderson was talking to was Royd's client. The pieces began fitting together. Henderson knew Manuel, his family, friends, or maybe his wife. When Manuel turns up missing, Henderson introduces those loved ones to Royd—everyone blithely ignorant of "them," the commando goons that Manuel had stirred up.

That still left the questions of what exactly Manuel had gotten involved in, and why Royd's client had insisted on hiring Nohar, and remaining anonymous.

"No," Henderson was saying, "something Manuel must have been involved in. They tried to kidnap *me* less than an hour ago, but he—"

She got quiet when Nohar stepped up next to her at the comm. The party on the other end began to say, "Sara?"

Then she got quiet as well.

Nohar looked at the screen, not quite believing. Now he knew why Royd's client had asked for him, and why she had required anonymity.

"Maria," Nohar whispered. All the breath had gone out of his body, as if he'd just taken a blow to the kidneys.

"Raj," she replied, using a nickname no one had used for nearly seventeen years. She hadn't changed, she had the exact same Jaguar face he remembered. Nohar began to realize why Manuel had looked familiar.

Maria had been on the cusp of Nohar's memory ever since he had seen Henderson crying. No matter how much time had passed, moreau tears always reminded him of Maria Limón. He always thought of her the way she'd been the second-to-last time he had ever seen her. It was on a battered comm screen like this.

Then she'd been at a public phone, streetlights behind her. Nohar could still remember a shimmer where the lights reflected off the black fur under her whiskers. He remembered the look of accusation in her golden eyes. He could still remember how the unnatural white of the streetlight refracted through a tear caught between the hook of her claw and the pad on her index finger—causing rainbow arcs across the screen.

He didn't remember the words. But he remembered the pain. He remembered her leaving. And he remembered the last time he'd been happy in a relationship with his own kind.

That had been seventeen years ago. But seeing her face again made it feel as if she had left him yesterday.

Seeing the curve of her black-furred cheek he could see echoes of Manuel's unhappy scowl. As he looked at her, a dread certainty began growing in the pit of Nohar's stomach.

He stared at Maria's face on the comm and could barely bring his voice above a whisper. "How old is Manuel?"

Maria looked pained. Her voice was tinny through the comm's speakers, as if she was talking down through all the years that separated them. "I'm so sorry, Raj."

"God *damn!*" Nohar yelled. The voice tore through his throat as if it was barbed and tore the flesh away as it escaped. Nohar slammed a fist into the wall next to the comm. It went through the drywall like it was air, and there was the sound of protesting metal as his hand struck a support. He felt the skin spilt open, and as he pulled his hand away, blood spilled from his knuckles, splattering on the ground.

The whole restaurant was staring at them now. A crop of beady little rat eyes and, close by, the smell of fear. The manager came forward, started to say, "Hey—" then either noticed Nohar's gun or his size, and backed off.

Henderson was backing away, too. "What's wrong?"

Nohar backed away from the wall, looking at his bleeding hand. "What's wrong?" He started laughing. *"What's wrong!"* Once he started laughing, he couldn't stop. It was like a stuttering roar that shook his whole body, belting out the frustration of not just the last few days, but the last decade, the last seventeen years.

He stood there gasping for breath, clasping his bleeding hand, and said, "He's my son." He stared at Maria's image through blurred eyes and said, *"He's my fucking son!"*

Chapter 9

"You should come here," Maria said. "I shouldn't say all this over the comm."

"Okay," Henderson told her. She was staring at Nohar wide eyed, with a barely concealed fear. He was leaning against the wounded wall, his whole body tensed, claws extending and retracting, tearing at the drywall.

Can't say it over the comm, he thought. *You* left *me over the fucking comm.*

Something was torn apart inside him. Somehow this was a worse blow than any pink bastard with a gun could deliver. Nothing he had felt in the past few days could compare with the wound this made inside him.

He kept telling himself that nothing had changed. He was the same person who had walked into the restaurant, and it was the same world outside it. But something drastic had changed. When he had come in here, he was alone by choice, someone who had decided to have no close connections whatever void it left inside him. Now, he was someone who *had* a family, had a connection to someone, and who had had it stolen from him.

It was as if all the emptiness of the last seventeen years was focused on that single moment. Compared to that, the fact that someone tried to burn down his house and kill him seemed minor.

"We'd better go." Henderson put a hand on his arm.

Nohar shrugged away from the touch, but he looked around the restaurant. People had shied away from the comm, and rats were standing up to move away from their tables. The manger had retreated to the back somewhere—probably calling the cops.

Nohar pushed past Henderson and headed for the door.

Maria Limón lived deeper in East LA, in a neighborhood of Hispanic moreaus. The place was better than Compton, the buildings newer. Here they'd actually rebuilt after the riots.

Most of the street signs were in Spanish, which left Nohar lost. Henderson, however, seemed to know where she was going.

They were as out of place walking down the nighttime streets of East LA as they'd been in the restaurant. It was another thing that made Nohar feel misplaced, alien. He was decades out of place here. He came from a time when moreaus were a single people. The idea of moreaus segregating themselves seemed sick and self-destructive. It was Moreys and the pinks; it didn't matter what nationality bred you, or what species. Those were dividing lines drawn up by humans. . . .

As he followed Henderson, he wanted to see some other moreaus, something other than the lab-animal descendants that the quantity-driven Central-American gene-techs had engineered forty years ago. He wanted to see something from Asia, a Chinese ursine, a Vietnamese canine, an African feline, even a frank from some long-lost black projects lab.

But the streets here were as racially pure as a moreau society could achieve. Enough that even Maria, a Brazilian jaguar, would seem as out of place as Sara Henderson.

Maria lived in a housing project that rose three or four dozen stories above the highway and surrounding shops. It was a modern building of flat white concrete. The windows were strips cutting deep black grooves through the floodlit walls. It had been built after the riots, but already looked heavy with age. Henderson led Nohar through a gate in the chain-link fence, and through an abandoned playground stranded in weed-shot asphalt.

The setting reminded Nohar of Saf-Stor. A concrete block where you stored stuff you didn't want anymore. The sight of the building shook him with a sense of claustrophobia.

They stopped in the playground. Henderson had led him in silence through the long walk. Now she looked up at him and asked, "What happened?"

"I knew Maria. She left me." Nohar shook his head. It was still hard for him to accept.

She walked up to him and put a hand on his arm. This time he didn't shrug away from the touch. "Is that it?"

"Yes."

No.

That wasn't it. But Nohar didn't know how to say it. He had been the product of two expatriate moreaus from the Indian Special Forces that escaped to the U.S. right as their homeland was collapsing near the end of the Pan-Asian War. He had probably been conceived on the airlift over the Atlantic.

His mother had died early, and he hadn't found his father until he was fifteen. That meeting with Datia Rajasthan left him despising his father.

Nohar had made a lifetime promise to himself that he would never be responsible for a fatherless child. He had never told himself that in so many words, not until now. He had never donated sperm to a Bensheim Clinic, even though every male moreau he'd known growing up had used it as a source of ready cash.

Nohar's greatest fear was that he would somehow become his father.

"Did you know your father?" Nohar asked Henderson.

"My mom went to a Clinic, like everyone else."

Like almost *everyone else.*

Nohar wondered what Maria had told Manuel about his father. Did she tell him that the Clinic had screwed up? That he was dead? That he just wasn't worth knowing?

Nohar stared up at the light-washed concrete. The sky beyond was dead black, as if the only things here were the building and the void.

"Let's get this over with," Nohar said.

The outside of the building was wrapped in graffiti that extended over Nohar's head. It poured inside, into the lobby, as if it were some fluorescent fungus infecting the building. Nohar looked at it as they entered the building, until he realized that he was looking for his son's name.

They took an elevator thirty stories up to reach Maria's floor. Her apartment was at the end of a graffiti-swathed hallway, the last of a long line of armored doorways. Above every door, cameras peered at them from behind their scratched shields of bulletproof polymer.

It took a long time for Maria to answer the call button. Nohar spent the time building up his anger, rehearsing in his mind what he was going to say.

How dare she keep this from him: How could she deny him that part of his life? They'd even been living in the same city. She should have told him. . . .

When she finally opened the door, all the words left him. The last time he had seen her, she'd been barely twenty years old. She was younger than he was, but right now she looked much older. She sat in a wheelchair, and the short blanket she wore across her knees didn't hide the fact that her legs were oddly twisted. Her free hand rested on her lap, open, claws partially extended. He saw the joints swollen with arthritis.

Her face, however, was the same. She looked up with a weak smile that turned up her feline cheeks, but didn't seem to reach her eyes. "Come in, old friend."

Henderson walked in, but Nohar stood outside, still staring, speechless.

Maria shook her head. "Come on, Raj."

"What happened?" The words came out in a whisper.

Maria's golden eyes turned down toward her legs and the hand in her lap. "Age, Raj. That's all." She lowered her other hand, which had been holding onto the door. It was as bad as the one in her lap.

Age? Your fur hasn't even grayed.

She rested her hand on a large shelflike brace set in the armrest of her wheelchair. She pulled her arm slightly back, the shelf rocked, and the whole chair moved backward to give Nohar room to pass.

Nohar walked in and closed the door behind him. As he did, he saw that the normal keypad had been replaced with an oversized handle. Seeing Maria like this made him angry, this time at the whole process of their creation.

The gene-techs had been making weapons, not people, and a long life was not part of the design criteria. Any problems that occurred outside a ten-year design window wasn't their concern. That meant that once moreys aged a little past their prime, they were prone to arthritis, degenerative hip dysplasia, multiple sclerosis, muscular dystrophy, Huntington's disease, a thousand flavors of cancer, and almost every other degenerative ailment that existed—including a few that were only native to some badly engineered species.

Nohar was lucky. His engineered joints were only slightly arthritic. Maria was only in her thirties. She might never reach Nohar's age.

He felt sick.

Maria rolled into the living room. "I'm sorry I don't have much in the way of chairs here. They're sort of a luxury for me."

There were two old wooden chars that seemed to have been refugees from an old dinette set. Nohar doubted the chairs could take his weight, so instead he walked to the window and stared at the blurry nighttime sprawl of Los Angeles.

The silence stretched uncomfortably until Nohar finally said it.

"Why didn't you tell me?"

He could hear her chair whir, smell her familiar musky scent. In his mind he could still feel the way she was then. Her lithe muscular body—

"I was going to tell you . . ." Her voice was soft, but Nohar could hear a painfully hard undertone to it.

"When?" Nohar's own voice was hard. "Seventeen years? Long enough for him to grow up. When were you going to tell me?"

"When I found out I was pregnant, Raj."

Nohar turned slowly around to face her.

"You stood me up that last time, and I just couldn't take it anymore."

Nohar remembered the call. He remembered Maria's tear-streaked face on his comm, telling him it was over. It had been the last in a long string of dates that had been sacrificed for his work. He couldn't even remember why he had missed it.

"You didn't have the right to keep it from me." In his own ears, Nohar's voice sounded weak and pathetic—the voice of a whining cub.

"Would you have changed, Raj?" Maria wheeled the

chair up to him. "You were married to that pink twitch before he was even born. Why *should* I have told you?"

"I'm his father."

"I'm sorry, Raj, but when did you ever have room in your life for that kind of responsibility?"

"I was never given the opportunity, was I?"

Henderson stepped between them. "*Please.* Manuel is the important thing here. Isn't he?"

Manuel. The reason his life was turned inside out. Nohar turned away from both of them and tried to calm his anger. "What happened?" His voice was quiet, almost a whisper. He felt that if he raised his voice, he would start yelling and clawing the walls.

"Manuel disappeared," Henderson said, "Two weeks ago now."

"I know." Nohar waked up to the window and leaned his head against the top of the frame, staring down into the darkness. "What I need is details. All the things that might be relevant. Where he disappeared from, where he worked, who his friends were, how you and Royd became involved, his habits, if he was involved in any illegal activity—"

Maria snorted.

Nohar shook his head. "You know the questions, and the answers. To get to the bottom of this mess, I need them, too."

For nearly an hour, he questioned both of them about his son. The questions were the sterile antiseptic details that he always ended up asking when he had been a PI. Somehow, though, there seemed a desperate urgency to the routine questions now that it was his own flesh and blood involved.

One of the most basic details was the name. The last name was a slight detail that Royd had left out of their meeting. Something as simple as that began painting a picture of his son in Nohar's head. The kid kept an unfashionable surname, perhaps as a way to distance himself from a moreau culture that would never fully accept him, the mule. It was an impulse Nohar could identify with.

Maria and Royd had expected him to take the case as soon as he looked in the little information file that Royd had left him. All it would have taken was the last name and the date of birth for him to have put it together. Of course, they hadn't figured that he didn't have a working comm out in the woods with him. *Everyone* had a comm. Why the anonymity? Maria thought that it was more likely that he'd look for his son if he didn't know who was hiring him.

Where did the fifty-grand offer come from? It's not like Maria could afford it.

They both looked surprised at that. Maria had only managed to scrape together five grand. It must have been Royd's money. When Henderson realized that, she broke down into tears. . . .

Nohar began to feel a little guilty about how he'd treated the late Charles Royd. He'd never thought he'd ever meet a rich pink who could turn out to be a decent person.

He drilled them about everything he could think of about Manuel's life. None of the answers seemed to lead to the Bad Guys. Manuel seemed pretty typical, if isolated. He'd gone through the accelerated moreau educational system, and had been working with a high school equivalency for the past three years. Maria said she had some hopes for college, but the way she said it made Nohar wonder if Manuel had the same hopes.

Manuel worked at the Compton Bensheim Clinic, mostly as a shipping clerk, not working with the patients. Nohar wondered if that was a bit of morey prejudice, *let's not have the mule working the desk where prospective mothers might see him.*

The only real friends Manuel had—that Maria knew about—were his coworkers. No school friends—Manuel's time in the morey excuse for a school system seemed predictably awful.

He'd left home at twelve. Though, despite that, he had come to visit Maria faithfully every Friday.

In fact, Manuel hadn't missed a single Friday until two weeks ago. When Maria called to find out what happened, no one had seen him since the Tuesday before. She had called the police and had gotten a sympathetic but nonproductive response.

When Maria was trying to discover where Manuel had gotten to, she discovered Sara Henderson looking for him as well. When Nohar turned around to look at Henderson, she said, "Me and Manuel, we—like—"

"I have the picture," Nohar said. Henderson and his son. He wondered what had brought the two together. How old was Henderson? She was in law school, that put her at least a couple of years older than Manuel, and only if she started college right after the morey public schools spit her out. It seemed an odd match, but Nohar had seen odder.

"Royd did some legal work for the Clinic," Henderson said by way of explanation. "I made a lot of trips there. That's how we met."

"It was Sara's idea that we get Mr. Royd to help us." Maria looked up at Nohar. "It was my idea we try and hire you."

"Why? It's been ten years since I had a case—"

Maria looked up into Nohar's eyes. "Because you'd take it, Raj. No one else would care."

"So what was Manuel involved in?" Nohar asked.

Both females stared blankly at him.

Nohar felt the edge of a growl creep into his voice. "I've been going over this for an hour. Neither of you have told me anything that might have dredged up an army of human commandos who've tried to kidnap or kill anyone who might be looking for him."

Maria looked at Henderson. "*I've* been looking for him."

Nohar was about to respond with a sudden realization struck him. Why wouldn't these people come after Maria? What were they after? If they were trying to cover up something that happened to Manuel, they were doing a shit-poor job of it. Just killing Royd increased the risk that someone would connect the whole thing to Manuel's disappearance.

What if Manuel was running from something?

What if he was running from the Bad Guys, and they didn't want someone else finding him? That almost made sense. . . .

"Does anyone else know I'm Manuel's father? Any records?"

"Only Manuel," Maria said. "And he only knows a little of what you were like in Cleveland—"

"What about Royd?" Nohar asked.

Maria shook her head. Henderson looked Nohar up and down. "I didn't even know. Not until an hour ago."

"I was afraid he might not hire you if he knew," Maria said.

Nohar tried to construct a sequence of events in his head. Manuel disappears. The Bad Guys start looking for him—probably the first to start looking. Then Maria and Henderson work out a deal with Royd. At some point after Royd makes his pitch to Nohar, the Bad Guys come in and torture the poor bastard. Probably still looking for Manuel. They don't find what they want, but they do they find out Royd had come to Nohar, and they decide they don't want any competition.

If the Bad Guys were looking for Manuel, their attempt to grab Henderson meant they hadn't found him yet.

That brought the question back to why they hadn't grabbed Maria. Nohar had an uneasy feeling that he knew the reason.

Bait.

If the whole point of all this was to find Manuel, you wouldn't strong-arm the kid's mother. You'd watch her apartment, bug the place, tap her comm, and wait for the kid to make some sort of showing.

Worse, that meant that where he had thought that he and Henderson had slipped away from these people, they had really stepped up under their noses.

Nohar walked past the two women and hit the light switch, plunging the room into darkness. He heard Maria's wheelchair spin around. "What are you—?"

Nohar raised a hand. Her eyes had adjusted, and she responded to his quieting gesture. He pulled his binocular camera out of his pocket and shifted its spectrum toward the infrared as he raised it.

He looked toward the window and saw what he had been afraid of. A small shimmering spot of infrared light sparkled on the edge of Maria's window. Nohar had a good idea what it was.

Someone had pointed a laser mike at the window, picking up every vibration their voices made in the glass. Nohar edged around until he could get a bead on where the listener was stationed.

He narrowed the source down to a window on a black van parked in the project's weed-shot parking lot. Nohar cursed himself for not noticing the out-of-place van earlier.

Nohar took a picture of the van and slipped the camera back into his pocket. He flipped the light back on. "Oops, sorry about that." His back was to the window, and he held a finger up to his lips.

Maria's voice was uncertain, but she went with Nohar's lead. "No, it's all right. . . ." She looked at Henderson, but Sara seemed just as confused.

"It's been a long day." Nohar walked through a short hall and found Maria's bathroom. Nohar noticed the long padded handles on the fixtures and felt an irrational wave of anger at all pinks, especially the ones in the van. "Do you mind if I spend a little time to clean up?" He turned on the faucets in the sink without asking.

"That's fine." Maria's voice hovered close to a question as Nohar slipped out of the bathroom and headed for the front door. Maria and Henderson followed him.

He opened the door and faced both of them. He pointed at both of them and then pointed at his mouth, then made yakking gestures with his hand. Henderson stared at him blankly, but Maria got the point. She reached over and tapped Henderson with the back of her hand. "Do you think these people got to Manuel?"

Henderson looked flustered. Still staring at Nohar she said, "I don't know. Why are they doing this to us?"

Nohar nodded encouragement, tapping the wall with his finger and pointing to his ear. *They're listening.*

Before he closed the door on their strained conversation, he pointed to his wrist and flashed them the fingers on his left hand twice. *Ten minutes.*

If he took longer than that to come back, he probably wasn't coming back.

He closed the door and began running for the elevator.

Chapter 10

It had to be sheer luck, but the bastards in the van weren't on to him as he reached the ground floor. He was hoping—counting on—the fact that they were listening, not watching, and they'd been doing it long enough to become complacent.

What really worried Nohar was who the men in the van might have called in when they heard him and Henderson arrive. The Bad Guys must have decided to let the pot stir to see if the three of them came up with what they wanted. But by now there had been enough talk for the Bad Guys to piece a lot together. It was only a matter of time before they made the decision to come down on them.

He had seven minutes.

Nohar left the side of the lobby opposite the parking lot that held the van. He headed straight out, keeping the floodlit bulk of the building between him and the watchers. He reached the fence ringing the grounds and didn't bother following it to a gate. He grabbed the fence, pulling himself up on top in a crouch that set off flares of pain in his bad knee. He stayed there as long as he could stand it, staring at the barbed wire angling away from him, over the outside of the fence.

Then he grabbed a strut holding the barbed wire in place, and vaulted over the wire.

He hit the ground in a stumble that fired pain off in his knee and his shoulder. He could taste his own exertion like copper in his mouth.

Six minutes.

He backed into the darkness and circled the property around toward the van. He could smell them before he reached the driveway that led to the project's parking lot. Three pinks had been here; their distinctive odor was as obvious as a neon sign. How the hell had he missed it before?

Nohar drew his gun and wondered if he was still capable of going through all this shit.

He edged up the driveway, sticking to the shadows on the upwind shoulder of the road. The van was twenty meters into the parking lot, on the edge farthest from Maria's building. The van was a modern Electrostar that looked out of place on the broken asphalt, in the midst of cars that were either headed for the junk heap, or customized beyond recognition. It was parked next to an old Ford Jerboa with a gold paint job, jacked-up rear, and a purple-fringed interior.

Five minutes.

Nohar was running on instinct. He wasn't sure what he was going to do, even when he started running up on the van. He held a dim hope that he wasn't going to shoot anyone. Knowing who he was dealing with, that seemed unlikely.

He closed the distance with the van in a matter of seconds. He landed between the van and the Jerboa, his back against the van's cold composite wall. He edged up on the passenger-side door. It had tinted windows that reflected the sodium lights of the parking lot.

Nohar sucked in a breath.

Four minutes.

He spun around before the men in the van would have time to react, bringing the butt of his gun down on the passenger window. There was a tense moment when the thought of armored polymer crossed Nohar's mind, but the window was just plain safety glass and exploded inward when the blow hit.

Nohar pointed the Vind in toward the driver's seat, yelling, "Nobody move."

Nobody did.

Nobody was there.

Nohar was pointing his gun at an empty driver's seat. He ducked his head in to look in the back. That was equally empty. There wasn't anyone in the van. The smell of the pink owners was strong, but ghostly. They hadn't been in the van for a while.

Nohar shook his head and lowered his gun. He did have the right van; he could see a portable comm unit in back, what looked like a satellite uplink, and what had to be the laser mike on a tripod, pointing toward the driver's side window, which was open a crack to let the beam reach Maria's window.

Chalk one up for the Bad Guys. Wherever they were watching, it was from a distance.

Nohar reached in and opened the passenger door. As he did, he heard the whine of the flywheel as the Electrostar's inductors were engaged.

"Shit!"

Nohar had a choice of backing up or diving in before the van pulled out. He dove into the passenger seat, broken glass digging into his knee as the van's autopilot engaged.

Nohar held on as the van accelerated over the parking lot's broken pavement. He could see a red light on the dash flashing the alarm he'd triggered when he busted the window.

There was little point to subtlety now. The Bad Guys had a live uplink to what was going on. They knew their van was compromised, and they probably had a video feed of him right now. He reached over to the dash and began flipping up the nav display. Security measures kept him from reprogramming the comm, but the Bad Guys left the display functions alone, so as the van tore out of the lot, swinging the passenger door shut on a sharp turn, Nohar managed to call up a map on the headsup with the van's programmed route flashing in red.

It was going for the freeway, then north to an address in Pasadena. That was all Nohar needed. He didn't want to follow the van into an ambush. He slipped into the back of the van, bracing himself in a crouch behind the driver's seat. Then he lowered his Vind and aimed at the nav computer.

The Vind exploded in the enclosed space, and a nasty hole opened up in the dashboard. The headsup winked out and the van rolled to a stop as the governors kicked in.

Three minutes.

Nohar backed into the van, checking over the equipment they'd been using to eavesdrop on Maria. It was sophisticated stuff. Nohar figured that the uplink alone cost a bit shy of ten grand. There was a set of numbers on an LCD set into the base of the uplink. Nohar noted them.

He probably only had a few more minutes before the Bad Guys descended on Maria's apartment complex. He had to get back and get both of them out of there.

"Is there a friend's place you can stay at?" Nohar ran into the apartment, gun still drawn, killing lights and going toward the windows. He looked out and cursed his bad vision. It had never been great for distance, but age seemed to have begun eating at his once-excellent night vision. He had to put the gun away and pull out his camera to make sense of the parking lot.

The van was still on the driveway, stalled, hazards blinking. No sign of the Bad Guys yet.

"What's going on?" Maria voice was strained.

"Like, what happened out there?" Stress brought out the Southern California in Henderson's voice.

"We don't have much time." Nohar kept scanning the parking lot, shifting through the spectrum on his camera.

"They were watching this apartment. They know I'm here with Henderson. If they're true to form, they'll fall on this place like a tac-nuke."

"But—" Maria began.

"They were watching here, waiting for Manuel to show, I think." Nohar lowered the camera and waved both of them into the bedroom. "Grab what you need. You help her. We have to get out of here before—"

They must have heard it about the same time he did. Nohar turned back to the window. When he placed a hand on the glass, he could feel the vibration caused by the rotors.

A black helicopter hovered over the parking lot, close enough for Nohar to make it out without the camera. It was heavy, armored, and three times as wide and twice as deep as a civilian aircar. The thing was matte black, and an even blacker hole was opening in its side as it descended.

Nohar raised the camera and saw it barely kiss the parking lot's surface. The camera was still set for IR, so the hole in the black helicopter's side was suddenly the brightest thing in the lot. The pit in its belly glowed, and Nohar saw the IR shadows of a dozen men spill out toward the building.

"Shit. We're moving *now!* Get out the door." They should have all been gone by now, before these guys showed up.

Nohar put away the camera and drew the Vind. How the hell were the three of them going to get out of here? He pushed through the door after Henderson and Maria. He felt a sinking feeling as he looked at her wheelchair. They couldn't get her down the stairs, and the elevators in the lobby would be the first thing the Bad Guys would secure.

"No chance of an aircar lot on the roof?"

"In this neighborhood you're lucky you have the roof."

"How do we get out of here, past them—" Nohar was at a loss, swinging his gun up and down the hallway, expecting commandos to storm them at any moment.

"Maria?" Henderson spoke up.

Maria and Nohar turned to face her.

"You have, like, a friend in this building, maybe upstairs?"

"I know a lot of people here."

"Come on, then."

Nohar followed, willing to try anything.

*   *   *

Maria had a friend on the forty-third floor. They were lucky on two counts. First, the Bad Guys hadn't seized control of the elevators yet, and second, the elevators only had up-or-down indicators on the outside, nothing to tell bystanders what floors the elevators were on.

When they reached the door to the friend's apartment, Henderson began pounding on it. Nohar nervously stashed the Vind in the holster under his shirt.

After a while the external camera swiveled to cover them and a whispery voice buzzed through the speaker next to it, "Ungodly hour, what is this—Maria, is that you?"

"Let us in, Sam," Maria said.

"We need to use your comm," Henderson said.

The camera moved toward Henderson, and the voice said, "Well, ain't you the pretty one? I guess for you, Maria—" The door slid open on a gray lepus in a ragged bathrobe. "Who's your friend?" the rabbit stared at Henderson.

Nohar pushed through the door, leading the other two in. "Where's the comm?" Nohar asked.

"If you're going to be like that," the rabbit said.

Maria wheeled up next to the rabbit and said, "Now, Sam. We need your help." She raised the back of her hand and patted his cheek with it.

Sam sighed and waved them into the living room.

Nohar led Henderson into the room, feeling time pressing on his back.

The living room was a wash of colored lights and incense. A black velvet couch faced a yellow comm that was two decades out of date. Above the couch hung a giant holo of "The Last Supper," the principals played by various moreys. Christ was an angelic canine, while Judas was some sort of ferret.

Henderson stepped in front of the comm and started to make a call. Nohar split his attention between her, the window at the end of the living room, and the door where Maria and Sam were talking. He expected to be on the wrong end of an assault at any minute.

"*Eye on LA,* Enrique Bartolo speaking. How can I help you—Sara? Is that you?" On the other end of the line was a fuzzy picture of a human. Nohar couldn't tell if the fuzziness was due to the connection, or because the pink had just woke up.

"Hi, Rick—"

"Christ, lady, where're you calling from? What happened?" The pink's face began to show some interest. Nohar could tell he was looking past Henderson at the rest of the apartment. Nohar stepped aside, out of view of the comm. He didn't know how much publicity there was connecting him to Royd's death, but he didn't want to test this guy.

"—this is hot, Rick. There's a SWAT team going into Pastoria Towers in East LA. Guns, armored helicopter, the works."

"No, shit, when?"

"Five minutes ago. They're running through the building right now."

"Christ! Then we've got to get a team moving now. Thanks. Where're you?"

"Where do you think?"

The pink's face went a little blank. "No shit? Well, we're—"

Enrique Bartolo never finished the comment, because the line went dead. A few minutes later the lights flickered and went out. "Just in time," Henderson said.

"What was all that?" Nohar asked, edging up to the window and looking at the helicopter in the parking lot. By now the commandos had found Maria's apartment empty, and were probably doing a systematic sweep through the building. Cutting the comm lines and the power would be the start of that.

"Rick's an old friend. Royd's office used to feed him stories all the time about folks screwing us—nonhumans—over."

"A reporter—" The more Nohar thought about it, the more it made sense. The Bad Guys weren't cops. They didn't like the daylight. Unless they were part of the Fed, the presence of cameras might scare them off. Even if they were Fed agents, cameras might keep them from summarily shooting someone.

With Maria in a wheelchair there was nothing more they could do but wait.

Nohar stayed by the window and pulled out his camera. It seemed that the commandos were everywhere out there, ringing the parking lot. He could hear noises through the skeleton of the building now. Odd thumping sounds through the air vents. Occasionally, Nohar thought he heard something that might have been muffled gunfire.

"What's going on?" Sam asked. For the first time Nohar heard in his voice how old he must be. His voice had become high and papery, the lisp much more pronounced.

Maria, sitting, was at eye-level with him. "Some people have broken into the building."

"Who? What people?" Sam walked into the living room. He moved slowly, limping on a bad leg. He walked up to Nohar and looked him up and down. "Oh, this is bad. It's you, isn't it?"

Nohar didn't know what to say, so he returned to watching out the window.

"You, you're the one who killed that lawyer." Nohar felt something soft strike his hip. *"Bastard."*

Nohar looked down and saw Sam pounding on him with both fists. Nohar barely felt the blows. Looking down at Sam, the only emotion Nohar could dredge up was a feeling of pity.

Henderson stepped up and pulled Sam away from him. "Calm down."

"Calm down? That cat's a terrorist. He's likely to kill everyone in this building. I saw it on the comm."

"You don't believe everything you see on the comm." Henderson led him back into another room. "Do you?"

"Why shouldn't I?" Nohar heard Sam reply.

Nohar shook his head slowly and raised his camera again.

"Do they want to kill us?" Maria's voice sounded small and weak. The words tore at his heart. Her voice hadn't changed at all from what he remembered.

"I don't know." Nohar shook his head. "I think they want Manuel, and they don't know where to find him."

"But why?"

"That's the big question." Nohar lowered the binocular camera and turned around. "Every time they show up, they seem more blatant. More desperate . . ."

Maria looked away from Nohar, toward the bedroom where Henderson had led Sam. Whispered parts of their conversation drifted toward them. Henderson seemed to be explaining the last few hours to the rabbit.

Maria looked back at Nohar. Her eyes were moist. "I saw about Royd on the comm, too."

"About me?"

"Don't worry, I know you didn't." She wiped her eye with the back of a twisted hand. "But were they right about what they did to him?"

All Nohar could do was nod.

"Could that happen to us?" Maria asked him.

Nohar walked up, knelt, and wrapped his arms around her. She rested her head against Nohar's shoulder and started shaking. "I keep telling myself I have to be strong for Manuel—but I couldn't take that. I can't take any more pain."

Nohar ran his hand over her head and whispered, "Shh."

"I don't have the right to ask you anything—"

"We'll get through this."

"—but don't let them do that to me."

"I won't."

Maria pushed him weakly, and Nohar let go of her. She was looking at him with a grave expression. "I mean this, Raj. If they're going to torture me to get information about my son, I want you to kill me."

Nohar looked into her eyes and couldn't find any words.

"Promise me." Maria held up her hands in a pleading gesture. They were cupped, as if to catch Nohar's nonexistent tears.

Nohar was about to respond when a wash of white light flooded the living room. Nohar spun around to face the window, where the light was coming from.

He headed toward the window, and behind him he heard Henderson rush out from the bedroom asking, "What's happening?"

When Nohar reached the window, he announced, "I think your friends are here."

He didn't need his enhanced camera to make out what was going on. Even his rotten vision could make out the two aircars shining floodlights on the scene around the building. The aircars looked like huge flying beetles with two huge fans in place of wings. On the sides, twinned pylons carried spotlights and video equipment that was probably more sophisticated than any recon unit had during the Pan-Asian War.

When the spotlight swept by their window, Nohar caught sight of the side of one of the copters. It was painted in fluorescent colors so that no one could miss the screaming red logo of *Eye on LA.*

Nohar raised his camera so he could focus on the parking lot and what was going on.

Henderson had called it right. The Bad Guys were in retreat. Nohar could see two on either side of the hatch in the helicopter, weapons raised as if they expected someone to fire on their retreat.

More of them poured from the entrance of the building, running for the helicopter. In a few moments the helicopter had lifted off—just in time for the groundcars of another half-dozen news crews to arrive.

"You did good, Henderson."

"Sara," she said. She had edged up to the other side of the window to see what was going on. One of the *Eye on LA* aircars was trying to follow the unmarked helicopter; the other still hovered over the building.

"Sara," Nohar repeated.

"So," she asked, "are you going to find Manuel?"

He nodded.

Chapter 11

They had to wait until the power returned before they could leave. By then dawn was breaking and about half the news crews had left. They managed to slip out from under the cameras. The reporters had their hands full with all the morey residents who wanted everyone to know how their rights were violated by these pink commandos—who everyone assumed were cops.

The Bad Guys had found Maria's apartment empty, then had begun systematically breaking into every apartment in the building. As Nohar escorted Maria and Henderson through the crowded lobby, he heard at least two stories about gunfire being exchanged.

They had to make their way outside the parking lot to

meet their taxi, because the police—real ones this time—had dressed up in riot gear and set up barricades around the building to keep people and vehicles out. Nohar worried about the three of them looking obvious in the sea of Hispanic rodents, but the cops were as overwhelmed as the reporters.

The cops had it worse than the reporters, the residents at least *liked* the reporters. Nohar had the feeling that if the cops weren't armed, they might not have survived being this close to Pastoria Towers.

They passed through the confusion, and to the taxi, without much difficulty. It was another automated cab, and Nohar let Maria direct it while he fell into an exhausted slumber.

Nohar dreamed of his father. They weren't pleasant dreams.

Nohar had been sired by Datia Rajasthan, commander of the mutinous airlift that brought almost all of Nohar's species into the U.S. just as the Indian military began collapsing. His mother had never told him who his father was. That was something he had to unearth himself, after she was gone.

He was only fifteen, still part of a street gang, when he'd found Datia. At first the discovery had impressed him. Datia had become, by then, a national figure advocating moreau rights. It wasn't until Nohar had met him that he'd discovered that Datia was a fanatic, more interested in controlling the destiny of the nonhuman population than he was in any family he might have had.

Datia couldn't have given a shit for Nohar.

They had only met once, and shortly after that the country erupted into riots—which many blamed on Datia Rajasthan. Datia was gunned down by the National Guard only a few dozen blocks from where Nohar was living. The only thing Nohar had ever gotten from his father was the gun he carried—something he received after Datia's death.

Datia Rajasthan hadn't even acknowledged Nohar as his son until he was dying in a burned-out building in Cleveland's Moreytown. There he mentioned his son to an audience of police, paramedics, and National Guardsmen. Nohar hadn't even been there.

In his dream, Nohar walks through the ruins of the

building where his father had been killed. He looks for his father's body. He finally finds a corpse, high up in the building, where no roof lies between him and a black rolling sky.

Nohar turns the corpse over. Manuel's face stares up at him.

Someone laughs behind him, and Nohar spins around to confront whoever it is.

Datia Rajasthan is laughing at him. In his arms he holds a young Maria Limón. She laughs at him, too. "Now," his father says, "you know how it feels."

Nohar crouches and growls. "Lying bastard. You're the one who died."

Datia shakes his head. "No. You died."

Datia points the Vind at Nohar and fires.

Maria's friend was an old canine named Beverly who lived on the fringes of Compton. Her eyes were clouded over, and Nohar thought she was nearly blind. Her eyes reminded him of Elijah, the half-blind dog in the hills.

But she walked with her nose forward, and it was hard to tell she couldn't see.

"Come on in, Maria. Introduce your friends." Beverly ushered them all into a two-room apartment. The inside was better kept than the hallway, which was wrapped in stains, trash, and graffiti. Beverly lived in a neat pair of whitewashed rooms. The apartment was in the basement, so there weren't many windows. Beverly compensated by having plants hanging from the pipes that ran across the ceiling.

The apartment smelled like a garden.

Maria rolled in first and said, "Sara, and Nohar."

"Pleased to meet both of you." She extended a hand and patted Nohar's forearm. "I'm afraid you'll have to duck a little. The ceiling's a bit low in here."

Nohar let Henderson go in first, then he ducked inside himself. He had to bend over more than a little. Not only was the ceiling low, but there were pipes, and below them the plants. He had to bend almost double, and he still set one begonia swinging.

Beverly shut the door and faced them. Her ears perked up, and Nohar saw her tail wag, a smile in compensation for her lack of facial expression. "Can I get anyone some tea?"

"I think we can all use something to settle our nerves," Henderson said.

"Sure, my dear." Beverly turned around and began opening cabinets in the other side of the living room. Nohar realized now that there was a kitchen hidden in that wall. As she filled a pot at a sink hidden behind a cabinet door, she asked, "Maria, what brings you here? The room's thick with worry."

Nohar could smell it himself. He just hadn't been noticing it since he'd been living with it for the past twelve hours.

"I'm sorry," Maria said, "I don't want to bring trouble to your doorstep, Bev."

"Shush. I'll take trouble to have some visitors. Tell me about it." She fiddled a few more minutes, then put the pot into another cabinet that apparently doubled as a microwave. "You aren't going to scare me after living in this neighborhood for twenty-five years."

"It's about Manuel," Maria began.

"Our son," Nohar said, almost involuntarily.

"Oh, dear," Beverly said. "This *is* going to be interesting."

Beverly fed them on Chinese green tea and a package of processed meat that Nohar supposed once bore some relationship to a pig or a cow. It was what passed for carnivore food in Compton. After all his years away from processed food, Nohar was glad that the strongest taste it had was the salt.

Maria gave Beverly an abbreviated version of what happened. At the end of it, Beverly shook her head and said, "Isn't this exciting?"

"That's one word for it," Henderson said. Her voice was weak and frustrated. Nohar looked down at her and saw how fatigued she looked. Her fur was sticking out at odd angles, and she seemed to have shrunk within her ill-fitting clothes. Looking at her, Nohar realized how bad off he must look. His fur was matted and still smelled weakly of algae. His shirt was an opaque gray, and his pants were torn badly enough to see his leg all the way up to the hip.

"Well, you all need some rest," Beverly said. "And to clean yourselves up. You're all welcome to my bathroom." She walked past Nohar and into the bedroom. "I'll find some comforters for all of you."

Her nose wrinkled as she passed Nohar.

"Did you fall in a sewer, my friend?"

"Reservoir," Nohar said.

Beverly shook her head. "Those clothes go in a disposal chute. And you get the shower first." She patted his shoulder. Even sitting, it was about even with her own. "I don't want to sound ungracious, but I don't want that smell sinking into my furniture."

Nohar chuckled a bit. It was the first time he had felt any real lightness since before this had all started. "Yes, ma'am."

Beverly chuckled herself. "I'll get you something else to wear," she said as she walked on into the bedroom.

Nohar pulled off his shoes and began making a compact pile of his wasted clothes. He emptied his pockets onto the coffee table. He used coasters to rest his possessions on, since most were still streaked with algae.

When he peeled off his shirt, Henderson looked across at him and said, "What are you doing?"

"You heard her. And I've wanted this pink crap off for days." He could feel the fabric adhering to his fur as he pulled off his shirt and stuffed it in one shoe. He began unhooking his holster, was stymied for a place to put it, then finally he hooked it on an overhead pipe next to a spider plant.

"But you're, you're . . ." Henderson seemed unnaturally flustered, and when Nohar started undoing his belt she just turned away from him. Maria was looking at her oddly, as if she was surprised at the way Henderson was acting, too.

It took a few long moments for Nohar to realize what was the matter. And realizing it made him feel all the more alien.

Henderson had inherited the human neurosis about clothing. To Nohar's generation, clothing was a contrivance used solely to appease the humans that most moreys had to deal with. To someone whose body was covered in fur, pink clothing was often useless and annoying, something to be used only when necessary.

To his generation, Maria's, too, stripping in front of someone meant as little as a pink taking off his hat.

Now, however, it was sinking in that, in his first foray into Compton, a place almost completely absent of pinks, he hadn't seen one morey going without the human-mandated clothing. When he was living back in Cleveland's Morey-town, half of the moreys he'd see would be going around with as little as possible.

Henderson's embarrassment made him want to cover himself up.

He sighed and shoved his pants into his other shoe. "I better go and shower off—" He glanced at Henderson, who still wasn't looking at him.

Maria looked at Henderson and nodded, as if she had just realized what was bothering her.

Nohar sighed and ducked into a bathroom that was much too small for him.

It took him nearly an hour to clean himself and dry out his fur. He could only fit part of his body in the shower at a time. He borrowed way too much of Beverly's soap. And he almost clogged the john with the clumps of fur he brushed off his body. He spent another fifteen minutes returning the bathroom to the shape he'd found it in.

He left feeling better now that the algae was out of his fur. He used the wall-mounted body dryer, but before he left, he grabbed one of the towels and wrapped it around his waist for Henderson's benefit.

When he left, Henderson wasn't there anymore. The only one in the living room was Beverly, who sat in a small easy chair in the corner of the room. She didn't look at him when he entered the room, but her ears perked up.

She held a canine finger to the tip of her muzzle, telling him to be quiet. Nohar nodded, even though he didn't think she could see him. He ducked into the living room, dropped the towel on the couch, and sat down next to it. It felt good to have his body relax for once, even in a space this small. The few snatches of rest he had gotten up to now didn't really count. He'd been too exhausted to receive any comfort. Even in the taxi coming here, his body wasn't so much resting as refusing to function.

Beverly spoke quietly. "I put Maria and her friend in my bedroom. They needed to get some rest." She raised a cup of tea to her muzzle and delicately lapped at it.

"That's good," Nohar's voice rumbled deep in his chest. "I wish they weren't involved—"

"From the sound of it, they involved you." She cocked her head as if daring him to tell her different.

"The Bad Guys involved me." Nohar sighed and reached for his own tea. The cup was small and nearly hidden in his hands. "They tried to kill me before I even knew Manuel had anything to do with me."

"You didn't know you had a son?"

Nohar stared into the cup he held in his hand, at the dark swirling liquid, and felt the knot of anger again. "How could you keep that from anyone?"

"I don't know, my friend. I won't condone it. But I've known Maria for years, and I knew she loves Manuel. Maybe she thought she was protecting him."

"We have it all mapped out." Nohar kept staring into the tea, the words pouring out uncontrolled. "We make kids at a Bensheim Clinic. It's so fucking common that fatherhood is reduced to a couple of sperm cells, even when—" The words choked off, and Nohar sipped his tea. He didn't know why he was babbling to this old canine. He was tired.

He shook his head. "It's as if it's abnormal to *care* about it."

"We're caught," Beverly said, "between nature, culture, and engineering." She made a small sound that was between a muffled bark and a sad laugh. "The balance we've struck seems equally unworkable on all three levels."

"I shouldn't unload on you." Nohar finished off his tea.

Beverly stood up and picked up the teapot. She managed to find his cup and refill it by touch. "Nonsense. You've had a trial. You can't bury feelings. . . ."

Nohar shook his head. "I've been doing fine till now."

How could someone do that?

How could a mother deny her child his father?

Why didn't she tell him?

When Nohar had that thought, he wasn't sure if he was thinking of Maria, or his mother.

Chapter 12

Nohar talked to Beverly longer than he expected. After sidestepping his personal life, they managed a few hours discussing the way things were twenty years ago, and how the changes since then weren't all for the best. It was the first real conversation he'd had with anyone in the past ten years. It made him fell a little less alien.

He could identify with Beverly. He had gone off into the woods, but she'd been as much in exile in this apartment, just as isolated, just as alone. Just as lonely.

Unfortunately, he wasn't free to converse. There was still Bad Guys out there, and there was still Manuel, somewhere.

Beverly had a comm and after they had finished their second teapot, Nohar planted himself behind it and began working on digging out of the hole they had all fallen in.

His first call was to a place in Cleveland that he hoped was still in business.

The line flashed a few times; the screen was distorted and out of focus. Nohar doubted that Beverly had ever gotten the picture properly aligned.

The blue AT&T test pattern dissolved into a shot of an office. Nohar saw the paneled walls and decided that Budget Surplus and his old friend Bobby were both long gone. He was about to cut the connection when he heard a familiar voice say, "Coming . . ."

The voice's owner walked in front of the screen, "International Systems and Surplus—"

The man on the other end of the comm stopped talking and just stared at the screen.

Nohar was equally speechless. The last time he'd seen Robert Dittrich, his old friend had been confined to a wheelchair—like he'd been since childhood. But there was no question that the man staring blankly at him was the same person, and he was *standing*.

"Good God!" Bobby exclaimed. "Is that you, Nohar?"

Nohar shook his head and said, "Bobby?"

Bobby pulled up a chair and sat down in front of the comm and shook his head. "And you still don't put on clothes to talk on the comm. Christ, what've you been doing with yourself? What, five, ten years?"

"Well, haven't been doing as well as you. What happened to 'Budget Surplus'?"

Bobby shrugged. "Got in on the ground floor of a good deal—passed someone on to a hacker acquaintance on the West Coast, and the deal was rich enough for the finder's fee to set me up for life. Managed to jack the place up a few notches on the respectability scale."

Nothing remains the same, Nohar thought. "Your legs—" He didn't quite know how to finish the question.

Not that Bobby needed him to. "Oh, I was still in the chair last we talked." He stood and slapped his thigh. "Good old American cybernetics—remember when there wasn't such a thing? But we actually managed to get a project going at the Cleveland Clinic a few years ago, reverse-engineering some old Japanese prewar technology. Finally got it working."

Nohar shook his head. He had known Bobby since they'd been kids. And even though Bobby had been wheelchair-bound, he'd always been the one who was going to take on the world. Nohar had never thought Bobby might actually win....

"Hey, enough about me. What can I do for you, old friend?" He glanced at the bottom of the screen, where the transmit information usually scrolled by. "You're still in Lala land, I see."

Nohar swallowed. He didn't feel quite right about dropping stuff into Bobby's lap after so long. But there wasn't anyone else he knew to call. "This wasn't a social call, Bobby."

Bobby sat down, and there was a grave expression on his face. Of all the pinks that he had ever known, Bobby had always been the best at reading Nohar's facial expression. Right now it was obvious that Bobby could still read him like a book. "What's the matter, old friend?"

"Do you still do miracles on the net?"

Bobby smiled weakly and shook his head. "You're

talking to someone ten years behind the curve. That's a young man's game. I do software, but I'm mostly a manger now."

"Oh . . ." Nohar frowned, wondering where he would go next.

Bobby smiled. "But there're perks to managing. I have a half-dozen bright young hackers on my payroll. What do you need?"

"I just have a number off the display from a satellite uplink. I don't know if it's an access code, a location, or what—but I want to know who was on the other end of the satellite."

"You don't go for simple, do you?" Bobby was smiling. "Give me the number, and the location of the uplink—I might be able to get the skunk works to pull something up for you."

Nohar passed on the information, and added, "Thanks for helping me out, after all this time."

"You're still a friend. And you have no idea how much I owe you. Now, where do I get hold of you?"

"I'll get hold of you."

Bobby frowned slightly. "Okay. Are you in some sort of trouble?"

"You don't want to know."

"That bad?"

Nohar nodded.

"Well, I hope I can help you with this. When will I hear from you?"

"I don't know. Next couple of days."

"Good luck."

"Thanks." Nohar shut off the connection.

Nohar spent another few hours on the comm searching through every local news provider he could access. He started with the story of Royd's death and worked from there.

It wasn't encouraging. Not only did the stories have video of him, big as life, taken from the little cop drones. But they had his name, too. "Nohar Rajasthan, ex-Private Investigator" was attached to every story in connection with Royd's death.

Somehow, the death of Charles Royd was linked to a

shadowy moreau terrorist group that someone had labeled "The Outsiders." These "Outsiders" had apparently taken credit for Royd, and the bombing at Alcatraz. The attack on Pastoria Towers was being billed as an antiterrorist raid to uncover a cabal of these "Outsiders—" That's how the press played it, even though no Fed agency was admitting anything to do with the raid, and a few said they were investigating it.

Most of the news seemed to have made up its mind.

Most.

A small news agency out of San Francisco, the Nonhuman News Network, had a different slant on things. They took the tack that the "Outsiders" didn't exist, and were a cover for covert actions by the Federal Government against the moreau community. The news was paranoid, involving everything from death squads to biological warfare. It seemed all too plausible from Nohar's vantage point.

He agreed with the NNN story: it was unlikely that any morey group would choose to target Royd.

Nohar couldn't find anything about Manuel in the public corners of the net. That didn't surprise him. If his theory was right, and the Bad Guys were looking for Manuel, they would have been watching the comm for him, too. They probably were a lot more sophisticated about it, too, judging by the hardware their grunts carried. There wasn't even so much as an acknowledgment that the cops were looking for a missing person of his description.

He also couldn't find any news about a shootout in Beverly Hills last night, or even something about a Mirador crashing to a halt. However, there *were* reports about Henderson's disappearance. Nohar wondered who had reported it, since the story'd come out about an hour before Henderson was due back at work.

Whatever the reason, the police wanted her for questioning in relation to Royd's murder. Strangely, Nohar didn't find any equivalent stories about Maria. Nohar wondered about that. The Bad Guys weren't cops—at least they weren't *the* cops—but they were certainly able to *use* the cops. Why not have them looking for Maria as well as Henderson and him?

Unless they were trying to keep the whole thing with Manuel under wraps. They didn't want the cops looking for Maria or Manuel, at least not publicly.

The last thing he did at the comm was patch in his old digital camera so he could get hard copies of what he'd been looking at the past twenty-four hours. He slowly managed to enhance a picture of the Mirador that had ambushed Henderson, but that was little use other than to see how they'd managed to obscure the ID tags on the car. He didn't even have a clean shot of the attackers' faces. That was a dead end.

There were a few other pictures. The only one that had much promise was a wide shot of the copter that had landed in the Pastoria Towers parking lot. The copter was unmarked, but he had a good shot of what the machine looked like, and it might give him a lead on who might own some. He also had a good shot of a few faces. The most promising one was the face of the first man out the door, apparently the leader of the raid.

He was a standout. Even with the glow of the IR view, Nohar could make out his face. He was tall, with Negroid features and a long jagged scar across his cheek that showed on the display as a cold spot. There was something deep and painful in that face, even at that distance and with the distortion of the heat patterns. Nohar thought he saw the eyes of a hunter there. . . .

Nohar spent an hour studying Scar and the rest of his boys—the ones whose features he could make out. He wanted to be sure he could pick these guys out of a crowd if he came across them. He would have felt better if he could catch their scent and the sound of their footsteps as well. Then he'd feel as if he knew these men. Just by sight, he'd only be good within a few dozen meters.

Beverly brought him lunch as he worked on the comm. This time it was an actual piece of meat, not something that had been mechanically processed into something the consistency of gelatin packing material.

"Are you finding everything you need?" she asked him.

Nohar stretched. The comm was in a corner of the living room, and all he had to sit on was a small stool. He had been bent over it, and all his muscles ached. "Everything I expected to find." Nohar stood and slipped over to the couch, taking Beverly's offered lunch. His head knocked a dangling fern, setting it swinging.

"Only so much I can do over the comm."

Beverly nodded.

"I need to see this clinic Manuel worked at, talk to his coworkers." Nohar looked down at himself. He suddenly found the whole idea of clothing an annoyance.

"I took some liberties," Beverly said and walked over to the door and picked up a package and handed it to Nohar. Nohar put down the plate he'd been eating from and opened the worn plastic. Inside was a whole new outfit.

Nohar looked up.

"I slipped out while you were working. There's an ursine I buy my tea from, and he had some old clothes I borrowed."

"Thanks," Nohar said as he pulled out the shirt. It was a giant tank top with an embroidered yin-yang symbol on it. With it was a pair of running shorts. He had to manhandle his tail through one of the leg holes. Not something your average ursine had to worry about.

It was enough for him to go out in public in. He took the old plastic box and put what was left of his possessions in it. "Thanks."

"It was nice to have your company."

Nohar glanced toward the bedroom. "Tell them I'll be back by evening."

Chapter 13

The clothing had Nohar thinking about protective coloring. His problem was his inability to blend into the surroundings. The cops and the Bad Guys were both looking for a tiger, and his species just wasn't that common. In fact, it was rare enough that the cops could claim probable cause on rousting any tiger they saw. It wasn't like pinks could manage to tell moreys of the same species apart—

Even moreys seeing the video the cops took would see

little more than a tiger in an out-of-style suit packing a big gun. Most wouldn't be sure about an ID without some non-visual cues. Scent mostly.

He needed to poke around the life Manuel left behind, but he also needed to disappear.

He had an idea how to do it. But first he needed some untraceable cash. Most of his cash cards had his name attached to them. Using them would be a dangerous prospect if the Bad Guys had any technical aptitude. And after the room, the car, and a Mexican dinner, he had about five dollars in cash left.

But he knew a quick and dirty way to get more cash, as long as his urban instincts held. Clothing styles had changed. He hoped certain other things hadn't.

He walked down the streets until he found a likely prospect. It was a hole-in-the-wall store at the base of an aging strip of concrete storefronts. The window was opaque with advertisements, and above it was a cracked yellow sign that read, "Beer, Wine, Liquor, Ganja." Three rats stood in front of the store passing a plastic liter bottle between them chattering in high-pitched rodent-accented Spanish.

This was what he was looking for.

He hugged the dirty plastic package to his chest as he ducked in past the steel door.

The cashier, a canine with the high narrow muzzle and gray coloring of central Asia, watched him enter from behind a wall of bullet-proof glass. There was suspicion in the dog's eyes, probably because the metal detector set in the door had set off a warning behind his desk.

Nohar didn't much care. He walked up to the counter, peered through the graffiti scratched in the manager's shield. "I found a live cash card on the street. It has a two thousand balance. I was hoping there was a reward for returning it." Nohar didn't try to make the story sound legit. He was better off if the cashier believed that he rolled some drunk pink for the card.

The dog cocked his head. "Slide it through the reader."

Nohar smiled to himself. He had a sale; all that was left was haggling. He pulled one of his cards out of the plastic case and slid it through the reader on his side of the bullet-proof glass. The cashier looked at the readout on his side of the glass and gave a jaded nod.

Nohar eventually left with seven hundred and fifty in cash.

He visited an overpriced convenience store and a second hand clothing shop in quick succession. Both were in the same building, with the upper stories abandoned and boarded up. After he left the clothing store, with all his new purchases in a battered engineered-leather backpack, he slipped behind the building and made his way to a fire escape.

He managed to kick his way through the plastic sheathing covering one of the busted windows, and slipped inside.

There was almost no light inside, but Nohar's eyes quickly adjusted to the darkness. Worse was the smell of mildew, which made him want to sneeze.

Nohar wandered through what used to be set of apartments until he came to what was left of the kitchen. Here, it smelled more of sex and beer than mildew, and the floor was littered with the trash of innumerable predecessors. The walls were wrapped in arcane graffiti. Nohar noticed a lot of used condoms, which still struck him as odd in a morey neighborhood.

Across the wall, above the counter that used to hold a sink—before someone had scavenged it—someone had spray-painted on the wall the word, *Genocide.*

A not so nice word, Nohar thought. It matched a not so nice world.

Nohar set his backpack on the counter and walked to the other side of the room, where sheathing covered the window. Sinking his claws into the plastic, he pulled the sheet back into the room, flooding the place with sunlight. Noise from the street below filtered in, but he ignored it.

He needed the light for what he was doing.

Nohar went back to the sink and took out a pair of four-liter bottles of "spring water." The labels were homemade, and he suspected that the bottles were filled from a still—if not a tap—in the back of the convenience store. Nohar didn't care. He didn't buy the stuff to drink.

He stripped off the clothes that Beverly had given him and put them on the counter next to the backpack. From the backpack he retrieved two small hand mirrors and a bar of soap wrapped in heavy foil. It wasn't ordinary soap—The foil bore warnings not to open except immediately before use, not to leave it exposed to direct sunlight, and not to use after the expiration date stamped in its side.

It had cost Nohar twelve dollars a bar, and he had bought three. It was a cosmetic beauty soap that had a special coloring agent in it. It wasn't a dye—which he could have gotten cheap, would have been hideously messy, and in the end would have *looked* like a dye job—the soap was doped with engineered enzymes that penetrated fur and chemically altered the pigmentation. It was a one-use thing that would last until the fur grew back its natural color.

Nohar had never tried it himself. But back when he was a part of the rest of the world, he knew moreys who swore by the stuff, people who preferred black to brown, or brown to russet. Nohar picked it because he had rarely been able to tell when someone had used it.

He didn't have the features of a black jaguar, and he was too big, but it would be enough for him to pass as a mule.

He uncapped one of the bottles and tore open the foil on the soap. He started with his left forearm, wetting it, lathering the fur, working the enzymed soap into it.

When he rinsed it off the fur on his forearm and on his right hand had turned a solid glossy black. Just like Maria's fur.

Nohar worked his whole body over. After getting the broad areas of his arms legs and torso, he used the two hand mirrors to locate hard to reach spots on his back. In the space of an hour, his russet stripes were completely gone.

He stood there, legs and arms spread, letting the afternoon sun shine through and dry his fur. He felt oddly different from himself, as if he'd done more than just color his fur. He felt as if someone other than Nohar stood here, a different feline, darker, colder.

He stretched, reaching, extending the claws on his hands and feet until he felt the joints pop.

Looking up, he saw more graffiti on the ceiling. *Shiva,* it said.

"... destroyer of worlds," Nohar whispered. His voice seemed to have changed as well, lowered in pitch, more dangerous. He knew it was only psychological, but he felt more threatening.

There was one thing left before he went out in public. He

rummaged in the backpack until he found a small makeup case. He opened it and began applying the contents to his nose, darkening it until the skin color matched his new fur.

It smelled dry and made him want to sneeze, but like the soap, it sank in and disappeared into the pigment.

Nohar had vanished.

When he returned to the streets, he was a different person. He could tell by the way the other people moved around him. He could smell tension precede him in a wave, and he noticed that everyone—even the hard cases—made sure they weren't standing anywhere that could be in his way.

His clothing still didn't match the current fashion, but that seemed to matter less now. He wore khaki pants and a matching shirt, the only ones he'd found that had fit him— well enough that they might have been military surplus from India. Over it he wore a black long coat that was sized for an ursine or something bigger. It hid the holster and his gun well enough.

The backpack he'd left in the kitchen, with his old clothes. The makeup he'd ditched several blocks away, in case anyone traced him to that point. He didn't want them to discover signs of his change in appearance.

It was a five-mile walk to the Bensheim Clinic. Nohar walked the distance without stopping. For once in a long while he wasn't feeling his age. The few times he caught his reflection in an unbroken window, it was a different person. Not just the fur, which lacked the gray streaks, and even seemed better groomed. His movements seemed younger, more fluid.

The Clinic stood out from the rest of the depressed architecture, a small white building squatting behind a wide well-kept lawn. The Clinic must have had the grounds regularly maintained, because none of the garbage that littered the sidewalks and the gutters made its way onto the Clinic's small greenery.

In front of the Clinic was a bronze statute of Doctor Otto Bensheim. They posed him with a canine, shaking hands. Around the doctor's neck was his Nobel Prize. It was the kind of thing that the Bensheim Foundation never would have permitted while he was alive. Dr. Bensheim never even wanted his name on the Foundation, or its Clinics.

He'd been one of the thousands of gene-techs who'd helped create the moreaus. Unlike all the other gene-techs, Bensheim had a conscience. He had created the Foundation and the Clinics to atone for his part in creating a new underclass. Reproduction, he had thought, was a fundamental right. The Clinics were there to assure that every female who wanted offspring would have the opportunity, whatever her species.

Of the thousands of species of moreaus that were created, each small genetic variation was listed somewhere in the Bensheim Foundation's confidential files. For a nominal fee, any female could walk in, get genetic testing, and be inseminated with the matching species of sperm. Any male could come in and receive a nominal fee for donating his own seed. The Clinics had gradually expanded their mission, to include neonatal and other aspects of reproductive health.

Nohar had never been inside one of the Clinics. He disliked hospitals in general, and something about the Bensheim Clinics had always made him uneasy.

He walked up the footpath, past the statue. It had the obligatory plaque, dedicating it on the occasion of the fifth anniversary of Doctor Otto Bensheim's death. That would make it nearly ten years old.

Nohar stopped and studied the doctor's face. He had seen Bensheim in news stories before the man had died. There seemed something oddly fake about the expression on the statue, as if the sculptor had never seen Bensheim smile. The look gave Bensheim the appearance of biting back some obscenity.

Nohar pretended to read the plaque while he covertly studied his surroundings. He didn't have to take his gaze off the plaque to realize that there were pinks around, ones more alive than the good doctor. The wind carried their scent along with the ozone exhaust of the passing traffic.

He wondered where the best place to hide them would be. They had to be watching the Clinic, since he couldn't think of any other good reason for humans to be in the neighborhood. Even the LAPD now hired moreys to patrol the Moreytowns, and Compton was about as nonhuman as you could get without leaving the planet.

So the pinks he scented, at least three, were almost

certainly the Bad Guys. Watching Manuel's old workplace. Probably watching for him.

He was going to get to see how well his new disguise worked. Either the Bad Guys were going to fall on him like a ton of bricks, or he was going to walk right in.

An apartment across the street, Nohar finally decided. There was a restaurant across the street, and above it were a line of apartment windows. The windows were broken and dark, but they had the only view of the front of the Clinic—and the wind was from that direction.

"We'll see," Nohar whispered to himself. He walked up the path to the Clinic door. The lobby was sparse and utilitarian. There weren't even fake plants to clutter the scenery. The lights were brilliant fluorescents that set off the blazing holo posters on the walls. The mylar holos were the only decor. He read one as he passed.

"Get the drop on the Drips!," it told him. *"A properly sized condom is your only effective protection from sexually transmitted diseases, including Herpes Rangoon."* There was a picture as well, of a peeved-looking rat who stared at an oversized condom covering his groin like a sheet, and of a smiling canine pulling one on that fit just right.

Nohar shook his head and walked up to the reception desk. A bored-looking lepus sat behind it watching some sort of comedy program on the comm set into the desk. Nohar noticed at least three security cameras as he walked up.

"What can I do you for?" the rabbit said without moving his gaze from the screen. He pulled a stalk of celery from a bowl on the desk and began chewing.

Nohar didn't want to attract any attention. "I'm here to pick up some extra money." *Just the regular crap that they get here every day,* Nohar thought. *Give them that, and they won't notice you.*

Lepus didn't even turn his head. He just kept eating his celery and said, "Donation? Fill this out." With his free hand the rabbit handed Nohar an electronic clipboard with an attached stylus. "You can go to the waiting room."

That was it. Having done his duty, the lepus ceased paying attention to him. Lepus could have looked up, seen a black-furred feline that was way too big to be a jaguar—or anything else with that kind of coloring—made the decision that his visitor was a mule, and saved the bureaucracy some effort by saying that they didn't want any from him. But the wonderful thing about bureaucracy was that no one was willing to spend the effort. Lepus would perform his job description even if a pink walked through the door.

Nohar took the clipboard and walked into the waiting room. There were more holo posters here, many warning of the dangers of Herpes Rangoon, a.k.a. the Drips. There were other posters that told people that every donation to the Bensheim Foundation was thoroughly screened for disease, and that no one could catch anything by donating.

Nohar settled into one of the larger chairs and rested the clipboard on his lap. He glanced at the glowing liquid-crystal page and read the first few questions:

"Have you ever been tested for Herpes Rangoon?"

"If so, what was the result of that test?"

"When were you last tested?"

"Have any of your sexual partners been tested for Herpes Rangoon?"

"Have you ever experienced nonhealing genital sores, itching, or difficulty urinating?"

Nohar read the list with a growing incredulity. It seemed to border on obsessive, especially if they were going to test the donors themselves. Nohar looked up from the clipboard's display. He began noticing how empty the waiting room seemed. He knew that was somehow wrong. The Clinic wasn't just for insemination, but it was a clearing house for all sorts of genetically related medical help, and it was all pretty much free. This was one of two Clinics in all of LA. The place should be packed, all the time.

There were maybe half a dozen seats taken, less than half the waiting room. Nohar noticed that they were all male, and most filling out clipboards like his.

Nohar looked at the person closest to him, a huge ursine who'd taken one of the five oversized chairs along the far wall of the waiting room. He wore what Nohar was thinking of as the Compton uniform, the pants mostly blousy strips, the vest little more substantial than Nohar's shoulder holster.

The bear was staring at the clipboard, puzzling over the form.

Nohar cleared his throat. "Ask you something?"

Ursine eyes moved slightly in Nohar's direction. There was a hint of menace in the bear's expression. However, it was undirected menace. It only took Nohar a few moments to see that this guy was just a kid, probably just hitting puberty for his species.

It was somewhat scary to think that this kid was going to get bigger with age. He was already bigger than Nohar.

"What you want?"

"Know why this place is so empty?"

"Why the fuck ask me?" The bear turned back to the clipboard.

Nohar sighed inwardly, but he decided that the angle was worth pursuing. He didn't know what had happened to Manuel, but his son's job was the one lead he had at the moment. If there was something odd going on with the clinic, he wanted to know—and he couldn't go harassing the staff here, not right under the Bad Guys' noses.

"Thought you looked like someone who knows what's what." Nohar did his best to stroke the ursine's ego; the kid was young enough that ego was probably the most important thing in his life. "Want to know if I'm stepping into something here." Nohar waved in the direction of the poster that proclaimed that no one could catch a virus by donating to the Foundation.

The bear looked across at him again. "So you asking me?"

"See someone better?"

That won the kid over. "Fuck no, got me there." He laughed and put down the stylus that he'd been filling out his form with. His voice took on a tone as if he was talking to his little brother. Nohar didn't mind. Even though he was probably thirty years this kid's senior, he didn't look it anymore.

"You don't got no worries. They only stick you to take blood to check if you're infected."

"What about . . . ?" Nohar made some stroking motions with his hand—

"Don't you know anything?"

"First time I've been here." That was the truth. But he said it in a way to sound lost. He figured that the easiest way to ingratiate himself into Bear-Boy's confidence was to act more naive than Bear-Boy was.

"You thought they let you baste some flesh here or something?"

"Well ..."

Bear-Boy laughed. "Look, it's just you and a little plastic cup."

Nohar did his best to look disappointed. Bear-Boy laughed all the harder and slapped him on the back. The blow ignited pain in the old shoulder injury, but he bore it with good grace. It took him a moment to think of something adequately stupid to say.

Nohar shook his head and asked Bear-Boy, "So that's why there ain't no females here?"

"Oh, fuck, are you lost! You never hear about the Drips?"

"You just told me—"

Bear-Boy shook his head at his new friend's ignorance, and it was all Nohar could do to suppress a smile. "Look, you'll be fucking plastic 'cause you're a guy. Female's got to have the wad of some stranger shot up her quim. Got me?"

Nohar paused a moment and then said, "Oh—"

"See my point?" Bear-Boy lowered his voice a bit and spoke conspiratorially. "Broad gets knocked up here with some hot juice, puts a damper on things."

"They say they test their donors," Nohar said, lowering his voice to be even with Bear-Boy's.

"Like they check them all? Fuck, boy, where you living? They got samples frozen from years before they named the Drips. Word is, females break out with this crap all the god-damn time." Bear-Boy winked at him. "Not that they admit it, or that their money's not as good as anyone else's."

"Thanks."

Bear-Boy straightened up, leaned over the clipboard, and said, "By the way, you ain't a mule, are you?"

"What's that matter?"

" 'Cause your come's dead if you are. *They* can't use it. Ain't going to pay for dead come."

Nohar put his head in his hands. "Where's the bathroom?"

"Down that hall, to the right."

Nohar nodded and went in the direction indicated. He was thankful that Bear-Boy was leaning over his clipboard chuckling. That meant he didn't notice that Nohar was just on the edge of busting out laughing himself.

Chapter 14

Nohar stayed at the Clinic for a little less than half an hour, filling out the form and surreptitiously watching the employees, looking for possible coworkers of Manuel. Staying longer would seem to be pushing things.

He went to the bathroom a couple of times. It gave him a view into the closed-off part of the building through an open door at the end of the hall. He could catch a glimpse of part of a storage area without being obvious about it. He could smell an odd scent or two from there, moreau types he couldn't quite identify.

It wasn't until the third trip that he caught sight of someone back there. The guy was in overalls and work gloves, and for a moment Nohar thought that somehow a dog and a rabbit had done the impossible and made a mule kid. Then, when the guy moved, he saw the broad tail and the barely engineered legs—

A kangaroo.

The guy moved so Nohar could glimpse his ID tag. The name was bold enough for him to read, "Oxford."

Not a difficult character to find again.

After that, Nohar sat and quietly filled out his form. He was especially careful to tell the Clinic people that he was a mule. Just as he wanted, once he handed in the form, they took a few minutes to say to him thanks but no thanks. He managed to get out of there without a single test.

And the Bad Guys hadn't budged.

It took Nohar less than fifteen minutes at a public comm to find out where Oxford the Roo lived. There were only so many Oxfords in the public database for Compton and vicinity. He kept connecting to each Oxford's comm until he came up with one whose recorded message was left by a person of the right species.

His quarry was Nathan Oxford of Lynwood.

Nohar walked away from the comm, and the clinic, and made sure he wasn't being followed. Only when he was sure that he was out of sight of any pinks did he find another comm and call a taxi to take him to Lynwood.

Nathan Oxford lived in a ranch-style housing project that was in bad shape. The lawns were dead, and the old brick residential buildings were covered in spray paint. Half the units had windows boarded over, and one set of units at the far end of the complex had been burned out, leaving nothing but a shell.

Nohar spent his first hour at Willow Estates looking for pink surveillance. He watched for a long time at a distance with his camera before he was certain that there wasn't any physical surveillance of the premises. That was good. If the Bad Guys were watching one random member of the Clinic's staff, they would be watching everyone.

Even for these people, *that* seemed a stretch. Nohar still wasn't sure that the Clinic had anything to do with Manuel's disappearance. All he was sure of was that the Bad Guys were set upon nailing anyone caught looking for him.

That might mean the Bad Guys were hunting down Manuel themselves, or it might mean that they had gotten him, killed him, and were trying to cover it up.

Nohar's anger flared when he thought of that. If they had harmed his son—

God help anyone who had touched Manuel then.

Nohar had Oxford's unit number from the comm, so it wasn't difficult to head straight there. He walked through the courtyards, listening to the yips of children playing and adults yelling. It was still daylight, late afternoon, and he had about an hour before Oxford would come home from work. More, if he did any overtime.

This place had had security at one point. Nohar counted a half-dozen brackets that used to hold cameras. The one that still held a camera was bent sidewise and dangled a severed power cord.

Oxford's unit faced the parking lot rather than one of the courtyards. The door was a security model, steel with an electronic dead bolt.

There was little chance of him breaking into the place by

brute force. That didn't concern Nohar much. While the place had once been secure, it had since passed into the bottom tier of such places. Where the buildings were this far gone, the corruption rarely confined itself to the physical structure.

Nohar walked around until he found what passed for the main office. It was two buildings down from Oxford, behind a door that was exactly the same except for the words "Rental Office" stenciled on it. Nohar leaned on the call button until someone answered.

The door was answered by a shabby-looking rat who smelled of beer. "What'cha want? Damn it." As the rat spoke, his triangular head looked at Nohar's feet and started traveling up. His gaze never passed above Nohar's waist, where Nohar held a c-note at the rat's eye level.

The c-note disappeared and the rat asked, "What you need, my friend?"

"You need to let me into an apartment."

The rat didn't even hesitate. "Which one?"

After two hours, and after Nohar had the chance to go over every inch of the apartment, Nathan Oxford threw the bolts on his front door and walked in. The door was closing as Oxford's odd, not-quite-canine muzzle sniffed the air. He knew something was wrong before Nohar ever spoke.

Nohar stood at the end of the hall opposite the front door shrouded in the gloom of the windowless kitchen. He held the Vind trained on the roo.

"Don't turn on the lights. Don't look at me. Don't move."

The door clunked home. Oxford stopped moving. He had stopped while facing the living room, in the act of turning around. Nohar could smell his fear. After what Nohar had seen in the kitchen and bathroom, he didn't really care what Oxford felt.

"What is it you want, governor? You can have it." The roo had an accent that had to be feigned.

"Living room, face the wall."

Oxford nodded and did what he was told. Nohar stood in the entranceway and faced Oxford, well out of range of his powerful hind legs.

"Who are you?" Oxford asked. "What the fuck do you want?"

"I have the gun, Nathan. I ask the questions."

Oxford nodded.

"You're a dealer, aren't you?"

"You want my stash, take it. More where that came from."

Nohar nodded. "The Clinic's well stocked."

"Yeah, sure. Anything you want, we can even special order it—"

What a scam, Nohar thought in disgust. This guy was working in shipping and receiving, and skimming a prime supply of any sort of medication you could name. His kitchen was stocked with everything from methadone to synthetic morphine. He'd been doing it long enough that he could make bookshelves out of crates addressed to the Compton Bensheim Clinic.

Oxford made Nohar sick. Not only was he a dealer, but he was ripping off a charity to keep himself stocked. And he had just as much as admitted that he could falsify orders to bring in whatever he needed.

Something grew cold inside him as he thought that Manuel was involved in this sort of crap. He had to suppress an urge to shoot Oxford. The only good thing about this situation was that there were few guys less likely to call the cops.

"I don't want your drugs." The assertion made Oxford smell of more fear.

"Look, you work for Sammy. Look, I'll quit selling across—"

"Shut up, Slimeball."

Oxford shut up.

"Say anything more that isn't a direct answer to a question, and I'm going to give you a twelve-millimeter gelding."

Oxford shook, and his tail twitched, its mass giving the impression of a coiled spring.

"Understand?" Nohar asked.

"Y-yes."

"Manuel Limón. You know him?"

Oxford nodded. "Yes." His accent had slipped almost completely away.

"Last time you saw him?"

"Two weeks ago last Wednesday."

"At the Clinic?"

"Yes." Oxford's voice was becoming shrill.

"I want a straight answer here. Was he ripping off the Clinic, too?"

Oxford hesitated a moment.

"Well?"

"Yes, damn it, everyone does it. It's not such a fucking big deal."

Nohar's disgust sank into his stomach. His voice lowered to a growl as he asked, "Drugs?" If this trash in front of him had gotten his son into drug-dealing, he was going to personally remove his liver and feed it to him.

"No, he never had the connections for that."

"What, then?"

"Hospital equipment, electronics, ramcards—"

Nohar didn't know if he was relieved to hear that or not. "Did he take anything the day you saw him last?"

"I don't know. That was a while ago."

Nohar cocked the action on the Vind so it made an ominous click. He could hear the echo from the kitchen. "I want you to think harder."

"Fuck, okay. I don't know what it was. Something came in that was supposed to go to the office in Pasadena. It was marked confidential, and he thought he had a gold mine."

Pasadena. That struck a nerve. The automated van was heading for Pasadena, and the Bensheim Foundation had offices there. Nohar didn't like the way this was going.

"How big was this package?" Nohar asked.

"It was a security envelope, for ramcards—stuff too sensitive for the net. Courier delivered. Marked confidential. Manuel thought it was corporate stuff that he thought some hacker friend of his could sell."

Hacking the Bensheim Foundation, Nohar thought. *How noble.* Though Nohar was beginning to wonder about Doctor Bensheim's charity.

"Did he?"

"What?"

"Have his hacker friend sell it?"

Oxford shook his head. "He vanished after that. I don't know. Maybe he did and bought a ticket out of LA."

Nohar doubted it. "Two more things and you might live through this."

"What?"

Chapter 15

Oxford's car was little better than his apartment. Nohar would've thought a dealer might have had something a little better than an aging Dodge Python. The oversized red car's fiberglass shell had been cracked in several places, and fixed with tape. Nohar could fit in it, at least from the legs down, but he had to hunch over to drive.

Still, he wasn't in a position to be choosy. He pulled out of the lot and hoped that Oxford wasn't the type to go making a police report about his stolen vehicle. Besides, he could probably trade some of his hoard on the street for something as good, if not better. The way the car smelled, Nohar suspected that was how he got this one.

The car's comm had been ripped out and sold a long time ago, so Nohar stopped at a public comm on the way back to Beverly's building. It was just as well. With all the attention focused on Manuel, he didn't want to risk anyone tracing the search he was about to make back to a comm anywhere near him.

He pulled over on a street that was mostly empty, flanked by boarded-up shops and a vacant lot. There was a kiosk with a public comm, wrapped in graffiti that looked like psychedelic urban camouflage. The only people around were a trio of rodents sitting in the doorway of the building across the street. They were passing something around between them. At this distance Nohar couldn't tell if it was alcohol or drugs.

Nohar left the car and walked up to the comm. He left the flywheel running in the Python in case he needed to make a quick exit.

He wasn't a hacker, and he was never much of anything with computers, but his job as a private eye had given him the opportunity to pick up a few tricks from Bobby. One of those tricks was picking up people from their aliases—the handle they used on the net.

He was looking for someone named "The Necron Avenger."

Necron was the name Oxford had given him, the only way Manuel had ever referred to his hacker friend. In his mind, Nohar was already thinking of Necron as a young version of Bobby. He couldn't help but wonder if Manuel had met Necron under similar circumstances. Were they drawn together because they were both outcasts? Nohar had been raised in a human neighborhood, and the only friend he had was the weak little kid in the wheelchair. A mule in a moreau community was in almost the same position.

Nohar told himself to stop speculating about the kid and started the comm cycling into the public news databases. Unlike the commercial news databases, where Nohar usually did his research, anyone and their second cousin could post an article on the public database. Even with the rough indexing the database provided, there was so much information—most of it trash—that any given article was lucky to receive a single reader from the millions accessing the net every day.

To find anything in that morass of home-produced programming, Nohar needed a series of very specific filters to weed out everything he didn't want. He had one very basic filter—Necron's handle.

In a few moments he indexed every article The Necron Avenger had made in the last month. He was in a hurry, so he put a few extra dollars into the comm to download the articles to a ramcard, which the machine spat out at him.

He wasn't after what Necron was saying right now. He was after where Necron *was*.

Even though the net was a high-tech colossus connecting every comm and most of the full-fledged computers on the planet, the way it propagated information hadn't changed much since the turn of the century. Everything, from phoned messages to news broadcasts, flowed along the optic cables from node to node, winding its way to whatever destination. Each node along the way left its signature on the transmission, and even at a public comm, it was possible to filter the headers on any particular message to find out where it originated.

In a few moments Nohar had isolated a set of arcane strings of characters. Each string pointed to a node somewhere that had received the article and passed it on, all the way back to the node that had first received Necron's messages.

The first thing Nohar did was check the first node for each of the messages he had for Necron, about two dozen. All originated from the same node.

That was promising. Almost everyone with a computer or a comm that wasn't in a high security situation left their access to the net on permanently. However, hackers were different. Many of them left their computers and comms isolated from the net, only connecting when they were doing something specific. A lot of them, especially those who skirted the law like Bobby used to, would manufacture their own temporary node on the net, complete with faux IDs. They would then use their temporary nodes to connect to whatever they were doing anonymously, then disconnect their computers from the net.

The fact that Necron's originating address was constant meant that he was using the same server each time he posted an article to the database. That meant either he wasn't a professional like Bobby, or he was sophisticated enough to manufacture a permanent bogus address to block tracers. Nohar doubted the latter; pros like that dealt in the shadows, and generally didn't post to the public databases.

Necron was probably just an amateur with a talent with computers. It also meant he probably didn't do anything much illegal. It was possible to do a business in data trafficking without necessarily skirting the law.

Nohar logged on to the server, and like most servers, it wasn't too protective of its user list. He managed to feed in Necron's handle and it spat back Necron's given name—or at least an alias that he was more likely to use in the world off of the net.

Oswald Samson.

It was another name that was easy to trace. There was only one Oswald Samson in the whole Compton area as far as the city directory was concerned. Nohar left the comm with Necron's address.

*   *   *

Oswald Samson lived in a little white one-family ranch house on the edge of where Compton began to bleed into the other southeastern LA suburbs. The yard was wrapped in chain-link, and the windows had the curtains drawn against the darkness outside. The sky was dark, and the streetlights lit the area like a stage set.

Nohar wasn't certain that this was Necron's residence. There was a good chance that Necron picked "Oswald Samson" out of the directory, just as Nohar had. There was also a chance that this wasn't the right Oswald Samson. However the fact that he was a resident in Compton made Nohar think that there was a good chance that Oswald was Manuel's hacker.

Nohar parked on the street and stepped out of the car. In the distance, music was blaring, and he heard the sounds of laughter and partying. Someone was having fun a few houses down. Nohar could smell the beer from here.

Oswald's house was quiet and dark.

Just looking at it made Nohar's hackles rise. He felt his adrenaline kicking in even before he realized why. He smelled humans. The scent was faint, but at one point there were enough standing around here to saturate the air with the odor of their sweat.

Nohar let himself through the gate and drew the Vind as soon as he was out of direct line of sight of the street. Now he was paying attention to everything. The lawn had been crushed. He could still see signs of footprints treading the weeds into the soil.

When he got to the front door, it was obvious that the doorjamb had been splintered by someone forcing the door. It was just closed now for appearances.

He began to feel ugly flashbacks of his visit to Royd's house. He was too late again; he could feel it. He was certain that he would find Oswald Samson's body somewhere inside the house.

He wanted to leave right now. A sudden certainty that the LAPD would descend on this place overwhelmed him. But he didn't really have an option. He had to follow any lead that might help him reach his son.

Nohar pushed the door open, keeping the place covered with his gun.

Streetlights filtered through the door and illuminated

what was left of Oswald Samson's house. Someone had been looking for something, and the way things looked, they hadn't found it.

Not only had they shredded the carpet, eviscerated the furniture, they had even gone so far as to tear the drywall out, exposing the wood frame of the building and the wiring. The lights were out because they'd been dismantled and were lying on the floor. The comm had been taken apart, and the electronics were scattered throughout the room.

Nohar wandered through the house. Floorboards had been taken up, pipes had been pulled from the wall and opened. The lining of the refrigerator had been torn out. The sheet-metal ducts for the air-conditioning had been slit open and peeled back. No object in the house had been left intact.

But there was no body. Oswald Samson hadn't shared Royd's fate.

By now, Nohar didn't need to ask what everyone was looking for. It wasn't Manuel, it was in that package he swiped, the one delivered to the Compton Clinic by mistake. From the look of the disassembled comm, Nohar suspected that it was a ramcard that was in that package.

He spent about half an hour sifting through the wreckage. There wasn't much here that told him what he wanted to know. He did manage to find fragments of Oswald's personal life. The guy was human, and had a teenage kid. He found holos of both of them, tossed in with piles of other junk. He didn't find signs of Oswald's wife, or signs that he'd ever had one. He did, however, find the kid's room. It was as trashed as the rest of the house, the comm just as disassembled.

It also didn't take long for Nohar to find something that didn't sync with the Necron he was looking for. He found a plaque honoring Oswald Samson for twenty-five years of service with the INS. That didn't make sense. First off, Oswald had a job working for the Fed. Nohar couldn't see Manuel palling around with a government agent, even if he was just an immigration officer. Second, that plaque put Oswald in his mid-forties at least, as old as Nohar. As Bobby had said, hacking was a young man's game. Lastly, Oswald was a pink. . . .

All of this made Nohar start wondering about Oswald's kid. The kid must've been around Manuel's age. . . .

Nohar walked around to the living room and picked up the broken holo of Oswald and son. He studied it, hunting for some clue to what had happened to his own son.

When he stepped out the door of Oswald's ranch, he was hit by a chlorine smell that made his nose itch. It was powerful enough that it overwhelmed anything subtler. Nohar froze in the doorway, looking around, searching for movement.

He could almost see the fumes hovering over the lawn.

Someone had tried to cover their scent, and had done a good job of it. He knew the smell; it was chlorine bleach. Nohar's hand hovered near the holster as he slowly made his way down the walk toward his commandeered car. At each step, he looked away into the darkness, down both sides of the street, checking for an ambush.

The only signs of life were from the party that was still going on down the street.

He reached his car without any incident. By now the bleach had numbed his nose to the point where the car could have been doused in it and he wouldn't be able to tell.

Chapter 16

"Nohar, what have you done to yourself?" Maria stared at him as if she couldn't quite believe what she was seeing.

"Is that you?" Henderson asked. Both of them were wearing blousy shirts and pants that were a decade away from any style. Nohar presumed the clothes belonged to Beverly. Maria was wearing green and Henderson was wearing navy. Nohar thought they should swap colors.

He stood in the doorway and said, "Can I come in?"

Beverly's voice came from back in the apartment. "He can't fit through with you both clogging the doorway."

The other two stared at him, as if they didn't quite trust his new appearance. But they moved aside so Nohar could duck inside the apartment.

Nohar ducked plants as he moved to the cramped corner where Beverly's comm sat. As the door shut, Maria swiveled her chair around to face him. "What have you been doing all afternoon?".

Nohar sat and took out the ramcard he'd minted at the public comm. "Checking out Manuel's acquaintances." He slipped the ramcard into Beverly's comm. "They're watching the Clinic."

Henderson sat down next to him. A ghost of chlorine still haunted his nose, but he could just make out the odor of her musk next to him. She touched his arm and asked, "You went to the Clinic? Wasn't that dangerous?"

The touch may have been innocent, but Nohar didn't feel it that way. He moved his arm from under it by turning on the comm and starting to run through the record of Necron's public messages. "The new coloring bought me some cover. Didn't stay long."

"Did you find out anything about Manuel?" Maria asked. There was a catch in her voice and Nohar couldn't bring himself to say that their son had been supplementing his income with petty theft. He sidestepped the issue.

"I found a coworker with a lead. Manuel may have a ramcard with information these guys are looking for."

"Like, what you have there?" Henderson asked.

"Another victim of the Bad Guys," Nohar said.

Beverly turned toward all of them from the kitchen side of the room. "Why don't you all take a break for dinner?"

Nohar ate dinner as he perused The Necron Avenger's collected works. Most were the typical hacker montages of sound video and text that were spliced together with little regard for form or sense. One article consisted of Mozart's *25th Symphony* conducted by electric guitars and overlaid with images of the Race—the one nonhuman species that wasn't created on Earth. It culminated with news footage of the bombing of Alcatraz.

That article was called "Requiem."

There was one called "Drips," more recent. This was a collage of human generals and government officials spliced in with combat footage of the Pan-Asian War, mostly moreau corpses. Spliced in with that were scenes of human-supremacy groups preaching that the moreaus were so much genetic waste from the war, and should be disposed of like any hazardous material.

Another untitled piece was strictly sexual images run through slide-show fashion, intercut with subliminal images of needles and surgical procedure.

Nohar didn't know what to make of Necron's work, but there was a theme running through it—a near obsession with the moreau world that was at odds with what Nohar had seen of Oswald Samson. It might explain a pink owning a house in Compton.

The more of his work Nohar saw, the more he realized how paranoid and apocalyptic Necron's point of view was. There was a sense of intractable evil in the world Necron portrayed, a cycle of pain that led inevitably to disease and death.

The subtext—maybe it was even the point of all the messages—was that the disease and death were engineered by those who ran the country.

Necron made him uneasy. . . .

He was on his seventh message from the Necron Avenger when the comm went dead. Nohar looked up at the other three. Maria and Henderson were quietly talking to Beverly, finishing the last of their dinner. None of them had noticed anything going wrong.

Nohar had a bad feeling in the pit of his stomach. He got up from the comm and started moving to the front door, ducking under the pipes and around the three females.

"Nohar?" Beverly was the first one to notice him move, though she wasn't even facing him.

"Shh." Nohar kept moving to take position next to the door. He didn't have time to reach for his gun. Almost at the same time, the lights in the apartment went out and the door flew open.

"Nobody move!"

Nohar saw the arm belonging to the owner of that voice. It was pointing something into the room. Nohar didn't wait to see what it was. He grabbed the wrist, moving his leg so he could pull the speaker into his knee.

When his knee struck flesh, Nohar brought his other hand down on the back of the intruder's skull. The person flipped over his knee, and landed flat on his back. Whatever he'd been armed with went sailing into the room.

Nohar placed his foot on the intruder's throat, immobilizing him.

There was a pair of light-enhancing goggles on the guy's face, and Nohar tore them off, revealing the intruder's face. Nohar recognized him from his picture—

Looking up at him was Oswald Samson's son.

Now that he was face-to-face with the kid, he could see the oversized skull and the elongated fingers. The kid was a frank—a genetically engineered human.

Necron finally made sense to Nohar.

The kid coughed and spat, and managed to wheeze, "Where's my father?"

After it was clear that the kid was alone, Nohar sent Henderson out to fix what the kid had done to the power. Nohar restrained the kid with a belt and threw him on the couch. He retrieved the kid's weapon, a government-issue .45 automatic that probably belonged to his father.

Nohar shook his head and turned to the kid. The aggressiveness was gone. The kid seemed to deflate on the couch. Nohar saw him clearly in the dark, but frank or not, without the light-amplification gear his eyes probably hadn't adjusted to the dark.

"You were trying to do what?" Nohar asked the kid. He looked at the gun and thought of a wild shot hitting Maria, or Henderson, or Beverly, and felt a lethal anger building. The adrenaline was still surging and hadn't found a true outlet yet. It was the kind of internal high that he could do anything on.

He leveled the Vind at the kid's forehead. "Explain. Now."

"I'm looking for my dad." His head tuned back and forth, as if he was trying to find Nohar.

"How did you get here?"

"Followed you."

There it was. This kid had come home to trashed house and missing father. When Nohar'd shown up, the kid had seen him and assumed he was one of the Bad Guys. He had even used the bleach to cover his scent. He'd probably been inside the house when Nohar had walked up to the door, and had slipped outside while Nohar was searching the place.

The lights came on again, and after a few moments the comm came back to life, still in the midst of playing one of Necron's messages. Nohar looked at the frank kid, no more than fourteen—for a human still a child—his eyes locked on the gun, and he could feel real fear begin to wash off of the kid in waves.

Nohar felt his anger fade somewhat. They were both in the same boat, and in the same position Nohar might have done exactly as this kid had. . . .

In fact he had done just that to Oxford.

Nohar lowered the gun. "The Necron Avenger, I presume."

The kid stared at him, and his eyes darted toward the comm. One of Necron's articles was playing the national anthem while panning across burned-out Moreytowns.

"The guys who took your father were looking for you."

Necron turned to face him. "I don't know what you're talking about." He shook his head and stopped when his gaze landed on Maria. He stared at her for a long time, as if he recognized her.

"You know my son, don't you?" Maria asked.

It was in Necron's eyes. He knew all right. He saw the same familiarity that Nohar had only gotten from a bad picture. The coloring was different, but Manuel had Maria's face.

It should have hit me. I should have known *the second I saw that picture.*

Nohar crouched so he could look the kid in the eyes. "I found your house because I traced your posts. The name I came up with was Oswald." He reached over and grabbed the kid's shoulder, pulling him forward to look at him. Necron was now completely limp, near panic. "You used your dad's account, didn't you?"

He nodded slowly. "What's happening?"

"Manuel Limón, they want something he has." Nohar leaned forward. He knew just being close to a predatory moreau like him was intimidating to most humans. He was hoping to make Necron as cooperative as possible.

"Christ—"

"They've killed at least one person already."

Necron stared at him with a hollow look. Nohar was cruel enough to let him think the worst for a few seconds.

"Not your father. We have to get to Manuel before they do."

Henderson came in the door, and Beverly drew her aside, away from the drama on the couch. The kid jumped when the door opened. Nohar could tell that The Necron Avenger was close to breaking. He eased back and let go of the kid's shoulder.

Maria leaned forward in her chair, reaching a cupped hand as if she was begging. In a way, she was. "Where is my son?"

"We were hiding him." The kid's voice came out in a breathless rush. "I promised—"

"We're his parents," Nohar said.

The kid was left speechless.

Nohar holstered his Vind and shook his head. "Helping us may be the only chance you have of seeing your father again."

There were a few more moments of silence, then it all came pouring out.

The kid's name was John Samson. His dad, Oswald, was involved in nonhuman immigration. When John was five or six, he'd been orphaned during a Pacific crossing in a cargo ship packed with too many franks and moreaus escaping Greater China. The mortality rate on that ship was close to sixty percent—and would have been higher if it hadn't been intercepted by the Coast Guard.

Oswald Samson had come across the orphan while processing the refugees and had decided to adopt him. The story came across in only a few terse sentences, but it was clear that John Samson remembered every bit of it.

He didn't even have a choice. His species had been engineered by Japan before the Chinese invasion, and one of the traits they'd been bred for was a photographic memory.

He and Manuel had met over the net. Some of his compositions seemed to echo Manuel's own world-view. That didn't surprise Nohar that much. Both kids had to feel similarly isolated, and had to have similar views on society as a whole.

Manuel was lost, as The Necron Avenger was lost. Manuel, like John Samson, watched the world pass by him with a fatalism that seemed truly frightening. The world was a burning building, a car wreck, an autopsy that had no emotional content because there was no connection between the watcher and the victims.

According to John, Manuel had no other close friends. He had tried at school, at work, but no one seemed to relate to the mule. He had even searched out other mules, but most mules had bodies broken, and brains damaged, and were too complete in their own isolation. Manuel's curse was he did not *want* to be alone.

John, the frank living in Moreytown, was the first person Manuel had ever met who seemed to relate to him.

The two of them had been talking over the comm for two or three years. And, lately, they'd actually been meeting in person. The data-trafficking had only begun in the last few months, when John had let slip that The Necron Avenger had some deep contacts in the data underground that could move that kind of merchandise.

They had moved about half a dozen pieces of such merchandise, making a total of about thirteen grand between them, when Manuel had showed up with the last package— the one that was not supposed to reach Compton.

"Everything was just like normal, until I hacked what was on the card." John Samson shook his head.

"What was it?" Nohar asked. "What happened?"

John looked up at him, his eyes blank and dead. "Fear is a natural thing, you know. Any rational person in this world has to be paranoid. There's no choice." John shook a little, and screwed his eyes shut. Nohar could sense the tension in John's posture. "No paranoid hopes he's right."

"What was it?"

"Imagine your worst fears about the world confirmed. Imagine the vilest betrayal."

Nohar wanted to lean across and shake him. "What?"

"The Clinics—" His voice caught. John took a few deep breaths before he continued. "The Bensheim Clinics are intentionally infecting people with the Drips."

Chapter 17

John Samson's revelation was like accusing the Red Cross of spiking their blood cultures with hepatitis. It didn't make any sense. The Bensheim Clinics were an international charity that had been around almost as long as moreaus themselves—and they certainly didn't have a paramilitary force to cover up this kind of discovery.

At least, Nohar didn't think they did.

He spent over an hour grilling the kid about what was on that ramcard. Nohar got the information in minute detail. The kid remembered everything, he rattled off the data as if he was sitting in front of a comm screen reading it.

The ramcard was, at the very least, an explosive set of case studies on the spread of Herpes Rangoon in the United States. John Samson had read several charts listing the spread of the virus from one person through several other partners. In each case study the original vector for the disease was a female moreau impregnated at a Bensheim Clinic. In about half of the cases the fetus spontaneously aborted due to the virus, and in half of the remaining cases the fetus was born infected.

What made the files all the more damaging was the way the data was slanted to highlight those moreaus that infected the widest segment of the population, over the widest area.

What John couldn't give him was any explicit statement from the data that the Bensheim Clinics were intentionally responsible for the initial infections. It still could be accidental. As the bear in the waiting room told him, it was probably a logistical impossibility to test all of their stock. Though even if that was made public, and the ramcard was just tracking the problem, it was bad enough to probably spell the end of the Clinics.

But John Samson hadn't read all the data. There were

several gigabytes on that card, too much to go through in the one sitting he had with the data. He had just read enough to set the natural paranoia going, and to believe that his and Manuel's lives had been in danger for being anywhere close to something like it.

That paranoia probably saved both of them.

"Where did you take Manuel?" Nohar asked.

"Safe hiding place," John said. "An old INS detention center on the border. I have my dad's access codes."

"That's safe?" Maria asked.

"The place has been abandoned for years." John looked up at Maria. "Sometimes, I think I'm the only one who remembers it."

Nohar freed the kid to take them all down to his vehicle. John Samson wasn't supposed to be old enough to drive, but he had followed Nohar in a decade-old van that made Nohar think of government institutions.

"There's a whole graveyard of trucks, vans, and cars abandoned by the Fed," John told him, as the four of them left Beverly's apartment building. Nohar believed what the kid said. Years of wind and weather had worn the van to a bone-gray. A thin layer of dust coated every window evenly, except where he had wiped clear the driver's side. The van still had government ID tags, and Nohar could still see the ghost of the word "Immigration" on the side of the van.

Henderson wheeled Maria out next to the van and stared at the vehicle. "It still runs?"

"That's why it took me over two weeks to get back here. Couldn't drive Manuel's car—they're probably looking for it. I had to work on getting this thing mobile."

Nohar nodded and walked to the rear and opened the back. The rear of the van was flanked by benches, separated from the driver's compartment by a wire mesh screen. It had obviously been used for hauling detainees around.

"Sorry you have to ride in back," Nohar told Maria. "Only place there's room."

"That's all right," Maria said. She grunted a few times as Nohar lifted her out of the chair and set her down on one of the benches. She felt way too light. All the muscle tone was gone. The sense of loss struck him again, the long path of years that could have gone in another direction.

Once Maria was settled, Nohar lifted the chair into the back. There were a few old elastic cords on the floor of the van, mixed with rats' nests and other debris. Nohar took one and secured the chair to the wire mesh separating the driver's compartment.

Once he had done that, John Samson started walking toward the front of the van. Nohar stepped out and shook his head. "No."

"What?" The kid turned around.

"You ride in back."

"Look we're on the same side—"

"You were waving a gun around, I don't trust you."

The kid looked at him and seemed to be gauging the probability of winning an argument with Nohar, or failing that, outrunning him. The kid had brains enough not to argue. He stepped in back with Maria, and sat down quietly.

When he did, Nohar grabbed another elastic cord and secured his arms behind him to a metal rod that was welded to the side of the van, seemingly just for that purpose.

He objected. "Hey, what're you doing?"

"You better hope," Nohar said, "that you gave accurate directions to this place, and my son is all right."

"What about my father?"

"That's my problem now." Nohar shut the rear door and walked Henderson up to the driver's side of the van. Henderson looked at him and said, "You're not driving?"

"I need to keep an eye on our boy back there."

Nohar opened the door for her, and after she stepped in, he handed her the .45 that John had been waving around. She stared at the gun.

"I'm going to have to come back to town." He needed to know for sure who the Bad Guys were. Until then, none of them were safe. "You'll need to keep an eye on him too. If he gives you any trouble, shoot him in the knee." Nohar shut the driver's door and got in on the other side of the van.

Nohar watched the abandoned red Python as the decrepit INS van pulled away. Changing vehicles was probably a good thing. He didn't want to get caught in a car someone else might've IDed. And who knew what warrants were out on that Oxford guy.

Once they headed out onto the highway, Nohar was lost in his thoughts, and he felt his gut twist.

There was nothing he wanted more right now than to see his son.

There was also nothing that frightened him more.

The ride took a few hours over the freeways of LA. Eventually, the traffic peeled away as they headed due east, toward Arizona. Buildings seemed to disappear into the desert as they left the fringes of civilization. The sun sank, and soon the old van drove along a tiny strip of the world carved out by its one working headlamp.

Nohar had the time to think of his son.

Seventeen.

At that age, Nohar had just stopped running with a local street gang and had started working for himself. He had started looking for people, a lot of folks got lost in Moreytown, and other folks would pay to find them. It eventually got to be a regular job. . . .

Nohar tried to reconstruct what it was like for him at seventeen. He had been physically adult for nearly ten years by then, and his brain was just growing into the body. He remembered his own isolation, a bequest from his father. He lived in an era that saw Datia as a hero, and he could never reconcile his own image of him with what the rest of the morey world saw. In the end, he was as surely isolated as Manuel was.

He hoped to God that he wasn't about to do to his son what Datia did to him. Though, in retrospect, it was hard to picture what Datia could have said to the young Nohar that would have fulfilled Nohar's expectations. How could anyone surmount the space of years that separated them?

Christ, it was probably too late for both of them.

The camp was unlit, so it was a complete surprise to Nohar when the gate sprang up in front of the van, caught in its headlight. It came at the end of a dirt track they'd followed off of the main road.

This was it.

The van stopped and Nohar got out, twisting the kinks out of his neck which he'd been straining, looking back at the Necron Avenger every few minutes during the ride here. Henderson walked up next to him, staring through the sliding chain-link fence, into the darkness beyond.

"Like a prison," she said, her breath fogging in the cold night air.

The headlamp threw their shadows through the gate and across an empty field. At the other end of the field, Nohar could see the abstract shadows of a guard tower blocking out the stars. At its base was another fence, which seemed more substantial than the chain-link in front of him.

"Let's get Necron," Nohar said, walking back to the rear of the INS van.

He pulled open the doors and John Samson looked at him. "Thanks for remembering me. I can't feel my hands anymore."

Nohar shook his head and stepped in. He looked at Maria and asked, "How're you doing?"

"Fine," she said, but her posture showed differently. The ride hadn't been easy on her, and the pain showed on her face.

Nohar turned and untied John, feeling the same undirected anger he'd been feeling every time he realized how deeply Maria's genetics had betrayed her.

"Hey, watch it," John said, pulling his hands away when he was finally untied. He began rubbing his overlong fingers together. "They're sensitive."

Nohar growled slightly, and John jumped out.

Nohar followed, "You have the access codes for here?"

Necron nodded and walked up to one side of the gate. He looked at Henderson and said, "You should get back in the van, and drive it through to the main gate."

Henderson looked at Nohar as if looking for confirmation. Nohar nodded. She got in the van and closed the door.

John walked up to the side of the gate, the light from the van's headlamp exaggerating his frank features. With the shadows cast by the light, his head looked grotesquely swollen, and his fingers seemed to stretch impossibly toward the ground.

He stopped by a small metal box mounted on a pole. It had a recessed cover that swung open when he pressed it. Beneath it, an alphanumeric keypad lit up.

He looked across at Nohar. "The access code, '01082034.' " He spoke the numbers as he typed them on the keypad. "Remember it, it gets you through the perimeter." He grinned and shook his head as the gate started rolling aside. "Someone in the INS must be from Frisco."

Nohar didn't know exactly what John meant. He followed the van through the gate, and it didn't strike him until he, Necron, and the van were all through and the gate was closing behind them.

"01082034," January 8, 2034—the date of the Frisco Quake. It was 9.5 and did a lot of damage to LA even though it was centered around San Francisco.

Nohar grabbed Necron, and they followed the van, on foot, down to the main gate.

The complex was a mass of dull cinder-block buildings surrounding an even bleaker central section enclosed by barbed wire. Nohar only saw glimpses of what had been the holding facility, barracks lined up with less than two meters between buildings. Even with the barracks, in the flashes of light Nohar could see the remnants of plastic sheets that had sheltered people who hadn't fit inside the buildings. The plastic was torn and fluttered weakly in the wind.

Nohar and John had boarded the rear of the van, and Henderson followed the Necron Avenger's directions, driving to the north end of the complex, where the main administration building was.

The van's headlight swept across the front of the building, and Nohar saw that the door was opening.

Nohar's breath caught in his throat.

A tall feline stepped out of the door, blinking in the light. His coloring was mostly black, with hints of russet stripes that faded to near-invisibility.

Nohar forgot Necron, opened the rear door, and jumped out. Looking at Manuel, his words were frozen in his mouth. Somehow, he had thought he'd know what to say. Now, every rehearsed opening seemed to fail him.

It was Manuel who spoke first.

"Who the fuck are you?"

Chapter 18

The headlight shut off, and his son squinted at the van. "Sara? What's going on here? You shouldn't be here, it's dangerous." He had the same husky voice as his mother.

Nohar was shaking his head. "You don't know how dangerous, son." His voice was barely a whisper, and he didn't know if Manuel had heard it.

Manuel turned to him again and asked, "And who the fuck *are* you?"

I'm your father. For some reason the words wouldn't come. Instead, Nohar said, "My name's Nohar Rajasthan. Your mother hired me to find you."

"Oh, fuck—" Manuel didn't get to finish his statement, because Henderson had gotten out of the van and had run up and hugged Manuel.

Nohar noticed that his son seemed uncomfortable with the affection. But Manuel raised a hand and patted Henderson's shoulder. "You weren't supposed to be involved."

Henderson gave Manuel's ear a nip and said, "Thank God you're all right. I really thought that they got to you." She pushed herself away and looked back at the van. "I need to get Maria."

"Mom?" Manuel's voice started out as a whisper, but a thread of steel started to emerge as he said, "You brought my mother here?" He looked at John, who had just slipped out of the back. Nohar saw his son's claws extending and retracting, and he could sense a dangerous uncontrolled anger building in him. "Are you *insane*? Someone in her condition—"

Nohar stepped between the two of them. "I brought her."

"Are you trying to kill her? She hasn't been out of her apartment in—"

"It's all right, Manny . . ." Maria spoke, and the words cut into Nohar's heart. *Manny.*

Manny was a name Nohar hadn't heard in ages. Manny had raised him, from the time when his mother died, until Nohar had left home. Manny, Mandvi Gujerat, had been the medical officer on Datia's airlift, one of the few nontigers aboard. He had delivered Nohar, and had taken in the cub when his mother had died. Manny had been the only real father Nohar had ever had. Manny had been dead almost twenty years.

Manny had liked Maria, and Nohar wondered if his son's name was a coincidence.

"I was trying to keep you *all* out of this," Manny looked at Sara who was helping Maria into her chair.

"We didn't," John Samson said. "They got my father, damn it! I get back, my house is trashed, and tall, black, and hostile here is sniffing around the remains."

Manuel turned to John, staring at him.

"They haven't found you yet," Nohar said. "That makes this the safest place we've got."

Manuel whipped around and looked at Nohar. "We, who the fuck is 'we.' I didn't invite you to this party, Mr. Rajasthan."

Nohar looked at Maria. "You never told him my name."

Manuel looked back and forth between Maria and Nohar. "What're you talking about? Who *are* you?"

Nohar tried to say it, but the words just wouldn't come. After a few minutes all he managed was, "I'm sorry. I didn't know you existed until a week ago." He turned away, toward the dark cinder-block building that Manuel had come from. "I didn't know who you were until yesterday."

Nohar shoved his hands in his pockets, feeling his own isolation crushing down on him. He had lost everyone who had once been close to him, his mother, Manny, Maria, Stephie—even Bobby probably only thought of him as a diverting curiosity now, not a friend. It was stupid to think that he'd achieve any connection with his son, now, after seventeen years. What would be the point?

Nohar let the others talk to Manuel. He heard his son say, "Someone explain this shit to me before things—"

"It's the card," John said. "It's hotter than we expected."

Nohar pushed through into the building and stopped listening.

That's not how it was supposed to happen.

The way it was supposed to happen—the son and father meet for the first time, their eyes meet, and there is supposed to be some paternal connect. They should *know* that the same blood runs through their veins. A bond like that shouldn't be erased by time. . . .

It was the way his meeting with Datia should have gone. He remembered wheedling a meeting with the great morey leader, knowing that when their eyes met, Datia would know and love him as his own son. The way it went was wrenchingly familiar.

"Who the fuck are you?"

"Who the fuck do you think you are?"

"Why the fuck should anyone else care?"

It was stupid and silly. No one else cared. Why should any moreau give a shit about his paternity? It mattered as much as the specific tiger who donated the first strands of Nohar's genetic code. It was an irrelevancy.

"That's where you disappeared to." Henderson's voice came from behind Nohar. Nohar turned around and looked at her. There was concern in her voice. More concern than Nohar had a right to expect. She pushed the rest of the way through the plastic sheathing that half-blocked the doorway. "I thought you'd want to talk to Manuel?"

Fuck. Nohar opened his mouth, but he couldn't form the words. Everything was tied up in knots inside him. "I do," he said, "but . . ."

He couldn't finish the sentence, because Henderson pulled Manuel in after her. Manuel seemed to have the same expression of combined unease, anger, and confusion that must have been on Nohar's face. Henderson looked from Nohar to Manuel and back again.

"John's going to show us where we can set up house," Henderson said. "I'll just leave you two to talk things over. . . ."

She slipped back outside before either of them could object.

After a while Manuel said, "Ain't this a mess?"

Nohar nodded.

"So now what?" he asked. "Do I hug you, or do I try to punch that face in?"

"I don't know," Nohar said. He wanted to tell Manuel that he knew how he felt. But he knew too well how that would sound. He swallowed and forced out the words that Datia had never said, "You shouldn't give a shit about me. I shouldn't matter to you—"

"That's easy for you to say—"

"—but if you do care, I'm here for you."

Manuel seemed to be taken aback. "Fuck, you don't know anything about me."

Nohar shook his head. "I know enough."

"You don't know shit. I'm an outcast, an outlaw, you're the last thing I need. What I need is a ticket away from ground zero."

"Do you even know what you've stepped in?"

"Yeah. The Clinic's giving people the Drips. Not like there haven't been rumors—"

"We have pink commando squads running all over LA. They've blown up my house, tortured and killed Henderson's boss, tried to kidnap her, and carried out an armed assault on your mother's housing project—all because you disappeared with that card."

Manuel seemed to deflate a bit and walked back toward the doorway. "You think I planned all this?" He shook his head again. "It was just supposed to be a little easy money—"

"No such thing."

"We knew we had something nasty. We shut up here hoping to keep everyone out of it—"

"You didn't think anyone'd look for you."

"Hell, I thought people would look for us, but I didn't think that'd get people killed." Manuel leaned his head against the doorframe.

Nohar reached out and put a hand on Manuel's shoulder.

"If anything," Manuel said, "I'm the one no one should give a shit about. I caused all this."

Nohar squeezed his son's shoulder.

"Why should you care about some half-breed misfit?"

After a long time Nohar said, "Back when I was your age, there was a saying, 'species before nationality.' There's another half of that saying that people tend to forget."

Manuel turned to face him and Nohar lowered his hand. "What?" Manuel asked.

"'Blood before all.'"

Manuel had inherited his mother's smile, and her tears. He grabbed Nohar's forearm with both of his and said, "So you're my father."

Nohar nodded, his voice failing him again.

"Damn," Manuel said. "I thought tigers had stripes."

There was a little nervous laughter. "Long story," Nohar said.

Nohar was impressed at their choice of places to hole up. The old federal buildings had been abandoned with piles of supplies and equipment. There was everything from cots to dried rations here. It had its own generators, still producing enough power to run the building and the security apparatus. In the room where John and Manuel made their home, there was a long desk with a set of inset comms linked to various parts of base operations and security, and behind it was a massive holo mapping out the whole complex. The map had several little digital readouts overlaid on what must have been a self-updating satellite image of the area.

The most distinctive feature was on the eastern side of the complex. There were acres of old government vehicles, parked between the inner and outer fences.

In a height of irony, the map told Nohar the official name of this place, "Camp Liberty."

Nohar helped bring out cots for the extra people, but as the night advanced toward midnight he decided he had to leave. They couldn't hole up here forever. The Bad Guys were still out there, and so was John's father. Someone had to go back to LA and try to deal with things.

Nohar had John copy the ramcard, which he said would take some time because of the encryption on the data. He gave it a few hours. Meanwhile he went out with Manuel to the vehicle graveyard.

"I don't know what you're looking for. The electronics on all these things are toast."

Nohar nodded as they walked past ranks of shadowed vehicles. Occasionally Nohar's flashlight would pick out a shadowed fender, a deflated tire. "I know, John told me how you spent a lot of time getting that vehicle running."

"Yeah—"

Nohar stopped at a small shack in the midst of the vehicles, playing his flashlight across the front of it. He hoped that it was what he had thought it was when he had seen it on the satellite map. Behind him, Manuel was still talking. "You know you can take the van...."

Nohar shook his head. "It's the only thing that'll move all four of you."

The beam of the light played across cinder block and old tar paper. The front of the shack was a rolling metal garage door. Nohar walked up to the side of the building, and found a cover that opened to reveal a pair of buttons, green and red. Nohar depressed the green one.

"There's my car—"

There was a screech of old and ill-maintained machinery as the green button lit and the rolling steel door began to ease its way open. "No. People are looking for you, remember?"

The door opened all the way, and the lights came on in the small garage. There were dusty tools hanging on the walls, but what interested Nohar was in the back. He walked up to a set of pumps on the far wall and examined them. As he was checking to see if they worked, he found the question slipping out, "Did you ever wonder about me?"

"Fuck, what a question—what do you think? She barely talked about you, I didn't know your name until a half hour ago. Do you know how many times I've cursed you for this genetic meltdown I got laid with, for whatever happened between you and Mom."

"We broke up, she never told—"

"Yeah. I bet that was just because you were such a great guy."

Nohar choked back a knot of rage, and felt his claws digging into the cinder-block wall next to the pumps. "If she had told me—" Nohar whispered. He couldn't finish.

The ugly silence filled the room, broken only by the ticking metal of the overheated motor that had raised the door. For some reason, Nohar was becoming aware of the peculiarly individual scent of the motor, a smell of oil, dust, and old electricity that was somehow distinct from the smell he remembered from the locker at Saf-Stor.

"What are you here for, Rajasthan?" Manuel asked.

Why? Nohar thought. What does a blood tie mean to a creature such as him? As any morey? At least Manuel had one parent. Maria had been there for him. Nohar's own blood had abandoned him. His mother had been taken from him, and his father had never acknowledged any ties to his son as an individual.

"I'm here," Nohar said, "because I don't have anything else." He rapped his knuckles against the side of the pump making a hollow metallic ring, breaking the oppressive quiet. "There's still fuel here."

"What fuel?"

"Diesel," Nohar said. "The military was still using internal combustion vehicles during this place's heyday."

"Huh? We just saw a lot of your standard induction engines."

Nohar turned around and nodded. "Sure. Most of the vehicles here are civilian. But if this is here," Nohar tapped the pump, "I bet there're a few old National Guard vehicles here at least."

"Why you want something like that?"

"It'll be easier to get running. Sturdier machine." Nohar walked toward the front and waved Manuel over. "Come on."

Manuel followed him into the darkened auto graveyard.

It wasn't long before they were pushing a forty-year-old Hummer into the garage. It was painted in brown-and-tan camouflage, and still had the markings of a National Guard unit on it. The tires needed to be inflated, the oil changed, and a few cables and belts needed to be replaced due to dry rot. Most of what needed fixing was self-evident. The most difficult thing was starting it. There were spare parts for the vehicles in the garage, but it took them ten tries before they found a battery that would hold a charge.

It took two hours, but eventually the Hummer was there idling.

"I guess I'd better get going," Nohar said.

Manuel looked at the vehicle, full tank, actually running, and ran his hand over the hood. "I wish I had thought of this. Easier than trying to refurbish a fried inductor."

Nohar shook his head, "I'm probably the last generation

that would remember these things. When I was a kid, there was still the occasional gas station on the corner. One or two I remember actually running."

Manuel turned to face Nohar, and the gulf of years between them was palpable. In a soft voice, Manuel asked, "Did you love Mom?"

Did I love her?

Nohar thought of that last message from Maria. The one where she had left him. He remembered how he had felt.

"Yes," he said.

Before the conversation could go any further, Nohar slipped into the Hummer and started backing out of the garage. He considered just driving away, but he sat and waited as Manuel closed up the small garage and jumped into the seat next to him.

He landed with a cloud of yellow dust. The grit seemed to cover everything, inside and out. Manuel didn't turn to face Nohar as he said, "Going to have to paint over those markings—thing stands out as it is."

Nohar nodded as he drove the Hummer back to the compound.

Manuel grabbed some spray paint and went over the Hummer while Nohar retrieved the copied ramcard. John was working at the comm, and when Nohar walked in, a shimmering rectangle popped out of one of the comm's data slots. John took it out and laid it in front of Nohar. Nohar stared at the rainbow-sheened ramcard as John said, "That's it. A copy anyway."

Nohar picked it up. Here was the thing that everyone was hunting for. It didn't look like much.

He made a cursory check to see that Maria and Henderson were all right, then he went back to the Hummer, which was now a collage of black-and-red spray paint.

When he reached the car, Manuel straightened up and asked, "Where're you going in this thing?"

"Back."

Manuel nodded. "Want to save the world?"

"Maria always said I was doing that." Nohar shook his head. "This is just self-preservation. The Bad Guys have your friend's father. He was INS. Only a matter of time before they figure out to look here."

Manuel had a fatalistic look on his face which told Nohar that he wasn't really surprised about that. "Need help out there?" he asked.

Nohar shook his head again. "We're better off if only one person's ass is in the line of fire. Stay here."

Manuel's look said that he wasn't too surprised by that either. "You coming back?"

"I don't know." Nohar looked down at the car, then across at the van. "If I'm not back in two days, get the hell out of here."

"Where?"

"South. Mexico."

"What about you? How're you going to find us?"

"I'll find you. It's what I do." He slipped into the driver's seat of the Hummer.

Manuel looked at him across the passenger seat; a cool desert wind blew through the open windows. For a moment the rest of the world seemed very remote, as if he and Manuel were the only living things left on the planet.

It seemed that some of that sense of isolation had reached Manuel. There was something very quiet, almost pleading, in his voice when he asked, "Why did you and Mom break up?"

Nohar sat there, letting the Hummer grind through a rough aged idle. He didn't have much of an answer for his son. *Why did they break up?*

"I wasn't there enough," Nohar said, the closest thing to an honest answer he could come up with.

Manuel looked at him as if he'd expected something more dramatic.

They stayed there looking at each other for a long time through the open window, the empty desert wind blowing past them.

After a while, Manuel exhaled. "This is all too sudden. I don't really know you—"

"I understand."

"I don't think I'm ready to be your son."

Nohar felt his heart sink. He turned away from his son and nodded. After all, what did he expect?

He heard Manuel walk around the front of the Hummer. At first he thought that Manuel was leaving, but after a moment he felt a hand on his shoulder.

He turned to see Manuel saying, "You seem okay, and you've done a lot for Mom, and Sara. So, *friends*, all right?"

Nohar looked at his son for a long time before he put his own hand on Manuel's.

"Friends," he said.

Chapter 19

Nohar drove back into LA. The suburbs passed by him like the circles of hell. He didn't reach the edges of Compton until about three in the morning. By then he was so exhausted that he just pulled off to the side of the road and slept where he was.

While he slept in the ancient Hummer, Nohar dreamed of his mother.

He is five again, sitting in the veterinary wing of the Cleveland Clinic. He is hunched over in a too-small chair. Whenever anyone comes near him, he growls. He is here to see his mother, and they aren't going to send him away.

Then the doctors and nurses are all gone. It is as if they have all abandoned the hospital.

He takes the chance and walks over to the big red door that leads to the feline ward. There are warnings plastered on the doors, but he doesn't read them.

The door opens on the smell of blood, feces, disinfectant, and death. He stands there, frozen in the doorway, his eyes unable to focus. He knows, somewhere in his head, that all the felines in this ward have died from a Pakistani-engineered variant of feline leukemia, a leftover from the Pan-Asian War. Everyone caught it from an improperly diagnosed jaguar.

Now it is different, the bodies lie in their beds, torn open. The ward is now a dead battlefield, the bodies scattered in the mud after a devastating attack. His mother, near to term with her second pregnancy, is facedown in the mud, clutching a rifle.

He hears gunfire in the distance, and walks through the

*mud to the tree line marking the edge of the hill the bodies
cover. He pushes through the brush and sees the war. A battle
rages below him, on the streets of LA. Black-uniformed humans fight heavily armed moreau forces equipped as they'd
been for the war. Ursines carry body harnesses linked to
thirty-millimeter anti-tank rifles. Rats scurry through the urban landscape wielding small submachine guns. Tigers, like
him, like his father, carry personal gatling miniguns that
spray three thousand rounds a minute into the human forces.*

*Above it all, flames race across the hills overlooking the
city.*

*At Nohar's feet is a weak bark. Nohar looks down and
sees one-eyed Elijah, the scarred brown dog with the electronic voicebox.*

"What's happening?" Nohar asks.

*"man," Elijah says in his electronic monotone, "is dissat-
isfied until he can destroy what he has created."*

The dawn sunlight woke him, the smell of smoke, blood,
and death from his dream following him into wakefulness.
His body ached, especially the base of his tail, from sleeping
in the car.

His first business was to find a public comm and call
Bobby back.

It took a moment for Bobby to recognize Nohar when
he answered his comm. But then recognition did dawn, and
he asked, "Nohar? Is that you?"

Nohar nodded. Dawn light was just reaching LA, but
where Bobby was it was nearly ten.

"What'd you do to yourself?"

Nohar thought he could ask the same question. Now that
he was over the shock of seeing Bobby on his feet, he could
see how he had aged. He could see the wrinkles starting on
his face. His hair was thinning and what was still there was
beginning to gray. Looking at Bobby made him aware of
how his joints ached from all the running around he'd done
yesterday.

"What have you got on those numbers?" Nohar asked.

"Not as much as I hoped." Bobby shook his head. "Posi-
tioning data for a satellite. But there's nothing that officially
occupies the area where your uplink was pointing—"

"There had to be something up there."

Bobby nodded. "It gets better. There is a satellite up there. Given time and location, my boys were able to find it. It's a Fed bird, and a black one."

"You sure?"

"My boys are sure, and I trust my boys. They tried getting into the thing's software, and they swear it was Fed defenses that locked them out. All we got on it is that it's in geosynchronous orbit over the central U.S., and that it's designed for extremely narrow-band transmissions. It's some agency's private communications center, private and secure."

"Any idea *what* agency?"

Bobby shook his head. "Could be anyone from the FBI to the IRS. My guess, though, would be the military. This is just a communications bird, not a spy satellite." Bobby leaned forward and asked. "What have you gotten into? I checked news reports on the coast, the cops are looking for you."

"If I knew, I wouldn't tell you—you've been dragged deep enough into this already."

Bobby shook his head. "You can't leave me like that, old friend. There's got to be something more I can do for you."

Nohar looked up and down the street. The sky was lightening, and with the dawn Nohar felt exposed. John Samson's paranoia was rubbing off on him. He felt as if he had spent too long standing in one place.

"Two things," Nohar said.

"Name them."

"Can your pet hackers get a list of people who did a specific search on the net?"

"That's not impossible."

"I need a list of people who've done a search for articles by a kid calling himself The Necron Avenger."

"That it?"

Nohar looked up and down the street again. The place was empty except for an occasional car. With the boarded-up buildings, this area of Compton looked like the aftermath of a full-spectrum war. It reminded Nohar of the pictures of African cities after the pandemic, after the genetech's microbes got out of hand.

"Do some research for me. The Bensheim Foundation and their Clinics. I need to know who runs what, especially in LA. I don't think I'll have time to hunt all that down myself."

"You got it." Bobby smiled. "You know, it's just like old times."

"Uh-huh. I'll call you back."

Nohar cut the connection, feeling older than ever. To his one-time best friend he was now nostalgia.

The Hummer—which only stalled out twice—got Nohar into Pasadena early enough for him to miss most of rush hour. Pasadena was pink territory, but nothing like Beverly Hills. Nohar didn't have to worry about cops stopping him just because he was nonhuman.

He was lucky, though, that no one stopped him because of the crate he was driving.

Nohar wasn't really sure what he was going to do eventually, but he was going to start by watching. He found a parking space in a garage that overlooked the main LA offices of the Bensheim Foundation in LA, the address where Manuel's ramcard was intended to go, and the place the van with the uplink was probably going home to.

The offices didn't stand out as much as the Clinic, probably because the building was nestled in among a series of similar structures which all seemed to have been built about the same time after the '34 quake.

Nohar chose his position before the start of business hours, so he could see the people coming here for work. He didn't know what he was looking for, but he knew that there was something here that would point to who was behind the Bad Guys.

If these people were going to such lengths to hide the information on that ramcard, that meant they were afraid of exposure. That meant that exposure was the one weapon Nohar had to end this nightmare—but he had to know what, and *who*, he was exposing.

His talk with Bobby confirmed for Nohar that whatever was going on went beyond the Bensheim Foundation. The Foundation didn't have paramilitary resources—at least they probably didn't—but Nohar was certain that they wouldn't be using a Fed satellite if the Fed wasn't somehow involved.

Nohar sat in the Hummer, on the top floor of the garage, and watched the entrance to the Foundation offices through his digital camera. It was a long and boring morning, watching the pinks move in and out of the building. He dutifully took pictures, low res so he wouldn't exhaust the camera's memory, just enough for identification purposes.

After about two hours, when it was nearing ten in the morning, Nohar finally got a break.

Walking out of the front of the building was a familiar face. It belonged to a tall black man with a jagged scar across his right cheek. It was the guy who had been first out of the helicopter at Pastoria Towers. The same bearing, the same arrogant hunter's stare. Nohar put down the camera when he saw that Scar was heading toward a dark Electroline van, twin of the one that had been watching Maria's apartment.

He pulled the Hummer out of its space and began peeling down the ramps of the garage. He only slowed to a normal speed—smelling what was left of the old brakes as he did so—when he reached the ramp out to the street.

He managed to pull out three car lengths behind the retreating van. Nohar slowed, matching the traffic flow, and wishing for a car less conspicuous than a spray-painted Hummer.

Fifteen minutes into tailing the van, the old instincts came back. He steered for blind spots in the van's rear view, using larger cars to run interference for him, hiding the all-too-conspicuous vehicle. It helped that the guy behind the wheel—whether or not he was aware of his garish shadow—wasn't doing anything to shake a tail. In LA traffic it would have been easy to get lost on the freeways.

Nohar stayed glued to Scar's van, down the Harbor Freeway, south, all the way to the coast.

He followed him off the freeway, until they reached the Long Beach Naval Station. . . .

When Nohar saw that, he just slowly drove by the guard shacks flanking the entrance. *"Shit,"* he whispered to himself as he watched the van pass through security in the rearview mirror.

Nohar drove into Long Beach and stopped at a public library kiosk to double-check what he already knew. The Long Beach Naval Station had been home to one of the country's top antiterrorism units during the last episode of rioting in LA. Apparently it had been a temporary assignment that had gradually become permanent.

That meant that the official news story about the attack on Pastoria Towers was probably right.

What scared Nohar was the fact that this all—everything that was happening—was a Fed operation. How could he fight against that kind of odds? The only reasonable option was to leave the country—and even that wouldn't put him and the others out of reach of this kind of operation.

He walked back to the Hummer, trying to think of what he could do.

They *had* run when the media arrived. The only real chance he had was publicity, widespread international publicity. That meant more than just Manuel's ramcard, that meant enough evidence of this Fed operation to punch it through the news filter of every comm on the planet.

There was little chance of him getting through the security at a military base, so he turned the Hummer back toward the highway and headed north, back toward Pasadena.

Nohar walked into the lobby of the Bensheim Foundation hoping that the pinks couldn't smell the tension around him. Luckily, moreaus weren't alien here, even in the Pasadena offices. The lobby guard didn't give him a second look, and Nohar saw a trio of female rabbits leave an elevator and head for the exit. From the way they were dressed, conservative, dark colors, lots of material, Nohar supposed they all worked here.

Nohar slipped into the vacated elevator, and the doors shut behind him. Out of the corner of his eye he noticed a security camera, so Nohar gave all his attention to the video display set into the wall of the elevator. It gave an office directory. He gave it a quick scan and highlighted the fifth floor—

The offices had their own on-site Clinic, and it was the least suspicious place for a moreau off the street to go. As the elevator rose, Nohar noted the other items on the directory. He scrolled through the items while looking as if he was fidgeting, tapping his claws on the screen.

Tenth floor, Systems and Building Maintenance. Ninth floor, Administration. Eighth floor, Accounting. Seventh and Sixth, PR and Community Relations. Fifth was the Clinic. Fourth was R&D and the Laboratories. Third was International. Second was Shipping and Receiving. First was Lobby and Building Security.

The strange thing was, this building was taller than ten stories. Nohar could remember that much from when he'd been watching it from the outside. He had this feeling confirmed as he looked at the display change floor numbers as the elevator rose.

Between the third and fourth floors there was a perceptible lag. Between every other pair of floors it took the number a little less than a second to change. Between three and four was almost three seconds.

Nohar could picture the side of the building. He had watched long enough to know that floor three was just as tall as the floors above and below it.

When the doors slid open, Nohar walked out into the hall leading to the Clinic itself. It was reminiscent of Compton, but this time the posters warning about sexually transmitted diseases seemed more ominous.

He made careful note of where the security cameras were located. Before he made it to the reception area, he slipped into the restrooms and entered a stall. He was improvising, and he wasn't quite sure what he was going to do—

What he did know was that he wanted to get a look at whatever was nestled between International and R&D. Nohar sat and thought of hiding until the building closed, but then he'd be dealing with active alarms and security that wasn't busy doing anything else.

He needed a distraction that would last long enough for him to get a good look around. If they were hiding a whole floor, how would he get to it? The elevator probably operated on some sort of code, so he couldn't use that. That left scaling the outside of the building, or the fire stairs.

That might be it.

Nohar left the bathroom and continued down the hall. He noted the presence of fire alarms and extinguishers. A false alarm was tempting, but there was little chance it would really empty the building before security discovered that there wasn't a fire. Besides, no one ever believes a fire alarm the first time it goes off. There's five to ten minutes before anyone believes it's the real thing, unless they smell the smoke themselves.

He needed another way to empty the building.

He walked into the reception area and took a clipboard form from the bored-looking human receptionist and walked around the desk. Instead of going to the waiting area, he walked to a set of public comms lining one wall around the corner from the entrance. He looked for security cameras watching the comms, and he seemed to be in luck. No cameras here, security was more interested in watching people come and go.

They'd eventually trace the call back here, and they'd have a video record of him all over the building, but at this point he didn't care. The only important thing was that they wouldn't connect him to this immediately. And all he needed was a little time.

Nohar slid in front of the clunky comm and ran his claws over the textured plastic. The rarely used keyboard was recessed beneath the screen, the keys had collected a lot of debris. He fed some money into the thing and switched off both the audio and video feed. Then he started a multiple destination message, composing at the keyboard. His message went to the Bensheim Foundation Administration, the police, and several news agencies.

The note was very simple. He claimed that the Outsiders—the same people who had taken credit for Alcatraz and Royd—had placed a bomb in the building and it was set to go off in ninety minutes.

They were good. It was only five minutes from his message—he had just walked into the waiting room and had sat down—when the klaxons of the fire alarms sounded, and the PA system came on telling everyone to evacuate the building in a calm fashion. They didn't mention a bomb, probably to avoid a panic.

That was fine as far as Nohar was concerned. He abandoned the clipboard and started out with the mass of male moreaus from the waiting room. Most headed for the elevator, but Nohar stayed with the ones who headed for the fire stairs.

The fire stairs wrapped around the inside of a concrete tube that did its best to amplify the klaxons, hurting Nohar's ears. The stairs were packed with people descending.

Nohar fitted himself into the crowd, hugging the wall. He continued down one floor, but at the next fire door he stopped, his back pressed to the wall, letting the people pass him. He stayed against the hinge side of the cinder-block wall, and waited.

Eventually, the fire door—which led to the anonymous floor between three and four—opened.

There wasn't a handle on the outside of the door, so Nohar grabbed the edge of it and pulled it all the way back toward him. Someone mumbled a "thanks" from the other side of the door.

Nohar stood there holding the door, waiting for someone to notice him. No one did. The moment the stairway seemed clear of everyone, Nohar slipped through the open fire door and into the secret heart of the Bensheim Foundation.

There wasn't anything that stood out immediately. Nothing to mark this place as something to be hidden. It was the same carpeted floor, same fluorescent lighting, same acoustical tile that Nohar had seen two floors above.

The fire door shut behind him, muffling the klaxons somewhat.

Nohar walked down the hall, passing ranks of offices, getting his bearings. At least it seemed that they had emptied this place as much as the rest of the building. Now he just had to figure out where to look. He had probably another fifteen minutes before the bomb squad brought their dogs and their chemical sniffers. . . .

Nohar turned the corner and was confronted with a much different hallway. The way was blocked by a heavy stainless-steel door that had the red biohazard trefoil etched into its surface. There was a portal in the door, and Nohar looked through it and saw a small chamber. Hanging on the walls were what looked to be human space suits.

Someone was working with some very dangerous stuff here.

Nohar backed up and took out his camera. He started taking pictures of the door and the room beyond.

He looked at the lock and decided there wasn't any time

to try to open the door. Not that he wanted to go anywhere that required a full environmental suit.

Nohar backtracked from the door and ducked in each office, hoping to get lucky.

He did.

In the third office he found a comm unit running, in the midst of some sort of database search. Its owner hadn't logged out of the system, leaving Nohar with a comm that still had full access to everything.

Nohar slipped behind the comm and figured he had ten minutes to get it to tell him what was going on.

Chapter 20

Nohar took a ramcard out of his wallet, his record of The Necron Avenger's public net activity. He felt okay overwriting it; he didn't need that information anymore. He slipped the card into the comm's data slot and tried to call up a directory, a database, or some sort of menu.

Nohar managed to back up from the financial information he was looking at until he hit a menu listing the databases he could open. There were the typical titles, "Accounting," "Inventory," and "Personnel."

But there was a group of other databases with more cryptic names, "Rangoon," "Tangier," "Congo," and "Niger."

Nohar entered the Rangoon database and was confronted with a history of the Drips. Vectors, case studies, maps of outbreaks, pathology, demographics. Everything that anyone could possibly want to know about Herpes Rangoon, down to its genetic structure.

He already knew that they were tracking the Drips from the information Necron had given him, so he only scanned the information before backing up and trying another heading. His next try was "Tangier."

What he saw was a hepatitis variant. This wasn't a disease that was making the news. According to the database it was confined to the canines inhabiting the Hollywood Hills. Nohar thought back to one-eyed Elijah, and the other dogs, the ones who were falling to some sickness. The people here were tracking that disease. Looking at the information gathered here, it was obvious that something odd was happening. Their reports on transmission vectors were as detailed as the ones for the Drips. The case studies of the disease's progress were as complete—and this was for a community of moreaus that never saw the inside of a hospital.

The genetic information was here, too. This time Nohar paid a little more attention. He wasn't a scientist, but he was beginning to get an ominous feeling from the databases. They didn't seem to be the product of doctors interested in curing, or even attempting to learn about a disease. The database seemed more a critique of the virus. Scattered throughout were words like "effective transmission," "efficient progression," and "optimum prognosis." As if they were rating the virus on how well it spread.

He scanned through the Tangier database, becoming more and more alarmed, until he came to a list of concluding comments, one of which was absolutely chilling.

"Hepatitis Tangier is not recommended due to an unacceptably high chance of transmission to humans."

Nohar started downloading the database to his ramcard. The comm flashed a warning to him, the comm's voice lost under the sounds of the fire alarms. "This is a secure database. Use is being logged. Do you still wish to complete this operation?"

Nohar hit "Y" on the comm's keyboard. His finger was shaking.

He had begun to realize that he wasn't looking through a medical database. He was looking at a military one. He was looking at an analysis of biological warfare agents.

He looked back at the Rangoon file, and found what he had missed before. All the signs that he was looking at something someone had engineered in a lab. More acceptable because the transmission rate to humans was nil. . . .

"Good lord," Nohar whispered to himself. He had expected to find some signs of a dark experiment, someone testing propagation of the herpes virus. He had never expected to find out someone had engineered the disease in the first place.

"Congo," was a flu virus. It had apparently ripped through

the moreau population in The States about two years ago. There had been a few fatalities, among the very old and very young. Nohar skipped to the conclusions—Congo had been abandoned because it was unstable, prone to mutate.

The last one, "Niger," was the most recent file. They had just completed the engineering of the organism. There were only two case studies, and there was no question that the victims had been purposely infected. Both had died within a week of infection.

The virus attacked the connective tissue of the body, and caused the internal organs to die off one by one. The victims bled from every orifice, the blood filled every cavity in their bodies. It refused to clot. And near the end, the rabbit that had been infected was vomiting up a black bloody mess that included the lining of his stomach, throat, and tongue. By then the file said the virus had undergone "extreme amplification," which meant that every drop of that rabbit's blood had enough virus in it to infect most of Compton.

The bastards had engineered a variant of Ebola Zaire. A variant that only affected moreaus. Somehow they had found a common thread in the genetics of all the moreaus that they could base their diseases on. Nohar thought of Elijah again—

All of them, all moreaus, shared some genes with those first creations. Something about their virus needed that to spread.

The conclusions found that the virus wasn't lethal to humans.

Suddenly, his concerns for his own safety, even that of his son, seemed petty. He was suddenly looking at the possibility of a genocidal plague in the hands of people who might actually use it. Not just that, but in the hands of people who could use it most effectively. They had been doing these studies for years, studying the propagation of these viruses. If they wanted to use their Ebola Niger, they would introduce it at multiple points, in victims who would assure the maximum spread of the virus. No quarantine would be able to stop it. . . .

The ramcard popped out. He had copied all of the databases.

Nohar reached up for the card, looking up as he suddenly sensed another presence moving toward the office.

The smell of humans was drifting toward him, and he could almost make out the sound of footsteps beneath the noise of the klaxons.

The owner of the footsteps knew exactly where he was going. A pink in a black uniform turned the corner of the office. He was armed with an M-303 caseless assault rifle. He leveled the oversized weapon at Nohar.

"Hold it right there!"

Nohar was already diving behind the desk as the guy let loose. The jackhammer of the rifle upstaged the klaxon as the office began shedding debris around Nohar. Paneling splintered, acoustical tile fell from the ceiling, fluorescent tubes shattered, and the comm exploded into a hundred fragments.

There was no room for negotiation with this guy.

Nohar felt a surge of adrenaline as he pulled out the Vind. He didn't have much time. His only advantage was the guy was firing wildly into the room, and had taken out the only light sources.

He waited for the gunfire to track into one corner of the room, then he sprang toward the opposite end, bringing the Vind to bear on the man silhouetted in the doorway. The guy caught the movement, and started to bring the rifle to bear, the bullets cutting a swath through the office paneling.

Nohar pumped off the two shots left in the Vind, one high, one low. The first caught the guy in the upper chest, the second in the left thigh. He wore body armor, but the first shot still knocked him backward. The second cut his leg out from under him, and he fell back into the hallway.

Nohar ran up and kicked the rifle away from the guy. He had managed to avoid killing the bastard, but Nohar couldn't bring himself to feel good about it. The hallway was rank with the smell of the blood that was pooling under the guy's legs, turning the blue carpet purplish-black.

"Go on," the guy said. His teeth were clenched against pain, and he sounded short of breath. "Kill me, that's what you're designed to do."

Nohar knelt over him, and saw that he was looking at a kid—at least in human terms. He wasn't better than nineteen or twenty. Still, Nohar held the empty Vind up to the kid's head and asked, "Who are you people? Is this a government operation?"

The kid spat at him.

Nohar didn't want to waste time. Everything was going to be converging on this office, the kid was just the first. He held the gun on the kid while he grabbed the M-303.

He was about to try another question, when he heard a door open down the hall, by the fire stairs. The elevators were back there, too. The kid smiled, and Nohar wanted to smack him.

Nohar holstered his Vind and ran in the opposite direction, toward the giant biohazard door. Before he reached it, he ducked into another office. This one had a window overlooking the parking lot. He shouldered the M-303 and picked up an office chair. He used it to smash out the window.

Below him he could see the flashers of the police and fire departments, and the crowd of people circling the building. He was in trouble. He had spent too long at the comm. He had planned to slip out with the last of the evacuees; now he was surrounded by cops and about to be hit by an assault squad with automatic rifles.

He looked out through the window. The wind whipped at his face as he looked four stories down to the pavement. Too far to jump, he'd break bones for sure. And police were already running toward the building. The crowd was all looking in his direction now.

"Fuck," Nohar said, pulling himself out onto the small ledge under the window.

He extended the claws on his hands to get some purchase on the concrete, and it made his fingers feel as if they were being torn apart.

There was a similar ledge on the floor below, and he desperately needed to make it. There were the sounds of shouting and commotion behind and below him, as he faced the wall of the building. More important right now were the sounds of running feet coming down the hall toward the office he'd just left.

There was little choice now. Nohar reached down so his hands gripped the ledge he crouched on. Then he pushed his feet off the ledge. His body fell from in front of the window, dropping from sight as the gunman reached the entrance to the office. He jerked to a stop that almost pulled his shoulders from their sockets. He held on to the ledge, feeling as if his claws would tear from his fingers. He fell against the window below. He swung a foot back to kick out the glass. He managed one solid kick, shattering the window. He let go, allowing his forward momentum to carry him into the blinds and the office beyond the broken window. Glass bit into him as he rolled across the floor at the foot of the window.

He got to his feet in a twin of the office above. He ran for the door. Even though the adrenaline was firing through his body, sharpening everything, he could feel where his body was screaming *enough*. His knee felt as if he had blown it out again. Every joint in both arms was on fire, especially the joints in his fingers. His claws felt as if they had locked in place.

He hobbled out of the office, through a forest of cubicles, and tried to think of an escape route. The more he thought of it, the less likely there was going to be one. He was going to have to deal with the security goons or the police. And it was looking more and more as if the police were the lesser evil.

Nohar crashed through the door to the fire stairs. He could hear a commotion a floor above. The security goons were hitting the stairs as well, trying to catch up with him.

The flights were side-by-side, with little gap between them. Nohar ran halfway down the flight and vaulted over the railing, stumbling on the concrete of the next lower flight. He almost fell headfirst into the landing, but he kept moving. He could hear the footsteps of the security goons above him.

The fire door on this floor was ajar, and Nohar pulled it open and slipped inside. He found himself in a large room, the walls piled high with packages and letters. There were several desks where packages were in the midst of being sorted.

Nohar stopped in front of one desk that was piled high with outgoing packages. He had no time, but he needed to get all the information off of him, he couldn't risk either the security goons or the police confiscating it.

He reached in, pulled out a handful of ramcard-sized packages. He dropped all but one with an address in Culver City that he'd remember. Opened the plastic as carefully as he could, though his rush left a jagged tear in the package.

He slipped the incriminating ramcards inside—his copy of Manuel's find, and the ramcard he'd just copied—and ran the opening through the sealer mounted in the desk. The plastic fused with a hiss, sealing the ramcards inside. The package didn't look great, but if they weren't looking for it, it might get through.

Nohar shoved the package back into the pile and ran for the other side of the room. Behind him he could hear the security goons slip through the fire doors. For some reason, they didn't fire at him.

Nohar crashed through the door on the other side of the mailroom, and came face-to-face with a half-dozen policemen in heavy padded body armor. They carried long rods which they were pointing at several corners of the hallway, and one held the leash for a black unengineered dog who had been busy sniffing the base of the wall until Nohar had appeared in the hallway.

Nohar looked at the Bomb Squad guys, raised his hands, and said, "I surrender."

Chapter 21

The police weren't that gentle, especially with the rifle and the gun on him. All the while, Nohar kept telling himself it was better than being shot. Though, after that victory wore off, he found himself in a bit of a bind. The cops still wanted Nohar Rajasthan for questioning in the Royd murder, and they had a weapons charge on him at the very least, and it didn't take a signed confession for them to figure that he had something to do with the phoned-in bomb threat.

He was driven to the Pasadena station in the back of a much-too-small Dodge Havier, his hands held behind him by nylon strapping because the cops didn't have handcuffs big enough for him.

When they got him to the station, they cut the nylon off and dumped him in a holding cell. The cell was a concrete cube with a single steel door. The unpainted walls were swathed in graffiti, and the concrete bench was too low and too narrow for Nohar to sit on. Nohar stood there for what seemed like hours, trying to think himself out of this mess.

All he got out of it was the full effect of an adrenaline crash. In about half an hour he was crushed by fatigue, leaning against the cold walls, feeling his muscles cramp, every joint in his body hurting as if it were grinding broken bones together. His hands felt as if they would be locked into the same arthritic claws Maria was left with. He bled from enough places from broken glass and shrapnel that the cops had handled him with latex gloves. His body felt like one massive bruise.

Eventually, after about four hours, the cops came for him. This time they had handcuffs that fit.

They led him out of the holding cell, and Nohar tried to walk without limping. Three cops escorted him, and he could smell their tension. He knew if he made a suspicious move, he would probably get a bullet somewhere inconvenient.

He passed lines of desks, and as he passed, the pinks stopped what they were doing to crane their necks and watch the huge moreau walk by. There were a few whispered words between them, and Nohar could pick up an occasional word here or there.

"—there's the Fed case—"

"—shoot-out with the Beverly Hills cops—"

"—why a morey would do Royd like that, he was almost one of them—"

"—probably another psycho. Killing's in their genes you know—"

His escort dropped him in a windowless interview room—a featureless place with walls of acoustical tile. There were a few uncomfortable chairs, a metal table, and a mirror running the length of one wall. Nohar looked at the mirror and sat down facing it. There was little else he could do, and it felt good to finally get off his feet.

They kept him waiting for another hour. Long enough that, despite everything, Nohar began to doze off. He suspected they'd been watching him all during the wait, because the door slammed open just when he was nodding off.

Nohar glanced up at the door, didn't see anyone, and had to lower his gaze until he saw a short man. He was balding on top, and wore a small beard and mustache, as if the hair were slowly sliding down his head. He placed a portable comm on the table between them and looked at Nohar. Even standing, his eye level didn't reach above Nohar's chest.

"I'm Detective Gilbertez." His tone was disarming. "Are you comfortable? Can I get you anything?"

Nohar's first impulse was to say, "A lawyer," but he held back because he wanted to hear what this guy was going to say. He just shook his head and looked at Gilbertez and tried to read what was going on behind his impassive face.

"Fair enough," Gilbertez looked at his comm and flipped open the screen. "Nohar Rajasthan." He glanced up from the screen. "Don't feel as if you have to respond to me. Just listen." He looked back down at the comm, still talking. "Never changed your name. Old-fashioned, or did you just not care?"

Nohar followed Gilbertez's suggestion, and stayed quiet.

"Most of the moreaus we see through here are half your age—most shed the surname. Like the place-origin names the INS handed out, way back when, were some sort of slave name." He shook his head. Nohar wondered if he ever paused for a breath. "Says here that you were once licensed as a private investigator, but you let that lapse about ten years ago. What've you been doing since then?"

"Retired." The word felt heavy with irony after what he had gone through the past few days. He flexed his hands, they ached, especially at the base of his claws. It felt as if his fingers were still tearing at the concrete outside the Bensheim building.

Gilbertez appeared to ignore the irony in Nohar's voice. "Yeah, we have records from the State and the Fed. You've been on one of the homestead projects. Getting the non-humans, especially the large predatory ones, out of an urban environment." Gilbertez looked up. "You know, for all the objections people made to that homestead project, from the hunting lobby to the Native Americans, I think it worked."

Nohar shook his head. This guy could change subjects on a dime.

"After they started that project the crime rate in their target neighborhood went down. They say it's just because the Fed moved the crime out, but the homestead areas haven't had any crime problems, nothing like the inner city. So what happened to your cabin?"

Gilbertez only paused long enough to look at Nohar's expression. Nohar didn't know why he should be surprised. Of course, if they hadn't known already, the first place the cops would have gone after seeing him at Royd's would've been his last known residence.

"Never mind, we'll get back to that. I take it you did a bit of hunting?"

"Have to eat," Nohar said. The shifts in this guy's conversation were giving him a headache. Gilbertez was wired, always moving, gesturing, talking. He had yet to sit down.

"Don't we all. And being that they gave you land without any income—Anyway, they found the buck you got last, all dressed up. Too bad the fire torched the carcass. Shame of a waste. Only had venison a few times in my life, but seeing those pictures made me want to cry. Which I guess brings us to Charles Royd."

Nohar didn't see the connection, but he let Gilbertez roll on under his own momentum.

Gilbertez started pacing in front of his comm. "Royd was another waste. Did a lot of good for this town for some asshole to torture him to death. He didn't go easy, you know—though I suppose you do, seeing the body and all. The Mayor, the DA, and the entire nonhuman population of this city want his murderer's head on a plate. Now I'm a nice guy, but I would really like to oblige them."

Gilbertez turned and leaned on the desk. With almost any other two people, the gesture would have him looming over his audience. As it was, he had to look up into Nohar's face. "Now I wonder if you feel the same way? We have the records from Royd's office, and you were up there, looking for him the same day. Weren't you?"

Nohar remained quiet.

"Then, after all that bullshit at Royd's residence, you turn up calling in bomb threats to the Bensheim Foundation. You've been very popular lately, and I suppose I should consider myself lucky that I've been the local boy assigned to this case." Gilbertez pushed away from the table. "You should consider yourself lucky you got me, too. I'm going for some coffee, want any?"

Nohar shook his head and watched Gilbertez pick up his comm and leave the room. *Just what that man needs, more coffee.*

Nohar sat and waited for the detective to return.

During the wait, it began to sink in that Gilbertez hadn't accused him of anything yet. Nohar couldn't help but think it was probably some sort of trap, but he began to wonder if he had gotten hold of a cop who might listen to his story.

Gilbertez returned with a cup of stale-smelling coffee. He set down his comm, leaving it closed on the desk. He gestured with his coffee and said, "You've had a little time to think. Do you want to contradict anything I've gone over?"

"I don't think I should say anything."

"Has anyone read you your rights?"

Nohar shook his head.

"Well, I'm not going to. Everything we say here's going to be inadmissible. Now—you have any problem with what I've said so far?"

Nohar shook his head slowly, unsure of where this all was going.

"Let me tell you about my day. Middle of the afternoon—I haven't taken my lunch break yet—I find out we got hold of this tiger that everybody and their brother in Fedland is looking for. Case falls in my lap, and shortly after, so do a bunch of Fed agents talking about nonhuman terrorism. Now I could hand you over and have lunch, but I don't like overbearing Fed agents, so I send them to the local judge, who'll spend at least forty-eight hours to decide if any of the antiterrorism acts cover the crap you're accused of. Then I bone up on all the records we have of you, and what you seem to be involved in." Gilbertez drained the coffee.

"What Fed agency?"

"FBI. Though every black Agency claims to be the FBI when they interfere with a criminal investigation. If they were FBI, they were FBI through some special forces branch. One guy had a unit tattoo on his wrist and the other had a big scar on his face—"

Him again, "Black guy?"

"—Yeah, know him?"

Nohar shook his head.

"Suit yourself. What I got is a two-hour rundown on you, and I have a lot of questions—"

"Like?"

Gilbertez looked over at the mirror and said, "Like why someone torches their own house after going to the trouble of hunting down and dressing a buck deer. The story we have from the antiterrorist people at the FBI has you blowing the place to hide evidence of bomb-making equipment, or it blew up when one of the devices malfunctioned. Now they have the site, can't get local boys there, but they did loan us some holos of the scene, which was enough to get my curiosity going. I mean there's the carcass right in the middle of the ruins, and then there's all the bullet holes."

"Bullet holes?"

"Or some frigging huge termites in the trees around your house. I got one pic I blew up that has a pretty good view of a forty-five-cal hole in a cinder block that used to hold up your cabin." Gilbertez finished off his coffee. "Then we got this story that you're supposed to have killed Royd as some terrorist act. Set aside for the moment that I've never bought these Outsider people as moreaus—their targets, except for Alcatraz, have been humans who were working with nonhumans. Bankers who do business in Moreytown, folks who set up shop to market to moreaus, factories that have liberal hiring policies. The whole Outsider manifesto about species separation never carried much weight with me—"

"Who are they, then?"

"I suspect they're some radical humanist organization bent on creating hostility at any point where humans and nonhumans seem to work together. They claim to be moreaus just to make it worse for the nonhumans, calling down all these antiterrorism acts on them. Anyway, that's all beside the point. You're supposed to be involved in Royd's death, and then, three days after the guy's killed, you visit his office looking for him, then return to the house with the body. Just as you're in there, somebody calls the Beverly Hills cops to report an Outsider hit squad in Royd's house."

Gilbertez put down his cup and leaned toward Nohar. "So what's going on here?"

Chapter 22

In the end Nohar decided that he had little choice but to trust Gilbertez enough to tell him. It was galling telling this all to a pink, and a pink *cop* at that. But, at the moment, Gilbertez was the only angle he had for getting on top of this situation. Nohar gave the cop a sanitized version of what had happened—he left out the names, and avoided telling him where Manuel and the others were supposed to be hiding out.

Gilbertez let him talk, even though silence seemed out of character for him. He flipped open his comm and typed notes as Nohar spoke. Nohar had spent an hour telling Gilbertez everything he felt he could.

Afterward, Gilbertez stared at the comm and nodded to himself. "Well, what do you know now? Your story had an advantage over the Feds'—over most of the stories I hear in here—it fits the facts. That's good. Though you do sound like every other conspiracy-mongering nonhuman I've ever heard. Really too bad that you didn't get a chance to copy that database you sneaked into." Gilbertez gave him a knowing look, as if he *knew* that was one of the few points where Nohar had lied. "I'd like to see this ramcard you say started all this bullshit."

Nohar shook his head.

"If you don't tell me where these people are hiding out, it sort of limits my options here. I mean I got a suspect the Fed wants, and a wild shaggy-dog story about one of the most respected charity organizations dealing with non-humans. I got to have more than just that if I'm going to do anything with this. Now I don't want to hand you over to these Fed guys, especially if they aren't FBI, but I gotta have something a little solid."

"I can't tell you where—"

"I know, I know. I *am* trying to work with you. Something

sour's going on here—not that I necessarily believe your doomsday scenario—and I'd like to know what these Fed guys are up to. I need something more than your story, though."

"What?"

"Maybe we could arrange a call with this hacker friend of yours. The one who looked up that satellite for you."

Nohar looked at him.

Gilbertez turned the comm around to face Nohar.

"Where the fuck are you?" Bobby said as his image came into focus on the screen. He was sitting in a darkened room, and what was left of his hair was mussed and pointing out at odd angles.

From behind the comm Gilbertez shook his head. Nohar guessed that Gilbertez's comm wasn't quite explicit when it came to identifying itself. "I need that information."

"Christ, you know what time it is over here?" Bobby reached off-screen for his glasses and a handheld computer. Bobby flipped open the small device, and Nohar could see a soft-green display reflected in his glasses. "Again, you got me wondering what you're mixed up in."

"You—"

"—don't want to know, right." He glanced up from the little computer and at the comm he was talking into. "You know that comm you're on isn't secure?"

Nohar looked at Gilbertez. "Didn't have much of a choice. Go on, what've you got?"

Bobby looked down at the handheld computer again. "We have a burst of net activity surrounding The Necron Avenger about six days ago. This wasn't some kid with his first computer either. Someone with access to a super-computer was looking for him. There're traces of this search everywhere on the net, and it all happened within the same five-minute period."

"Who was it?"

"We traced it as far back as a Fed node on the net, a naval gateway we can't get past. Whoever did the search did it through the Long Beach Naval Station."

"You mean the navy—"

Bobby shook his head. "All this means is that was the point they accessed the civilian part of the net. The search could have started anywhere in the Fed's net. Hell, it could have even originated outside the Fed net—they could have entered through some other gateway entirely, and have it routed through Long Beach. The fact is just that we can't backtrack it past there."

"What about the Bensheim Foundation?"

"That takes a little more explaining—"

As Gilbertez looked on, Bobby gave Nohar a rundown on the Bensheim Foundation. All the time Dr. Bensheim was alive it had been run by an independent board based in Geneva. After the founder's death, there was an internal struggle between the various arms of the organization and the board, ending with a multiple schism of the original Foundation. It split along international lines, so the Geneva Board still ran the Bensheim Foundation in Europe, but there were different Bensheim Foundations in the Far East, Africa, and in North America.

The Bensheim Foundation in North America struggled along by itself, near bankruptcy, for a couple of years until a corporate white knight came along to bail it out.

The white knight was named The Pacific Import Company.

"Why is that name familiar?" Nohar asked.

"Probably because of the congressional hearings back in '62 over alleged government control of a company called VanDyne Enterprises. All of it had to do with aliens, corporate shell games, captured extraterrestrial technology, and the habitat on Alcatraz."

"What does Pacific Import have to do with that?"

"VanDyne was a Race front. The Fed took it over through Pacific Imports. Pacific Imports is an open secret, most likely run by the CIA."

"The CIA runs the Bensheim Foundation?"

"Didn't say that. Pacific Imports could have funneled money from just about any covert arm of the Fed. And there was no other record of any involvement with the Bensheim Foundation. As far as I could discover, the Bensheim Foundation is still an independent entity. Their headquarters happen to be in LA, Pasadena."

Nohar's talk with Bobby helped convince Gilbertez that there was something to Nohar's story. Even so, Nohar didn't feel good about it. The last thing he wanted was a confirmation that it was the Fed that was engineering what he had seen in the Bensheim database.

Gilbertez took him back to a holding cell. As they walked through the station, emptier now that it was on the night shift, Gilbertez talked nonstop. "You might have something here. I don't know, but I got to check some things out myself. But if this does pan out, you have to take me to these people who're sitting on this evidence you keep talking about. In the meantime you should think about whether or not I'm your friend. From your story you have reason to be paranoid, but I think that just means you really want me on your case rather than these Feds who're waiting for me to turn you over."

Gilbertez opened the cell for him and removed Nohar's cuffs. Nohar rubbed his wrists as Gilbertez said, "Think about it."

The door shut, leaving Nohar in the same cell with only a concrete bench. As Gilbertez asked, Nohar thought about it. He couldn't decide if he was for real, or just a clever Fed plant trying to get the only real information Nohar had, the location of Manuel and the others. The location of the ramcards.

Even if he was legit, Nohar had no illusions about any local agency standing up to the Fed on any level. Gilbertez might get everything, but that didn't mean he'd be able to do anything. Publicity was still their only hope. When the Fed no longer had a secret to protect, they might be safe.

He had to think of something.

Nohar lay down on the concrete floor of the holding cell. It was the only place he could rest, and even there he couldn't recline fully. He needed to get the ramcards—the ones he sent to Culver City—into the hands of a reporter. As far as he knew, even if Gilbertez was a Fed agent, no one knew that the database ramcard existed.

All he needed was to contact a reporter on the outside, get one to pick up the ramcards. The database spoke for itself, loudly enough that the pink news would pick it up. The fact that the CIA—or whoever—was using biological warfare agents domestically, for whatever reason, would set off the alarms. It would remind people too much of what had happened in Africa.

Nohar closed his eyes and tried to sleep. He dreamed of his mother again. This time she wasn't dying from Pakistani-engineered feline leukemia — this time the Fed had injected her with Ebola Niger.

Gilbertez didn't return until early the next morning. Nohar only knew the time from the sense of activity beyond the holding cell door. Gilbertez was accompanied by a uniformed cop, and he looked as if he hadn't had any sleep. He tossed a pair of cuffs on the floor next to Nohar.

"Put those on. You got to take me to these people hiding out before all hell breaks loose around here."

Nohar looked up at Gilbertez and tried to get some clue as to what he was feeling. It wasn't hard to pick up the scent of fear. Something had really disturbed him. The uniformed cop was wary, but Gilbertez was really scared.

"What's going on?"

"Somehow they got a judge. Someone's walking downstairs with transfer orders for you. We have to be on our way before those Fed agents show up, or I'll *have* to hand you over." Gilbertez glanced at the watch on his wrist for emphasis. "We don't have much time. If we don't get a case put together fast, you're going to disappear into the Federal machinery. You don't want that to happen while you're still an accused terrorist."

Nohar stood up, holding the handcuffs. The uniform took a few steps back. "Are these necessary?"

"You're still a suspect. Play along, and we can get out of here smoothly."

Nohar put the cuffs on his wrists as loosely as their size would allow. "And him?" Nohar gestured to the uniformed cop with both hands.

"A concession to regulations. Suspects are escorted by at least two police officers. This has to be by the book, or anything that gets turned up'll be tainted. You don't need to worry about Ortega. I know his uncle."

The uniform nodded, but the set of his expression did not inspire much trust in Nohar. He couldn't help feeling as if this whole situation was some sort of setup.

Gilbertez and Ortega hustled him out of the holding cell and took him past the elevators and toward the fire stairs. They certainly gave the impression that they were sneaking out. Nohar kept an eye out for security cameras, and didn't know whether to be reassured or dismayed by the fact that all the cameras they passed were inactive or pointing the wrong way.

They led him up the fire stairs to the rooftop parking area. In the rear, past the banks of black-and-white aircars, was an unmarked Plymouth Pegasus. Its sleek lines were at odds with the forced aerodynamics of the cop cars. The police cars were heavy-duty bubbles, where the Pegasus was a cream-colored arrowhead.

Gilbertez led them straight to the Pegasus.

Hackles rose on Nohar's neck as they approached the car. A car like the Pegasus was out of line for someone on a detective's salary. That meant someone had provided the car. Nohar didn't think the LAPD was in the habit of handing out sports cars as unmarked vehicles. He could see Beverly Hills detectives tooling around in a Pegasus; a Pasadena cop, no.

But Gilbertez pulled out a remote, pressed his thumb into the sensor, and the gull-wing doors swung open to accommodate them.

"Nohar better sit up front, more room there. You get in back, Ortega." Ortega glanced at Nohar, and again his expression was less than reassuring.

Nohar slid into the passenger seat in front of Ortega, and he couldn't help thinking that it gave the cop a perfect shot at the back of his head as he wedged himself in the tiny space in the front of the Pegasus.

The fact was, there wasn't any way they could've fit Nohar in the back anyway.

Gilbertez slid into the driver's seat and fired up the fans, and the Pegasus sluggishly rose. It was obviously overloaded with Nohar in it, and Nohar tried to avoid looking down as Gilbertez slid away from the garage and out over Pasadena.

The way tension was rolling off of Gilbertez, Nohar almost expected a troop of Fed agents to run out on the roof and attempt to shoot them out of the sky.

The Pegasus climbed, and Nohar watched the headsup display, a green vector map of the airspace corridors. A few lines in the display were a warning orange because the Pegasus was hugging the bottom of its legal flying space.

Strangely, Gilbertez was quiet through the whole ascent. It seemed unnatural to Nohar—the man seemed to run on nervous energy.

Nohar looked across at Gilbertez and asked, "So what did you find out?"

"Huh?" Gilbertez slid the Pegasus into the civilian air corridor above Pasadena. The Hollywood sign slid by the passenger window as the aircar turned for an approach on downtown Los Angeles.

"You said you were going to check things out. Did you find out anything more about these people?"

Gilbertez glanced back at Ortega before he answered. "No, nothing more than you told me."

You're lying. Nohar could feel it. He wanted to look back at Ortega himself, but there was no way he could move his head in the small space provided by the Pegasus. *I bet you don't have any clue who Ortega's uncle is.*

"Okay," Gilbertez said. "Where are we going?"

Nohar started talking, uncomfortably aware of Ortega's presence behind him.

Chapter 23

The aircar banked over the Santa Monica Mountains and Nohar could see the surface of the Hollywood Reservoir shimmering green in the dawn light. "Down there?" Nohar heard Ortega say, the first words he had spoken in Nohar's presence. It wasn't a voice that inspired trust.

"Yes," Nohar lied.

Gilbertez was nervous. Nohar could feel it, but the mood didn't make it into his voice. "This was where you ditched Royd's car. The police and the Fed have combed this place with a fine-toothed comb."

"That's why I picked it. Why look somewhere you've already searched thoroughly?"

No one expressed any further doubts. Nohar knew that his story stretched belief, but he hoped that it was plausible enough to get them clear on the ground.

"Land near the harvesting pylons," Nohar said. He peered through the window, trying to make out details on the ground. There was a fuzzy patch in a clearing and he pointed toward it. "There."

Gilbertez obligingly aimed the Pegasus for a landing in that clearing. He looked across at him and said, "Are you sure?"

Nohar nodded, wondering exactly what was going to happen when they landed and found nobody there.

The Pegasus put down in a clearing about twenty meters from the tree line. Opposite the trees was the edge of the reservoir, alive with shimmering engineered algae and the rotating booms. Near the edge of the water sat a squat little cinder-block building. It was windowless, and only had a single steel door.

Gilbertez got out first, then Nohar. He stood looking over at the building, shaking his head. "They're in there?"

It did look bigger when we were in the air. Nohar nodded. "Let me show you."

Nohar took a few steps toward the structure.

Ortega's voice came from behind them. "Why don't you stop right there?"

Nohar turned around, slowly. Gilbertez was already facing Ortega. He didn't seem very surprised by seeing his uniformed cop holding a gun on them.

Ortega held his automatic, covering both of them. Nohar noticed that he'd waited until he'd walked far enough away from the car. There was now no way that he could clear the distance between them before Ortega fired.

"I don't think there's anything in there," Ortega said.

"Why don't we just look—"

"We will." Ortega pulled a card-sized radio from his pocket, flipped it open. "As soon as my backup arrives." Not too surprisingly, the radio Ortega started talking into wasn't police issue.

Nohar glanced across at Gilbertez and said, "He's not talking about LAPD."

Gilbertez shook his head.

"This was all a setup," Nohar said.

"Only so much I could do with a gun to my head."

Nohar looked back at Ortega, watching him, waiting for

his attention to shift. "You found out more than you told me." *Come on, start talking, Gilbertez. It's what you're good at.*

"I made the mistake of checking up on the credentials of the two Feds who showed up for you. Didn't have fingerprints, but I had their pictures from when I scanned their ID. Now the ID turns out to be legit, there are two FBI agents with those names and ID numbers—" Gilbertez turned to look at Nohar, "—but the FBI says that they're on assignment in Orlando, Florida."

"So they're not FBI agents?"

Gilbertez looked back at Ortega, who was putting away his radio. "It gets better. I ran their pictures through a half-dozen criminal databases, including Interpol. The one with the scar is a native of South Africa, named Tabara Krisoijn. He's a mercenary wanted by a half-dozen countries from the UAS north."

"They'll be here in a few minutes. Just keep talking." Ortega had a nasty grin.

"What's he wanted for?" Nohar asked, hoping for something in the conversation to agitate or distract Ortega. From the look of Ortega standing there and holding the gun, Nohar doubted that he was going to let that happen. He was too damn confident having the upper hand like this.

"It amounts to terrorism under the guise of antiterrorism. He's worked for a number of governments within the UAS, the Islamic Axis, and even Europe, but the folks he's hired to hunt down are usually outside the nation's borders—civilians, too."

Nohar nodded. Ortega was unmoved. That probably meant that he didn't care what information he had. And *that* meant that he was probably not meant to survive whatever was going to happen.

Nohar kept thinking of how he found Royd....

Gilbertez was still talking. "The other guy is in the terrorist database for involvement in extreme humanist activities. He's ex-Navy, ex-Special Forces. Name's Frank Trinity."

Nohar's attention was caught by a familiar scent. The algae covered every scent in the area like a shroud, but he could still make out a vaguely canine subtext to the air. He listened carefully, tuning out Gilbertez, who was going on about Trinity's history in the military.

Beyond Gilbertez's voice, and beyond the constant whir of the pylons behind him, Nohar could hear rustling in the woods. Four or five large animals pushing their way through the brush.

". . . this guy." Gilbertez gestured at Ortega. "I don't know who he is, other than he works for the same people. The only thing I found out about the antiterrorism unit at Long Beach was that it was supposed to be decommissioned by Congress a few years ago."

Ortega spat, for the first time reacting to what Gilbertez was saying. "Those shitheads on the Hill didn't know what they were doing."

Nohar jumped on Ortega's reaction. "You're part of that unit?"

Ortega gave Nohar a stony expression. "I don't talk to fucking animals."

"You are part of it, aren't you?" Gilbertez asked, seeming to clue in on what Nohar was doing.

Keep him distracted.

"You make me sick, you know that? Sticking your neck out for a furball like this pile of garbage." Ortega shifted the gun a little toward Gilbertez.

"There's a murder here, and this furball didn't do it."

Ortega shook his head. "Fuck Royd. He was no better than these engineered *things.* Killing him didn't mean any more than killing one of them."

"Is the Fed behind this?" Gilbertez asked. Nohar didn't know if Gilbertez could see the mixed Rottweiler slip out of the woods behind Ortega. It was Blackie, from Elijah's pack.

Ortega chuckled. "This government doesn't have the *balls.*" There were three or four dogs behind him now, approaching with a deliberateness that was out of sync with their appearance. "They set up an operation to take care of a threat, and they didn't have the will to see it through."

"What threat?" Gilbertez had to see the dogs now. Nohar was impressed with his ability to stay focused on Ortega.

"If you can't see the threat, you're part of it. Nothing worse than a traitor to your own species." Ortega raised the automatic and leveled it at Gilbertez. "You know, we don't even need you anymore."

It was the distraction that Nohar had been waiting for. He dove for Ortega. Gilbertez ducked. And Blackie came out of nowhere to seize Ortega's wrist. He fired a wild shot, then Nohar had his arms over the bogus cop's head, and the handcuff chain around his neck.

Blackie shook Ortega's wrist until the gun fell. Gilbertez took a step to recover the gun, but Blackie placed a possessive paw on the weapon and growled at him.

Ortega stopped struggling, and Nohar dropped his limp body to the ground. He checked his neck for a pulse.

"Is he still alive?" Gilbertez asked.

"Yes." Nohar was unnerved to realize that there was slight disappointment in his answer. He fished around for a few minutes until he found some handcuff keys on Ortega.

Gilbertez kept turning, looking at the pack of dogs that surrounded them.

Nohar fumbled with the handcuffs until he got them open. He flipped Ortega over and handcuffed his hands behind him. Nohar had to close them all the way to get them to fit.

"What are they doing?"

"Watching us." Nohar carefully reached for the gun, and this time Blackie backed away from him. "Be careful. They have no love of humans."

"What are they doing *here?*"

"we return the help that no-har gives us." Elijah's electronic monotone came from the rear of the pack. The others parted to let Elijah's brown form through. He focused his good eye on Gilbertez. "more men come. we watch men approach, land. see no-har threatened."

Nohar nodded as he began manhandling Ortega back to the Pegasus. Gilbertez looked toward Nohar. "What are you doing?"

"We both have to get out of here before Ortega's backup arrives. We only have a few minutes." They had less than that. Nohar was beginning to hear the resonant hum of approaching aircraft.

"They have a tracking device on the Pegasus," Gilbertez objected.

"You aren't taking the Pegasus." Nohar's mind was leaping ahead, coming up with some sort of workable plan. He turned to Elijah. "Can you get this man down to the city?

He's going to help me expose the men who gave you the sickness."

"this man." Elijah's monotone spoke. The whole pack started in on a chorus of staccato barking.

Gilbertez backed away from the sudden canine debate. "What are you talking about?"

Nohar wedged Ortega in the passenger seat. "Ortega's people infected them with an engineered form of hepatitis."

"I'm going to help you—how?"

"I'll fly decoy in this thing. You get back to Hollywood and get a cab to Culver City."

"Culver City?"

Nohar wedged himself into the driver's seat in the Pegasus. Now that his hands were free, he could ram the seat back as far as it would go. If he'd had the time, he would have liked to rip out the seat and sit in the back seat, that would give him just about enough leg room.

"A Doctor Brian Reynolds is getting a package from the Bensheim Foundation. Inside it are two ramcards, information detailing everything they're responsible for."

"But I need a warrant—"

"Don't *arrest* anyone. Get it to the media. The ramcards, and the story I told you. If this is a rogue operation, that will be enough to shut these people down."

Nohar fired up the fans on the Pegasus, and the grass ripped around the pack's feet as the engine powered up.

"we will escort this man." Elijah's electronic voice was barely audible over the sound of the Pegasus' fans. He turned his good eye to Nohar.

Gilbertez looked from the brown dog to the closing doors of the Pegasus, as if events were moving too fast for him. "What about—" the closing door cut off the rest of Gilbertez's question.

Nohar shook his head as much as the cramped space would allow. "No time."

The Pegasus lifted off from the clearing and Nohar kept an eye on the rear video as the pack led Gilbertez back into the woods. That was it, then. He had made his decision. He was the decoy. His job was to distract these people long enough for Gilbertez to get the information to the media.

He couldn't help regretting the fact that this meant that

he was probably never going to see his son again. But his son was probably better off without him. . . .

He eased the Pegasus into the civilian air corridor, the vector display on the headsup flashing yellow, orange, and red at him. He had only flown an aircar twice in his life—and once was into the reservoir beneath him—and he wasn't terribly good at it, especially in a sports car that was overburdened with his weight. His presence shifted the aircar's whole center of gravity, and the nose kept dipping on him.

He cleared the trees, and the proximity radar began beeping all sorts of warnings at him. He looked for the radar display, but before he found it on the dash, a huge shadow shot over the top of the Pegasus. A matte-black helicopter flew across the Pegasus' path, barely ten meters above him. He had to pull the aircar all the way to the right and down to avoid a collision.

At that point, Nohar ignored air corridors, gaining altitude, or even leveling out the Pegasus. All that mattered was speed, and being pointed away from the helicopter.

He shot north, the belly of the aircar almost brushing the tree line, and flew right under another black helicopter, just like the one that had been at the assault on Pastoria Towers. *Might even be the same one.*

The two helicopters flanked him, easily matching the Pegasus' top speed.

The mountains dropped away and Nohar could see Burbank ahead of him. He had the feeling that he would never make it there. A pair of red dots appeared on the windshield and made vibrating independent journeys across the headsup display, across the hood of the car, ending at each of the forward fans.

The Pegasus shook as two shots, fifty-cal or better, pounded into the forward fans of the Pegasus. The air in front of Nohar was alive now with flying chunks of fiberglass. Part of the fan housing smashed into the windshield, fragmenting the headsup into a million emerald-and-ruby pieces. The front of the car dropped while the rear stayed under power.

The Pegasus did a somersault.

Nohar tried to control the crash, cutting power to the

rear fans. Trees tore at the car, the left side of the Pegasus smashing against the side of a tree and bouncing off. Branches crashed through the windows as the aircar tore through the cover. Nohar had barely shallowed out the angle of descent as the aircar plowed into the ground, throwing up showers of topsoil and setting off the airbags. Nohar felt the car roll once before he lost consciousness.

Chapter 24

The first sensation that Nohar was aware of was agonizing pain in his left arm. His awareness filled out, cataloging each pain as it came to him. His neck, the base of his tail, every joint in his legs, even the muscles in his jaw ached.

Water splashed across his face. He sneezed and opened his eyes. He expected to see the wreckage of the Pegasus around him. The last thing he remembered was the airbag deploying.

He didn't see the Pegasus when he opened his eyes. His upper body was taped to a heavy chair. He couldn't see much, because a bright light was focused on his eyes. What he could see of the room was a concrete floor, and he could smell the must and damp, as though they were in a basement. There were two people here. He could smell their confidence. The fear and tension he smelled was his own.

"Time to finish." The voice had a faint accent. It took a while before Nohar recognized it as Afrikaans. The speaker moved near Nohar, close enough for Nohar to make out his face past the light. He was a light-skinned black man, with a large scar on his right cheek.

"Krisoijn," Nohar whispered. It even hurt to talk.

The man reached out and grabbed his face, clenching Nohar's jaw shut. Nohar was too weak to resist, and his neck hurt too much for him to turn away. Krisoijn's muscles stood out like steel cables on his arm.

"You'll only speak now to answer my questions." Krisoijn leaned in. "You fancy yourself a hunter—but man is still the most dangerous predator on this planet. Your ancestors only survived because man permitted them to live. Your kind exists now only because man permits them to live. You only live now because I permit you to live. Do we understand each other?" He withdrew his hand.

Nohar wanted to rage at the man, but he knew that there was little point in antagonizing him. He consoled himself with the thought that Gilbertez was talking to some reporters even as Krisoijn was talking to him.

It didn't last.

"I mean it when I say it's over." Krisoijn waved over the other man in the room. Nohar recognized the scent before he saw the man.

"Too bad about Ortega, but we all have to make sacrifices when the species is at stake." With every word Gilbertez spoke, Nohar felt his gut sink. Gilbertez held up a ramcard that shimmered like a rainbow in the spotlight. "You saved us a lot of trouble tracking this down. The session was logged, so we knew you copied the databases. They'd been tearing the Pasadena building apart looking for where you stashed it." Gilbertez placed the card on a cart on top of its twin.

They both lay next to a makeshift electronic device covered with silver-gray duct tape. It took Nohar a moment to realize that it was Elijah's voicebox. Gilbertez noticed Nohar looking. "Too bad we had to deal with them like that, but you had to let slip about Tangier, didn't you? That's one of the keys to the whole project, you know, engineer a virus that twigs on just the few proteins that are common to all moreaus, on the genes you inherited from the first few dogs. Had to start with them. If that tidbit got out, it could unravel everything. The rumors about the Drips are bad enough."

Krisoijn reached out and pulled Nohar's head to face him. "I am leaving you in Gilbertez's capable hands. I know you're thinking that you're strong enough to stay quiet—or maybe you're hoping that you'll die before you tell us anything more. It's a vain hope."

Krisoijn let go of Nohar's head and walked out of the room. Nohar heard a door shutting him in with Gilbertez. Nohar turned to face Gilbertez and said, "You?"

"Surprised? I find that gratifying." Gilbertez walked over to another cart and rolled it near Nohar's chair. Nohar saw the spotlight glint off the metal of surgical knives and a set of needles. "It's nice that we're not going to be pressed for time here, like we were with Royd. You've been a pain in the ass, and I'm going to enjoy this."

Gilbertez looked at the cart and looked at Nohar. Somehow his tense movements, and constant chattering were taking on a whole new sinister cast.

"It was all a setup." Nohar's voice came out in a groan.

"That's what you first suspected, wasn't it? I had to bring all my talents to bear to get you over that first impression. That was work. Trying to sympathize with a moreau, that was effort. My first hope was to talk out of you what we wanted. You were a little too cagey, so we absconded with you. When you led us to a dead end, Ortega pulled his trump. Between us we were supposed to overpower him, and do it a bit too late. The dogs were a bit of a wildcard that almost screwed everything up."

"You wanted me to tell you where Manuel is," Nohar said. "I'm not going to."

"Yes, that was the idea. But that's sort of moot now." Gilbertez picked up an air hypo and checked the charge in it. "You see, we managed to piece it together, once we knew that we didn't have the real Necron Avenger. You told us our quarry was still at large, and with Manuel and the data. We just had to press on Oswald Samson a little to get him to talk about his adopted son—"

Nohar stared at Gilbertez.

"Oh, you think less of Oswald now," he smiled.

"Don't. No one can hold up under a professional interrogation." Gilbertez turned to face Nohar, his expression telling him that he was enjoying the process of revelation. "We got enough from him before he died to get a picture of The Necron Avenger. From there it was just a short step to double-check the Government net and find old INS sites that've seen recent net activity. Krisoijn's on his way to clean that up now."

No . . .

He had screwed up. Failed in the worst possible way.

Gilbertez pushed up Nohar's right sleeve and pressed the hypo into the exposed part of his uninjured arm. Nohar started to struggle. It seemed useless. The chair was steel and anchored to the concrete floor. He was held down to the chair by straps across his chest and upper arms. His forearms were strapped to the arms of the chair. Even his thighs were held down by a belt strapping him down to the seat. Only his lower legs had any freedom of movement.

Pain flared in his left arm and Nohar stopped struggling.

Gilbertez smiled. "I've just injected you with a synthetic drug. It doesn't even have a street name yet. It's a cousin to flush, it has hallucinogenic and stimulant qualities. The important thing for you is to realize that its main effect is to sharpen perceptions."

Nohar felt as if the world were suddenly trying to tear open his brain. Gilbertez's voice was painfully loud. The spotlight seared his eyes, even through closed lids. Worst was the pain in his arm, magnified a hundredfold.

"Most important for you," Gilbertez's booming voice said, "is the perception of pain."

Nohar clenched his jaw and whispered, *"Why?"*

"'Why' what, my friend? Why the project? Or why are you strapped to that chair?" Nohar didn't answer. His jaw was clenched tight enough for his own fangs to bite into his gums. That pain, even amplified, was nothing compared to the feeling as Gilbertez unstrapped his wounded arm. "The project," Gilbertez continued, "is the ultimate solution to a problem the government saw during the last riots here. The riots, and the nonhuman population, were becoming a threat to national security. This antiterrorist unit here—it never even had a proper name—was formed to meet that threat, and it recruited men who saw the threat. The operation grew to a point that, when our government arbitrarily decided to ignore the threat, we didn't abandon the fight. The threat is still here, in this country, and there is only one way to eliminate it."

Gilbertez bent his arm upward and Nohar roared. The sound tore at him as if it were ripping the skin out of his throat. "I'm afraid it's broken. That'll do for a start." Gilbertez held Nohar's arm, and Nohar could feel the adrenaline surge of combat. He could feel the chemical rush as it flowed through his system. His nerves screamed.

"As to why you're strapped here—You were very cagey with your information. Even though we have that ramcard you copied, the ramcard stolen from Compton, and the location of Manuel Limón, we can't be sure what else you might be hiding. So I'm going to go over it with you a few times." Gilbertez turned Nohar's wrist, and the broken bones in the forearm grated against each other.

Nohar roared again. The conscious part of his mind wanted to start talking, give Gilbertez what he wanted to gain some respite from the pain. But the adrenaline was in control now. The thinking part of his brain was already pushed aside by the Beast created by the gene-techs.

His good arm balled his hand into a fist, and the tension in his own muscles felt as if it could break the bones in that arm. He opened his eyes, and the world stood out in a relief so sharp that the edges of every object were painful to see. He could smell Gilbertez, smell the fleeting traces of Krisoijn and the three other men who must have strapped him here. He could hear Gilbertez's heartbeat, and the breathing of the guard outside the door. He could feel the grain on the leather strap on his wrist, and he could feel the slight change in tension as the bolts holding the arm in place began giving way.

Gilbertez was still talking, but the part of Nohar's brain that listened was shut off, drowned in the tide of chemicals. The Beast had always been there, but Gilbertez's injection actually seemed to strengthen it. . . .

Gilbertez moved Nohar's arm again. Pain shot through Nohar. He arched his back and roared again. His arm strained against the chair and the room echoed with shearing metal. Nohar's right arm came free with a ten-kilo piece of the chair strapped to his wrist. The belt holding down his chest and forearms was anchored to that part of the chair, and it fell away as he raised his arm.

Gilbertez turned, letting go of his other arm. He was backing away, but the world had slowed for Nohar. Gilbertez barely took a step before Nohar's arm connected.

Nohar's fist, with ten kilos of extra weight attached to it, slammed into the side of Gilbertez's head. Gilbertez's head snapped back, and he flew out of the spotlight. Nohar could hear him thud limply against one of the concrete walls.

He was still strapped to the chair, but now half the chair was dangling off his right arm. His left arm didn't want to move, but he brought the buckle on his right wrist in reach of his hand so he could peel it off.

He'd just gotten it when he heard the door begin to

open. He grabbed the arm of the chair with his newly freed right hand. When the guard stepped into the room, Nohar threw the jagged wreckage of the chair at about where the man's head should be. Nohar still couldn't see past the spotlight, but he heard the sound of a sickeningly soft impact, and of a body striking the floor.

He tore away the remaining restraints on his legs and sprang out of the chair, clutching his broken arm to his chest. Once he stood, he punched the spotlight, Glass fell into the suddenly darkened room and Nohar could smell burned fur and blood. He paid little mind; adrenaline and Gilbertez's drug still raced through his blood, coating everything with a razored immediacy.

The room shot into monochrome focus when the light died. Gilbertez was crumpled on the ground, his neck bent at better than a forty-five-degree angle. He didn't breathe. Nohar marked him as dead the moment he saw him.

The guard lay in the doorway, still alive, making choking noises as he clutched his throat. Arterial blood was collecting in a pool under him.

Nohar stepped up to the cart where Elijah's voicebox sat. Next to it were the ramcards, gray in the darkness. Nohar grabbed them and slipped them into a pocket.

On the way out, he bent and took the choking guard's sidearm.

Chapter 25

The door led out into a hallway with the same cinder-block walls, and the same concrete floor. Naked fluorescent tubes lit the hall with a vibrating white glare. Overhead pipes hugged the ceiling, low enough that Nohar had to duck as he ran down the corridor. He passed security cameras, and he could hear an alarm going off somewhere.

He made it to one end of the corridor and had to stuff the guard's automatic in his pocket so that he could open the door to the stairway. He still clutched his broken arm to his chest.

As soon as the door opened, he could catch the scent of

at least three humans coming down. Their steps echoed in the stairwell. Nohar slipped inside before the door was open fully and pulled out the gun. The first man turned the corner a flight above him, just as Nohar flicked off the safety.

Nohar saw him, a kid dressed in a Marine uniform. Nohar was running on screaming instinct, and it didn't register that the pink facing him was a kid, or a Marine. What Nohar saw at the top of the stairs was an enemy with a rifle.

The kid's posture stood out in relief, like a neon sign advertising his intent. Nohar didn't hesitate.

Nohar's stolen sidearm was a submachine gun disguised as a pistol. One pull of the trigger sent five shots into the rifle-wielding Marine. Every shot hit, and the kid never had time to react. He hit the wall behind him, splattering blood, then he fell face first down into the stairs, rolling toward Nohar.

Nohar started up the stairs before the Marine had fallen halfway. He had to jump over the body, and he managed it without thinking of anything but the two enemies that were still up there.

Nohar was moving faster than he had a right to go, and his nervous system was screaming at twice the speed his body was moving. The world seemed suspended in gelatin around him. As he dove around the corner of the landing, he ducked low, almost to the ground. The two other Marines had heard the gunfire, and had barely enough time to bear their weapons. Their aim was a meter off.

The bullets from their machine rifles tore parts of the cinder block away from the wall above Nohar, showering him in a cloud of dust and concrete shrapnel. He had already had his gun pointed where he wanted the bullets to go. The automatic emptied itself of the remainder of its ammunition as the shots tore up the stairway, through both Marines. The gun was empty before Nohar's dive hit the ground.

Neither Marine got up from the crumpled heap they formed in the stairwell.

He had landed on his broken arm, and he pushed himself upright with an inarticulate roar. The pain was intense enough for his vision to black out and for his stomach to heave. But it didn't stop him moving. The pain seemed to sharpen his perceptions even further. All of the thinking part of his brain was now devoted to tactics, getting him out of here alive.

Nohar tossed the empty automatic down the stairs.

The enemy was converging on this point. He had to get out of here before they blocked off his escape. He ran up the stairs and grabbed one of the machine rifles. It was awkward, and probably dangerous one-handed, but he didn't have time to fiddle with a holster.

Nohar ran up the stairwell. He had to keep moving, keep the enemy reactive. The moment they had the chance to think, to plan, he would be crushed by sheer numbers.

He needed to know where he was, find a point of escape.

He passed two more doors as he ascended. They were marked with numbers that decreased as he went upward. Nohar didn't stop until he reached the next door. It was marked with a zero.

He had to put down the rifle to open the door, and every nerve in his body primed itself for an attack while he was vulnerable. He managed to get through the door without being ambushed.

The door led to a massive, dark chamber broiling with dry heat, and filled with the deafening resonance of dozens of giant fans. Under the high ceiling, ranks of massive metal boxes led away from the door. Above the humming machinery, massive fans fed huge vents in the ceiling.

Air-conditioning for an immense underground complex. The units were probably here to hide the heat signature from a spy satellite, the fans above dispersing the heat to dozens of widely separated points on the surface. It meant that he was a floor or two away from the surface himself.

As the door shut, he could sense the closing noose of troops behind him. He could hear movement above and below, even over the resonance of the air-conditioning units.

Nohar looked up to the massive vents in the ceiling. They were being fed by slow-moving fans about three meters across. The vents had to lead to the surface.

Nohar tossed his rifle on top of one of the huge air-conditioning units. He grabbed as high as he could reach with his good arm and pulled himself up, pushing on the sides of the unit with his feet. He managed to lever himself up on top of it. Beneath him, under a wire mesh screen that dented inward with his weight, a ferociously spinning blower shot near-searing hot air into him. It was like lying on top of an oven. He rolled off and stood. As huge as the unit was, there was still enough clearance between it and the ceiling for him to stand upright under the vent above.

The vent, and the fan feeding it, was protected by a set of metal bars. Nohar reached up and grabbed the center bar, putting all of his weight into pulling it free. It came loose so easily that he almost tumbled from his perch.

The fan in the vent moved slowly, but not slowly enough for him to climb into the vent while it was still moving. The fan was mounted above a metal strut, and beneath that, the motor was exposed. Nohar could see the metal sheath that fed the power cables into the fan. He grabbed it and yanked. After the second try the cables came free with a shower of blue sparks.

The fan slowed to a stop and Nohar pushed the rifle up into a horizontal pipe that fed into the side of the vent above. Then he grabbed the strut bracing the dormant fan and hooked his feet through the grating that he had pulled off the vent.

Pulling himself up was agonizing, especially with the extra weight on his feet. One-handed he managed to chin himself up to the strut. Even then, he had to raise the elbow of his broken arm up on top of the strut to give him the leverage to pull himself the rest of the way up.

Pain clouding his vision, doubled up across the strut under the fan, he managed to reach down for the grate. He managed to keep hold of it with his feet, and he got hold of the center bar so he could pull it shut behind him. He was even able to wedge back into place the way he had found it.

He wished he could start the fan again, but there was no way to do it safely from above, even if he could reattach the wires he had yanked free.

He couldn't stay where he was. He stood, precariously balanced on the strut between two fan blades. The side vent where he had pushed the rifle was too small for him. So he had only one direction to go.

Nohar looked up, but the vent above was shrouded in gloom that even his good night vision couldn't penetrate. The rifle had a shoulder strap, and he slung it on his back.

The strap was too short, and it hung wrong, but he couldn't afford to leave his only weapon.

He turned around until he found a ladder set into the wall of the vent.

Slowly he began the painful ascent.

To his telescoped sense of time it seemed it took hours for him to reach a horizontal vent he could fit through. The ladder was designed for pinks and his feet could barely find purchase on it. He also had to use the elbow of his broken arm to keep his balance every time he reached for a higher rung. Once he twisted the broken arm, blacked out from the pain, and nearly fell.

His ears were numb from the echo of the blowers beneath him, and even with the fan disabled, the heat was burning and almost unbearable. His eyes watered, and his fur itched, and all he could smell was the dry scent of heated sheet metal.

He might have missed the passage if the ladder he was climbing didn't end there. He reached for another rung, and his arm met empty space. He managed to pull himself into a horizontal vent about half the diameter of the vertical one. He crawled forward, his digitigrade legs slipping into a horizontal gait, limping on one foreleg.

Twice, now that he wasn't in immediately physical danger, the adrenaline-fueled Beast left him in a state of collapse in the vent, blacking out from pain and exhaustion. Each time it took a severe effort of will to keep going.

It took an eternity for him to move down that darkened tunnel. Eventually, his progress was stopped. A carbon-black barrier walled off any further advance. The thing was louvered and spongy, and felt as if it was formed on a metal framework. Combination of heat dissipation and security. To keep people like him from wandering around the ventilation system.

Nohar moved back until he was well clear of the barrier. Then he unslung the rifle and made sure it was on full auto. Then he emptied half the clip into the blockage. The sound was deafening in the enclosed space and his nose was seared with the smell of the gunfire. This rifle wasn't caseless, and burning hot cartridges bounced all around him.

In front of him, the black material tore away from a network of copper pipes. The pipes leaked cold water into the vent, and Nohar could suddenly smell salt.

Nohar edged back up to the barrier. It was damaged enough that he could form an opening he could squeeze through. He bent two broken pipes back to the walls of the vent, and he forced the remaining horizontal pipes to bend up enough to allow him to crawl through on his stomach. It was a tight fit, and he had to leave the rifle behind until he made it through. Then he pulled it after him.

Time was precious again. They might have missed his entry into the vent, but between the gunfire and the damage he had just caused, they were sure to know where he was now. He probably had only a matter of minutes to make it outside.

Fortunately, the reason for the heat barrier was that he was within twenty meters of a vent to the outside. He only had to crawl a short way until the vent emptied into a concrete chamber that was topped by a square grate that looked up at the sky. Under the grate there was enough clearance to stand upright. The grate was heavy, iron, and padlocked shut. He didn't know what was out there, but he could see the edges of the landscaping camouflaging the vent outlet.

Nohar didn't want to start shooting, alerting whoever was above, but he had to break the lock.

He raised the butt of the rifle and slammed it into the lock. It took him five tries, and a split in the composite stock of the weapon, before the padlock popped open.

He slung the rifle and started pushing the grate up. It was hinged at the base, and it was heavy. It took all of his strength to push it up with enough force that it arced over into the bushes.

Nohar scrambled up out of the vent and crouched behind the bushes to get his bearings. He could hear alarms, and people running. He looked around and saw low military structures, and a lot of armed Marines running toward the building nearest him.

Opposite the Marines was a concrete landing pad on which sat two of the black helicopters he had seen too much of lately. The twinned rotors on the one nearest him were starting to move. He could see a pilot seated, and the door in the side was hanging open.

The copter had probably been all set to leave when the alarms sounded.

Nohar sprang from his cover and ran for the helicopter. He heard commotion behind him, and a few seconds later he heard the sounds of gunfire. A few bullets tore into the asphalt as he ran, but the shooters were far enough away that the sight was completely disconnected from the sound.

The pilot must have seen him, because the door on the helicopter started closing. It was too late. Nohar managed to dive into the body of the aircraft before the door had closed completely. He landed on his bad arm, and he roared in pain and dropped the rifle.

The pilot stood, scrambling to get out his sidearm. Nohar grabbed the rifle and put a shot into the front windscreen. The broken stock hammered into his shoulder, but he managed to keep hold of the gun. The area where it struck the armored glass starred and rippled in rainbow colors where the bullet was suspended.

"Take off now!"

The pilot sat back down, and Nohar heard the obliging whine of the rotors picking up speed.

Nohar looked around him. The rear of the copter was in disarray, as if its inhabitants had had to leave in a hurry. *Probably bugged out to hunt me down,* Nohar thought.

The copter rose, and the adrenaline high finally began fading from his system. He couldn't ignore the pain in his arm anymore; it was slamming him like a jackhammer.

Now that he was aware of the future beyond the next thirty seconds, he began to think of Krisoijn.

Chapter 26

The helicopter levered itself into the sky.

"Toss the gun back here," Nohar said.

After a few seconds, the pilot's sidearm slid along the

floor next to him. Nohar dropped the rifle and picked up the pilot's automatic, checking to be sure it was loaded and the safety was off. He lay there for several minutes, the pain from his injuries racing through him in shuddering waves. He wanted to collapse. He couldn't allow himself to do that.

With agonizing slowness, one-handed, Nohar pulled himself up off the floor of the helicopter. It took him three tries before he could manage it. He made it to the front of the helicopter, and through the broken windscreen, he could see the skyline of Los Angeles scroll by as the helicopter banked over Long Beach.

"East," Nohar told the pilot. He collapsed into the seat next to the pink. It was too small and he was hunched over, giving him a chance to feel the bones grinding in his forearm every time the helicopter changed attitude.

The pilot looked across at him. "What the fuck do you think you're doing?"

"What matters is what you think I'll do if you don't do what I say." Nohar had to aim the gun across his chest, to point at the pilot's head. "East, where the other helicopter was going."

"I can't do that."

Nohar put another shot, past the pilot's face and into the side window. The bullet was suspended in the armored window, throwing rainbows across the surface of the broken glass. Nohar leaned toward the pilot. "I don't like defeatist attitudes."

Nohar could smell the fear emanating from the pilot. He was another kid, barely twenty. Nohar remembered the kid on the stairs. He couldn't get that image out of his mind.

It was a good thing pinks were rotten at picking up emotional cues, or he'd know that Nohar wasn't going to kill him. Nohar could tell he had the kid on the edge, so he pressed while he had the advantage.

"There's at least one helicopter that had a lead on us. It's fully loaded. You're not. That means you can catch up."

"You don't understand what you're asking—"

"One more word, and I put a bullet through your cheek."

The pilot shut up.

"I can read your radar. Follow him as fast as this crate can go."

The helicopter banked west, and the pilot didn't say another word. Nohar watched for signs that the pilot was holding back on the acceleration. He knew less about helicopters than he did about aircars, but from the looks of the displays in front of the pilot, the speed on this thing was maxed out. Looking out the windows at the angle of the coastline told him they were traveling in the right direction.

Once the towers of LA drifted behind them, Nohar lowered his weapon. He glanced down at the console in front of them.

"You're not going to see them on that," the pilot said.

Nohar looked up.

"Go ahead, shoot me. Even if they were within short-range radar contact, they'll only show if their FOF transponder's on."

"How much of a lead?"

He could see the pilot debating with himself over his cooperation. "Fifteen minutes."

"Distance?"

"Ninety to one-fifty klicks."

Nohar didn't know whether to curse the distance, or be thankful that Krisoijn hadn't reached his destination yet.

The pilot looked at Nohar. "You know, I'm worthless as a hostage. They're not going to hesitate shooting us down."

"Then get moving."

Nohar looked down at the console. His vision was blurry with fatigue and pain. He switched the automatic to his other hand, clutched to his chest. He hoped the captive pilot wouldn't try anything while he held the gun in his broken arm.

Nohar began flipping switches on the helicopter's comm.

"What are you doing?"

"How do you get a civilian channel on this thing?"

The pilot looked at what he was doing. "They'll be able to monitor everything you say on that."

"As long as the person I call can read me."

"The first dial to 'CIV,' the second to 'DAT,' and the third to 'TRN/RCV.'"

Nohar did as the pilot said. After going through an on-screen menu he managed to get the familiar blue AT&T test pattern logo. He was never happier to see that image.

He slipped a ramcard—the one he had copied from the Bensheim database—into the comm's data slot.

"What are you doing?" the pilot asked. He still smelled of fear, but he had recovered enough for Nohar to trade the automatic back to his good hand. It hurt to move his broken arm toward the console, but he could move his fingers enough to operate the comm.

"What are *you* doing?" Nohar said.

"What?"

"What is the mission of that military cabal you work for?"

The pilot looked at Nohar as if he was nuts. "What do you think is going on here?" Nohar said.

"You obviously escaped from detention..." Nohar would have laughed if his arm didn't hurt so much. He began typing in Pacific Rim Media.

"Why was I being detained?"

"I don't know." The pilot paused. "You obviously are a morey terrorist—"

"Why else would I hijack you, right?"

The pilot nodded.

"You don't have any idea what their agenda is?"

"Whose agenda?"

"The people you work for."

"The Marines?"

Nohar shook his head as a receptionist came on-line to take his call. The man on the other end of the comm was an immaculate Asian gentleman who was just imperfect enough to be flesh and blood and not a computer facsimile.

Nohar knew he was a real person when he saw the expression of shock at the sight of his caller. Nohar didn't know if the handgun was in the frame, but the man could certainly see the ragged blood-spattered clothes and the broken arm.

"Pacific Rim Media." The man announced it in such a way that Nohar knew in his secret heart he hoped the response would be, "Oops, wrong number." The man never even gave Nohar the obligatory, "May I help you?"

"Not the Marines," Nohar said.

"What?" said the man on the other end of the comm. The man's movements were jerky with interference. Nohar stared into the screen. "Connect me with Stephanie Weir." The receptionist looked unsure, so he added, "Tell her it's Nohar calling. She'll talk to me."

"Just a moment." The receptionist's face showed the relief he felt, putting Nohar on hold.

Nohar hoped he was right, and Stephie would talk to him.

"What are you doing?" the pilot asked.

"You'll see it on the news, if we live."

He shook his head and stared out the distorted windscreen. The eastern half of Los Angeles slid underneath them. Aircars passed above them as they flew illegally low over the suburbs. The helicopter had maxed out at about two-fifty klicks an hour.

"Making demands to the media won't help. They still won't negotiate with you. If you gave up, they might not shoot. . . ."

"No demands," Nohar said. "No negotiation." Stephie's face replaced the Pacific Rim test pattern and she started off on him before the video had fully resolved. "What the hell do you think you're doing, calling me at work like th—" When the video was fully on-line, Stephie stopped talking and just stared.

"Get a blank ramcard ready to download."

"What happened? Where are you—"

"Do it."

Nohar saw Stephie fumble around her desk, eventually sliding a ramcard into her comm. "What's going on?"

"Something for your news division." Nohar pressed the button for a burst transmit of the ramcard's contents to Stephie. Once the data started shooting through the comm network, Nohar said, "Make copies of this. Transmit at least one overseas. They're monitoring this comm."

Stephie shook her head. "What is this?"

"A rogue military operation. An antiterrorist action gone out of control. That card you're downloading is a database detailing domestic biological warfare experiments, using the North American Bensheim Foundation as a front."

"What?" The word came from Stephie and the pilot, they had almost the same expression. The display on the screen showed the card almost downloaded to Stephie's comm.

"No time. The database has enough for the story." The display started flashing that the transfer was complete. Nohar swapped out the card, painfully with his broken arm, and slipped in the other one.

"Get moving once this thing downloads. You aren't safe until all this information is public."

"But—"

The second card, the one that started all of this, didn't take nearly as long to transmit. It was over before Stephie could ask him any more questions.

Nohar cut the connection. He hoped that he hadn't just condemned her like he had condemned Elijah.

"We're being ordered to land," the pilot told him, holding a hand up to his headset.

"That isn't going to happen."

"Look at the radar," the pilot said. He flipped a switch so Nohar could hear the audio he was listening to.

". . . repeat, you are being ordered to land. Acknowledge, or you will be forced down . . ."

Nohar glanced at the radar. There were two blips following them, both had the letters marking an active transponder. They were closing fast.

"Those are two Vipers. Fully armed attack copters. This is a troop carrier. Which do you think's faster?"

Nohar gripped the gun tightly. "Landing isn't an option." In the background the commands from the Vipers continued in a monotonous litany.

"Don't you understand? They are going to shoot us down if you don't let me land."

No, they would've already. For a moment Nohar wondered why they were still airborne—they were well within missile range. Then he looked down at the suburbs sliding by below them. They were waiting for them to clear the civilian population. . . .

"Hug the freeway," Nohar told him.

"What?"

"Get over the freeway, as low as you can without hitting any cars."

The pilot hesitated a moment, then he banked the helicopter down toward the Riverside Freeway. The Santa Ana Mountains filled the front of the windscreen as the copter dove toward Anaheim. As Nohar's stomach dropped out, he looked in the rear video and saw the Vipers on their tail. The black copter he was in resembled a grotesque beetle under its counter-rotating props, the two Vipers were as narrow and lithe as dragonflies. Even at this distance Nohar could see their stubby wings, there to carry weaponry that couldn't be attached to the Viper's narrow fuselage.

"We're aiming right toward March Air Force Base—"

Nohar didn't respond. He watched as the mountains slid by the helicopter. Below them, traffic sped by in a blur, rolling along an endless ribbon of concrete. It felt as if Nohar could reach down and slap the roofs of the cars as they shot by beneath them. Air Force base or not, as long as they were so close to traffic, the pursuers wouldn't dare shoot them down.

The problem was going to come when they ran out of traffic. The freeway they were on would take them to I-10, which would take them all the way to the Arizona border, where the camps were. At some point, over the desert, they would have to turn south, giving the Vipers a clear shot at them.

Nohar didn't know what he was going to do then. He hoped to catch up with Krisoijn before then.

The copter blew past March on the northern turn up toward San Bernardino and I-10.

"We're headed toward Norton now."

"Just take Ten east." Nohar stared at the radar, where other blips were joining the Vipers. They were far away, but from the speed he could tell that he was looking at a pair of conventional aircraft taking off from March, fighters. . . .

The pilot looked at Nohar as he took the turn onto I-10. The traffic was lighter, and the population of Greater Los Angeles was now mostly behind them. Ahead lay mountains, desert, and a clear field of fire.

"We have to put down," the pilot said. "I can radio that we'll put down at Norton Air Force Base—"

Nohar shook his head; all he could think of was Maria. "How close are we to them?"

"What? The other helicopter?" The pilot shook his head. "There's still at least seventy-five klicks between us."

Nohar gripped the gun and pressed it into the pilot's head. "We're supposed to be faster—"

"The jog north, following the freeway, it eats up time."

They'd never catch up with them at this rate.

The board in front of the pilot started coming alive with red lights and buzzers.

"What's happening?"

Over the speaker Nohar heard the tinny voice of one of the Vipers, "You are ordered to land *now*. This is your final warning."

"One of the Vipers has a radar lock on us." The pilot turned toward him. "We have to land *right now!*"

Nohar tasted copper on his breath, and felt the rush of his pulse in his ears and in his wounded arm. "No." The word was almost a whisper.

"Fuck this," he said. "Shoot me, then."

The copter tilted and ducked toward a clear spot beside the highway. Nohar gripped the gun, but it was pointless to shoot, even if he could. There wasn't any way they could escape the pursuit.

The pilot yelled into the radio, "Hold your fire, I'm landing."

The alarms didn't go away, but the missile didn't come.

They were almost on the ground when a new voice overwhelmed the channel the Vipers were using. "Two unidentified attack helicopters, disarm your weapons now! Desist pursuit and accompany us to March Air Force Base."

The pilot's expression changed.

"What is it?" Nohar asked.

"The fighters..." The pilot shook his head as if he couldn't understand what was happening.

Nohar heard the Vipers talking back, "We are on an authorized antiterrorist mission. We have been ordered to stop that helicopter—"

The fighters called back, "You are following illegal orders. You are to accompany us or be fired upon."

There was a long pause before the Viper said, "We require confirmation from our command—"

The Viper didn't even finish getting the whole phrase out. Another voice, weaker with distance, broke in on the channel. "Black four and Black five, your mission is aborted. Repeat, your mission is aborted. Follow the fighters to March Air Force Base as you've been instructed."

"We need to hear from Colonel Shuster—" said one of the Vipers. "This is a matter of national security."

"This is *General* Thomas Charland, and Colonel Shuster is under arrest pending a court-martial."

There were a few more exchanges, and the pilot's face grew more incredulous as he listened. On the radar, Nohar could see the blips of the fighters looping around to escort the two attack copters.

"Colonel Shuster," the pilot whispered. "Arrested?"

There was only one way Nohar figured that could happen so quickly. The command at Long Beach had been monitoring his transmission to Stephie. General Charland must have decided to cut his losses.

"What's happening?" The pilot whispered.

"Don't land," Nohar said. "Follow Krisoijn."

"Why—"

"Your general decided that the project was blown."

"What project?" The color drained from the pilot's face. "Not that bullshit you were talking about."

"Move this thing."

The pilot looked at Nohar's gun, and banked the helicopter southeast, accelerating toward Arizona. "Biological warfare?" The words were almost inaudible. Nohar could sense the pilot's fear again. This time the fear wasn't because of him.

The kid had just realized that what Nohar had told Stephie might be true. Of course no one had ever told him what the unit at Long Beach was doing. As far as the pilot could tell, Nohar was just another violent morey with a conspiracy theory.

That was until his superiors reacted. The pilot knew as well as Nohar did that the only explanation for the recall was that someone had monitored Nohar's comm transmission, and had responded to it.

General Charland had to be in command, running the show. That was the only way he could have reacted so quickly to the leak of the biowar database. There was probably a plan set in place, with predesigned evidence, preselected fall guys. There was probably a script waiting for this Colonel Shuster laying out exactly what he would say to the Congressional investigating committee when they subpoenaed him. There would probably be stories of how an internal investigation had been onto these folks all along, and just about to hand out indictments when the news broke.

General Charland had just decided to "discover" the conspiracy and arrest its ringleaders before the news started making headlines. His ass was going to be covered.

"Will they recall him?" Nohar asked.

"Who?"

"Krisoijn, the other helicopter."

The pilot shook his head. "He's supposed to be radio silent. It might not even be on."

This General Charland, Nohar had too good a picture of that Machiavellian bastard already, might shout orders, but it was too easy for Nohar to believe that they'd let Krisoijn go through with his objective, just so there'd be an example of what a loose cannon he was. It would help distract attention from the officers in charge of this mess.

"We're going to catch up with him," Nohar said.

The pilot didn't contradict him.

Chapter 27

With the pursuit gone, the helicopter sped across the desert, in a straight line for Camp Liberty and the Arizona border. The pilot didn't talk much anymore, but he flew the copter where Nohar wanted it to go.

While southwestern sand and rock blew by underneath them, Nohar used the comm. He called a half-dozen media outlets, spreading the information on what was going on as widely as possible. Half of them treated him like a psychotic, the other half humored him long enough to download the database on the ramcard. He told everyone who would listen about the coming attack on Camp Liberty, down to the location.

One of the people who seemed to listen was Enrique Bartolo from *Eye on LA*, the reporter that Henderson had called at Pastoria.

Nohar was on his seventh call when the pilot said, "There they are."

Nohar looked up through the bullet-scarred windscreen and saw a dot hanging over the horizon. The black dot seemed to grow as Nohar watched. His rotten day vision couldn't make out any details, but the coloring and the position were right.

"How long before we reach the base?"

"Five minutes."

"Can we beat them there?"

"Barely."

Nohar watched the fuzzy black dot of the other helicopter. It grew, but much too slowly. The difference in the helicopter's load made only a slight difference in speed.

If they could reach the place first, he could get everyone out.

If . . .

Suddenly, the fuzzy black form of the helicopter rose and banked to the left. "What are they doing?"

The pilot shook his head. "They know I'm compromised."

"How?"

The pilot turned toward him. "Someone looked back. You kind of stand out."

"Fuck—" There wasn't any way they could have missed him in the copilot's seat. Even if they'd missed him, the bullet in the windscreen was a giveaway.

The other copter was sliding close, too close. Nohar could see the copter lining up with them on the left and above. He started to make out the landing gear and the massive side door. It was sliding open as Nohar watched.

"Can you get more speed out of this thing?"

The pilot shook his head, more out of stress than negation, and dipped the nose of the copter. The machine started tilting toward the desert floor, just as Nohar began to hear gunfire over the sound of the rotors. It sounded distant, almost fake.

The smell of panic filled the cockpit as the bottom dropped out of Nohar's stomach. The copter fell toward the desert floor. At the last minute the pilot pulled up and the copter shot by about ten meters above the ground. Rocks and cactus seemed to reach up almost far enough to grab them out of the sky, and sand billowed in a cloud behind them.

"Fuck," the pilot said, "They're above and behind—"

The dive had added about fifteen or twenty klicks to their speed. They started banking, back and forth, evading the copter behind them, and large rock formations that sprang up ahead of them.

Nohar heard more gunfire behind them. The sound still

seemed distant, but this time he heard something pounding the outside of their helicopter.

"*Shit,*" the pilot said, pulling the copter up into a climb. The desert fell away and was replaced by sky. Just as the horizon slid under his feet, Nohar saw sunlight reflected from something on the horizon.

A window. It had to be a window in the distance.

More gunfire, and an explosion rocked the helicopter. The cabin filled with the smell of ozone and fried ceramics. The rotors began making ugly rhythmic knocking noises, and half the lights in front of the pilot began flashing red.

"What—" Nohar started.

"The primary inductor blew. I have to put her down."

The copter was shaking itself apart now. All over the console, things buzzed for the pilot's attention. The knocking and the shaking were getting worse. "Losing alignment on the rotors—" He said it through clenched teeth, and Nohar didn't know if the pilot was talking to him or not.

The nose of the copter dipped.

The gunfire continued, as if they couldn't tell that the helicopter was in trouble.

Nohar dropped the gun and tried to pull the safety harness around himself. It didn't fit, and he had trouble doing it one-handed. He roared as the attempt jostled his busted arm, sending fiery waves of agony through that half of his body as the bones ground together.

They were barely fifteen meters above the ground when he got one strap fastened. They were slowing, but not enough. The helicopter was trying to shake itself apart as it shot over the four-meter-high perimeter fence.

Suddenly, below them, the desert floor was covered by ranks of vehicles. An endless parking lot spread out below them. In front of them, in the distance, was the fence and the low buildings of Camp Liberty.

The pilot tried to bring the nose up, tried to slow. But the helicopter began pitching against him.

More gunfire, and this time he heard a sickening screech of abused metal. The two rotors had gotten out of sync enough to touch. Nohar saw a shower of ferociously turning metal erupt from above the helicopter and tear into the cars below. The copter was now completely dead to the pilot's control. It nosed straight down into the ranks of parked vehicles.

An INS van flipped up and smashed against the nose of the helicopter. Nohar was thrown against the single safety strap holding him into the seat. His head struck the armored windscreen, which was the only thing between his face and a jagged mass of twisted fiberglass and metal. The van slid with the helicopter, its body tearing through the desert floor and screeching like the damned.

The copter pushed the van about thirty meters before it stopped moving.

The body of the helicopter fell back, tilting the nose up, away from the damaged van. The rear of the helicopter slammed to the ground with a screech of twisted metal.

The pain in Nohar's arm was so intense that he had to look down to assure himself that it wasn't a stump. His breath came in ragged gasps, and he could smell his own blood leaking from gashes in his forehead.

The pilot was in better shape. He looked as if his nose was broken, but he didn't seem injured otherwise. He was shaking his head and saying, "My God, we made it."

Nohar wasn't so sure.

He unhooked the harness that was still attached to him, and picked up the gun. As he stood, he could feel the line of bruises across his midsection where the harness had bit. His legs buckled and he had to sit and breathe for a few moments before he could stand again.

"Any weapons on board?" he said between ragged gasps for breath.

The pilot looked at him with disbelief in his eyes. "Do you know how lucky we are to be standing? You can't be thinking ... ?"

Nohar raised the gun at the pilot.

"You want to commit suicide, be my guest." He gestured toward the end of the compartment. "There's a heavy machine gun that belongs to a mount in the door."

Nohar pocketed the automatic and found the weapon the pilot was talking about. The thing was nearly two meters long and fed from a belt. It was a fifty-cal at least. It was obviously intended for a door gunner, the only support on the frame was a ratchet meant to slide into a preset mount.

"This is it?"

The pilot looked at him and nodded.

Beggars can't be choosers.

Nohar picked up the belts of ammo and draped them over his shoulders. The weight bore down on him, lighting fires in his old shoulder injury as well as his broken arm. For the first time in ages, Nohar tried to force the Beast to come out. He tried to conjure the adrenaline and the engineered combat machine that lived in his genes. He was so close to the edge, he couldn't tell if his biochemistry responded.

After standing and sucking in breaths for nearly a full minute, psyching himself up for the insanity he was about to step into, he managed to lift the fifty-kilo weapon one-handed.

Carrying it balanced, one-handed, was awkward.

"Open the door," Nohar said.

The pilot nodded, and the doors in front of him began to open with a rattling hydraulic wheeze.

Once the other helicopter passed from above them, Nohar stumbled out. He ran, each breath feeling as if it were tearing burning holes in his lungs. He loped past the wreckage of dozens of abandoned government vehicles, many now sporting fifty-caliber bullet holes. To his right, over the edge of the compound ahead of him, the other helicopter was banking, preparing to land.

Nohar ran for the compound thinking twinned thoughts, that the pilot was right when he said that he was committing suicide, and that in there were Maria and his son.

In the daylight, Nohar could now see the whole complex. It must have covered a hundred square kilometers. He was heading toward the inner fence that separated the vehicles from the compound and could just glimpse the dozens of buildings through the small vents in the heavy steel fence. The place shimmered in the daytime heat, like a mirage. Nohar ran through the heat, and it felt as if he were slogging through mud.

He made it to the fence about the time the other copter was dropping troops at the southern end of the compound.

Nohar realized that the commandos had no idea where Manuel and the others were in there. That was his only chance. Nohar ran along the fence line and found an access gate. He had to drop the machine gun to flip open the keypad access. For a few moments he almost blanked on the access code that John had given him.

Then he remembered earthquakes—

"01082034"

It slid open for him.

Nohar grabbed the gun and ran inside. The small pedestrian gate was next to a much larger gate that was designed for vehicle access. The gate was plastered with red signs that said "Access Forbidden" in about twenty different languages.

Between the pedestrian gate and the large vehicle gate was a small guard shack that offered some cover. Nohar dove into it and forced the barrel of the machine gun through the window facing the Bad Guys' helicopter. The window shattered, and Nohar braced the gun on the guard shack's desk.

The ratchet of the gun wedged in a control panel, and the barriers on this side of the vehicle gate began raising and lowering.

Nohar concentrated on getting the belt of ammo off of him and feeding it into the weapon. He ducked down behind the machine gun and sighted on the helicopter. It was still unloading, three or four pinks were rappelling from lines dangling from its sides.

Nohar let the copter have it.

The sound was deafening. Each sledgehammer shot shook the guard shack and slammed the ill-braced weapon into Nohar's bad shoulder. The small room filled with the smell of gunsmoke and heated brass. The barrel wanted to travel, but somehow Nohar kept pulling the weapon back on target. He could see sparks flying off of the side of the helicopter. And he tracked the shots until he was firing into the door.

The dangling pinks dropped so quickly that Nohar couldn't tell if it was panic or free fall. Two others fell out of the side door, unattached, tumbling to the ground.

The helicopter banked and started pulling up and away to the left, empty rappel lines still attached to it.

Nohar tracked upward toward the twin rotors.

By then the helicopter had turned and brought its own fifty-cal to bear on the guardhouse. Nohar caught the hint of a muzzle flash and ducked under the console. The little building shook as the copter strafed it. It offered cover, but no protection. The slugs carved through it like paper. Nohar could only hope that they didn't have a steep enough angle to get a good shot at the floor.

The building shook with each impact, and electronic debris showered him from the console as it was torn apart by gunfire.

The gunfire suddenly became erratic. He could still hear the fifty-cal jackhammering in the distance, but the shack no longer shook with the impact. Nohar didn't risk a look out until the gunfire ceased completely.

When he looked out he could still see the enemy copter. It was banking to the left, but the steepness of the turn told Nohar that it was uncontrolled. The fifty-cal was almost pointing to the ground as the copter tried to pull an impossible inside turn.

Nohar's shots inside must've taken out part of the navigational controls.

The copter tried to spiral upward, turning so steeply that its rotors were almost perpendicular to the ground. At that point there was no way the pilot could maintain stability. The nose pitched down and the whole thing corkscrewed into the ground, out of Nohar's view behind the buildings. Though he couldn't see it, Nohar heard the impact and the secondary explosions of the inductors letting go.

He struggled to his feet. Each time it was becoming more of a trial. Pain was no longer localized in his arm. He felt bruised in his abdomen, the old wounds to his knee and shoulder, the cuts on his face, and a half-dozen places where pieces of the guard shack had cut into his flesh. Breathing was pain.

But he couldn't stop.

He looked down at the machine gun. There were a half-dozen shots left on the belt. With a shaking hand, he removed the empty part of the belt from the other side of the gun. Then he grabbed it, the heat of the barrel searing his knuckles when they brushed it, and started after the commandos.

Chapter 28

In the daylight, the camp seemed like a waiting room for hell. Heat rippled off of every surface. The smells were of metal and hot asphalt. The buildings were whitewashed cinder block the color of bleached bone. The few windows were boarded over with gray plastic construction panels. Everything was dry, functional, and dead.

Nohar limped along the asphalt strip between buildings, listening, concentrating on odors, trying to sense how close he was to the Bad Guys.

He was heading toward the south end of the compound, toward the Bad Guys and away from Manuel and the others. He was hoping to harass the attackers enough that Manuel and the others might have time to escape.

All he needed to do was buy time. The next helicopters were going to be news crews. Then it would be over.

Nohar didn't know how much time *he* had. His broken arm was clutched to his chest in a twisted parody of Maria's arthritis. He had to strip off his jacket and shirt because of the heat. His new black coloring made things even worse. His breath would come only in coppery gasps, and the fifty-cal machine gun felt as if it was about to tear his good arm out of its socket with every step he took.

The Bad Guys were quiet. For a while it seemed as though he were the only living thing moving between the whitewashed buildings. The only things he heard were the dry wind and his own breath. The sense of isolation was so complete that he almost missed the first commando.

He was just about to turn a corner, heading toward the southern end of the compound, when he realized he smelled tension and exertion that wasn't his own. He paused long enough to hear two sets of footsteps, running lightly. The sound would have been quiet enough to miss beneath the noise of his own breathing if not for the tearing sound of the soles adhering to the asphalt.

Nohar had just stopped at the corner of the building when one of the commandos sprang around at him. He was ducking around the corner to cover the intersection. Nohar was right there. The man's submachine gun was up, but it was covering the street. It was a miscalculation, because the guy had to back up and turn to cover Nohar. Nohar didn't give him that chance.

The fifty-cal had a barrel that was nearly half the length of the distance separating them. Nohar jumped from the wall, pivoted on his good leg as if he were throwing a shot put, and swung the gun up so the barrel slammed into the man's chin.

The guy dropped like a sack of wet flour.

He had a partner.

As the weight of the fifty-cal still carried Nohar in a circle, the other one sprang up while Nohar's back was to the corner. Nohar could feel the man's presence, even before the first wild shot went off.

Nohar didn't let the new guy get a second shot. He swung the fifty-cal back in an arc, slamming the stock into the new guy's upper body. The impact shook Nohar's shoulder, sending daggers of pain through the joint. He heard another wild shot, and he smelled gunsmoke and the char of something ricocheting off of cinder block.

He also heard the body strike the asphalt.

Nohar turned back toward the downed commandos, carried partway by the pull of the swinging machine gun. Both were out of it for the foreseeable future, unconscious. The lower part of Number One's face, and Number Two's neck, were both turning a violent shade of purple.

Nohar dropped the fifty-cal. The sound was like another helicopter crashing into the ground. He couldn't carry the thing any farther.

He checked the intersection to be certain that there weren't more Bad Guys about to drop on him, and then he bent and grabbed one commando's gun. He had to fight a wave of nausea and vertigo as he bent over. The only reason he didn't vomit from the pain was because his stomach was completely empty. He stayed bent over, vision blacking out, for a few long moments before he could retrieve a weapon.

When Nohar straightened, he looked at what he'd picked up. These guys weren't prepped for stealth. Instead of the covert Black Widows, these submachine guns were matte-black Glock 23s, a common enough weapon for antiterrorist forces, as well as terrorists. The lightness of the weapon was a relief after the machine gun. It almost disappeared in his hand. The barrel on the thing barely extended beyond the trigger guard, just enough to prevent someone from accidentally shooting off a finger.

Nohar checked once more to assure himself that the two downed commandos weren't getting up, then he started a quiet halting run in the direction from which they had come.

The next set of Bad Guys, he heard in time.

Nohar was padding next to one of the dull cinder-block buildings, his shoes lost somewhere with his shirt and jacket. He heard movement from the other side of one of the gray panels boarding over the windows. He could hear whispered voices, though the words were unintelligible. He had time to force his mind away from his injuries, time to steel himself for a confrontation.

Nohar circled around until he found the entrance to the building. It was another panel of gray, leaning loosely against a hole in the cinder block twice as high as the windows. Nohar pushed it aside for a moment with the Glock, listening. When he was sure the movement was deeper within the building, he slipped inside.

After the blinding-white desert exterior, the inside of the building was midnight black. Nohar had to stare into the darkness for a few moments before his eyes adjusted to the monochrome gloom.

The first detail that Nohar could make out was an IV drip bottle hanging from a stand in the corner. The sight was like a lump of ice in his gut. He turned slowly and saw a stretcher, a desk, a cart carrying a few items of monitoring equipment.

He had stumbled into the camp's infirmary.

The sounds came from down a corridor to the rear of the room where he stood. Nohar walked across the linoleum floor, his steps stirring small clouds of dust that made his nose itch. Naked fluorescent tubes hung dead from a corrugated metal ceiling. The corridor was flanked by drywall, the whitewash not quite covering the joints.

He passed two open doorways and checked briefly into each one, making sure they were as empty as his other senses told him they were. One was an operating theater, the overhead light dangling like a spider about to feed on the table beneath. The other was a small ward with a half-dozen bedframes, mattresses gone.

Nohar moved down the corridor, hackles rising as he closed on the commandos. In his mind he was already picturing hospitals, like the one where his mother had died. He could imagine them filled with moreaus dying of an engineered plague. He could imagine the virus spreading through the hospital until the corridors were coated with infected blood and a stay there was a death sentence. He could imagine the pink doctors wading through the gore, unconcerned and uninfected, disposing of bodies. . . .

The copper taste of blood in his mouth wasn't exertion or fatigue anymore; it was anger. The humans who had created Nohar's kind would never accept them.

Man is dissatisfied until he can destroy what he has created.

At the end of the corridor hung a pair of swinging doors. There were two windows of dirty plastic that looked into the room beyond. Even before Nohar had reached it, he could hear that was where the Bad Guys were. He could make out two of them from their voices and the sound of their footsteps. One was about five meters from the door to the right, the other was two meters away and to the left.

Nohar swallowed and shouldered through the door and leveled the Glock at the nearest commando and fired high, above the body armor. The man took a slug in the back of the neck and fell face first into a pile of old boxes. Nohar swung the Glock over to where the other was and found himself facing a stack of more boxes—

Fuck!

Nohar ducked to the side just as the other one flung himself around the obstructing boxes and started firing. Nohar swung his Glock around to fire at the same time. Nohar was faster, but he was falling backward and his aim was off. He felt something slam into his thigh as his own shots slammed into the commando's chest and neck.

The guy fell back through the swinging doors as Nohar hit the ground.

Nohar groaned. A bullet had torn into the meat of his left thigh, and it felt as if someone was drilling a hole in his leg with a dull bit. For a moment or two, the new insult flared greater in his awareness than his broken arm. Somehow, though, the anger seemed to feed on the pain, growing stronger with it. He lay there, feeling blood spread beneath him and the rage ignite within him.

He shouldn't have been able to move at all, he had been running so long on the verge of collapse.

But slowly, his broken body fought for each movement with a flare of pain. His breath shuddered and his limbs shook. He dropped the gun. But Nohar made it to his feet.

His leg wasn't broken. It bore his weight, the wound burning with the fire of torn muscle. Nohar forced the leg to move despite the pain. He moved deliberately, as if a sudden motion might split his skin and send his insides spilling on the ground in front of him. He bent down, feeling waves of nausea again, and grabbed the Glock from the man who'd gotten shot in the back of the neck. It lay on top of a pile of boxes, easier to reach than the one he had dropped on the floor.

Limping, Nohar pushed his way out of the building. He stopped in the lobby to tear some remnants from his pants to tie around the leg wound with one shaking hand.

Nohar made it all the way back to the wreckage of Krisoijn's helicopter. He stood at the edge of a debris field and stared. Unlike the one he'd flown in, this helicopter had been aimed straight down into a building. It looked as if the rotors had torn into its body and had ripped it apart. There were pieces of helicopter scattered for fifty meters in every direction.

Nohar could see two bodies. One was out on the asphalt, the rappelling cord wrapped around him, his head turned ninety degrees from the rest of his body. Nearer the wreckage was a victim of the helicopter's rotor. The blades had torn him nearly in half.

But there wasn't a sign of Krisoijn or any living Bad Guys.

Nohar didn't believe he had taken out all of them, and that meant that they had slipped by each other as Nohar made his way south. As Nohar turned around to catch up with the enemy, he heard the rapid hammer of a Glock echo in the distance. He started a limping run toward the source of the gunfire.

In addition to the rattle of the Glocks, he could hear the cough of a forty-five automatic. Nohar felt a sinking feeling.

He had left Necron's forty-five with Henderson.

He ran with a bobbing gait, pushing his burning leg harder than it wanted to go, his broken arm clutched to his chest as if it were fused to his body. He could feel tacky warmth seeping down his left leg, matting the fur beneath the makeshift bandage. The edges of his vision had turned black and every breath was an effort. He lost track of how many times he stumbled; his thoughts were losing any linear cohesion under the physical assault to his body.

Nohar ran down the center of the complex's main roadway, focused only on moving toward the small cluster of buildings where he'd heard the gunfire. Nohar knew where the shots must be coming from. It was the only thought that seemed to remain clear and focused through the red haze of pain.

The sounds were from a low undistinguished structure that squatted at the northern end of the main strip of asphalt. The main administration building.

There was a period of time that seemed to black out from his memory, and the next thing Nohar was aware of, he was leaning against the nose of the INS van that Henderson had driven them all here in. He stood on the cracked apron surrounding the administration building.

The gunfire had ceased. The silence was a sickening hole in the pit of Nohar's stomach.

The two swinging doors, metal and chicken-wire glass, showed two bullet holes near the top. Nohar could see lights in the hallway beyond the doors, and barely stopped to look through the glass. His consciousness had shrunk to a singularity that contained only the awareness of combat. His body was moving long after it should have stopped.

Nohar opened the door with his bad arm, unwilling to drop the Glock even for a moment. It felt as if a knife were slashing through his arm from the inside. He could feel bone grinding and muscle tearing. His jaw clenched shut, keeping him from crying out.

Even so, they must have heard him, because a pair of

human forms turned the corner to face Nohar down the length of the hall. Nohar didn't hesitate. He sprayed the Glock, firing through the window at the two men. Fragments of glass bit into his skin, through the fur. He emptied the clip, and when the Glock was finished firing, Nohar realized that the deafening sound was his own roar.

Both of the men lay heaped at the end of the corridor.

Nohar stepped into the building, tossing away the empty gun and pulling out the pilot's sidearm. The air was rank with the smell of blood, human and feline.

Some of the feline blood wasn't his own.

The sounds coming from Nohar's throat had lost their resemblance to speech. He loped along the corridor, listening and trying to make out the scent of the enemy. There was no mistaking the smell of humans here. There had been five of them.

Three now.

Nohar stopped by the bodies, crouching, concentrating on where they had come from. His breaths were ragged and quick, and the pain in his arm and his leg had begun to tighten on his chest. Every sensation filtered through the pain, fragmenting everything into a series of disconnected moments. Through it only one thought managed to retain its focus, a hard kernel of anger that told him to kill the enemy.

Kill the men.

Kill the humans. . . .

Nohar moved through the building, the twists of the halls lost to him. He barely perceived the halls he passed through. What drew him was the scent of man, and the scent of blood.

Footsteps came toward him, and he faded into the shadow of a nearby doorway. The pilot's gun fell to the ground, forgotten.

When the commando ran past Nohar, toward his downed fellows and the sound of gunfire, Nohar reached his intact arm out of the doorway, his claws fully extended. He caught the man in the midsection, and the man's weapon went flying down the corridor. Nohar had time to see the man's eyes widen, before he kicked out with his good leg, tearing from the groin down, and throwing him into the opposite wall. The effort dropped Nohar onto the ground as his left leg collapsed, but he rolled and pushed himself upright with his good hand. His hand slipped a few times in the man's blood, but he managed to struggle upright.

Nohar left the man to slowly go into shock as he limped toward the last two enemies.

The scent of blood became stronger as he approached the heart of the building. Human and feline, and other scents merged into an all-encompassing odor of death. Nohar knew he smelled his own death, and his son's, and especially that of the humans who had brought this down—

Nohar sprang through a doorway, and into the maw of death itself.

The first one was right beside the doorway, guarding it. Nohar knew exactly where he was from the sound of his breathing and the smell of his sweat. Nohar turned, his good hand reaching the man's throat, the claws biting into the trachea. He was nowhere near quick enough. The man's weapon fired once as Nohar pulled the man's neck free. The shot slammed into Nohar's abdomen, Nohar stumbled back into the room, feeling a fire in his gut worse than anything he felt in his arm or leg. He could feel blood sheeting across his stomach, and down his back.

His back hit the wall of the room, and fragmented images—pieces of the scene in front of him—began sinking into his consciousness.

The Necron Avenger, John Samson, lay on the floor unmoving.

Near the doorway, at Nohar's feet, lay Sarah Henderson. Necron's automatic had spilled from her hand, and her eyes stared upward, glassy and unmoving. She had taken a half-dozen shots, one right in the chest. Nohar was standing in a pool of her blood. Maria's wheelchair was behind a large desk with an inset comm. Her face was swollen where someone had struck her, probably breaking the cheekbone. But she still breathed.

Standing behind that desk, facing him, was his son. "Manuel." Nohar's voice was a ragged whisper. He spoke as if the flesh had been scoured from his throat.

Nohar tried to take a step forward, but an Afrikaans voice said, "Don't move."

Krisoijn stood behind Nohar's son, holding a gun to his temple.

Chapter 29

Nohar froze, and that gave time for his brain to start working again. He had screwed up. He had let anger override everything else. Now here he was with his guts leaking out everywhere, his body racked by so many insults that he couldn't distinguish separate sources for the pain. The pain was an omnipresent haze that he sucked in with each breath. Every few heartbeats his vision would black out for a moment as another wave of agony broke over him.

He shouldn't have been able to stand, but, seeing Manuel, he managed to.

Seeing Manuel had an almost supernatural force. He could see everything that he had missed before. Maria's bone structure, the shadows of his own coloring. Manuel's eyes could have been born directly from Nohar's mother.

"Nohar?" Manuel had the same husky voice as his mother. He tried to take a step forward, but Krisoijn held him back.

"No one moves," Krisoijn said. "This is messy enough already."

Nohar shook his head and forced the words out, "It's over. Long Beach, the Clinic, it's all exposed...."

Krisoijn laughed.

Nohar stared. "He knows," Manuel said. He reached onto the console and tossed a ramcard over at Nohar's feet. "He doesn't even care about this anymore."

Nohar looked down at the card, glinting rainbows in Henderson's blood.

"Why?" The question felt as if it tore the flesh from inside his stomach. He was beginning to feel dizzy and light-headed. "Why go through with this—" He felt his knees giving way. He dropped next to Henderson's body. His good hand caught himself on her stomach. Her flesh was blood-soaked deadweight.

"You, Nohar," Krisoijn said. "I wanted to see you die."

"You got what you wanted," Manuel said. His voice was quick and strained, showing the pull of adrenaline. Nohar recognized it. "Why don't you go meet your plane—"

Nohar stared into Henderson's unmoving eyes, feeling his life pump out of the hole in his stomach with every heartbeat. "Plane . . ." Nohar whispered. He barely heard the word himself beneath the sound of his heartbeat.

"You cannot attack such a threat on a single front." Krisoijn was distant, the Afrikaans accent just cutting through Nohar's pulse. "Your escape from Gilbertez compromised this operation. The whole enterprise had to be terminated. You've done us damage, but you haven't come close to stopping our effort."

The operation at Long Beach was only a small part of something much larger. Nohar didn't know if Manuel realized it, but the fact that Krisoijn had even hinted at that meant he didn't intend to leave anyone alive. The bastard knew the media were coming, but he planned for them to find an inexplicable bloodbath where his own corpse was absent. The soldiers he had brought in with him, the bodies scattered around this abandoned place, they probably hadn't known that much.

Nohar forced himself to look up at Krisoijn. The man's eyes were dead, black, and showed little trace of any emotion. Nohar looked at Manuel and saw the fury burning in him, mirroring his own. Nohar could see the tense muscles, the strain of reining in all the instincts to flee or fight. "I'm sorry," Nohar said to Manuel. He was apologizing for his failure, the entire string of events that had begun with denying him a father, and ended with him impotent, bleeding on the ground only three meters from his son.

Krisoijn spoke. "We are the dominant species on this planet, and we will not tolerate a threat to our existence."

Nohar knew that he was about to shoot. He had to do something. He tightened his stomach muscles, and held his broken arm to the wound, pushing himself up against Henderson's body. "You murdering bastard. There's no reason for this."

"No reason?" Krisoijn said, his voice raising. For the first time there seemed some emotion in his voice. Nohar struggled to his feet as Krisoijn spoke. "Do you have any idea

what you engineered monstrosities did to my homeland? A whole generation of my family was lost during the war, and in the revolution that followed all of my brothers and sisters—all of them—were killed. I took a machete to the face, and barely survived myself. I was six years old."

Nohar tried to focus. To fix the room in his brain, to connect the impressions through the fog of pain he walked through. His son and Krisoijn stood behind the central control panel, in front of the giant holo map of the complex. On the map, lights blinked, showing the status of the compound. There were two flashing red lights where the two helicopters had gone down.

Maria was in a corner, sitting in her wheelchair, still unconscious. He could hear her breathing, ragged but steady. Two guns lay on the floor. The dead human's Glock lay on the floor near his body by the wall opposite Nohar. Less than a meter away from Nohar was the forty-five that Henderson had been using. Beyond that, in front of the console was John Samson, face down. . . .

For the first time Nohar realized that there was no blood coming from John Samson's body. His clothes were splattered with blood, but from all appearances it was Henderson's. And, if he concentrated, Nohar could hear him breathing. It wasn't the slow rhythmic respiration of someone who had lost consciousness.

"He didn't kill your family," Nohar said, waving his good arm at Manuel. "Let him go."

Krisoijn shook his head. "Every one of you is a danger to the species." He cocked his head toward the door. "How many people have you killed today?"

Nohar took a step forward. "You had my son."

Krisoijn pressed the Glock into Manuel's head and said, "I'll make you a deal. You give me back one of my brothers, and you can have him."

Nohar staggered forward another step, and his foot was next to the forty-five. Nohar stared at Krisoijn, keeping his attention. "How many men have you killed, Krisoijn?"

"In defense of the species."

"Royd, Samson, how many others?" Nohar shook his head. It was cruel, but he was hoping that word of his father's death might prod John into action. "You're just another fanatic. Just like my father."

"Do not compare me to an animal." As Krisoijn spoke, Nohar's foot kicked the gun gently. It slid across the linoleum and stopped next to John Samson's head.

"Both of you wrapped up in your own righteousness," Nohar said. "*They* wronged you, and *they* must pay. Datia saw humanity as the enemy, you see the nonhumans—it's just revenge."

"You are a danger to the survival of the species—"

"And you don't hesitate to engineer the same kind of weapons that devastated your homeland. Your brothers died in the revolution. Which one of the plagues killed your parents?"

John realized a gun was in reach. He inched his hand toward it. His effort was too slow, especially since Nohar could see plainly that he was on the floor out of Krisoijn's view behind the console. Samson obviously didn't realize that, and he moved cautiously.

"I think this has gone far enough," Krisoijn said. Nohar could see the tensing of the muscles in his arm as he prepared to squeeze the trigger.

"If you shoot him, what's going to keep me from tearing out your throat?" Nohar tried to take all of his resolve and put it into his voice.

"You'll be dead before you cross the table." Krisoijn's voice was confident, but Nohar could see the hesitation in his arm.

Samson's hand touched the butt of the forty-five.

"I know you," Nohar said. "My family was killed by the enemy, too. My mother died carrying my only siblings, from a virus designed in some human lab. My father was shot down by pinks in the National Guard."

"You don't know me!"

"We know each other, Krisoijn." Nohar stared straight into Krisoijn's eyes as he listened to Samson moving. "You know what drives me. If you put a bullet into my son's head, you *know* that nothing will stop me from tearing your heart out."

Krisoijn was backing away from Manuel, the Glock trained on Manuel's head. "Maybe so," Krisoijn said, reaching the wall and edging toward the door. He was angling around the console to bring both of them under the stare of the submachine gun. "Maybe I have to kill you first—"

Krisoijn's gun moved, just a little, toward Nohar. Samson had been paying attention. He rolled out from behind the console, aiming up at Krisoijn. The automatic fired twice before it clicked on an empty chamber.

The Glock fired as Manuel ducked. Krisoijn fell back toward the wall, the two bullets lodged in his body armor.

Nohar leaped at him.

The jump at Krisoijn felt as if it tore his intestines loose from his abdomen. His broken arm wouldn't move, so Nohar shouldered into Krisoijn's gun arm. The Glock kept firing, blowing holes in the holo map, throwing sparks across the room.

When Nohar's full weight connected, the drywall gave way and they blew through into the neighboring room, a massive chamber divided into office cubicles.

They stopped moving forward when Krisoijn slammed into a cubicle wall. The Glock had stopped firing. Nohar heard the trigger click a few times before Krisoijn brought it down on the side of his skull.

The impact caused Nohar's vision to black out, and he stumbled back on his wounded leg.

Blood clouded his vision, it took most of his strength to yell back through the hole in the wall. "Manuel, get Maria and John out of here—"

His words were cut short by a stabbing pain beneath his ribs. His vision cleared enough to see Krisoijn's hand removing a knife from his side. He slashed again, but Nohar managed to block the thrust with his good arm.

Krisoijn faced him with almost a feral grin as he waved the knife between them. He'd tossed away the empty Glock. "I don't need a gun to finish you off."

Krisoijn swung again, and Nohar blocked the thrust with his good arm. This time he felt the blade take a part of his bicep with it. He could feel his strength ebbing. Pain and fatigue were pulling him down with iron bands. There was no way he could hold off Krisoijn for any length of time. Defending himself was pointless as near to the edge as he was.

"Me, maybe . . ." Nohar said.

Krisoijn must have seen the resignation in Nohar's eyes, because he grinned even wider. He dove with a fatal thrust toward Nohar's neck.

". . . but not my son," Nohar raised his hand for a block,

and the blade passed through the palm and out the back. The pain of the knife stabbing through tendon and bone was distant—everything seemed distant, as if he was watching at a remove.

Krisoijn's expression changed when Nohar's hand grabbed his own. Nohar's hand enveloped Krisoijn's in a crushing grip that drove the knife even deeper.

Nohar pulled back, dragging Krisoijn toward him.

Krisoijn beat at Nohar's hand with his free hand, but Nohar barely felt it as he bit into Krisoijn's wrist. The man screamed as Nohar's fangs sank into his arm. Nohar twisted Krisoijn's hand until he felt the bones separate and Krisoijn dropped to his knees.

Krisoijn fell to the ground holding a stump of a right arm. Nohar's right hand slowly, painfully, unclenched, letting go of Krisoijn's hand. The hand fell, and the knife slowly slid out of the wound to fall next to it.

Krisoijn got to his feet, clutching his bleeding arm to his stomach.

Nohar felt his legs give way. He fell, unable to raise either hand to protect himself. He landed on his left side, barely turning to avoid falling on his broken arm.

The world was turning gray. Even the pain seemed distant, felt through a gauzy haze. He couldn't find the strength to move any more.

He stared upward, at the corrugated steel of the ceiling, sensing that he was dying.

Dying wasn't good enough for Krisoijn. He stepped into Nohar's field of vision, holding the knife in his left hand. He knelt, putting a knee on Nohar's chest. Nohar didn't feel his weight, he didn't feel much of anything anymore.

Krisoijn raised the blade, and Nohar waited for it to bite into his neck.

Before the blade descended, Krisoijn turned to look away from Nohar. A look of surprise crossed his face. Then a spray of bullets took away most of that expression above the lower jaw. He fell, his scar the only recognizable piece of his face left.

Nohar turned toward the wall they had broken through, and saw Manuel standing there holding a Glock.

The one the last Bad Guy dropped, Nohar thought.

He might have smiled before he lost consciousness.

*   *   *

It might have been hours later, but Nohar managed a small episode of lucidity. He opened his eyes enough to see the faces of some pink EMTs manhandling him into another helicopter. He was assaulted by the sounds of dozens of people crowding too close. He saw flashes of sunlight off of vid cameras, past the guys carrying him.

Fuck, hate hospitals.

He turned his head and saw the IV bag above his head. He was strapped down, immobile. He could feel burning tightness in his leg, his arm, his hand, and especially in his stomach—which had the weird feeling of having been melted away. He was light-headed and everything seemed far away.

Painkillers, he thought, his brain refusing to put together complete sentences.

He was still trying to figure out why he wasn't back home at his cabin.

"You're going to be all right, you hear me?" Nohar turned to see a familiar-looking face. *Knew his mother.* Nohar managed a friendly expression, through the drugged haze. He tried to say something, but his vocal cords didn't seem connected to him anymore.

"You hear me?"

Yes . . .

"You're a hero, Dad. You know that?"

Dad. He wondered at the word for a few seconds, then decided he liked it. *Manuel,* the name came to him finally.

Manuel reached out and touched his shoulder before the EMTs hauled him into the helicopter.

"A hero," Manuel shouted above the rising sound of the rotors.

Nohar shook his head.

No, Nohar thought of his father. *Not a hero.*

He looked at his son, feeling his head clear for a moment. "We're going to be fine." He managed to whisper. "Both of us."

Manuel nodded, though Nohar didn't know if he could hear him above the noise of the helicopter. Then the doors slid shut on him, and they were taking off.

Was it enough? Nohar wondered as he closed his eyes.

It was better than his own father.

It would have to do.

Afterword

Frankenstein in Utopia (Part 1)

Just about two hundred years ago Mary Shelley composed what Brian Aldiss would call the first true Science Fiction story.

While the body of Frankenstein is stitched together from the tropes of Gothic Romance, within its heart beats what I, and many others, see as the central conceit of what, a little more than a century later, Hugo Gernsback would term "Scientifiction."

That conceit is the Enlightenment idea that the universe is subject to rational laws, laws that can be understood through human reason.

The Creature in *Frankenstein* is not animated by supernatural forces, gods, or spirits. Within *Frankenstein* is the idea that the universe, including creation itself, might be unknown, but it is knowable.

Contained within it is also the reaction against this view of the universe. *Frankenstein* removes God from the universe and replaces Him with man, and the results are not pretty. Or, to put in terms a bit more palatable to a modern sensibility, *Frankenstein* is a case study in what happens when our knowledge and technical capacity outpaces our moral and ethical development.

The Creature is not evil in and of himself, nor is the process used to bring him to life: the evil in *Frankenstein* is Victor, the scientist, who at every turn is repulsed by his own creation, denies it, and attempts to abandon it.

The central flaw that drives the events in *Frankenstein* is not in the Creature, but in Victor. In that sense it is as much Tragedy as it is Horror. It also has a subtle political message about human nature, holding Victor Frankenstein's hubris up as a counterpoint to that scientific, rational Enlightenment Universe. A recognition that the same Enlightenment that gave us a Jefferson, also gave us a Robespierre.

Frankenstein is about hubris.

Given the novels you've just read, it should be apparent that *Frankenstein*'s story about humanity's moral failures with technology has been an influence on my stories in more than a metaphorical sense. Beyond the homage I've paid to both *Frankenstein* and its younger sibling, Wells' *The Island of Dr. Moreau*. That homage, the slang usage of "franks" and "moreys," was a deliberate acknowledgement that my story, in many senses, covers the same moral ground as those two stories, as well as countless others.

I also thought it was cool.

When I wrote *Forests* I was in my mid-twenties, unpublished, in any way you might measure, a neophyte novelist. So I honestly had no particular grand plan when I wrote *Forests of the Night*. Not even any particular plans for a sequel.

At that point in my career, planning out what would eventually become ten thematically interconnected books over the next twenty years would have been hubris on *my* part. The homage to prior work was intentional only because it was obvious.

But while my other decisions with that book were all to service the immediate story I wanted to tell, a genre potboiler with a humanoid bipedal tiger as a Chandleresque private eye, the decisions I took with building that world would unconsciously draw on themes and patterns I would echo and revisit through my entire career.

First among these themes, and one that applies to everything I write, is the idea that actions by those in power always have effects that are orthogonal, and often opposite, to their intent.

The origin of the moreaus in *Forests of the Night* is an example of this.

The United Nations in this world had drafted a treaty to ban the genetic engineering of humans. This was, like all efforts as arms control, an attempt to curb the effects of unconventional weapons. But it was also a broader attempt to prevent what could be seen as atrocities in the making.

In practice, the ban resulted in a creative arms race that led to a menagerie of creatures treated as less than human despite having human intellect. All of which were definitively non-human enough to avoid sanctions via the treaty, and all definitively non-human enough to be treated as slaves, bred to fight and die on the battlefield.

This was far from the intent of the drafters of that treaty. It might be argued that it eventually turned out to be a worse outcome than had they done nothing.

The second detail I added to the historical background of *Forests* illustrates the same unintended consequences of well-meaning acts by those in power.

Again, it was originally driven by literary decisions about what I wanted to write about—in this case the non-human subculture my tiger PI would be part of.

To allow my protagonist a legal status to act as my PI needed to act, I added an amendment to the US Constitution that gave the sapient products of non-human genetic engineering the protection of the Bill of Rights.

A writer with more faith in the ability of intent to shape outcomes, especially someone with my admiration for the ideals that shaped the founding of this country, might have left it at that.

However, the realist in me could not write believably about a United States where simply enshrining a principle in writing, even in our supreme legal document, would change either human nature or reality. I could believe we might enshrine this ideal when there were few enough non-humans to make much difference.

But then the refugees would come.

In the world of *Forests*, as so often happens in the real world, our ideals ran aground on the shores of reality. With waves of uncontrolled immigration came all the problems that accompany it; the problem of racism, because the moreaus are more instantly identifiable, more different, than *any* combination of human racial and ethnic signifiers; the problem of xenophobia, because our fear of them is justified, the moreaus were engineered for warfare and are deadlier than any human; and, most importantly, the problem of assimilation, because in many cases the moreaus' non-human biology prevents them from adapting to human culture.

As an example, the rats of my world are unpleasant. This

is not due to any species bigotry on my part, but because of the unintended consequences of the way they were engineered. The rat moreaus physically mature at two years and have a life expectancy of around twelve. However, their brain is largely human, given that was the only model the engineers had to use. Studies of human moral development generally show that we don't develop conventional morality until somewhere in our early teens. My rats, as a species, never have the opportunity to reach that stage. Morally, they are children given the status of adults, which leads to a gang-like social development that few, if any, are able to ever grow out of.

And for all the ill feelings on the human side of the equation, the moreaus are justified in reciprocating—after all, we created them in bondage, and in many cases, we did not engineer them to survive well off of the battlefield. The rats being an obvious case in point.

Of course, none of this was envisioned by the people who drafted the legislation governing this world.

Forests has been held up as an allegory on civil rights and the racial divides here in the United States—an inevitable consequence of the world I chose to write in.

I'd like to think the issues at play are of a more universal significance, drawing not just from the African-American experience in the United States, but more generally from displaced immigrant and refugee populations, from the re-assimilation of conscript soldiers into peacetime, and most generally, from the friction that inevitably happens when one culture is completely surrounded by, and ruled by, another.

The plots of these four books—in this omnibus and the next—are deeply informed by these issues. But they are not *about* them. These themes were less the result of planning on my part and more a result of my attempt to create a plausible background for my noir storylines.

As a result, I think what I wrote about these issues in my mid-twenties is truer than anything I might have developed if I had planned a polemic. If I had naively gone that route, I suspect I would have inevitably removed many of the shades of grey in this world. I would have made the moreus more clearly the oppressed victims. I would have made the humans more clearly the oppressor.

And I would have lost the resonance these books have with the moral complexities we deal with in the real world.

Because I was writing to create a setting I believed in, not to make a point, my world is not so clearly delineated. It's messy. It's a place where the Pope has decreed that moreaus have souls, and the US Supreme Court has only recently ruled that the non-human rights amendment applies to human products of genetic engineering. It's a place where there are rodent street gangs and human supremacy movements, and human-founded fertility clinics devoted to the right of every sapient being to reproduce.

And, as in the real world, I don't have any easy answers.

There is a temptation to look for those easy answers, in the real world and especially in fiction. There is a utopian impulse, a very human need to see an endpoint to history, the thought that if we conquer just one more evil it will all be all right.

But history didn't end with the Emancipation Proclamation, with the end of Jim Crow, or with the election of a black president. It did not end with the fall of Nazi Germany or the Soviet Union. It doesn't end by electing the right people or by fighting the right wars.

It doesn't end by not fighting them.

It. Just. Doesn't. End.